The potion went blazing down her throat...

He brought his hand up, framed her face in a curve of black fingernails. Stomped the glass to shards and claimed her with a serpentine kiss. A flaming match dropped onto a kerosene-soaked effigy, the anathema of cheating came on with a strange, self-destructive euphoria, the sharp tear away from the person she loved and had been so stupid to love. The hurt would be coming, oh yes, but right now, her shape was changing within his embrace, already somebody else. Devon's hands raced with heartbreaker voodoo along the thin fabric of her dress, every second decimating the girl she used to be, the fit of her new flesh just as intoxicating as this forbidden kiss. No one would mistake her for a virgin princess ever again...

Goddess of Thunder

Lilah Wild

Leopard Moon Press
NYC

Leopard Moon Press, NYC.
www.leopardmoon.com

This is a work of fiction. All names, characters, events, and incidents depicted herein are either a product of the author's imagination, or are used fictitiously.

Cover photograph © 2017 by Lilah Wild

ISBN-13: 978-0615647784
ISBN-10: 0-61564-778-2

for John

Goddess of Thunder

Prologue

1968

"I'm your scarlet woman," she said.

And that changed everything.

No one was here yet. She was sprawled out on the altar, her long blonde hair flowing down the marble, her wrists and ankles lost within huge bells of black lace. Above her, his arched eyebrows rose, the half-arranged candlesticks and this evening's festivities momentarily forgotten. For the first few seconds, she mistook his expression for respect.

None of the girls had ever been much more than set dressing, in her opinion, the bait of naked skin like a Playboy Mansion promise beneath their ceremonial velvets. But there was magick here, no doubt. She'd been with him long enough to know it, had stepped forward from the line of infernal dolls across the ritual chamber floor and gained his eye, and a place in his luxuriant bed. She was top girl now. His favorite.

And what happened in the park, up on Strawberry Hill…that could only cement her ascendance as Witch Queen.

She wouldn't be dancing at that North Beach go-go joint forever. And she refused to camp down with those silly flower children in the park. She was destined for better things.

She gazed up at him. The shaved head, the mustache that tickled her face when they kissed. The conniving carny heart beneath the tailored suit, parading his mod succubi in luscious defiance of the straight, uptight world, golden tongue of outlaw power that kept them all returning to the infamous black Victorian. Such a force of persuasion, intelligence, cold splash of left-hand reality that told her not to waste her love, not to turn the other cheek, to be strong and beautiful in the way that only she could be. He was teaching her freedom. It felt right. Even though she had to follow his directions like a marionette, speak the words and raise the cup on cue, this was the right path to follow.

That surge she'd felt—up on the hill, alone above the city, visualizing the fire of her birth element while the mist dampened her face—she'd closed her eyes and slowed her breath, lost herself, opened herself. She could feel the power building

(without him)

the roots of the trees pulsing beneath her feet, restless with a feral heat that soared up through her limbs, her sex, her heart. The earth called to her—wonderous flame, cherished daughter—and she called back, exuberant.

This was where the rites were meant to go, she knew. Stripped of speech, of all artifice, down to pure animal form. This flash of intuition meant she was climbing up to where he was. Power of her own to wield, to match him in the dance.

Yes. She should be mistress of the house. Absolutely.

He looked down at her, stretched out on the marble, eyes dreamy beneath a thick valance of kohl. They regarded each other, the wily organ-grinder and the young witch perched at the threshold of secrets.

Outside, it began to rain.

He seized her shoulders, kissed her, tore at the delicate crochet. She gasped, twisted herself inside his grip to shed the restrictions of dress, her hair tumbling down in a shining mass. He unfastened his pants, pulled her down to the edge of the altar and she cried out as his hands sought her hips, brought her closer, deeper, driving himself into all that gold, all that light, with such force as if to knock her off the pedestal.

Nine months later, he had.

Act 1

Chapter 1

1987

Lavender. Lemongrass. Lobelia. Plastic boxes were spread out across Starlight Occult's second floor. The herb stock hadn't been cleaned out in years, and Danae's hands were filthy with decayed roots. She dumped yet another box in the trash, wiped her fingers on her jeans, hoped there were no more disgusting surprises after finding a nest of larvae squirming around inside the linden. Death Angel raged from a small boombox beside her.

Why did her mother even buy this stuff in the first place? The customers didn't want to muck about with mortars and pestles. The real money was in the oils, the love perfumes, and the clientele was steady enough to pay the rent on the Tenderloin storefront, and their little apartment above. With Danae as the built-in maid. She sighed and got to her feet, pushed her dirty blonde hair behind her ears and sneezed on the foul-smelling air. The M's were next, almost halfway through. Time for a break.

She crossed to the residential side of the apartment, passing the stairway leading down to the shop. As she stopped to wash up in the bathroom, she heard the telltale sound of glass sliding on glass. Seven-day candles on the counter, pushed towards a worried customer.

"We've been married seven years. He's all I've got. I don't know what I'd do if he's got someone else on the side…"

Those candles were red, no doubt.

Danae opened the door to her room and flung herself on her bed.

Cassettes were scattered across a scratched rolltop desk, classical and metal. In her closet, cotton and denim hung in sharp contrast to the aristocratic jewel tones of her mother's wardrobe. On her dresser, a carved stone box of silver jewelry sat next to a small TV set. Candlewax dribbled down the side of a nighttable, makeshift altar. The one window overlooked the street, the convenience store across the way like a derelict stage. After hours, she'd sit with the window open and listen to the night, the fights and propositions and gossip. She'd roll her desk open, savoring the clack of wood on wood, and dig through the pile of tattered drugstore notebooks for an empty page. Celeste bought them in bulk during the fall, always muttering about getting more involved with Danae's homeschooling, but they ended up with poetry dancing across their college-ruled lines. Demons conjured from violin strings. Ghosts disrupting weddings with unholy screeching, or pining away in a deserted attic. Witches calling what they needed from the earth. Strong women, like her mother.

It stung Danae that she was called upon to blend the oils or dress the candles, but was trusted with nothing beyond running the shop. Celeste hadn't stopped her from practicing her small magicks in her room, but neither had she shared her secrets, keeping her vast knowledge to herself with a dismissive smile. Danae had been allowed to start counseling the customers a couple years ago, and she hoped that someday her mother would overhear one of those conversations, advising someone to heal a relationship or change jobs, and something would persuade her that her daughter was wise and worthy. Not young and stupid, as Celeste surely considered her.

Witch to witch. Mother to daughter. A tiny family of two, but they could be so powerful together. Why was her mother holding out on her? She'd swept that fucking storeroom enough.

Outside, a couple of voices cackled about champagne rooms and neon g-strings. Dancers on their way to the lunchtime shift at the O'Farrell Theatre. She sighed again.

The brass bells over the shop's door announced a new customer, and she was already bounding down the steps before Celeste could yell for her, *Dannay*, two syllables like a high-pitched leash. The dusty rose lampshade in the tiny tarot room was on—her mother had talked the anxious customer into a reading.

Slouched against the counter, Zolo. *Shit.* A bald, lithe dancer wearing his customary leer and leather. With him was Julia, a tall brunette who had worn her work outfit to the shop, a rhinestone-studded strapless gown that she kept having to yank up. Inevitable condescension, along with the highlights from his latest S&M party, one of her more dreaded customers. Julia had spotted the new display of crystal necklaces glittering from a small tree, and was loudly begging him to buy her one.

Another girl was over by the bookcases, squatting down on pink spike heels in the Magick 101 section. Long black hair in a French braid, blue jeans embroidered with butterflies on the back pockets. None of the girls Zolo brought in had ever bothered with the books—just the love oils and jewelry. And endless money spells for more tips. Danae took her place on the stool behind the counter.

"Can I help you?"

The girl turned her head. Thick dark eyebrows, skin like a warm summer beach. Fuschia lip gloss turned up in a smile. She rose and walked to the counter, swaying her hips a little. A rhinestone bowtied bunny hung from her neck.

"Yeah. There's all these books and I have no idea which one to start on."

Cool. Open-minded beginners were fun to help, and Danae enjoyed recommending books, being a good influence in someone's magickal life. But...the girl's gaze was so direct, magnetic brown eyes, and the way she was leaning on the counter...*is she flirting with me?* And for one hot moment: lace on lace, dreamscape of skin. What would it be like to undo that braid, draw her close, mess up that lipgloss...

Danae brushed the image aside quickly. Ground and center, she'd deal with her libido later. The feminist-minded authors were the best place to start for a woman mixed up with Zolo. She was about to walk the girl back to the bookshelf, when Julia's voice broke in.

"Princess! Princess, look at this one."

Julia had fastened a pentacle around her neck. It made Danae wince to see someone as vapid as Julia treating that star as mere exotica for her act, nothing more. Princess walked over and slid her hand beneath the charm.

"Pretty."

Ah. The smile was probably the same one she shone at her customers. Silly to think it might have been real.

Zolo turned to Danae. "Hey, Glinda the Good Witch. You should have been at my place last night. I had Julia on the cross, and there was this cute little redhead crawling around on the floor—"

"Quiet, Zolo. I don't need to know."

Suddenly, a voice was raised in the tarot room. "No way, not her. She would *never* do that to me."

"I tell you only what I see in the cards."

"I've known her since we were kids. What the hell is this?"

The customer flounced out of the tarot room, whirled angrily in white bohemian lace. Brown hair pulled back in a chignon, gold bangles on her wrists, a Haight-Marina hybrid of sixties groupie and eighties money, rockstar's girlfriend made good. "That's the *worst* reading I've ever had. I want a refund. *Immediately.*"

Celeste came out behind her. Long blonde hair, blazing blue eyes, regal in flowing burgundy. The bearing and mystique of a true witch, icy calm against the wealthy tempest raving away among the gemstones. Refusing yet again to bullshit the customers' egos with the predictions they really wanted to hear.

Zolo snorted. The customer realized she had an audience, and her eyes darted around the shop. Zolo all sleaze, Julia falling out of her dress. She threw her head back with laughter to erase her embarrassment. "What was I thinking? What a joke this place is. Keep the money, you need fifteen bucks a lot more than I do." She whooped her way out the door, banging the bells against the glass.

Danae started towards Celeste, an apologetic, comforting *Mom* on her lips, but Zolo stepped in front of her.

"Oh, Celeste. Don't listen to that crazy bitch. You know women always have to tear each other down…"

Danae watched her mother's face soften with the flattery. *Mom, can't you see what a worm he is?*

"You know what you were, back in the day, Celeste. What an incredible woman you were. You still are, and people like that are threatened by it."

Celeste's eyes had gone to slits as her gaze drifted over to her daughter. The kind words died in Danae's throat as she watched her mother appraise her, look her over as Zolo's words drifted in the background, stroked her with past glory.

(Your mother is jealous of you.)

The thought barely had time to form before Julia broke in. "Ohmigod! It's quarter of! Princess, we gotta go!" And she made for the exit, but not before Danae ran past the counter and put a hand on her bare shoulder.

"The necklace?"

Julia looked more petulant than apologetic. But Julia spent a lot of money here.

"We can hold it for you, if you want to come back for it later."

"Take it off me?" Julia lifted her hair, a lush fall of auburn, and Danae thumbed back the clasp.

"Hah. Usually you've got to wave twenty bucks to hear her say *that*," said Zolo.

Julia tripped out the door, followed by Princess, who smiled at Danae with a soft *I'll be back later*, and finally Zolo. Danae walked to the crystal display and fastened the necklace back to its branch. Before today, she would have hoped her mother saw this small act of theft prevention. Attention to detail, care for the store. Qualities in a good witch. But how many more days would this go on, trying to win her mother's regard, hanging on for pennies of respect, while Celeste placed someone like Zolo before her own flesh and blood? The customer's laughter rang in her head. Maybe there was a place for her elsewhere, better than this.

Danae walked back through the center of the shop, narrowing her eyes at Celeste as she passed between the counters. Celeste stared back, ringed hands clenched inside flowing sleeves, as if she were trying to hang on to something that had already left. Danae shook her head slowly, then charged upstairs into her room and grabbed her backpack. Fuck all this. After years of hearing others' fortunes, it was time for hers to unfold.

* * *

Golden Gate Park was quiet. Danae stood at the stone wall and swept her eyes across the misty darkness. She'd spent the evening wandering the city, the night alive with thousands of voices: the clink of wineglasses from a second-story townhouse window, the cheerful blare of salsa from a taxicab, miles of sidewalk passing beneath her sneakers. Now, her feet had grown tired, and she was getting sleepy.

A trial awaited her. Was she brave enough, strong enough, to fall asleep within the primal heart of the trees?

Metal videos came back to her, girls in long gauzy nightgowns walking into the forest. Innocent and wide-eyed, leaving their bedrooms to answer some call. A demon, a dragon, maybe she'd get lucky and find a band. There sure were enough of them dragging their equipment out to some secluded glade and rocking out in their videos.

But, seriously. If she could spend the night in the woods, alone...what wouldn't she be able to face, after that?

She found herself heading for the hill, thinking about curious strangers. Most people didn't bother with sleeping bodies, really, just walked past them when they were lying on the sidewalks, curled into doorways. Out here, she was away from casual foot traffic. And even if someone stumbled upon her, most likely they'd pass her by, leave her in peace. Still, she took out her can of pepper spray and tucked it into the front of her bra. Ran through a mental chart of pressure points on the body, places to hit when attacked, recalled from afternoons reading about eastern medicine. And if things got really bad...her athame, the ultimate last resort, if it came to it.

The lake splashed softly in the darkness, punctuated by talkative quacks as she crossed the bridge and walked to the park's highest point, pushing small branches from her path, tripping here and there over jutting rocks, using her hands to guide herself through the uneven terrain. Nobody here, so far so good. Most of them were probably camped out near Stanyan, or within the gnarled trees along the road. Elsewhere.

She reached the top. She navigated her way to a small copse of trees, put her backpack down and swept the ground smooth of leaves. Far away enough from the trail that she wouldn't be spotted by early-bird joggers, and the morning light would awaken her before anyone else got out here. She shook out a sweatshirt to curl up on, rolled up a t-shirt for a place to rest her head. Her bed made, she settled back down inside her leather jacket.

Where did those video maidens in their floaty nightdresses end up going? A diabolical spirit tempting her soul, a coven welcoming her into secret lunar ceremonies, a lover drawing her into the shadows for a passionate tryst…there was no one waiting for Danae inside the park.

And now there was no safe bedroom for her to run back to, if things went wrong.

She closed her eyes and listened to the forest. Night creatures, soft wind. The scent of the dirt, the way the moonlight turned her hands blue. There was much to fear out here, sure, but there was much that was beautiful, too. And plenty of things that were useful, if you knew how to use them. Fire, air, water…she wasn't alone. As she passed into sleep, she reflected on how good it felt to have the whole earth at her back.

* * *

Princess sat on the steps outside Zolo's house. Behind her, through the windows, she heard the crack of a whip, commands delivered in a snarl. Some of his friends were up from L.A. for the weekend and they had free rein of his harem. She'd watched their methods of play and was beginning to regret showing up.

Zolo. He'd been so used to getting his way that he'd actually raised his eyebrows as she withdrew her consent, as if asserting a boundary were grounds for punishment. She'd grabbed her leather trenchcoat and gone out on the porch for a smoke.

Her mind wandered back to her altar as she rooted in her purse for a cigarette, lit up. She'd gone back to the botanica but the witch's daughter wasn't there. Hadn't been there all last week, or this one, either. She couldn't get the girl's face out of her mind—her eyes bright with knowledge, contrasting with the sweet, unsteady way she'd met her gaze.

Princess was working her way through the beginner's section on her own, and the books were bringing her back to Mexico City, her grandmother's house, the Virgin of Guadalupe hot in her halo and ringed with dolls, photographs, candles within a shrine that never stayed still—a small temple to everything momentary and domestic, fed with flowers and copal and hot chocolate. The first witchcraft author she'd picked up, a bearded white guy with a mischievous smile and lots to say about solitary practitioners, was telling her to follow her instincts in building her sacred space; she gathered pictures of her friends and lovingly draped their faces in her jewelry, scattered seashells at their feet. In the middle, two goddesses: Frida Kahlo and Nina Hagen. Wax splattered down the wood of her dresser as she cast for a good direction, a wide and general spell to get started on. Specifics would come later.

Inside, she heard Julia laughing. Fake and witchy. The wrong kind of witch, not even really a witch at all. Just cruel. This crowd had great toys but no imagination. All these occult tools, all this expensive dungeon gear, and cliched psychodrama was the best they could do?

What am I doing here?

She dropped her cigarette to the sidewalk. As she crushed it with her boot, her necklace slid off her neck, the catch broken. The rhinestone bunny.

Maybe the spell's working already!

She shushed the excited inner voice away, but a smile formed on her lips anyway. She got up and headed off to hail a cab. If some lucky nightcrawler didn't snatch it up from the sidewalk first, let it be a sign to Zolo that she was through with him.

* * *

6pm, time to flip the sign from OPEN to CLOSED. Celeste shuffled to her office in the back, grateful for the solitude.

Where's your daughter? When's Danae coming back? Celeste had been surprised at how many people had come into Starlight asking for her. A single mom trying out incenses to get back into the dating scene. A teenage punk with a pierced lip and too many smartass questions about something called chaos magick. A dancer from the club down the street, who was burning a lot of gold candles, must be working on a job change. Couldn't blame her—the girls, coming down off the stage and into the audience! Onto the customers' laps! To think about all the heat she took back in the day for dancing topless on a piano.

Zolo had offered to go out and look for Danae, but she politely refused; he'd be a terrible huntsman, much too lecherous. He was a pale shade of her devil man, mere arrogance no substitute for that pervasive, insidious charm. She'd tried to put her original tempter out of her mind, her sweet serpent, but he had just appeared on a talk show last night. The mustachioed, scandal-chasing host had flashed a portrait to the audience—posed on a carousel, clad in darkness, leaning against the gaily-painted horses of his carnival barker past. Sinister and beautiful and utterly fearless. Celeste had turned off the television and reached for a drink.

She slumped down at her desk in a rose mesh dress, something with huge swooping sleeves that looked great over a tarot spread but felt limp and annoying today. She'd tried her hardest for almost two decades to get over him, but had never been successful. Danae had been a daily reminder of the life she used to lead, before pregnancy banished her from his house. She had never been able to forgive her daughter for it, and yet, Danae was her only connection back to him. A Magickal Child created through the union of their enchanted blood. A little girl loved and cherished until her body started to mature, when it finally dawned on Celeste that he was never going to change his mind. She was left to raise the child alone, who would grow into a woman blessed with the benefit of his genes.

Right before Danae had left, right as she'd walked up those steps, he had looked out at Celeste from her daughter's eyes. Glowered with Danae's features. A woman who was half of what he was, would be automatically stronger. No way was Celeste igniting a competition in which she'd surely lose. But Danae would find out the truth, sooner or later. And had to be subdued while Celeste got her back under control.

She took a deep breath and glanced around her sanctuary. Hundreds of oils, jars of powdered incense, her desk in the center. A small collection of antique perfume bottles ringed an art nouveau mirror, each one filled with a personal potion, just for her. She stared at her reflection. Thick locks, soon to turn white, features deepening with age. She pulled her hair off her face. No. Soft skin, sparkling eyes. She still had it.

Danae had it too.

Her daughter. An awkward, stumbling girl in her late teens, trying to make fairy dust from piles of ash. If she had any of his fire, she'd be very, very good at it.

Celeste gazed at her perfumes. Slices of rounded glass to drag across her throat. Atomizers to squeeze small poofs of scent into her hair. Woman after woman through that door, day after day, slapping their dollars on the counter and asking her how to find a man. *Her* of all people, a charlatan who couldn't hang on to the one she'd really wanted. Nor move on past him, his hold on her too strong, surviving spell after spell to make her forget. She smiled bitterly, and the mirror smiled back.

Love oils. Satin soaked with lavender. Women playing their little erotic tricks, while the club down the street upped their ante with strippers bumping and grinding in the seats. She was losing her taste for tarot readings. Tired of getting that personal with strangers.

Maybe it was time to try something else. Up the ante of her own. Bring a little of that Green Door magic down her way.

Danae could be the attraction. An irresistible doll of sympathetic magick to beckon them in, a threat contained in a safe place, until Celeste figured out what to do with her daughter. It would require deception, which she hated, but it would be in the service of self-preservation. The greater good.

Brilliant.

Celeste rose from her chair and ascended the steps into Danae's bedroom, the binding practically writing itself. Hairs collected from her pillow. Necklaces that had rested against her skin. Candlewax from her altar. Her daughter hadn't bothered to clean up her work before running out of the house. Careless, careless.

She brought the taglocks down to her desk and added supplies from around the shop. A red candle shaped like a woman. Magnetic sand. A small forest of tapers burned from every shelf, every counter in the office.

Find her. Bring her back. Break down whatever will she has, and bring her home.

14

When the candles had burned to stubs and the incense was nothing more than a lingering scent, she concocted a love brew of sugar and honey and rose petals. Nothing dangerous, nothing lethal. The only poison in this apple would be an unexpected dose of maternal sweetness.

* * *

Danae sat on the ground and leaned against her tree. *Her* tree, yes. She might not have been able to string jewels across its branches or nestle teacups in its roots, but it was a home.

After the trepidation of that first night, she'd picked up the rhythm of living outdoors, stretching out the little money she had. She'd showered in a Mission high school that opened its doors to the homeless at night. A group of men in top hats handed out bowls of stew in the Panhandle. Even though she'd run across small clusters of friendly punks, she kept to herself—she didn't want to get mixed up in other people's problems, but more importantly, she needed the seclusion.

She closed her eyes and breathed in the sunlight. The traffic around the park faded to white noise, and the breeze was cool on her cheek. She opened her hands, turned her palms outward, flexed her fingers up like starbursts. Concentrated on the circulation of her blood. A meditative exercise she'd been developing over the past couple of days.

Footsteps. Probably just someone wandering through. She'd been getting used to it, no longer jumping at every noise. But the crunching was getting louder, definitely heading in her direction. Her mind raced. Should she stand up? Stay down? Suddenly a pair of feet came into view. White boots, ringed hands shaking an eyelet ruffle free of clinging twigs.

Celeste.

This couldn't be her mother. This woman was dressed in mint. *Pastels.* There was even a breathtaking hint of tie-dye in her broomstick skirt.

"Danae." Celeste was smiling. Why? Shouldn't she be screaming her head off, having some sort of meltdown? Instead, she looked more balanced and healthy than Danae had ever seen her.

How the hell did she find me?

(Need you ask, neophyte?)

"I've done a lot of thinking, and I'd like us to talk."

No. No. But her eyes. She'd waited so long for her mother to look at her like that.

"Danae…" Celeste looked down and sighed. "Danae, this is very hard to say. I'm hoping you give me a chance. Come on, I'll take you out to lunch."

Just an hour or two. If Danae slammed the door, she'd never know. Not to mention, she was *hungry*.

"OK."

Celeste stretched out her hand, but Danae got to her feet without help.

"Well, first of all, I have some ideas about Starlight," Celeste began, as they walked down the hill. "You know how everyone pretty much came in for love spells. I was thinking about carrying lingerie, specialty candles, romantic things. I want you to come back with me and help me put it together. I didn't realize how much you did around the shop until you left. It's been so quiet without you." Celeste smiled.

It was sweet to hear it, finally, after all this time. But Danae had gotten a taste of independence. And the woods were teaching her so much.

They reached a small cafe directly across from the park. Painted porcelain and delicate embroidery, fresh flowers on every table. They took a table by the window, and Danae fell back into a worn canebacked chair as Celeste ordered tea sandwiches.

"Here. I brought this," Celeste looked around to make sure no one was watching, lifted a small bottle of wine from her tapestry bag. "It's a special occasion." She turned over the empty glasses on the table. Danae went rigid despite the growling of her stomach. This was all going too fast. The change of clothes, the new business, her mother speaking an alien language of love and honor. What would Celeste say when she told her she wasn't coming back?

And what was in that bottle?

Danae popped the cork and sniffed. Apples. She'd never known Celeste to dabble in the poisoning arts. And they were in public, within the safety of other people. Why was she being so paranoid? This was her *mother*. Children ran away and then made up with their parents all the time. This was classic American dysfunction, not unusual at all. And the wine...Celeste was treating her like an adult now. Why not enjoy the moment? Celeste poured them both a glass, hid the bottle behind a vase of baby's breath, and raised her glass.

"To family."

"To family." Danae smiled and took a small sip. It tasted like liquid autumn. Her mother letting her drink underage, *encouraging* it, awesome. This was how she wished it could have been—locking the shop's doors, opening a bottle, chatting over the day's customers. She felt warm, opened to strange suggestions. Maybe she could go back, but part time. Keep a foot in the park. The heat spread out across her shoulders, down her stomach. Why was she so tired all of a sudden? The flowers were crawling out of the walls, off the china, into her skin. Her arms sagged. Celeste drifted in a blonde haze, swam in petals as she tucked the bottle back in her bag. The glass rolled from Danae's hand and smashed on the floor. She struggled to keep her eyes open, heard the footsteps of a waitress, Celeste's voice.

"My daughter's not feeling well. Could you call us a taxi?"

Danae struggled to speak, resist, but she couldn't move. She felt rings across her face, fingers sliding down over her eyelids.

"Sleep, child. I'm taking you home."

* * *

Princess was pissed. It had been a hard night between the table of gropers and the jackass with horrendous breath. And if the DJ announced her as The Spicy Hot Tamale one more time...*argh*.

As she stepped out in front of the theater, a group of guys waited for the 38 bus. Whistling, talking shit. She crossed the street before they noticed her. Oh, to be home already, to sit on her bed and count the cash, and then a long soak in the tub, and then crash. Perfect. She headed toward Van Ness, wondering what was left in the fridge.

A light burned up ahead, electric violet making the filthy sidewalk glow. The botanica—finally back open, after a week with the shades down. What were they doing? She ran up and looked in the window.

The walls had been papered pink with a pattern of roses, blasphemously spiked with X-rated movie posters. A mannequin stood in a black lace bustier and stiletto heels, her face obscured by a fall of shocking pink curls. Her eyes were closed, and dried roses were scattered at her feet. Beside her, a red mesh negligee was draped over the velvet cushion of a small chair, and flesh-colored toys lay across the top of an old-fashioned vanity, three mirrors to reflect it all. A room sliced from a dollhouse of perversions, Aphrodite caught and pickled for the Tenderloin tastes.

Princess shook her head, trying to separate the two worlds; the bitchy grind of her job, the flickering light of her altar, separate realities that would never meet. But the mannequin looked so real. Her eyes followed the line of her body. Shockingly, her chest rose and fell with breath.

What the hell!?

Princess put her hand up to the glass, and sharp pains crossed her forehead. It didn't matter that she was still new at all this—that setup was crawling with bad energy. Had people been passing by the window all day without realizing that this was a live human being? She had the feeling she would have done the same if she hadn't spent the last few weeks trying to expand her senses.

Beneath the ache, beneath the horror, way down in the darkest waters of her psyche…something smiled.

Charged with newfound power, she looked around for something heavy, hitting the nearby trashcans until finding a dead fire extinguisher in a vacant lot around the corner. She headed back to the window and swung it. The first couple of blows cracked a spiderweb, and Princess aimed straight for its center.

An alarm went off, and the violet light sizzled out, but the mannequin didn't stir. Princess stepped up into the window, kicking away videotapes and shards of glass, and stood up next to the sleeping girl, brushed her hair from her face. The pink wig fell off, revealing tangles of dark blond.

The witch's daughter!

Half from fairy tales lodged in her subconscious, and half from sheer delight at finding her, Princess took the girl's face in her hands and kissed her.

Awaken!

* * *

Danae took a deep breath, and opened her eyes. A girl with long black hair was staring at her—the pretty customer, the dancer. Behind her, a broken window. The shop's window. She looked down, saw vibrators and dead flowers circling her spike-heeled feet. The eyes of pornstars surrounded her.

Mother…this is where you've brought me?

She hugged herself against the night's chill.

"What am I doing up here?"

"I don't know. I was just walking home and…I found you."

Princess backed out of the window and helped Danae get down to the sidewalk, wrapped her trenchcoat around Danae's shoulders. "I'm headed back to my place. You should come, you need to get out of here."

Danae looked into the girl's face, her glitter-swirled eyes filled with concern. "I remember you. The books."

"I'm Princess. No! Pam. My name is Pam. Sorry, I just came from work."

"I'm Danae." She braced herself against Pam's shoulder to steady herself, and felt a supportive arm curl around her back. "Sorry, I'm not used to walking in these things."

"Oh, it's cool." That flirty smile again. "Are you OK? Other than freezing your ass off? You're not hurt, are you?"

Danae shook her head. "I'm fine. I'm just…this is weird."

"I'll make you some tea. Come on, before the cops show up."

Just then, Celeste appeared at the door. As Danae laced her fingers through Pam's, she turned and looked her mother in the face.

I can do it without you.

Celeste was left alone, staring as the women walked hand-in-hand up the sidewalk, into the shining forest of city lights.

Chapter 2

The day was warm, and bright yellow light was making good on every painted-lady promise. Shouts from volleyball games, pop tunes blaring from boomboxes, the rhythmic scrape of roller skates, the sounds of Golden Gate Park all faded to a cheerful background clamor in this unmapped bit of enchanted forest. Secreted behind the trees was a small grove, a circle of stumps hidden from well-worn paths. A new sanctuary, since Celeste had invaded the old one.

Legs crossed, eyes closed, facing each other. Palm to palm: bright pink fingernails pressed against kitchen scars, a slight shake running through their fingers. One day it would go smoothly, they knew. They'd be expert witches, high priestesses, years of concentration to streamline them cool and confident. Right now was the early part of the scrapbook, the first polaroid pages sunblurred with laughter at fuckups and open delight when it all went right.

A breeze made Pam's bangles tinkle. Danae opened her eyes. Stole a moment to gaze at Pam, still deep in trance, so solemn and intent while loosened hair danced across her cheeks. Leaned forward and told her with a soft kiss that the meditation was over.

Pam took a deep breath, rolled her neck, stretched her back. So in tune with her body, Danae noted—dancing for six hours in spike heels would demand it. Right now she was grounding herself after a working, letting all the energy out into the world to manifest, without even knowing it.

Warm brown eyes looked back at her from within a dusting of gold glitter. A smile followed.

I'm not alone anymore.

The wave of happiness was almost painful. Danae jumped up and hit Pam on the arm.

"You're it!" She dashed off into the surrounding trees, leaving Pam to curse, dust off her jeans, and pursue.

Back and forth, side to side, scampering maypole-style around the twisted trunks as Danae tried not to let her laughter slow her down. Bark shattered beneath her grasping hands, roots tried to trip her up but she jumped away. Pam jingled behind her. Danae envisioned a sparkling strand shooting backwards from her heart, wrapping a thread around the grove of stumps. *I'm weaving a web, what will I catch?* She realized she was running clockwise. Deosil.

She felt a sharp tug on the collar of her jean jacket and hit the ground as Pam straddled her, pinned her wrists to the dirt.

"Gotcha." The word summoned her back to Pam's bedroom, long hot nights of sweat and candlelight, the slow delicious ruin of her purity. As far as Danae was concerned, she was utterly disqualified as a virgin sacrifice. All the fight went out of her body. Limp. *Yours.*

Pam leaned down and kissed her without releasing her wrists. Danae wanted to touch her face, run her fingers through her hair, but Pam wouldn't let her go.

Something crawled beneath Danae's back. She squirmed.

"You're not the only one who likes biting me. C'mon, let me up."

Pam sat up, brushed dirt from her Cathouse t-shirt and got to her feet, pulling Danae up with her.

Back through the woods, onto a tiny weedy path that circled back out to the main drive. A drum circle was going in the next field over.

"Zolo came into the club the other day. He's been taking Starlight's powder, dividing it up into little bottles and reselling it to all the dancers, for like four times the price. His special secret love stuff."

"That man *has* no secrets. Every time he came in, on and on about another party. In graphic detail."

Down beneath the bridge, up past the swampy little lake, through the clusters of backpacks and torn denim and long stringy hair. Whispers of *I got acid, I got pot*, back pockets filled with dimebags of fresh white sage.

"It's like he totally forgets there's a world out there that has nothing to do with the club."

"He must, it would explain the time he came in wearing assless chaps."

They reached Haight Street, dodging the outstretched legs of panhandlers, the lollygagging of tourists. The air was thick with cheap incense, honking buses, sizzling meat, classic rock anthems. Dead icons peered down from bright murals, faced shrouded within clouds of spraycanned poetry. Cameras pointed up towards street signs, shop windows, eager to capture the last wilted petals of flower power.

"You know he still lives with his mother?"

"Get out."

"He does! One of the other dancers told me that she's got the top floor of the house, all those parties go on and she's just rocking away upstairs, oblivious."

Down past the fog-frosted woods of Buena Vista Park, down to their Victorian castle. Up the battered wooden steps, past the stained-glass mandala set inside the front door, up to the cozy little nest on the third floor.

Countless ceramic masks awaited their entry, wrapped within the reds and pinks of secondhand scarves. Pewter candlesticks, silk flowers, peacock feathers and *who did your decorating, Prince and the Revolution?* But Danae had meant it as a compliment: Pam had given her a place to stay, a warm shelter of dimestore splendor.

Danae shed her jacket, threw it to the couch. Felt slender arms curl around her from behind.

"I am Master Zolo. And tonight, you will be my love slave." Pam breathed heavily into her ear. "Come. I will flex my buttcheeks of supreme command. Doubt not their power, foolish mortal."

They started cracking up again as Pam pulled her towards the bedroom.

Dull brass shine, pink satin sheets. Small bites along her neck as she buried her hands in Pam's hair, silently blessed this torrid, passionate girl who had invited grubby little *her* into her bed, ragged fingernails, dirty sneakers, utter amazement that someone so beautiful, someone at *all*, would want to bring her to ecstasy. Now it was her turn to be a good student, and show Pam what she'd learned from her.

The Cathouse shirt hit the floor, followed by the jeans. Danae felt the knowledge blooming steadily in her fingers, her lips, the incredible power she could wield over another person, her hands a pair of hungry pale stars trailing down Pam's writhing body.

I touch you here, and you're mine, she thought as she unclasped Pam's bra, leaned down to kiss where the underwire had been. Pam arched her back, stroked Danae's hair. *And you're mine*, as she curved her fingers below the waistband of those pink bikini panties, over the triangle of carefully-tended stripper fur. *Oh yeah. You are totally mine.* A thousand awful rock ballads exploded from the back of Danae's mind as she caught the sweet surrender in those sexy, half-closed eyes, returned that lascivious smile before bringing her mouth down.

* * *

Curled together in the afterglow, Danae soon heard a tiny snore. Pam was prone to falling asleep—mostly from the exhaustion of her job, or maybe she really was throwing around major energy today.

She rolled over and looked around the room, let her eyes roam Pam's altar for the current spiritual forecast. There was that strip of photobooth pictures from the pier last weekend, already dotted with candlewax. Phone numbers scrawled on rips of paper. Customers? Co-workers, other dancers? She imagined wealth runes scratched beneath tabletops, hips stroked with bayberry oil just before stepping onstage. Above, a Hanoi Rocks poster was tacked up next to Danielle Dax. New, but not surprising. Pam had a thing for big hair and big voices.

Danae grabbed her clothes off the floor, closed the bedroom door softly behind her. Dressed, she sprawled out on the couch, once again wondered if there was a way to lure Celeste out of the shop so she could sneak back and grab her stuff. If any of it was even still there. And even if it was, left unharmed. Her leather jacket, her athame. Her poems. All those notebooks, filled with night after night of poetic scrawl…

Danae sighed, tucked her legs up beneath her on the couch. Building a new life demanded resourcefulness. And it was already starting to come together, in little ways. The blessing of an Exodus t-shirt in the Salvation Army the other day. A pack of Rider-Waite cards spread out on the Haight sidewalk, fortune-seekers' fives and tens making their way into her hands. She was lucky to even be sitting here, in the living room of a kind person.

Her old bedroom, her home, crumbled into the ash of memory—no way back, the journey was underway whether she liked it or not. What kind of world awaited her outside the shop? Celeste was not blocking her way anymore. It was time to find out how good her magick was, for real.

And magick or no, she knew how to live in the woods. Something, she realized, that Celeste probably didn't.

Pam had left her a couple of white tapers on the coffee table. A pen knife, a lighter, a little sage. Danae picked up a candle, carved a small star clockwise into its base, left it otherwise unanointed, nothing but her fingerprints pressed upon its surface. She thumbed the lighter.

I want a home. I want a family. I want to make some kind of art, and be really good at it. I want to be strong. I want to know where I fit into all of this.

The wick lit tall, a promising sign. She set the candle down in a silver holder and the flame danced a little before settling down, bright and strong. And she picked up a notebook, and started her life over on the next fresh page.

* * *

There was music coming from the grove.

Danae softened the tread of her sneakers. The chords of an acoustic guitar wove their way through the trees. For just a moment, all was as it must have been, twenty years ago: notes pouring forth in an intricate stream, giving voice to the leaves and the sun. You didn't come here if you were in it only for the fame and the groupies. She imagined a legendary rock star taking a break from his good fortune to practice his art alone, without an audience, no adoring fans at all. Just the wind, and the forest creatures, and whatever benevolent deity might be listening. *This is my gift, that I give back to you.*

She was torn. It wouldn't be polite to intrude on someone's communion, and this felt like nothing less. But the gentle tune had gotten a hold on her. And...

So, spider, what have you caught?

She stepped through the trees.

The guitarist's face was tipped downward, lost in concentration, framed by waves of waist-length hair, brown so dark it was almost black. Biker rings a row of scowls and sneers across his olivine fingers, big and rugged and *how can he play with those things?* she thought, as he realized he was no longer alone and looked up at her.

Silence, as the world seemed to stop, his storm-gray eyes at the very center. Expression neutral on a face that took her breath away; not smiling, but not *go away* either. He ran a hand through his hair as he stared back at her.

Holding his gaze, she settled on a stump and pulled a notebook from her backpack, nodded at him: *go on.* The song resumed while she dug for a pen, and she envied how well he played, fingers so sure of which fret to slide onto next. And that they weren't shaking like hers were, badly, barely able to get the pen cap off. She took a deep breath, touched ink to paper, and let his music fill in the lines.

A pathway. Dirt pounded hard by generations before, thousands and thousands of footprints to follow in. Swirls of fog, silver and cool against her face as she walked forward, a floating veil lit up by the moon. She added the tracks of her boots to the trail, like signing her name to a crowded book. Ahead, a shimmer. Up three stone steps to a small courtyard. In the center, on a stone platform, a glass bowl of water. Clear as crystal, sparkling, inviting. She plunged in her hands, cupped them together, drank. It tasted like absolution. Her mistakes washed away, all sins drowned down the back of her throat. But cold. Very cold. Beyond the bowl, a fire. She stepped down into the next courtyard, held her hands out to the fire. But it made her feel colder. She reached out to touch the flames, and as her fingertips skimmed the edges, she began to bleed. Bright red oozed out from beneath her nails. She felt it pour from her mouth, saw it splatter against the stone. Any forgiveness offered so easily promised utter corrosion.

She realized the grove was silent, and looked up at him.

His hands were clasped together beneath the guitar's body. Eyes watching her.

She blinked, centered herself back into the warmth of daylight. Where had he just taken her? Inside his dreams? To some hidden alcove of her own mind? She'd never written anything like that before.

It was *awesome*.

Sitting in repose like that, he looked so much the early 70's album cover longhair, but for the hi-tops and the Armored Saint t-shirt. The dark gift of this conscious nightmare could only be answered with something beautiful. She leaned down and plucked a couple of yellow flowers, threaded their stems through the headstock.

There, now you're a proper hippie. She couldn't stop herself from breaking into a smile.

He smiled back.

She was out on the main road before she could see the world clearly around her again. The brush of his fingers against her hand, electric before he packed up his guitar and walked off to whatever part of the city was his. She unfolded the memento he'd given her. Within a small galaxy of scribbled stars:

RESTLESS DEAD PRODUCTIONS PRESENTS!
13 CHURCHES
ENSPELLED
AXENHAMMER
$5
ALL AGES!!!

* * *

It was just a guy in a t-shirt. On a barstool. All she had to do was walk up and hand him five bucks. Right? She should have asked Pam before she left. All these years reading about shows in *Blast!* and *Aardschok America* and it only just now occurred to Danae that she didn't know how to get through the door. Sure, she knew all about who gave an amazing live performance, but the reviewers never mentioned anything about needing ID. And despite what the flyer said, this place kind of looked like a bar. Any kind of velvet rope, even one so mangy, made her anxious for not understanding how it all worked.

What spell could she cast, to get the door open? She was flipping through the runic alphabet when two kids walked up and handed him their fives, got their inner wrists inked in return. That was all. Feeling silly, she walked up to the door and held out a five to him with a small smile. He didn't even look at her, eyes pointed elsewhere down Mission as he raised the stamp and told her to turn her wrist over.

The stage was straight back. Bleacher-type seats descended from the wall all around the room, giant steps covered in black carpet. She sat down on the lowest step and commenced people-watching. The first band had already finished and were hauling their equipment offstage. Some flyers for upcoming shows were scattered nearby, local groups hoping to follow in the arena-bound footsteps of their Bay Area brethren. Their videos would play on Headbanger's Ball, and Saturday nights she'd turn her TV up as loud as possible despite the abysmal sound. The city was their backdrop, slamdancing in the cells of Alcatraz or speeding through the steep streets when they weren't wailing away before rabid crowds.

A guy in a Giants cap was talking about some blood-soaked show he'd been to last week; she couldn't tell if he meant the band's shock rock performance or an actual fight. Another guy in a handcuff belt was going on about his first lesson from a killer guitar teacher in the area. All around her, biker pins and embroidered patches, white basketball sneakers smudged over from mosh after mosh, punctuated here and there by spiky fingernails. Teased hair. The girls. Smudged black eyeliner, cigarettes tucked between filigree rings. One of them further up in the bleachers was wearing an amazing pair of spike-heeled boots, shiny buckles climbing up her calves, the perfect shoes to crush a man's heart. And Danae hadn't even known how to get in the door. A black wave of utter loneliness came rising up within her.

And then, before it could crash, a bass guitar came strumming up through the amps, followed by the guitars, quick sound check. She stood up to see the band—*oh*.

Him.

They looked just like anybody else in the crowd, the four of them: torn jeans, scuffed sneakers, leather bracelets. On the bass drum: ENSPELLED in angry black paint. She got up, slung her backpack over her shoulder and gently nudged her way to the front, the crowd letting her through, saving themselves for the headliners. He stood behind the mic, spotting her just as the drums kicked in. One nod, just to her: *I have a show to do, but I know you're here.* Four cymbal crashes and the guitars came to roaring life.

Distorted riffs came galloping hard from the amps, mean and foreboding, a spiked gauntlet thrown straight into her bloodstream. The drums came in to nail down the sinister pace, and then the lead guitar sparked a breakneck tempo change, summoned double-blasts of percussion at manic speed, and they all jumped into the pandemonium at maximum volume.

And his voice joined the cacophony: guttural growling over the chaos, his dark side unleashed as the lights played over his face. The boy from the woods— onstage was his photonegative, wrenching all the doom possible out of a human voice, the guitar in his hands now electric and arachnid and obsidian.

The others she caught in glimpses: the lead guitarist whipped a long mane of straight black hair around a determined sneer, plucked the notes from the neck of a flying V; the bassist, shaggy blonde hair that dusted his shoulders, tall and solid and holding it all together from the low end, glancing at the others as if keeping them in line; the drummer, a blotch of eyes and curls and sticks and derangement.

Most of the metal she knew was the kind conjured from leather jackets and beer cans, sweat-soaked missives that raged against conformity, corruption, the lies of the family and state. Fast and severe and truthful. Then there were the glam acts from L.A., spandex and sequins and rock'n'roll benders. Fun, but they were the junk food of metal, Pam's favorite but not hers. And then there were those who dabbled in arcane lore, singing of ancient battles and spirit evocations, but she hadn't heard anyone do it with this kind of ferocity.

And the stories they told. A cathedral full of murderous ghosts. Wasting away from a flesh-eating disease. Planet Earth, poisoned to death. Dark visions, all; and, she noticed, not one word about fallen angels or eternal damnation, no supreme being above to defy, no infernal puppetmaster pulling the strings from below. That eternal game, that endless source of lyric fodder, completely absent.

Beside her, the rest of the front row was a line of crossed arms and hard eyes: *impress me.* A few of them were nodding their heads, only a couple dancing. This was the mad whirl around the bonfire, the destination of all those witches on their broomsticks, delirious rites of yore reincarnated right here between pawnshops and discount clothing stores. All this bedlam, for only five dollars, and hardly anyone was enjoying it. What *idiots.*

She dropped her backpack to her feet, banged her head. *I understand this. I like this.* Her hair flew, her fists clenched, lifted up on all that sound, and she escaped inside the pounding drums, the shrieking guitars, ravenous for whatever horrific scenario they would fly her to next.

Three furious riffs to end it all, and the lights went on. The audience broke up behind her, knotted back up in their cliques, lighting cigarettes or going off for cokes. Wow. Just…*wow.* Whatever wild art the white candle was nudging her towards, whatever form it would take, it was definitely here. She rummaged in the pocket of her jean jacket. She needed her notepad. Her mind was on fire.

Sneakers hit the floor in front of her. She looked up.

Hello, said the gray eyes.

What to say? *You were great?* No. They were no mere "great." *I found it to be very…*ugh, too pretentious. He was staring at her. She had to say *something.*

Your band is fucking amazing, she was about to blurt, but——

"What were you writing?"

Deep voice. Totally hot. Writing? Writing what? She hadn't even gotten the notebook out of her pocket yet. What did he mean——

"Yesterday."

The word, that shared sunlit stretch of time in the grove, it shone like a piece of gold. She didn't even know his name yet and already something was *theirs.*

"Poems. Well, not really, not like rhyming stuff, more kind of freeform."

He said nothing, just waited for her to go on. She felt her chest tighten as she saw all her work, all the dreams she tried to capture with words, and tried to figure out how to cram them into the tiny box of her next sentence.

She took a deep breath, and continued.

"I was writing…I was just listening to you play. And the wind, and the trees, like the forest was part of it. Like some kind of instruments themselves. I listened to all of it together and tried to follow where you were going. It was like you were painting pictures, and I wrote them down as I saw them."

"What'd you see?"

She paused, thought about the harsh gloom his music had cast over her hand. It was like her mind wasn't even there, just the conduit of her pen pressing onward into the paper.

"At the end of it…blood. Lots of blood."

His eyebrows lifted. "From…*that*?

She shrugged and nodded and tried to slow down her pulse.

"I wanna hear more. Come back with us."

She followed him up onto the stage as he led her through the rest of the band, still packing up. The platform beneath her feet was just one foot up from the rest of the club, but a whole other world—like standing on a giant altar, where all the power came from. A hallway appeared beside the drumkit. Oh, yeah. Her first night at a show, and already she was going backstage.

* * *

Danae.

Little blonde thing, squeezed in between Matt and Gnash in the back. Alex had expected her to insist on shotgun like his last ex, but not only had she jumped in without complaint, she'd helped out getting their equipment into the van. They found out on the way over that her mother owned Starlight Occult. That place he'd always meant to stop by, but somehow never did.

The guys had unloaded everything back into the jam room before heading down the street for a post-gig drink. As usual, commentary.

"That's the girl you met in the woods? Isn't she a little plain for you?"

Ronnie tossed a handful of picks into his guitar case, curled his lip towards the living room's pocket doors, where she waited, out of earshot.

"She's cute." Matt shrugged on his jean jacket, shot Alex a look, *don't listen to him.*

Gnash bounded down the stairs in a flash of chains and blonde hair and they were out the door, Vic Rattlehead glowering from the back of Matt's jacket.

Alex headed to the living room, stood at the threshold. Watched Danae walk around the comfortable shabbiness of the band's house, reaching out to trace the hammered curve of a chalice, the carvings on a cinnabar box. He thought of Kaylee, with her pewter dragons, bragging about her trips to Salem, sapphire-jewelled fingers hovering over the latest tarot deck, *you're so grim, Alex*. He scanned Danae's jean jacket for any sign of common ground, some patch or pin of allegiance to one band or another, but there was nothing. Not even any makeup.

But she'd listened to an acoustic guitar—acoustic! not plugged in! not loud!—and heard blood. *That* interested him.

She looked around at the antique incense burner, a chunk of quartz, all trinkets given to him by one ex-girlfriend or another, pretty little presents meant to convert him to Wicca. He had the woods, and playing music, parties on the full moon to give thanks for the house, and that was all he needed. He had no interest in New Age trappings.

But Danae was not gazing at everything with the admiration he'd grown accustomed to. There was something else in her expression.

Scrutiny.

What formulas spelled themselves out across the back of her mind, what energies was she picking up from each knickknack? Could she tell they were devoid of ritual, spiritually empty? He felt thrust beneath a different kind of spotlight, much more focused than a crowd he was never sure was showing up for tunes or beer.

"Drink?" As much for himself as for her.

She nodded, and he went into the kitchen. He pulled down a bottle of cheap white wine—the drink of choice when girls were over, a habit picked up from Catrinel—and set it down on the counter, turned his palms down onto the cool cracked white of the sink. Leaned forward, closed his eyes and steadied himself on wood, stone, the foundation below. Conjuring up a home was no small feat, no matter what she thought.

His house. *Their* house. Its roots were in the Inner Sunset, Outer Richmond, random Sunday treks down the peninsula, garage after garage and playing with whoever else had turned up. Covers, Celtic Frost and Angel Witch and always some Led Zeppelin somewhere, floating through the haze of a slightly drunken afternoon. It wasn't too long before he'd found himself somewhere in the Panhandle, someone's Victorian loaded up with amps and cords and a cooler of cold beer. Ronnie, his best friend since forever, had been there, Matt too, solid, from prior jams. Gnash had drifted in from out of town, new face, X factor. The sound they made…something in the heaviness caught and held. The improvs crept in natural, an extension rather than a distracting tangent, each one taking a turn to lead the others, *here's what I'm bringing*. Afterward, a climb up into the gray mist of Strawberry Hill where talk became lyrics, beats pounded out on denim-clad thighs, the ideas coming almost too fast to catch in a battered notebook. When night fell, they'd come back down as Enspelled.

Alex pushed himself off the sink and grabbed the bottle, a couple of glass goblets.

He sat next to her on the couch, popped the cork and poured her a glass as a high-pitched yowl startled them both. A small ragged ball of gold had made its way into the living room, glared up at the couch with suspicious blue eyes.

"Oh, how cute! Boy or girl?" She stretched her hands out, made feline summoning noises.

Alex took a sip of wine. "That's Weedy. Matt—our drummer—he's a vet tech, she's one of the rescues that never found a home."

Weedy jumped up on the couch between them, sniffed at Danae, allowed three strokes on her back before turning her head and sinking her teeth into Danae's hand.

"Ow!" Ears flattened, tail lashing, but the little cat sphinxed herself firmly against Danae's thigh.

"Yeah, she's tough. It's why nobody wanted her."

Danae shrugged. "What's wrong with being tough?" She lowered her hand, gently tickling the cat's face. "She's purring. See, she likes this." Weedy rolled over and grabbed Danae's hand with her front paws and started kicking with the back, gnawing her fingers. Blood started to rise from the small scratches. Kaylee would have freaked out by now. Danae just laughed.

"She's just playing. Sad little shelter cat, it's probably the only way she knows how."

OK, now he *had* to know. "The poems you wrote…"

"Oh yeah." She disentangled her hand from Weedy's jaws and reached into her backpack. Dug out the notebook and flipped through, found the page, handed it to him. Went right back to teasing the cat.

The path, beneath his boots. Stepping right in her footprints, the latest person who'd walked this track, made this metaphoric mistake. It was like looking at his music from the other side of a mirror.

Not bad. Not fucking bad at all.

"It was the first time I'd ever written anything like that. I mean, I've had really vivid dreams, but never when I was awake." He looked up. Weedy was curled up in her lap, motor running, tamed for the moment.

"You've never done a spirit journey?"

She shook her head, smiling. Matt was right—she *was* cute.

"Really? And you worked in that shop, with all the candles and the oils and stuff…"

"I did a lot of New Orleans. Doesn't mean I did Native American. Or Celtic. Not my specialties."

The admission she didn't know everything, and so casual about it, *yeah, whatever.* He felt all the tension evaporate at the same time her cred skyrocketed.

"So…do you guys have an album?" she asked.

"Just a demo tape, three songs." He got up and grabbed one of their tapes out of the jam room. "We did it in ten hours. No worries about overproduction," he snorted. "But it's all our own material. No covers."

She turned the cassette over and looked at the cover. A serpent curled itself around a skull. Eternity winding around mortality, something Gnash had sketched one rainy afternoon. She gave it an approving look, stuffed it in the inner pocket of her jacket.

"So you've got practice space in here too?"

After that fateful day, the band had immediately set to casting for a house. Somewhere they could be together away from prying parents, hippie roommates, bitchy landlords, somewhere that had room to rehearse. It had taken months to put the decrepit house in Potrero Hill in order, but they prided themselves on something missing from the typical crash-and-burn rock'n'roll trajectory: discipline. They'd seen too many good bands draw no more than crowd of about a hundred, only the front row of about fifteen getting into it with a tiny pit, and that's as far as they'd go.

And they wanted to get a lot further than that. Badly.

He got up and opened the pocket doors into the jam room. Boxes of cassettes lined the walls, tapes to trade, tapes still to be listened to. A silver boombox was covered in stickers. All over the place, flyers, good nights promised by ransom-note fonts and badly-drawn demons. Beer bottles, torn notebooks, someone's plaid shirt tangled into a pair of dirty sneakers, a broken chandelier above it all. And everywhere, candles.

She sat down on the floor against a raggedy cushion. Looked up at him.

Play for me.

No fluttering of eyelashes, no leaning in to touch his arm or his thigh while flashing cleavage. It was usually at this point they would slide along the staircase, hinting to be taken upstairs. Not that he needed much encouragement. He hadn't found his muse yet, but he'd been having a lot of fun trying to find her.

Maybe you should start looking for her somewhere besides your bedroom.

Something was beginning here, very possibly something he'd been searching for, for a long time: duality. Enspelled was an outlet, a potent one, but playing music was as far as it went with them, with Gnash and Matt anyway. He wanted someone to trust within the opposite sex—a girl to share the grimoire with, balance him out. A safe place within her heart for passion, but also truth. Not the pretty stories skimmed off the major arcana, not the nebulous futures fudged from astrological charts, but hand in hand headfirst into the shadows.

(She has to come to you. Lay a hand on her in anything but friendship, and it shatters.)

Yeah. Yeah. He struck a match and lit three white pillars, turned off the overhead light.

"Acoustic? I'll have to grab it from upstairs."

"No. Electric."

"It'll sound incomplete," but he dragged a practice amp over anyway, sat on top of it. "It's not the whole sound, just one guitar."

"I know."

He reached into his case and brought out the solid black Warlock, goofed around a Metal Church lick.

"Those can make it sound different." She nodded towards a mess of pedals.

He looked over. "Wait. Yeah. You'll like this," he said, grabbing the cord of something bright orange. He struck a chord and stomped it, and suddenly it turned deep and spacey, shot through with echoes.

She nodded. "Yeah. Yeaaaaah."

He realized that he'd hardly asked her anything about her life—and there was so much he wanted to know. Bands, and shows, and neighborhoods, where she lived, where she hung out. *You worked at Starlight all this time? How come I've never seen you around? Who ARE you?*

She dragged her notebook onto her lap, clicked her pen over a blank page, and the way she smiled up at him…his fingers flew down the neck as he set his mind against hers, curious to see what morbid spectacle would emerge this time, determined to draw forth something brutal.

He caught her staring at the complicated fretwork, the light-speed exactness of his hands, kept his grin strictly internal. He hadn't meant to show off.

Alright. Maybe just a little.

* * *

Sunlight, ugh. Danae blinked awake, threw a hand up against the bright hot torment streaming in through the blinds. Stretched, tasted sourness. Her head spun slightly from the wine, but it couldn't stop the joy soaring through her body. She looked down at the phone number inked across her palm.

Getting up to leave the rehearsal room, handing him the pen. He'd nodded towards her notebook, a lot less empty than when the night began, but she shook her head, turned up her hand, the one she'd kept away from Weedy.

No. Here.

The writing was the doorway in. She had no friends to pave the way, no shared local history of detentions and concerts and bonfires on the beach, and she couldn't even begin to think about the exes that were surely lurking around in his past. All she had was her notebook.

Last night, sitting in front of the amp, letting the cold dribbling riffs guide her forth, scratching it all down as fast as she could. He sharpened her. Put edges on her dreams, still vague but beginning to catch in places. She needed to hit the sidewalk today, tarot for tourists, but for the moment, rent money could wait.

She dug the demo out of her jacket pocket. She loved how crude and homemade it was. The shop had kept her too busy to jump into metal's underground lifeblood of tape-trading—here was her first one, and already she knew the singer.

The front door banged open. Pam was home from the lunch shift.

"Hey! I was wondering what you'd gotten up to last night."

"I went to a show."

"Speed metal, right?" Pam wrinkled her nose. "I hope you had a good time, as much as you can with all that death and murder and stuff."

Fuck yeah, I did, and Pam was pulling off her heels, coming over to flop on the couch for one of Danae's foot massages. Before she realized what she was doing, Danae angled her hand so Pam wouldn't see the inked number. It didn't matter, when Pam threw her head back against the arm of the sofa and closed her eyes.

Bright pink toenails beneath her hands, so charming just yesterday. The trips to the park, trying to meditate together—having to *try*—where she'd just settled right into trance with Alex. Things were changing. What she'd wished for, coming almost sickeningly fast.

Chapter 3

Darkness. Sweat. An aching jawline, ringing ears, small prices to pay for all the fun she'd just had. Danae came back to earth as she walked up Market Street, Alex beside her, the lights of the Warfield fading behind them.

The night sent a chill through her damp hair as she rewound the evening. Three bands, all local thrash groups just starting to break big, Alex was friends with the first band's drummer and guested her in. The sound was massive, at least a thousand other people in the building, maybe *two* thousand. Hair in their eyes, stagelights reflecting off the sheen of their faces as they banged their heads and flashed devil horns of appreciation at the bands, *yes yes yes. More!*

"Shit," rubbing the heel of her hand below her chin, not displeased.

"Yeah, that's gonna leave a mark, "Alex said, shrugging on his leather jacket.

Her adrenaline was still surging. She'd been completely gone in the second act's frantic drumming when out of nowhere a huge body came flying right into her, *bang,* two panicked seconds of falling before Alex's pit-seasoned hands grabbed her shoulders and caught her. Back on her feet, his voice at her ear, *you OK?* She managed a dazed nod. It was total show etiquette, picking up the ones who got knocked down, he would have done the same for a total stranger. Somehow the brief embrace was even better for that. More pure.

"But it doesn't feel bad, you know? It hurts, but it hurts good."

"Souvenir you'll be feeling all day tomorrow."

"Fuckin' A."

Taxicabs cruised by in an endless 2 a.m. river to the left. Traffic lights dangled over the street, big yellow lamps to guide the way, steadfast counterpoints to the martini-shaped neon and rundown hotel fluorescence dappling the rest of the street. A pair of dirty white heels click-click-clicked ahead of them on the sidewalk. Ragged shadows slinked against the wall, peering through the smoke of ten-cent cigarettes. In the distance, the hills of Upper Market twinkled, twelve blocks and a whole other galaxy away.

Coming up on the right, the curve of Polk Street, Starlight lurking in the distance. Row after row of glass candles, bottles of oil, jars of incense, just waiting to be activated by a prayer, a chant, a fervently whispered wish. Going to the shows was bringing out energies within her that could never be summoned by intense introspection—it was like a big piece of the puzzle that the books, so insistent on quiet meditation, were leaving out.

"We should go up the woods. See what happens when we're completely out of the city," said Alex.

"Should I bring a picnic basket?" Half-kidding, thinking about cakes and wine.

"We'll go up to Tamalpais. There's spots there, totally hidden. Golden Gate, you can kind of still hear everybody, you're still surrounded by the world. This is better for when you need to get really far away."

The sign for Haight Street loomed above. Time to part. Sigh.

"I'm headed home." She nodded up the incline breaking off from Market.

"I'm off to work. Check it out, we've got a new flyer. The manager's coming in late tonight, we're all hijacking the copier." He pulled a drawing from the pocket of his leather, Gnash's artwork again, a skull with bat wings flapping above Olde English lettering, a show in North Beach this time.

"Next Saturday. You know you're on the guest list."

"You know I'll be there."

She reached out to hug him goodnight, breathed in cedar and cinnamon and the musk the show had wrung out of him, restrained herself from burying her face in his hair. He hugged her back hard. A metal hug—roughness shielding deep affection, she'd watched guys at the show practically knock each other over with saying hi.

She reluctantly lifted her head and he stepped back, let her go. In fifteen minutes she'd be crashed out while he was just starting his shift at the 24-hour print center, but for now, standing at the bottom of Haight, bathed in her own perspiration, exultant. Secret hideaways up in Marin, huh? She stuffed her hands in the pockets of her jean jacket, walked a few steps backwards.

"Later," giving him one last smile through a tangle of hair before pivoting towards the incline.

"Later," behind her, silent for a few seconds before she heard his footsteps resume the walk up towards Duboce, and her fingers went up to her face and she hoped she woke up tomorrow with the biggest, ugliest, most lingering bruise her skin could manage.

* * *

"My name is on the guest list."

"I'm sorry, sir, I don't see it. I'm afraid I can't let you in."

"Bullshit, he said my name was on the list. Don't you know who the fuck I am? I'll have you fired if you don't let me in, right fucking now."

Dance music slithered from beyond the silver double-doors of a nightclub, the kind of place where the guys wore suits and the girls all had perfect manicures. Danae glanced at scuffle breaking out at the head of the line and smirked. No silly velvet ropes where she was going.

She maneuvered through the flashing angles of North Beach, the tourists and the drunks and the clubgoers clogging up the sidewalks. She passed the tawdry pink of a strip club; the guy out front stepped into her path, *wanna make some money, honey?* She elbowed past him and wondered how Pam put up with it. Wove through knots of chattering people outside an Italian restaurant, crossed to Broadway before a line of impatient headlights. Up ahead, jean jackets, back patches. Her people.

An hour later, she was standing at the back of the club, halfway through Enspelled's set. She badly wanted to be in the crowd, dancing with the two or three other people getting into it, but no. She needed distance to study the whole thing, take it apart. Figure out where she belonged. This was only her third show and already she knew that being an appreciative audience member was not going to be enough.

Being in a band sounded so glamorous, but quickly she was coming to realize how much climbing the local circuit could suck. A new hurdle lurked at every turn of the labyrinth: walking into a club with what looked like a healthy turnout, just to see them all leave when their friends in the first act packed up their stuff and split. Other bands taking forever to break down their gear, biting into precious stage time. Indifferent audiences, or hecklers that wouldn't shut the fuck up. But turning down the 1am slot at a local dive was one less chance to get noticed.

Matt had chatted with her before the show. *Alex says you write poems. Cool.* Now, behind his drums, he was bursting with the need to smash and conquer. Her hand was still healing up from Weedy's bites—the same feral energy glimmered all around him, but he'd focused it to do his damage on the skins. She hardly knew him, but already she could tell that Matt was someone you didn't want on your bad side.

To the left, Ronnie. Ronnie. Ronnie was going to be difficult to work with. Where Alex was trees and forests, warm earth, Ronnie was the cold violet of deep space. She watched his hands disappear into a complex solo, total concentration to make sure every note was firmly fixed in place. The planes of his handsome face were etched with disdain, driven by a perfectionism that made the expression perhaps permanent. Her body didn't care about this and craved the touch of his long, slender fingers.

She shook her head, moved her eyes to the right. Gnash. Thrashing his head in time to the beat, strumming a pick down on the bass strings, his energies should be coursing off him like sweat right now, but he was smooth and clear as glass before her probing mind. The wyrd rune, tabula rasa, powers undiscovered, untapped? Or…perhaps mastered. There was an odd serenity about him in the midst of the madness, the way he watched over the other three. She wondered what kind of art he did when he wasn't sketching out generically macabre heavy metal cassette covers.

She walked to the stage when their set ended.

"OK, so I've got the flyers for the next show," said Alex, lifting a stack of paper from his guitar case.

Ronnie grabbed them and scanned the art. "Not bad, Gnash. You're starting to not suck."

"Fuck off."

"Whose turn is it to hand them out?" said Alex.

"Mine. On my smoke break, hah." Ronnie grabbed his leather jacket from the back of the stage.

"I'll help you." Danae stepped onto the stage.

"Hey Alex, when did you decide to put the groupies to work?"

"Dude, she's not a groupie."

Ronnie's foxlike face swept her up and down like a laser beam: no makeup, hair back in a ponytail, baggy t-shirt. "No, I guess not."

She tightened her face, tried not to think about all the girls who'd come before her. The ones she'd just been compared with, who'd had their shit together in a way she only dreamed of. She grabbed half the flyers out of his hand, stepped back down to the floor.

"Whatever, *rockstar*," turning around, threading her way to the door. Back out into the night, she glanced down the street at the glittering lights of other clubs. Wondered who else in North Beach just had a shitty moment. She felt a tap on her shoulder.

She turned around. Ronnie.

"Hey, sorry about that. I can be an asshole sometimes."

Maybe he was genuinely sorry, or maybe he was just doing it because Alex told him to, either way it felt good to have that pretty face asking for her forgiveness.

"Forget it," she said, shaking it off.

She moved a few feet away from him, leaving him near the curb while she backed towards the wall, angling so the clubgoers would have to walk between them to get back to the main drag for their post-show drinks and slices of pizza. She held one out to a guy in a SFSU t-shirt, who took it.

Ronnie lit up a smoke. "You worked at that witch shop in the Tenderloin."

She nodded, keeping an eye on the door, both to watch for potential show-goers and to avoid the directness of his gaze.

"You must know a lot," he said.

"I know some things."

"I dunno, I never went for all those smelly perfumes. I like doing it all from the mind."

It was meant to be an insult, but she couldn't help snorting. It was the standard line of the New Age Girl's Boyfriend—one of the archetypes who approached her counter again and again—this was the guy who hung back while his girlfriend leaned forward to ask about zodiac signs and moon phases. He'd always glance around the shop with a faint look of amusement, so cool and removed, just here to indulge the silly whims of his woman. Yeah. Ronnie was that guy.

"So you're like Wiccan?"

"No."

"So what *do* you do?"

What a nosy little fucker. As socially inept as she felt, even she knew you didn't go around asking people straight-up what they practiced. It was something you waited patiently for them to reveal, if they ever felt like it, if you ever earned it. But she saw no reason to withhold the information, at the moment.

"Right now, just writing. Just making art." More flyers left her hands. She hoped they weren't ending up in the trash can down the block.

"Sometimes I think that's the best thing to do," he said. "Like yeah, circles and chanting and all that, but you know when books tell you to stare at a dot on the ceiling for an hour and that's true focus? What the fuck. I'd rather play, that's just as much true focus, actually more because I'm actually *doing* something with the concentration."

Hm. "Yeah, and you ever notice that good things start happening when you do it? Like the universe knows, and it's trying to help you out."

"Totally. Although I'd really like it to hurry the fuck up with a recording contract."

She nodded and handed out the last flyer, walked back over to him.

"All gone already?" he asked.

She glanced at the sheets still left in his hands. "Alex didn't bring that many."

He looked away, dragged on the last of his smoke. "It's just 'cause you're a girl."

"They still took them, didn't they?"

He laughed. It was one of those sneaky laughs, as if he was enjoying a personal joke on everything, and keeping it completely to himself. He dropped his smoke to the ground, thrust the rest of his stack at her.

"Then we'll let you do all the promoting from now on. 'Cause you're so *good* at it," he said, going back into the club.

Her hands itched to drop the flyers to the ground, *fuck you*, but no. She couldn't take it out on the rest of the band. She went back to stand by the wall. Alex walked out right as the last one left her fingertips.

"Van's loaded up. C'mon, let's go get a slice."

They walked up into the thick of the nightlife, Alex already into plans for the next show back down in the Mission. She stayed silent and nodded at the appropriate points while she wondered what to do. Saying something would make her look weak, whiny, unable to take care of herself. And he'd known Ronnie longer, she was the one who had to tread carefully. How to slay this dragon, or at least get it to quit breathing fire at her?

Her tongue would have to remain firmly bitten. Fine. But if Ronnie insisted on being an asshole, she would make him into a useful asshole. By the time they reached the pizzeria, half a poem had written itself across the inside of her skull. It involved white-hot pits of flame and the merciless laughter of a demoness. And it still wasn't evil enough.

* * *

Dirty crystal glasses caught the afternoon sunlight in the Duboce Triangle, sent it shining across chipped china. Pam picked up a long, slim fork shaped like a trident, tapped it against the heel of her hand. She'd improvised playthings out of household objects less elegant. It had potential.

"How much?" she asked the silver-haired gent behind the table.

"A dollar." There was a conspiratorial look in his eyes, as if recognizing her intentions, fellow traveler on the path of perversity.

She gave him a crumpled bill and a sly grin over tarnished stemware, carefully tucked the fork upward into her fringed leather bag. She looked over at Danae, who was rooting through a box of hardbacks. From the size of the seller's collection, that would take a while. She lit up a smoke.

"So this Ronnie guy sounds like a real piece of work."

"He's nice, then he's a dick, then he's nice, then he's a dick again." Danae was flipping through something on the medieval castles of Europe. Some Noe Street yuppie was replacing the book on their coffee table, unknowingly sparking metal lyrics with their stylish discards.

"He sounds like the kind of customer I absolutely loathe. The ones who hold out the dollar and then yank it away."

"Are you serious? People have actually done that to you at the club?"

"Well, nobody's actually gone, 'here, stripper stripper!' but yeah."

Last night, in fact. The only sour note in a very, very good evening at work. She was glad Danae was finally sharing her secret—Pam had known there was someone else, almost definitely a guy—but she wasn't about to share hers in return. No way. She'd spent way too many hours before her shrine, candles ablaze, casting about madly for a way out of the club. It might have appeared in the form of Tommi Roxx.

His band was in town—Vicious Vice, their music videos were all over the place right now—and they'd come in, all bright spandex and hairspray partytime. Julie had literally jumped off the stage and into the guitarist's arms. Someone had rushed to the DJ to cue "Savage Romance" up in her set, someone else was digging through her costumes for a blue lace dress just like the girl in their video had worn. Anything, anything to show them *I'm hot, I'm sexy, I'll do anything, Mr. Beautiful Rockstar God.*

Pam's heart had skipped a beat along with everyone else's, but she refused to pander. She changed into a purple metallic bikini and had the DJ spin Sade, throwing aside the rock'n'roll strut for earnest soulful heat, offering the band the same quiet storm as the rest of the patrons. No special treatment, nothing to give away the huge crush she had on the lead singer.

Tommi was a man internationally desired for a sweet face and tight pants, and he would pay *her* to dance for him.

Tommi's hands reached for her, but she willed herself to dance away from that long blonde hair, that sexy surf-dude voice, stay out of his reach. When it came time to work the floor, she changed into a long silver gown. Played a game of hide-and-seek all around him, slipping into a darkened cluster of tables for a little while, then emerging triumphant to disrobe directly across from him onto another paying lap, only to disappear again, forcing him to wonder where she went, and with who.

When she finally walked nearby, he caught her arm and offered a pair of aphrodisiacs: deep blue eyes and a hundred dollar bill.

His hands were draped over the sides of the leather armchair—he knew the drill—as she slid onto his thighs. Pure enjoyment lit up her face as she tossed her hair, stared into his eyes and melted the dance over into genuine foreplay. The songs flowed into each other, turned from three-minute chunks of purchased time back into party tunes. She flirted, vamped, ground herself into him until she ended up in his arms, somewhat spent, lying back on his chest, clad in only her g-string.

"You are incredible."

She said nothing, let his voice caress her cheek.

"Come back with me to my hotel."

She turned around to look at him, but still said nothing. She got up to leave, *time's up*, and she cloaked her lust in polite refusals, denials, she hid a smirk as he actually pushed Julie out of the way to run after her.

"Please. I wanna talk to you."

She carefully unspooled the evening through an all-night diner, then a park, so by the time the magic moment arrived, he'd been too exhausted to chase her around the hotel room. There were promises to see her again, take her down to L.A., time would tell if the trysts would materialize into something real.

Danae was handing over a couple bucks and sliding the castle book into her backpack.

"I gotta run," said Danae. "The Goodwill's gonna close in an hour."

"S'alright. I'm gonna fall over if I don't get some sleep." Not a word. Even though she was so excited she could burst, not one word. Secrets needed to stay bricked up to retain their strength. That, and she knew Danae would just laugh at her. At him. *Oh, that poseur*, she could already hear Danae saying, so casually stepping hard on her dreams.

"Sleep late. Tomorrow I'm gonna be up north."

That was okay. Pam no longer had time for the grove, either.

* * *

It was a beautiful day for a journey out of the city, in the chariot of a green '77 Camaro, borrowed from Matt's brother. The sun glinted off Alex's rings as he drove them north, Iron Maiden's second album blaring from the stereo. No operatic wailing yet, no massive stage shows, and Danae liked them better that way, back when they were all gruff vocals and black leather jackets and London streets full of nightmares. Paul D'Anno begged for his captured soul, voice swerving from gentle to ragged and back again, guitars lit up with sorcery and clear azure skies as they crossed the Golden Gate Bridge. Beyond, clouds piled thick on the horizon, a silver feather boa dropped by a careless ocean goddess to float on top of the water.

A picnic basket sat at her feet beside her backpack—grapes and cheese and walnuts packed into a lidded wicker bowl with a couple of sodas, thrift-store score along with a tattered quilt. So tempting to throw a handful of rose petals inside, her hottest wish scribbled seven times down a sheet of notebook paper and hidden at the bottom, but no. This afternoon would unfold without any glamours at all.

To the left, a breathtaking drop of pure green forest. Alex swung onto a shoulder of dirt, pulled a U-turn and drove back to park where the asphalt curved outward, one of the gawking spots scattered along the road. Way up from the touristy boardwalk of Muir Woods proper, nothing but virgin earth as they got out of the car. He led the way, a gym bag slung over his shoulder, stepping between the trees, angling down carefully into the drop. Danae followed, praying she wouldn't fall on her ass, which looked terrifyingly easy to do.

"Just go slow."

"Like I have a choice!"

Tree to tree, free hand clutching onto bark, connecting the dots. Dirt crumbled beneath her sneakers. The shade gave way to a patch of shine, and a break in the steepness turned their feet level again, towards a meadow dotted with pinkish wildflowers, perfect spot to drop their gear.

No path to lead the way here, complete invisibility from the road. The hill descended sharply into a valley, and she relished the bucolic danger that lay before her, thousands and thousands of trees bowing in the wind. She thought of landscape painters gingerly making their way down the hill, risking a deadly fall to capture the scene before her in strokes of oil and watercolor.

She spread out the quilt, opened the basket and plucked a grape from its green plastic cage.

"So, when you guys are writing—what comes first, the music or the lyrics?"

"I write some words, and then Ronnie writes the music around them. But I was thinking about what you did that day in the park. Letting the music write the words."

He lifted a tape recorder out of the gym bag—ah, she'd been wondering why he hadn't brought his guitar—and hit PLAY. Electric chords rose up from the ground, a riff that no doubt sounded powerful onstage, but here, dwarfed tinny. But work was work, and she focused on the rhythm as she drew out her notebook and two pens, lay down on her belly to put the blank page before them both. Thick, heavy sludge, chug-chug-chugging over and over, then a climb up the fretboard, then a plunge down the lowest strings, then the sludge again, over and over, waiting for a voice. He stretched out beside her.

The first idea darkened the paper with his handwriting. *Fist, and fire. Fist, and fire.* Orange and yellow, aggressive and red. The Inquisition? Pitchfork revolt? Fist vs. fire, or were they working together? She didn't know, but that was OK, specifics could come later. *Burning ever higher,* he added. She frowned—they could do better than that—but it filled in the space of the sludge, gave them something to build on.

That stage growl came pouring out of his mouth, picking it up, setting it down within the tempo, trying it out. *Fist, and fire. Fist, and fire. Burning ever higher.* Leaving the climb and the plunge blank. Two more cycles, and she broke in on the climb, just as guttural: *Raging through the dead of night.*

The plunge stayed empty as he turned to look at her. The sludge came back around, and he sang again, nodding at her to take the climb. And then she took the plunge: *Through the ash, the witches' light.*

She jotted the lines down. He raised his voice, dared her to follow. Hear herself. It took guts to make that leap. Did she sound stupid? He pushed her. *Louder*, he commanded her with his own volume. *Open up.* Her vocal cords thrummed. Something uncurled from her chest, made its way out uncertainly. No amps to accompany her, no volume to bolster her confidence, just the trees where her voice unexpectedly hatched and stood naked before him.

The riff faded away into silence.

He rewound the tape.

"Again. There's more in there."

Growling back and forth, back and forth, drawing out new pieces. The page filled up with lyrics, and the page after. She quickly saw the limitations of doing it this way: while the riffs were heavy and evocative, they locked you in. There would be no screaming away into the yonder past that eighth beat, if a good line surfaced to mess it all up.

That, and she realized for such a pagan-sounding band name, the lyrics were all over the place. Violence and darkness, but nothing cohesive around a theme, which should be esoteric, given the name. This thing they'd just done? Witch burnings. Enspelled should be building on that.

Alex spread out his leather jacket and lay down on his back. She scooted beside him and rested her head on his shoulder. Together they watched the clouds, the forest all around them quiet and alive, and she was ecstatic to be back within that cinnamon-cedar scent again.

Pam's hands and the grove meditations flashed across her mind, and just as quickly disappeared.

The sky's shifting light cast down gray chill, bright yellow warmth. Now somebody else had entered Danae's notebook, tangled his handwriting together with hers. A lock of his hair brushed her cheek, and she closed her eyes.

"Can I record you?" asked Alex.

Her heart jumped. "Why?"

"Because it sounds cool."

The thought made her excited and nauseous in equal amounts. It helped that she knew all their songs, at least all the ones on the demo, by heart already.

"Gimme a minute."

"Don't be nervous."

"I'm not," she lied. "I just wanna watch a few more clouds." *And I want to remember every detail, before I scare you off with how much I'll suck.*

* * *

The jam room was fully ablaze for Danae's ordeal. Candles burned from every pewter stick, every empty bottle. Alex had brought home a couple of six-packs, made sure everyone had a few beers to loosen up, break the ice of getting to know her. He remembered clearly how hard it was, the first time you had to impress a bunch of strangers with your music, and not even with an instrument, but your voice, your own raw soul roaring out of your body. She'd have to be tough to handle it, in all kinds of ways. But she was walking into an existing group, the newcomer, there'd be no laid-back afternoon in someone's Upper Haight garage for her. The least he could do was mellow things out, just a little. He lit a stick of sage and let it smolder away in a bronze dish.

Flames, and swirls of smoke, a touch of inebriation, sticks and picks and the circle was cast. The slow drip of melting wax turned every rehearsal into a ritual, atmospheric reminder that the mistakes, the aching fingers, long hours spent confined within this room, all the banes of fledgling bands everywhere, this was their offering to get better, better, *better*. And in front of the right people, someday.

He'd given Danae a few songs to learn, verses she could break in on, lines to sing back against him. Her response to his call changed with each drama: an ally, an enemy, another voice there to challenge him, push him further. How would this play out onstage? It wouldn't be all on him to carry the crowd anymore, but two voices to tell the story.

He hadn't bothered recording her after all; the tape recorder wouldn't do justice to her voice the way live, warm sound could. But he'd run it by the band, what the hell, *let's bring her in for a rehearsal, try this out.*

"We don't need a girl in the band," Ronnie had said.

"What, you don't like Bolt Thrower?" Gnash sounded offended.

"Bolt Thrower are OK. But that girl's a bass player. Not a singer."

"Dude, why not? It'll be interesting, at least," said Matt, knowing how important it was never to regard practice as a pain in the ass. Gnash agreed. And that was that.

And here she was, in the middle of it all, with her crooked little smile. The world was not so gray with her in it. How could it be, when she smelled like cookies. And she was taking forever to make a move. An audition, yeah, serious business, but he felt like messing with her head.

"Figures this is happening on the hottest day of the year, right?" lifting his t-shirt over his head. No big deal, right, watching her eyes.

"Oh, fuckin' A," said Matt, pulling his shirt off too, before Alex had a chance to catch her reaction.

Gnash and Ronnie stripped down as well, and she glanced around with a priceless look on her face, *is this part of the test too?* before she shrugged and yanked off her shirt, joined them in a little black crop top, inadvertently destroyed Alex.

Now—taking up the spare mic, Matt clacked his sticks together, 5-6-7-8—

Come the dusk the dead will rise
Rotting flesh and bleeding eyes

There it was. All this time, he'd been regarding the feminine principle as a lover, never thinking to seek her out as a fellow artist. Now, she was entering the most powerful place in his life, the band. Her voice rushed out from beneath his like a hidden wave, throwing in emphasis or running off with the narrative completely. Now the songs were dialogues, meanings completely shifted when the verse came from a different person. Throwing back her hair, wild eyes, she was loving it.

Trapped into this dance of death
In this moment, your last breath

A few songs spilled over into a half-hour, then an hour, they called it quits when her newborn voice couldn't take it anymore. Dark by this time, the chill getting their shirts off the floor and back onto their shoulders.

Danae went off into the kitchen for another well-deserved beer. Matt got up from his kit and followed her, pausing at the doorway to turn back and nod once to everybody.

Ronnie pulled out a pack of smokes, headed out to the backyard.

"Dude. I didn't know you wanted your girlfriend to join the band." He lit up.

"I haven't done anything with her." Yet. "She's here because—dude, didn't you fucking *hear* her?"

Gnash stepped outside to join them, thumbed the lighter on a menthol.

"I like it. She makes you sound different—the way her voice is coming in and out of yours, like she's the girl version of you. But can she put up with the rehearsals and late nights and shit, is what I wanna know."

"I'm guessing yeah. She has no problems shedding blood."

Gnash's eyebrow went up, awaited an explanation.

"She doesn't freak out getting banged up at shows, kind of likes it, actually. And she thinks Weedy's hilarious."

"Oh yeah, Matt's in the kitchen with her already talking about a song idea."

"That just leaves you, Ronnie," said Alex.

Ronnie took a long drag, sighed out the smoke. "At least she'll be good for promoting the shows."

"OK, then. It's done." Alex opened the door back into the kitchen, took down a set of shotglasses. The flu herbs to take care of her throat would come later. Right now was partytime.

Danae was trying to keep her face neutral, but the brightness in her eyes gave her away as he opened a bottle of Jagermeister. Breaking out spirits generally didn't mean *no.*

He poured a heavy measure in each glass and handed them out, lifted his up.

"Cheers to Enspelled's new singer."

They all lifted their glasses as Danae blushed, grinned, tried to control at least six warring emotions. She'd have to get that under control before she got in front of an audience, but for now, she was allowed to be adorable.

"Blood, sweat, and rage," said Matt, bumping his glass against hers.

"Bring us your best screams," said Gnash, with a clink.

"Hope you're ready to bust your ass," said Ronnie, hitting her drink hard enough to make a couple drops fly out.

Chapter 4

The moon shone fat and full in the sky over Potrero Hill. Danae heard the party before she spotted it, laughter and guitars and people enjoying being loud, staggering off the porch onto the sidewalk. Her excitement quickly plummeted into anxiety. All these strangers—all these people who would now be looking at her as Enspelled's new singer…

(The new singer. Yeah. A position you earned by being good with your voice and your imagination. Go forth and be proud.)

She was still glad for the thyme she'd sprinkled in her sneakers beforehand. The herb for good first impressions.

She stepped up onto the porch, nodded at the curious glances thrown her way. Nasty Savage blared through the open door, and the air was thick with the earthy, friendly smell of good weed. Candles lit up the crowded living room and a tarot deck was spread out across the bottle-cluttered coffee table—the Motherpeace, she'd know those round cards anywhere—beyond, the jam room's pocket doors were closed. Smart move, not chancing open beers—or enthusiastic drunks—around the equipment.

"It's never a good thing to have your cards read by someone known to yell 'See! See, I told you!' after one of their readings proves true. It sounds like they're trying to cover up all the times that it *didn't*," said the girl presiding over the reading, her green fingernails skipping from card to card.

"Oh, you mean like Alessandra? She's a poseur anyway. She doesn't know the runes very well, she looks down on people who aren't into tradition, and besides, she stood me up. Hey!" Matt disentangled himself from the fortunetelling circle and rose to greet Danae. Hard squeeze that took her breath before turning her around to face the group, "This is Danae, she's our new singer."

Danae smiled at three girls parked on the couch as she sat down cross-legged on the floor.

"Congratulations," said the girl giving the reading, authoritative in a long black braid, full-figured and giving off Botticelli vibes in a long black dress and a necklace of tiny daggers.

"I know you!" On the left, brown feathered hair, overlapping teeth, a name necklace that spelled out MELISSA in silver cursive script. "You're the girl who used to work at Starlight Occult! You sold me my first deck! And now you're in the band? You're gonna kick ass!"

"Thank you," small shy grin.

"Yeah, that's great. Now can we get back to the reading? My life is hanging in the balance." Red curls glinted from the other side of the couch. "No offense, but I gotta find out if this guy is gonna work out."

"Linda, no. Anybody you meet in a bar who starts bragging about his past lives is *not* someone you can build a future with. Hell, your ex Steve is better than this guy," said the Botticelli girl.

"And all that stuff about martial arts? Not that martial arts are bad, but seriously, it's like these kinds of guys are always going on about how tough they are, how smart they are, just because they took some Tae Kwan Do classes," said Melissa.

"Oh, yeah. Watch out for those."

"The kind who's always blowing his own mind with how powerful he is," Danae chimed in.

"Oh, he's blowing *something* all right, and it's not his mind," said Botticelli Girl, and everybody cracked up as Matt returned with a beer, dropped the cold can into Danae's hand, filled her in. "That's Catrinel. Gnash's girlfriend. She's good people."

"A good practitioner doesn't pull that trip. Like a lot of people think being a high priestess means getting to boss people around, but somebody's who's really good doesn't need to push to get their shit done," said Melissa.

"A good priestess is a good psychologist, really," said Danae.

"A good priestess knows first aid and how to resist arrest," said Catrinel, arching an eyebrow at everyone.

I like her.

"So to answer your question, Linda, no. And you don't need the cards to tell you that. Just fuck him and get it over with and don't attach any more importance to it. Now, where did I put that wishing shit?" She rummaged in her tooled leather purse.

Melissa's eyes fixed on something behind Danae.

"Matt," she said, and gestured with her chin.

Behind them, a very drunk guy was holding a distraught Weedy up by the scruff of her neck. Before he could make the obvious joke, Matt sprang up off the floor and got in his face.

"You put my cat down right fucking now. *Right fucking now.*"

The guy dropped Weedy onto the floor, held up his hands, *I was just playing* while Matt grabbed the collar of his shirt.

"Do you know who that guy is?" Danae heard Catrinel ask, behind her.

"No idea," said Linda.

Weedy wove around everyone's legs and made a mad dash upstairs as Matt dragged the guy into the hallway.

"You're getting the fuck out of my house. Don't you ever fucking come back here." The people hanging around the front door took one look at Matt's face and quickly scattered. Danae got up and drifted into the foyer as Matt pushed the guy out the door. A ponytailed girl ran up to Matt, tried to intervene, but Matt wasn't having any of it.

"He used to get into a looooot of fights before he became a drummer," drawled a voice behind her. Ronnie was coming down the stairs, slowly, sliding a little against the bannister. "Music's what keeps him sane. Mostly."

He slung his arms around Danae's shoulders, too rough to be friendly. Whiskey breath warmed her face, and his sudden weight threatened to pull her down.

"You know I can be a real asshole, right?"

"You're being one right now."

Her libido snuck past her repulsion and liked his embrace very much. She pushed the thought aside as he pointed out a girl standing on the porch.

"That's Kaylee. She used to date Alex. Isn't she hot?" Wavy brown hair, cleavage peeking through a laceup top, tight jeans that showed off her curves, rocker pixie straight off a fantasy canvas.

Why lie? "Yeah, she is."

"What are you, a fucking lez?"

She turned towards him and her voice dropped an octave. "Then why'd you ask me if she's hot?"

Ronnie went silent, then clapped her on the shoulder.

"You'll be a good cheerleader," he said, laughing to himself and stumbling towards the porch.

Resisting the urge to kick him in the seat of his pants, Danae made her way to the kitchen, toward an intense huddle of black leather and cigarette smoke.

"…and that's what he told you? Bullshit, they didn't go on late due to technical problems, it was because they were too fucked up to play."

"But what the fuck else is there to do in Bumfuck, Illinois?"

"It's that bass player's fault. They've been going to shit ever since that shithead joined the band."

"S'cuse me. Hey, Gnash."

"Hey, Danae. Guys? This is our new singer. Danae, this is Mike and Bobby. They're in Axenhammer."

"Hey, what's up." She offered them her hand, received two crushing shakes in return.

"Can't wait for your next show. We'll be there. Our singer can give you stuff to take care of your throat," said Bobby.

"Alex has me covered. Where is he, by the way?"

Gnash nodded towards the sliding door. "Out in the yard. Uh, he's pretty wasted."

"I'll have to catch up, then," she said, grabbing another beer from the cooler.

"So anyway, yeah, you know the only reason he's playing bass is 'cause he sucks the worst on guitar—"

"Fighting words, asshole," she heard Gnash growl against a sudden apologetic protest, as she stepped back out into the night.

The new Slayer album blasted forth from the boombox, enthroned before a bonfire lighting up the center of the yard. Everywhere, bodies spun and smashed against each other. A big white sign was stabbed into Alex's herb garden: TOUCH THESE PLANTS AND I'LL KICK YOUR ASS. A few lawn chairs held party guests both animated with gossip and totally passed out. A bespectacled girl in black sat with a leg crossed beneath an oversized notebook, pencil tucked into a sensible bun. She smelled like art school.

"I'm doing a series of sketches called Drunken Men," she said, very soberly.

Danae raised her can and tipped her head forward—cheers to *that*—and sorted through headbanging locks of brown, black, blonde. There—wrestling against a kid in a muscle shirt, both of them cracking up as a third guy threw himself into it and everyone fell to the ground, laughing. A surge of affection bloomed from her heart towards the boys rolling around on the grass, the tarot girls inside sharing secrets by tiny fires. She hadn't even stepped onstage yet, and already there were people who were cheering her on.

A hand shot out from the pile of boys and grabbed her leg. Alex had found her. She dropped her beer as she was pulled down into their sweaty hands and dirty jeans and violent euphoria. Pushing to get away from someone, pulling to start it against somebody else. A couple of girls saw her out in the mayhem and joined in. Bruises accumulated on her knees and elbows but she soared above it, black and blue such a small price to pay for turning her aggression loose.

The tape ended. The ground rang out with cries of *Flip it over! Flip it over!* And soon, that half-hour of absolute evil was screaming itself out through the yard all over again.

All around her, kids just as filthy and amped as she was. She felt cold water hit her sneakers—someone had turned on the garden hose.

"Rob! You *fuck!*" as someone tackled the guy responsible, someone else snatched the boombox out of harm's way, and the fracas dissolved into a vigorous mudfight. Cautious partygoers emptied the chairs in a hurry while more raucous guests ran out of the house and dove in. Alex caught Danae around the waist and pushed her into a puddle. She smeared mud into his hair. Everywhere, faces disappeared behind masks of raw earth, and the sludge people howled and battled and wallowed in a night that would be talked about for years to come.

One of us. One of us.

* * *

The green of Golden Gate Park, the ferocity of Holy Moses. Tonight Danae hit the stage, and she needed some time away from everybody. Back to the grove, her Walkman blocking out softball games and barking dogs, another woman's guttural vocals for company.

She was no longer the girl in the nightgown, walking at midnight towards her doom. Danae was now what was waiting in the woods.

Through the tangle of weeds to the narrow path, and she was at the circle of stumps. On her jacket, a few band patches, a couple pentacles mail-ordered from pagan catalogs. The back, the all-important declaration of total fandom, was still blank. In her backpack, a fresh notebook. Cassettes to consume, then throw back into the trading pool. A couple copies of *Kerrang!* New albums from Heathen and Testament, local success stories. *If they can do it, so can we.*

On her left hand, a bandage.

Chopping tomatoes in Pam's tiny kitchen, something to make the store-bought spaghetti sauce taste a little better—so *sick* of ramen—Pam on the couch, flipping through one of her metal 'zines.

These are some fucked-up people you're running around with, Danae.

What are you talking about?

This shit. Holding up the xeroxed, staplebound compendium of album reviews and show reviews and all kinds of other things worth having an opinion about, opened to a page of fan art. A crude sketch: a skeleton loomed over a naked woman, drawing a knife across her stomach and pulling out her intestines. Her breasts were perfectly round and intact.

It's just some stupid teenage boy thinking he's tough, that's all. Chop, chop, chop.

Some guy thinking it's hot to carve you up, that's nothing?

It's just a fucking drawing. Not some real-life girl dancing around in a video like some asshole's trophy.

Some real-life girl who's fucking alive.

Being somebody's hood ornament is not my idea of being alive.

So it's better to be somebody's corpse?

The knife sliced down through the meat of her thumb. No further discussion, as Danae refused to go to the emergency room and Pam sprinted to the drugstore.

Danae dropped her backpack on the grass, pulled off her headphones, rolled her shoulders. She settled onto a stump and pulled out her notebook. Her first poems about ghosts and witches and demons seemed so cartoony now. Menacing shapes, but no real emotion behind them, back then.

I hadn't met Ronnie yet, ha ha.

The trip to Tamalpais had knocked her somewhere else. Higher. The natural majesty of such a place warranted harder work, a better tribute.

She closed her eyes and breathed in the forest air. Tonight she'd be thrown in the arena. Would she emerge a victor? There'd been all those lines to memorize, and so many sudden time changes just waiting to trip her up. Day after day of practice, tromping off to the jam room, taking up the mic to sing it again, and again, and again. She was counting beats in her sleep, making sure she'd fill the right measures. Gods forbid she accidentally sang over one of Ronnie's solos.

No rehearsal today; they'd studied enough, nothing to do but chill out before the test and hope it had all sunk in. She lit a stick of incense and stabbed it down into the earth beside the stump. Started jotting down stream-of-consciousness poetry as she willed her onstage persona, whatever the hell that was, to come forward. Because she needed to *do* something up there, and unlike Alex, there would be no guitar to stand behind. Her left hand ached; she ignored it.

Failure was not an option. The band was giving her a chance to prove herself, the way Celeste never had. She could not fuck it up. But she knew that it would all fall into place, somehow, as long as she kept writing. And now, singing.

Once upon a time, she'd lit a candle to power her words. Until she had met Enspelled, it had never occurred to her to write the words to power her candle.

* * *

A soundtrack of King Diamond wailed across the club as strings were strummed and bass drums rumbled in a quick soundcheck. Before Danae, the mic awaited, shining in the dark. Behind her, the grounding presence of Gnash. Above her, the lights, which she hoped would get turned down a bit, those fuckers were *bright*. Beneath her, the very stage she'd first seen Enspelled play on.

Beyond—*them*. The crowd, gathering in front, or scattered across the carpeted steps in back. How many nights Alex had faced all this on his own, but now it took on a different flavor as curious eyes looked up at her. *Who's this new girl?* Catrinel was out there, so were Bobby and Mike and Melissa. Definite friendliness, ready to clap and yell and put up an encouraging racket. But there was also a streak of hostility, small but definitely present. Creeping through the letters sections of the magazines, muttered around her at shows, she knew exactly what a certain fraction of the audience would always, always say about any woman who dared step up onto the stage: *whore*, she knew at least a few of them were thinking, depressingly pervasive demand she be twice as good to be taken seriously. She caught it in a girl's expression, unhappy her boyfriend would be staring at another chick for the next forty minutes. Saw it in the hard set of a guy's mouth as his eyes wandered up and down her body, ready to blow her off as untalented or ugly. Forget the audition, *this* was the real trial.

She cast about for something to banish stage fright, just one small sign to boost her spirits. She scanned the crowd, caught on familiar swords crossed in an almost-pentacle. Yeah. Pray to Saint Araya, *he'd* never let the crowd intimidate him. Another set of swords, a few feet away—and another, on the other side of the room. She snorted as she realized at least three people were wearing the same Slayer shirt.

You silly little sheep, I almost let you scare me, smirking and stoked as the

Mercyful Fate and house lights dimmed.

Up here, beside him, beneath the lights herself. The thought nearly took her breath away, which she was about to need. *Be happy later, get to work now.*

Alex and Ronnie built the intro: slow guitars like the clack of a rollercoaster climbing up that first rise, it didn't matter if this song was on her Walkman or the boombox or best of all live in a club, it never failed to get her blood jumping, and *I'm right in the middle of it about to SING it* and Ronnie was winding it up, Matt following on a cymbal, *bang bang bang* and down they all dropped into full-speed wrath.

Alex stepped up to the mic, took the first two lines.

> *Born beneath the blood moon*
> *Destined for insanity*

Here it comes, the moment she could ride or ruin. She closed her eyes, grabbed the mic stand, and dove in.

> *Locked up in your raging tomb*
> *Soon I'll tear you free*

Whoa. The fury she'd honed through all those rehearsals was completely freed out here, fed by the crowd, a few of whom were dancing. Bobby? Catrinel? No, total strangers. Unbiased. *Yes.*

> *Raging eyes are blinded black*
> *To the end there's no way back*

She threw her head back, shook her hair off the first break of sweat as she battled Alex.

> *Now I'm gone, no longer sane*
> *Locked into a life of pain*

Alex took the exit line—the victor in this song, but there were others where she got to win. Three riffs and a break, and that was when she noticed drops of blood coursing down from her death grip on the stand. She'd been so caught up in the moment, she hadn't noticed she'd reopened her injury.

She pulled off the gauze. Her hand was a wet red mess. Someone she recognized from the club's management was at the side of the stage, making gestures for medical attention. Fuck that. She shook her head at him, glanced back at the rest of the band, who were wearing a collective look of *uh, are you sure?* She nodded at them. Fuck yeah.

"It's just a flesh wound," she murmured into the mic, and she heard a few cheers around the dark.

Gnash strummed into the next number and she was back in it, fighting Alex over something else. Halfway through she ran her palm across her mouth—*why not, it did wonders for Alice Cooper*—squeezed down hard and centered on the pain. A few more people joined the dancing in front of the stage and she brought her whole body into it, foot up, howling down into the mic, eyes closed, hair loose around the sheen on her face. Reaching down deep to give them everything she had, they were moving faster now, the frantic push of a small pit and it bolstered her, pushed her harder, wreaked an exhaustion as sweet as sex. The white candle's wish was granted in a storm of cheering and devil horns and the thrilling spark of the next riff: *This is where I belong.*

And then: *How far can I go?*

The lights came on along with Sentinel Beast and she caught Gnash nodding approval at her, *good work* before the staff guy got in her face, pleaded with her, and she let him lead her off towards the first aid kit while the rest of the band broke down their equipment. Couldn't keep the smile off her bloody lips as hands came out of the crowd to clap her on the back, *awesome* and *sick* and there was Catrinel trying to get into the white box of bandages, she was certified in these things, thank you very much.

Four, to five. It was official. The final point in the pentacle had arrived.

* * *

The Upper Haight sun shone down through a haze of smoke and Dead Can Dance, glimmered off the jeweltoned velvets of Catrinel's bedroom. The walls were covered in fantasy art: maidens with flowing hair and heavy gowns walked through castles, woods, snow, hoisting swords or shooting fire from their fingertips, every one of them in firm command of the captured moment. The bed was a jumble of silky tapestries, a soft place to sprawl out and read rock magazines. A sad little prom gown drooped from Catrinel's dress form. Her scissors flashed in the afternoon light.

"Are bodysuits really supposed to look sexy? It looks like she forgot to put on a skirt." Danae held up the page for Catrinel's glance, the publicity photo eliciting a dismissive grunt from around a cigarette. Danae sipped a glass of white wine and perused the singer, fuschia eyes peering seductively from beneath a poof of bleached blonde hair. Her band was glam, but she had serious pipes, totally wasted on hungry hearts and playing with fire. Too bad. A few pages over, a couple more girls in another glam band. There were conchos. There was somebody in a fringed suede jacket.

"The green on that tiger-print spandex is hurting my eyes," said Catrinel.

"Does this guy really think those pants are gonna get him laid?"

"Well, standing on a stage makes anyone at least fifty percent more attractive, you know."

The ad opposite showed three women in leather bikinis and spiked gauntlets. They wielded whips and cold stares, flanking a guitarist holding a Flying V like a sword. *Choose the best weapon*, read the headline.

"They're dressed like warriors, but how tough can they be, posed around one guy. Pfeh."

"Are you even bothering to read the interviews?"

"Why? They're all gonna say how hard they worked on their album and how much they love their fans and how they're totally gonna rock the world, blah blah blah."

A few pages later, romantics. Bustiers beneath blazers, pearls, the ones trying to be respectable and mystical at the same time. Love songs made of prisms and mirrors, and walkin' the edge—but never falling over it, that was for the acts who went with bandannas and motorcycles. They looked so self-assured beneath their manes of huge, perfectly-fluffed hair. They probably rode horses.

"Ooh, the one all the way to the left, I like her top. All those ruffles." Catrinel leaned over.

"You *would.*"

Flip, flip, whoa. Devon Dare. Danae shifted the magazine slightly, went quiet while Lisa Gerrard's haunting voice filled the room. Devon Dare. He smoldered at her from a velvet couch, jewelled hands clasped together, regarding the world with those famous kohl-smudged bedroom eyes. Black leather vest, tight leather jeans, dark hair teased in a corona of spikes. No trying at all in his expression, so many attempts at hard-rockin' attitude in this magazine and his sexy little smile was the real deal.

He'd done his time on the L.A. glam-metal circuit, well-documented in countless interviews, his brilliance with image and sound and soundbite catapulting his band into arena-level success by his utterly iconic second album. She knew his stuff—everybody knew his stuff. She'd seen clips of his shows while waiting for the thrash videos on Metal Meltdown—pop but heavy, incredibly catchy actually, a genuine artistic wisdom at work behind the careful makeup. And a talent for playing with his appearance, cycling through various archetypes the way fashionable women did, presenting a different persona for every photo shoot. Now he was moving into his next incarnation after a glossy third album: time off to play kingmaker for Nemesis Records, with his uncanny eye for the future. Determining who got deals, who got airplay, magazine coverage and spots on tours and the whole fucking grail. Perverse imagination set free by immense wealth, millions of worshippers, there was no higher throne in the enchanted rockstar dynasty.

How many women would throw their lives away to crawl towards the crook of his beckoning finger—be real, how many already *had*—just to trace the perfect curve of his jawline, kiss that smirking mouth. Danae quickly flipped the page and drank some more wine. He was a secret pleasure, total blasphemy within her speed metal circle. But so very pretty.

"So Gnash said you'd found a costume or something? For the shows?"

"Oh, right!" Catrinel tossed her scissors on the bed and opened her closet door, revealing a rack of dresses that were all long, dark, and romantic-looking. She rummaged around on the top shelf and tossed a heap of black fabric onto Danae's lap. "I found this at the Salvation Army the day after I watched you first sing with the band. It's like it was meant for you."

Danae unfolded the mass of chiffon and held it up by the straps. Inside, a label: PROPERTY OF THE SAN FRANCISCO OPERAHOUSE. She jumped to her feet, shucked off her jeans and t-shirt, and pulled the dusty, voluminous dress up over her body.

"I wasn't sure of your size, but this was on the big side. It can be taken in, easy." Catrinel did up the hooks on the back of the bodice.

Immediately Danae felt her petite height take on a kind of power. Special clothes for singing, like a ceremonial robe for the stage. All that writing, and practicing, and *work*...it really warranted something more dramatic than jeans and sneakers, now that she thought about it. She tried to walk to the full-length mirror but Catrinel stopped her.

"Wait. Let me do your makeup. And your hair! It won't look right 'til you're totally done up. Here, sit down on the bed and let me get my stuff."

Catrinel pinned Danae's hair back and went to work on her face. Foundation, eyeshadow, blush, soft bristles caressed her eyes and cheeks in short, expert strokes. Pam should be doing this, thought Danae, Pam and her box of stage makeup tricks. She pushed the thought aside as mascara was brushed onto her lashes, heard the heavy trod of boots and Gnash's "Hey, babe," as he crossed into the bedroom.

"Hey babe, yourself," said Catrinel, as Danae opened her eyes.

Gnash dropped into an overstuffed armchair and whistled. "Damn."

"Uh-huh," Catrinel concurred. "If she's prone to doing things like bleeding onstage, she should really be outfitted for maximum drama. Although Danae? It's perfectly OK to use blood capsules. Didn't hurt Ozzy Osbourne's credibility, now did it?"

"Ozzy plays stadiums. And he already bit the head off a bat. His reputation is *made*."

"Still. We need to keep you in one piece, makes it a lot easier to tour." Gnash lit up a cigarette and picked up one of the magazines. Danae swore he had a secret double life playing bass in Guns'n'Roses.

Catrinel pulled the pins out of Danae's hair and went to work backcombing her whole head with a round brush. Green fingernails curled against her forehead, protected her face from a fragrant rain of Aqua Net, and then Catrinel's hand was in hers, tugging her up and stopping her at a pair of low black heels, a size too big but they fit good enough, and then leading her towards a full-length mirror beside the dress form, accidentally knocking a shoebox full of craft glitter from the edge of her dresser. It fell and exploded at Danae's feet.

"Shit!" Catrinel coughed and fanned the sparkles away.

Shit, indeed. Within the mirror, a woman appeared within a cloud of glimmering dust. Her eyes were those of a cat, traced with black, shadowed in gray, framed by thick, dark brows. Fading slashes outlined her cheekbones, and her lips were kissed bright crimson. Her hair stood out in a witchy storm that gave her more height. The dress itself was loose, ghost rags that hung from her body like a shroud. She turned her face from side to side, stunned to encounter this darkly glamorous woman who had been hiding inside her, all this time.

Eat your heart out, Mom.

"Well? What do you think?" Catrinel lit up another smoke, sat down in Gnash's lap.

"I feel like…I've become everything I've been writing about."

"You look totally fucking evil," said Gnash. "So babe, are you giving the rest of us makeovers or what?"

"I've said for the longest time you should go more theatrical, Nashville."

Danae's eyebrows shot up towards Gnash.

"You never heard that," he said, caught out. She pantomimed zipping her mouth shut and throwing away the key, with a smirk.

"But yeah, the crowd went nuts over the blood. Maybe we should jazz it up a little."

"Would you let me put lipstick on you?" asked Catrinel.

"Only if it's black." Danae caught the pink of his tongue slip into Catrinel's grinning mouth, such casual sensuality, the easiness between them.

They'd been together for close to a year, and instead of that first fire cooling, she knew they'd be on the bed as soon as she left the apartment.

I'm ready. Right now.

"I gotta go. Thank you *so* much."

"Where you going?" Catrinel settled back on Gnash, arms lazily winding around his neck.

Danae said nothing, just grabbed her backpack and went out the door.

"Go get him, vampire queen!" she heard Catrinel yell as she ran down the stairs and headed for the bus stop.

* * *

Danae climbed the steps to Enspelled's house. Rehearsals had done away with the need to knock: *come on in, sister of the flame.* She looked down at her hand as she turned the knob, nails bare of paint. A gap in the costume, a detail that needed adjustment. Later.

Inside, sunset honey dripped through the living room windows, caught on crystals and glass, lit up this house so scuffed and garrulous and *fun.* The strums from an acoustic guitar drifted down the stairs. Everything turned hazy as she ascended.

Halfway up, footsteps. She drifted to the top, spotted Ronnie at the end of the hallway. Watched his face change from confusion into recognition as he made out her features through the frightwig hair, the kabuki makeup. She gazed back, cool, put a hand against Alex's bedroom door.

I'm going in, and you can't follow.

Fingers on the chipped white paint, one push, and everything would change. Ronnie still stared at her from the end of the hall but he didn't exist right now. One push could make it stronger, or smash it all to pieces. The time had come to find out. She pressed gently, and the door swung open.

Familiar by now: the line of plants along the windowsill, sprouting from their coffee cans. Small bookcase of fantasy novels, music studies, a couple of monster hardbacks on botany. Candles blazing away from within twists of gnarly twigs on his altar. Alex was sitting on his bed, hair tied back. The light from the hallway fell across the strings and he looked up.

Surprise in those gray eyes as he drank her in, this totally unexpected incarnation. She stepped inside and closed the door behind her, let him look, loved him looking, as his gaze traveled from the ragged hem of her gown to the wild tease of her hair. He lifted the guitar up from his lap, leaned it back in its stand at the foot of his bed. Slowly, she moved forward, and he stood up as she drew close. Nothing, no *wow* or smile or sudden embrace to tell her this was okay, this was wanted. The risk of shattering everything between them was completely on her shoulders.

Total vulnerability shimmered within her Cleopatra eyes as she looked up at him, lifted her hands to his face. Thumbs so gentle against his jawline, still no reaction, not *yes*.

But not *no*. She brought her mouth to his, asked the question with a soft kiss.

The answer: his lips parting and the sweet slide of his tongue against hers, kicking up the jackhammer beat in her heart. She felt his rings glide against her back, run up into her hair and she let herself fall, breathless as a broken spell, sinking to the bed and taking him with her.

She lay within the circle of his arms, breathed in spice and woods, pulled at the rubber band to release the dark curtain of his hair. His body was strong, solid, like clinging to a tree in a storm. So tender with her in these first fragile moments, silent confessions crossing through their hungry mouths, he was open to her now; through the moshpit and the mudfight and watching the clouds, the audition and bleeding onstage, dizzying to think of those moments again when all along, the answer had been *yes*.

She wrapped herself around him, meaning to take it slow, draw it out. The impatience to explore soon took over. Her hands slipped beneath his t-shirt, traced the spot of light fur on his lower back. Like a satyr. A creature of the woods, to the core. Her fingers sailed over his ribcage, found the stiff peak of a nipple. She pushed his t-shirt up and nipped him gently, and a soft moan escaped his throat. He pulled the t-shirt over his head and she clawed down a dress strap, to bare herself to the waist, feel the heaven of his skin on hers, but he stopped her.

"No. Leave it on."

A fetish? Or something more esoteric? The gown hadn't been washed since the thrift store, and probably still bore the stage sweat of the woman before it. Now she was adding hers. Theirs. He was right. Charging it with first passion would turn it into more than just an erotic memento, but a potent talisman when she put it on for performances.

"But I can do this, though," he whispered, reaching around her back to undo the first few hooks. Lightly sucked at her throat as he tugged the bodice down. Another kiss as he played with her, hard and pink beneath his fingertips. She ground against him as he moved his head down and returned the bite.

She ran a hand over the front of his jeans, exulted in how badly he wanted her. He lifted her skirt, traced her through her soaked panties. She sighed against his mouth and parted her legs, agonized beneath the long tease before he pushed the thin black cotton inside and slipped his fingers within the slick folds of her flesh.

Her whole body reached for him, breathing coming faster. Rising, she could feel it building as his thumb circled her precisely, her hands crabbing into the sheets. He lifted his head to watch her, and those beautiful gray eyes brought her over. She jolted against his hand, ravenous for him.

"Now."

"But—"

"Now." *Please.* Pushing him up, frantic kisses as she tore at his jeans, the dark gold of his skin revealed totally—*holy shit he's gorgeous*—a condom snatched from his bedside drawer, her skirts pulled aside and she came for him, chalice over athame, eased herself down onto the hard euphoric sting of his body. So hot where she held him completely, those first delirious waves coursing through her flesh, speeding up her motion. He pulled her down onto his chest, brought the growl of the stage right up to her ear. Held her tight as he took her, faster and faster until one deep plunge and his rhythm went spastic. She couldn't resist looking up to watch his face: the way his eyes closed, the snarl contorting his mouth, as she savored every inch of temporary insanity.

Slowly, his grip loosened.

"*Now* you can take your dress off."

She laughed as she slid away, got up and checked herself in the compact mirror Catrinel had thrown in her purse, while he did whatever you were supposed to do with condoms when you were done with them.

He stared at her with an afterglow grin. "C'mon. Get your ass as naked as mine."

He stretched out on the bed, hid nothing from her, shameless as the big bad wolf. It was ridiculous to feel like there was anything left to be afraid of, but still.

Her reflection was still so alien, so easy to forget how bewitching she appeared. She looked like a woman who had secrets, features wise and knowing from many torrid midnight adventures. Strong and glamorous and dark. An illusion to grow into, come true over time. Right now was an excellent place to start that journey. Continue the one she was already on, really.

She stretched her arms behind her back to undo the rest of the hooks. The dress dropped to the floor. She lifted her hands over her head, not with the obvious flesh-house confidence of Pam's moves, but just taking her time. Plain black cotton, but she may as well have been wearing the world's most exquisite lingerie, the way he was looking at her. She undid the clasp on her bra; the elastic of her panties whispered down her thighs. Her makeup was smeared, and her hair was surely deranged by this point. She didn't care. She stood before him, showing herself completely.

"You know what I was doing before you came over?" he asked.

She half-smiled as she climbed back into his bed. "Playing acoustic."

"Yeah. Thinking about you."

Total skin to skin now, and she pushed her face into his hair, breathed him in. His hands drifted down towards the small of her back, caressed her with calluses and rings.

"Although I never imagined you coming to me like *this*."

How thrilling it was, when you *fit* with someone. She thought of Catrinel and Gnash on the other side of the city, probably doing the same thing right now.

"I've been dreaming of this moment," she said.

"So have I." He kissed her, brought his mouth down beside her ear, soft. "A *lot*."

Nothing in the world but lips, and hands, and warmth, slow as they started again. Nothing beyond the bed. No idea that on the other side of the wall, a bristling rage was listening to their every sound, guitar in hand, answering each cry with a curse for the lovers' destruction.

Chapter 5

So how bad do you want it?

The eternal question simmering away in the background, behind every band. As if the rigors of the club circuit weren't enough, nor bad reviews, nor the ever-present threat of infighting. To step onto the stage of the shittiest club on the emptiest night demanded sacrifice. Long days disappearing into practice. Quitting jobs. Quitting school. Less time spent with girlfriends, boyfriends, having to give them up completely if they threw down that notorious ultimatum, *it's either the band or me*. Any reason for saying no was met with the same ass-prodding taunt: *you just don't want it bad enough*.

Life blurred into a relentless cycle of rehearsing, sleeping, partying, writing music, and most importantly, performing. Gnash made backdrops, repainted the bass drum with their new logo: a triple moon worked into the intricate lettering, tempting doodle fodder for the paperbagged covers of high school textbooks. Alex printed up t-shirts and stickers for the merch table, run by Catrinel. Ronnie wheatpasted flyers onto telephone poles and left them in record stores. Danae typed up newsletters and sent out upcoming show dates to fans and fanzines. Matt booked the gigs, and got friends in other bands to get them onto bills as well.

They recorded another demo to get Danae's vocals into tape-trading circulation, scattered the seeds of a hundred cassettes to take root in the scene. The sound of her own voice surprised her—what she'd always taken for a generic female midtone revealed a madwoman's roar she'd never known she possessed, just waiting for a chance to lead everybody off into the dark.

Driving the van up to gigs in Sacto, down to Santa Cruz, benefit shows in San Jose and Oakland. Crashing on dirty floors, subsisting on various forms of pasta. Her true relationship with Alex was kept secret. Nobody would take the band seriously if the romance between the lead singers got out. The rest of Enspelled knew, and Catrinel, but no one else. It remained suppressed in front of the fans, and the full moon parties, hidden behind a platonic front until the first available door was closed and it all came bursting out.

But it was all worth it. They were getting a good name as a live act, slowly building a fan base of people coming just to see them. The merch table was making a little money—fans paying for the privilege of promoting them!—and a couple of college stations were playing them on the metal hour. Fanzines were writing them up. Headlining weeknights soon became headlining Fridays. And best of all, more bands with the fast, evil sound were popping up all over the place. Incredible tapes coming out of Stockholm, Tampa. More bands to share flyer space with. More bands to spread the virus.

Five dark figures took the stage when Enspelled came to play: gone were the blue jeans and basketball sneakers, now it was just black, black, black. Combat boots, thick leather belts, t-shirts of other friends' bands, smudges of black shadow beneath their eyes. Danae's hair grew long and wild down her back, she'd kept the makeup but not the hairspray, that was too glam. They'd thought about props—swords, setting things on fire—but decided the blood capsules and Danae's ghost rags were as far as they should go. *Our songs are strong. We don't need to be Blackie Lawless about it*, Matt had said.

But, catharsis, thought Danae. Faces in the front row slicked red from her fingertips, giving themselves over completely to Enspelled's special brand of madness. If a good priestess offered herself as a channel to the community, as an outlet for their rage, then she'd become a priestess. Suck on *that*, Celeste.

Exciting times, as Danae jogged up the steps of the Victorian. Matt had floated the idea of a mini LP, six tracks, somebody in Axenhammer already volunteering to do the production. Something to throw on the merch table and actually earn money from, unlike the demo, which was purely to get the word out. The money was there, pooled from their jobs, taken in from the shows. The mythical next level looked within reach.

She flung open the door of the apartment, and was greeted by four bare white walls. All the masks, all the scarves, gone. She peeked into Pam's bedroom—the bed was still there, and the dresser, those were the landlord's headaches now, but the shrine had vanished.

Danae's own stuff was still right where she left it, her toothbrush, a couple pairs of black jeans, not much. A note lay on the dresser next to a scrap of white cloth. She dropped her messenger bag onto the bed and picked it up.

Danae ~
    I was walking home from work and I ran into a bunch of your friends. Take a look at what they did to my shirt.

Danae unfolded the white cotton. POISON in bright green, pink pouts and flawless blush, four faces that currently decorated the walls in every teenager's bedroom across the country, torn out at the neck and across Rikki Rockett's wink. Danae had laughed when she'd first heard about thrasher kids clawing pop metal t-shirts off the backs of the lightweights, now her heart sank as she thought about Pam walking home alone from work, in the dark, dog-tired. Figures blocking her path, mocking her, a swarm of strange hands reaching for the clothes on her back. Danae had no idea who had done it, but her throat thickened with guilt.

    They let me keep it, as a reminder not to be such a poseur. How nice of them.
    I've told you these people are fucked up. I don't know what you see in them, but it's only a matter of time before they rip you apart, too. But you don't want to listen. You're not even really home anymore so what do you care.
    I'm off to L.A. where I belong, with the rest of the poseurs.
    Don't say I never warned you.
    Pam

Danae collapsed back on the bed, looked around the stripped room. The sanctuary had crumbled beneath her feet, and she'd been so busy with the band she hadn't noticed. They'd been gradually drifting apart—different crowds, different versions of happiness—but Danae still felt like she'd let something vital wither up and die.

Long black hair brushing her face, wicked eyes gently pushing her further. *The second you don't want this, you say stop. 'Cause I'm gonna keep going.* Candlewax splashing Danae's collarbone. *The way out is right in your mouth. Say stop, and I'll stop.* Liquid heat spilling down the curve of her breast, Pam's fingers pulling down the cup of her bra...

She squeezed back tears. What a shitty way to pay back her white knight.

Her thoughts arranged themselves into verses, out of sheer habit. But she didn't reach for her notebook. There was no time. She didn't know how long the note had been sitting here, but her key would not open the door for much longer. She blinked the grief from her eyes, gathered up her things, and split, closing the door on Happily Ever After.

* * *

Ronnie snarled as he wove through the Wiggle, the flattest bike route from Market up to Golden Gate Park. The last run had been a breeze, pick up in SoMa to drop off in Chinatown, no monster hills, no oversized packages, just contracts, nice and easy. Ice queen receptionists at both ends, both melted by his smile, the bad boy striding through a tailored gray landscape of nine-to-fivers. One of them had given him her number, but it wasn't enough to shake his bad mood. His next job wouldn't be for an hour. Time to catch a smoke break with Gnash.

He zigzagged through the lower Haight as he ground his gears against the interloper. *Her.* He'd worked his ass off for Enspelled, just for this bitch to show up and snatch it all away. Biking around the city exhausted after a late night hauling around equipment. Saving up bits of paychecks for the next effects pedal. Everyone off at the bar or someone else's show or living their fucking lives while he sat in his room and composed the riffs, interpreted Alex's words over into notes. All of it, for nothing.

It was all too easy to see it, if they ever got famous, the girl front and center in all the publicity shots, the guys fading into her background props.

She'd definitely get the upper hand now that Alex was fucking her. Hell, she'd *moved in*. Gnash and Matt were fine with having her there, more help with the rent, the housework, but just having a woman around…

Ronnie, you play songs about death and destruction, and you can't handle a pair of bloody panties in the bathroom? They'd all roared over that one. Now Catrinel had an ally. Just great.

He loved Alex like a brother. Their history ran deep, through so many memories. Riding up on his BMX, holding up the first cassette that had arrived from their tape-trading letters. Finding out about that fundamentalist church in the east bay burning rock records, going down with a bag of pot and throwing the seeds in their garden while Ronnie stood lookout. A true friend, right beside him through all the mistakes and frustrations and eventual command of learning to play guitar, through the sacred teenage vices of liquor and sex and witchcraft. But fuck, he could be so fucking *blind*.

All caught up in writing the lyrics with Danae, *here, write some riffs around this*. And then: *the words busted out of the measure, could you rewrite this part?* Cold fear that Enspelled had actually gotten better with her arrival, what a nightmare, that people liked them more now. Already a couple of his solos had been shortened for more of the singing. And the songwriters were the ones who made the money. A third person would bite into that cashflow, if it ever happened for real.

Ronnie hit the Panhandle, breathed in the trees as he zoomed across the asphalt paths. His best friend was slipping away. Gone were the nights of secrets, the world hush of 2am and soft conspiratorial laughter. Not the crystal queens and their bite-sized enlightenment, trying to turn Alex Wiccan, not the ones who *cared*…but the other girls, the ones in between, fearless sluts slinking around the edges, dark and ripe with nihilist fire. After shows, up the steps to Ronnie's room where clothes were shed and the rites were performed. Two on one within the circle of black candles, hot wax splattered across some thrashing nympho's body, pornographic sprites restrained in silk. Mouths damp with red wine, arcane symbols painted onto glowing flesh, lips and legs spread to receive them both, all touch reduced to the honesty of pure lust, nothing more. *Freedom.* There was nobody else in on the taboo, nobody else who could be trusted that much. A cute brunette was waiting for Ronnie to call her tonight, and he'd go. But nothing compared to those quiet ceremonies of the forbidden. Alex had left them behind, now that he'd found something better.

If Alex preferred just Danae to an endless number of occult playmates, Ronnie could only wonder what he was missing out on. Someone who would have brought her own ideas to the black candles. The way this plain peasant girl had grown into an enchantress…what immense powers of transformation she wielded. And he'd been too careless to see.

His big mouth had already alienated her, no chance whatsoever, might as well keep going. He dropped hints of those nights, the rites she hadn't been a part of. She played like it was all beneath her, but it wasn't. He saw doubt creeping into her eyes, envy maybe, even better. *I was there and you weren't. I know Alex in a way you never will.*

That afternoon in the hallway, that look she'd shot him right before entering Alex's bedroom…he should have left the house. He should not have stayed in his bedroom, and listened, wanting to tear them apart as badly as he wanted to join them. Desire surged through his body and he hated himself for it, so easily satisfied in his hand but no, don't give in, and more importantly, don't waste it. He'd picked up his guitar, willed himself to grow cold and concentrate. Focus on the maps, the charting of journeys that was his magickal signature, the solos as aural representations of travel. Every howl that crashed over him, he channeled into a cluster of notes, sharpened the edges of a hex, a musical sigil to slip within the new material, unlockable by blood. A burst of carefully harnessed rage to aim in her direction, push her back, *get her away.*

But for now, he could sow dischord on the more mundane level.

He turned up Shrader and coasted onto Haight, down from the Ashbury intersection where he knew she laid out her tarot cards. He swung onto the sidewalk, locked up and headed into Final Vinyl. *Daydream Nation* was on and Gnash was at the register, a junior high kid stabbing at the glass counter beneath, down at the secondhand cassettes.

"You're charging only two bucks for Venom? When everybody else is four? Are they worth only two dollars because you think they suck?"

Gnash shook his head. "I dig Venom. The manager did that."

"That's such disrespect, man, like all these bands are better. *Two dollars* better."

Ronnie caught Gnash's glance and rolled his eyes. Gnash called out to a green-haired girl to cover for him, grabbed his leather and they headed through the stockroom out to the weed-strewn patch of yard in the back.

"Dude, you have *got* to hear Morbid Angel," said Gnash, handing him a demo. Having a band member regularly patrolling the indies and imports definitely had its benefits.

"Matt was saying something about them, yeah," he said, slipping it into his back pocket. "So, there's this Girls of Rock feature that some skin mag's doing, Danae turned it down."

"Really," said Gnash, lighting up and passing the flame over.

"She doesn't want it bad enough."

"Posing naked, yeah, that's an *awesome* way to tell everybody how great our music is. Do you really want any more assholes in the front row screaming 'show us your tits?'"

"You're just taking her side because you're getting to do bass solos now."

"Hey, why don't *you* pose in *Playgirl?* That guy from Ratt did it."

"Fuck you."

"Do it for the band, Ronnie!"

Ronnie dragged on his smoke, changed the subject to Monsters of Rock tickets, and felt the walls close in. Everyone was solidly behind Danae's decisions, and he should have known better than to stir up shit with Gnash, the way he was dating somebody like Catrinel. No idea what he saw in that stuck-up ren-faire bitch. What was it like to be so utterly possessed by another human being? Was that what love was? He hoped he never found out.

* * *

Onscreen, *The Texas Chainsaw Massacre*. Long seventies hair and chicken feathers and terrified eyes were given an alternate soundtrack of Napalm Death. Around the room, the messy, comfortable world of Matt: bowls of half-eaten ramen, broken drumsticks, cat toys, the only television in the entire house. A copy of *This is Spinal Tap* sat on top of the VCR, they all knew it by heart, every metal musician did. Weedy was nestled in Danae's lap.

"This is good. Solid, if you're into tradition," she said of the big blue book Matt had handed her. Her hair had a couple of red streaks from Catrinel dyeing it in the sink. Not perfect, but better than just plain natural.

"I'm not. Linda shoplifted it for me," said Matt.

Danae snorted and sipped her beer. "Glad you never came in my shop. OK, next one."

Matt handed her a pink paperback. A serene man in a caftan was lighting a stick of incense beneath an orange sky, the embodiment of every cringeworthy New Age cliche.

"This author is actually really good if you're on your own, lots of room to do what you want, what feels right. Everything's a starting point, not law."

"Cool. He's got a bunch of stuff out so he's got to know something, right?" Matt killed his bottle and reached for another.

"Not necessarily. He just happens to have a lot more substance than the other popular authors, although you'd never know it from this cover. Next one."

A small green swirling font proclaimed something about True Witchcraft. "Total garbage. It's all about destroying rivals at parties and petty bullshit. It's pretty funny if you're reading it like you'd watch a cheesy horror movie."

"She seemed like she had a few issues."

"Just a few."

"None of her stuff worked, either."

"You actually tried this stuff? She's all about controlling spells."

"Well, not to control anybody…just to find someone."

"Some nice pagan girl to settle down with." Danae's kindly-grandmother tone quickly disappeared into silence when she realized how serious he was.

Alex walked in and dropped a box of cassettes into the middle of the mess. "Look what Gnash dragged in."

The three of them dove into the box, pulled out new tapes. Ooooh, Siren's Dirge. Lucifyx. The third one stopped her cold, turned her stomach to ice.

A nude woman lay on a bed within a circle of three demons. One between her thighs, one at her mouth…her bright red guts lifted up into the teeth of the one in the middle. Danae winced as she caught the name—a band that was professional, whose dark, twisted sound she really, *really* liked. She looked up. Matt and Alex had the gatefold open on another tape, scanning through the credits for a mention of Enspelled, high-fiving when they found it. Immune to this gutpunch—no album cover would ever tell them they didn't belong here. Metal was the loud, raucous, exhilarating place she ran to get away from the world…and the same old hateful assholes were in here, too.

More stupid art, so what, she thought, tossing the tape aside. They're just trying to be shocking, and I almost fell for it. Who am I, Tipper fucking Gore?

The phone rang. Matt leaned over, clawed the cord to pull it within reach.

"Hey. Chris, what's up?"

Chris? From Stolen Hope? Alex and Danae looked over at Matt.

"Yeah? They did? That's too bad." Winding the curly green cord around his left hand, thumping one foot against the floor at a phantom kickdrum. Silence, as his eyes slowly lit up.

"Really. Yeah, we can be there. No problem, we'll manage."

Matt was nodding, a few more *Yeahs* before hanging up. Turned back with an expression of near-disbelief.

"You know who just called?"

"Who?" they both practically yelled back at him.

"The next level."

* * *

The venue was one of the city's great old dancehalls, with a gilded balcony and glittering chandeliers and a bawdy burlesque history. Getting loaded and rocking out was just the latest form of raising Cain to a century-old locale that had seen it all. Not only was it the most distinguished stage Enspelled had set foot on yet, it was their first night playing to a crowd of over a thousand people.

Danae's first fan letter was tucked into her bra, over her heart, a lucky charm against whatever hecklers and venomous glares might be lurking out there. *Thank you for being up there—thank you for singing that lyric*—she drew strength from the handwritten words, this stranger, a teenage girl who saw herself in Danae's success. She would do her best not to let her down. These anonymous people, calling themselves fans—whoever they were, she loved them.

Stolen Hope had asked them to open—the slot had been emptied by a group whose tour had ended suddenly, no word why, the gossips were speculating on broken hands, old grudges, divorce papers. Whatever. One band's tragedy was another's windfall, and this one came with roadies and equipment. It followed selling out their first club date a couple weeks ago, all their hard work speeding up into a thrilling momentum.

From the stage, the crowd looked massive. Even though the notice had been short, a lot of them had come for Enspelled, curious to see what they'd do with this level of volume, ready to brag about being there from the beginning. The blood packets were ready, secreted within Danae's skirts, and she was equipped with the arsenal of familiar songs, plus the debut of the new material. Their instruments were prepped, the lights went down, and on they walked to a boisterous welcome.

No hello, no introduction. No stage patter at all. Just five people dressed in black, picking up their weapons. Gnash strummed out a mean bassline, and Danae howled into the mic as she counted off the cymbal crashes. Three...two...one...*go!*

The guitars pulsed with dark aggro fire as the pit sprang to life. A *big* one. Danae kept her excitement in check, focused on the lyrics and refused to process the scene before her until the verse jumped to Alex, ten seconds free to watch the dancers bang themselves against each other, big tough guys going absolutely apeshit. Yes! *Yes!* Her hands itched to burst the blood packets now, but no, not until the third song. *Don't blow your load right away,* thanks, Gnash.

The verse came back to her, and she threw her voice into it. It sounded so fucking *good* in here, in a room specially designed for loudness. She took the mic off the stand, walked along the front of the crowd, picking out faces to sing to. A couple of guys in jean vests banged their heads and flashed her devil horns. A blonde girl in a shredded t-shirt thrashed wildly beside them. Arms ringed in sweatbands and bike-chain bracelets reached for her, eyes transfixed from behind shaggy bangs, voices screaming along with her. Three deep they hung on, the pit boiling with bodies behind them.

Three final chords ended the first song, no break, immediately into the next one. One that had Danae taking all of the vocals, leaving Alex free to shred away. She glanced at Gnash, The Tall Blonde Control Tower she'd privately nicknamed him, and wandered back into the fray. She lifted her gaze, trying to connect with the faces further back. Sneakers appeared at the edge of the stage, a skinny kid lifting his arms. She threw him the horns before he jumped back into the crowd.

Third song. Time to pull the trigger. Alex was back up at his mic, speaking the invocation to release the drama. Danae found the first packet, responded to his call with her mic in one hand and a fresh burst of crimson in the other. She went down on her knees to paint the faces in the first row with a concoction of chocolate sauce, karo syrup, red food coloring. The jean vest guys received her touch with closed eyes, and the blonde tried to lick her fingers. A hand shot out and grabbed at her dress, but she leaned backwards, stood up to continue the anointings.

Lost beneath the wounded skies within the dead of night
My only friend the howling wind
No other soul in sight

Alex shot her a look from across the stage, mad grin: holy shit we're HERE.

Alone I walk this path of dark, through a hateful seething land
My only friend the brewing storm
The knife within my hand

Time had never gone so fast. Before she knew it, they were on the second to last song. A brand-new assault to drop on the fans, to mark the occasion.

She heard Ronnie's fingers crawl down the fretboard, then Matt coming in on the kick drum. She dipped her head in time, counting off the beats until the first verse, Alex halfway through the line when she felt a blast of something hot against her back. It hit her like a shockwave, a bone-deep buzz that made her teeth ache on its way through, drenched her in a storm of pain that was as intense as it was fleeting. It blew right through her, towards the frenzy of the crowd.

Danae turned around towards the direction it had come from, spotted blood on Ronnie's guitar strings.

Wait, I didn't touch him.

She'd never lost count. It was time to come in, and she spat out her two lines, tried to concentrate on getting through the next four minutes. Watched in horror as the malevolent energy slowly spread itself throughout the pit, turning the friendly pushing and shoving into genuine violence. She spotted a face covered in blood. A couple of security guards charged into the crowd, and two fists became ten. Twenty. A folding chair came flying down from the balcony, barely missing the chandelier, right as the song ended. The lights came on and left nothing in the air but an ugly roar.

A few angry fans began climbing up, but security was pulling them back down, screaming at everyone that the show was over, leave immediately. Gnash unplugged his bass and dropped it into the stand, jumped down from the stage and pushed his way towards the merch table, bellowing for Catrinel. The other bands were pulling the curtains aside, peering out onto the chaos, falling bodies and vicious beatings and flames lighting up the balcony and not the night they'd shown up to play at all. The stage manager, walkie-talkie in hand, was screaming at the roadies. "What the fuck are you staring at? Get your asses out there and get the equipment!"

Matt's temper was awake and uncoiling itself towards the management, Alex trying to hold him back. Danae grabbed Ronnie by the elbow, hauled him towards the open door of a utility room. Pulled him beneath the harsh yellow of one bare bulb and kicked the door shut.

He lifted his chin, defiant. Slitted eyes, closed mouth. Oh, he'd fucked up, all right. There was no protest to contradict her. Those lovely eyes gave her nothing, just glared. Ready for her to hit him, scream at him, something angry and spiteful and utterly impotent. As badly as she wanted to strangle him on his leather choker, she knew that hate would not do it.

But something completely unexpected, would. Bottled up for so long inside, that awful, persistent, maddening thirst she'd been unable to sour, an unwanted craving that she never thought could come to any good but right now, let it out, let it *devour*. Furious as she was, it was shamefully easy to let it take over.

She stepped back and spread out her hands. Her eyelids drooped as a small smile twitched the corners of her mouth. *Yes*, she beamed at him, *yes*, serene as she opened her heart, let unbridled lust come coursing out in a flood of shivering stars towards his hips, that tender place to sign her name. Back in the house, in the hallway, her hand upon Alex's bedroom door, she reached out to him. *Yes. Follow.* She took his bleeding hand in hers, lifted it to her mouth. Calluses, like Alex, what a dream to be between their hands, where all the songs came from. Stared through the merciless light into his eyes as she ran her tongue along his index finger, sucked hard on the end before bringing her lips down completely. He made no move to stop her. Working down his hand, finger by finger, licking the blood clean, making a big show of swallowing when every last red drop had been lapped up, neutralized.

She took a deep breath to scatter the stars, clear the room.

"I've got you under my skin. Hurt me now, and you hurt yourself." *And you just stood there and let me do it. Idiot.*

She dropped his hand with a look of disgust and pushed by him to open the door.

Things looked like they had calmed down some. The cops had shown up, paramedics too, and Yanni played from the speakers in an effort to drive the rest of the crowd out. A couple of venue staff were having an argument, and someone else was screaming away on a telephone. She headed in the direction of the dressing room when she felt a tap on her shoulder.

She turned around and faced a tall, wiry guy in a Carcass t-shirt, short buzzed hair, and thick black glasses.

"Hi. I know this is a hell of a time to meet." British accent.

"It really is, man." Danae suddenly felt bone-tired and wanted nothing more than a shot of whiskey. And a sink to get this blasted corn syrup off her hands. And Alex. Who was now walking over with a *where'd you go?* look on his face. Please, please don't be a crazy weird guy, she prayed silently. Ronnie stopped beside her, all tensions shoved to the background, shiny united front whenever band business came up.

"I'm from Migraine Records. And we're very interested in signing Enspelled."

Chapter 6

It was warm up here in the lights of Manhattan, looking down on the intersection of Something Street and Whatever Avenue. Danae had changed out of her stage dress into jeans and a Godflesh t-shirt, broke away from the backstage swirl to climb up onto the roof, be alone for a little awhile. This was the closest she could get to the peace of the grove while she was on the road. Her hands were still sticky with traces of stage blood—the sink in the bathroom had been filthy.

A half-moon bathed the city in pale light. In her hands, Enspelled's new album. No worries about scraping together the cash for that mini-LP after all. Migraine had been really cool about everything; they knew the sound was going to suck if it came out too polished, and this was not a label that ever had an issue with censorship. She toyed with a brand-new set of black rubber bracelets someone had given her in Texas, stared at the cover.

Gnash hadn't gotten to the do the art, and he was miffed at the implication that his work wasn't pro quality. Ronnie had wanted to go with something violent and shocking, but he'd been overruled in favor of the band's logo, sharpened and refined around the edges, red on black and that was all. She opened the plastic case. Inside, the five of them stood before a weathered mausoleum somewhere in Colma's rolling hills of eternal sleep. Leather jackets, the white of stone and sky, the shadows of their faces picked out in high-contrast black and white, defiant and grim against the hard afternoon light.

Look at us. Fuck. We did it.

So far, the reviews were as good as could be expected. The mainstream critics wrote them off completely. The alt weeklies hated metal and never gave anybody a fair shot. The metal mags loved them, but so far, only one of them had mentioned Danae, and only for her opera costume. But the crowds were a different matter. Little gifts of skull necklaces, bags of homemade incense, girls had started showing up in black dresses and mouths streaked with red lipstick. The fans, bless them, would never let anyone tell them who they were supposed to like.

The pumpkin of the van was traded in for the carriage of a third-hand camper, and Migraine had arranged for them to share roadies and equipment with the gore-for-gore's-sake middle band. Six people in a camper was enough, she couldn't imagine a stranger or two in here as well. Especially not that morning, in the top bunk trying to be really quiet with Alex, Catrinel and Gnash in the bed below them. Ronnie and Matt were out with some girls they'd picked up the night before. A soft rustle of sheets, Catrinel moaning, *shhhhhh* from Gnash, kisses. Danae let out a loud gasp in response, *it's OK, we're fucking too.* Catrinel cried out, and they quickly struck up an erotic cacophony over who could have the louder orgasm. Danae could still feel the hard slam of Alex's hips into hers, both of them turned on like mad. After, she'd whispered in his ear: *we should invite them up here sometime.* Before he had a chance to react, Gnash let out a huge belch, and the camper exploded with laughter.

City to city, the hands of friendly strangers inking the roadmap towards the next venue, detouring into bars and record stores and parties. Sleep deprivation, birdbaths in rest-stop sinks, a steady diet of fast food, small discomforts for such rich rewards. Although it would be nice to change up from playing the same songs over and over every night. Space out the days a little, break up the endless stretch of highway, if it were possible to afford it. If she wanted to bitch about monotony, there was always a tarot deck and a Haight Street sidewalk waiting for her ungrateful ass.

Their cassette in her hand, the Big Apple skyline beyond…

Is this all there is?

The troubling little thought barely had time to surface when a bottle of beer appeared before her, smuggled up to the one last underage band member, which she gratefully accepted as Matt sat down beside her.

"Hey."

"Hey."

They drank and watched a bunch of kids skateboarding on the church steps across the street. Windows winked squares of light on and off, the comings and goings of the night owls. He tipped his head onto her shoulder, and she put her arm around him, and before she knew it, he shifted over and put his head in her lap, something he only did when nobody else was around. Absentmindedly she ran her fingers through his hair while she gazed out into the night. She swore she could hear him purring.

"Weedy must be bouncing off the walls by now."

"Nah, she's getting spoiled at the clinic. Hardly anybody's boarding there right now and they always need some animal to take it all out on. Tuna, and attention, she's *fine.*"

Silence for a little while.

In another life, the one where she had a mom and a dad, and she'd gone to high school, she and Matt lived in a little house with a white picket fence. It was in the middle of deepest, darkest suburbia, full of jocks and conservative Christians, every day a total struggle to be yourself. But there were lots of other kids in the neighborhood who listened to metal. In this life, she and Matt cut class and got drunk in the woods, spraypainted ZOSO on cliff faces and camped out for concert tickets. They pulled sweethearts up through their bedroom windows and covered for each other, to their parents, teachers, cops, anybody who ever gave them shit.

"You're the brother I never had," she said.

He took her hand and kissed the first knuckle.

I light a thousand red candles in your honor. May the damsel be worthy of you, when you find her.

And: *if I'm in the middle of a national tour with two other bands and dreaming about life out in the middle of nowhere, then I have definitely not had enough to drink.*

She finished her beer. "C'mon, lets go back downstairs. And grab me another one of these."

* * *

Green leaves, gray sky. Danae gazed up at the canopy of trees, Alex's hand in hers, centering warmth through the chill of the day. No show tonight, time to stop and rest and wander through one of the cities they were playing in. Catrinel and Gnash had gone shopping in the punk district. Matt and Ronnie had gone drinking, probably in the same part of town. Danae had wanted nothing more than a walk in the woods.

The earth was damp from recent rain, soft beneath their boots. A path cut through tangles of wild green, thorny loops like barbed wire sprung straight from the ground. The air was thick with the scent of soil, punctuated by bird chirps high up in the branches, the jingling of the zippers on Alex's leather jacket. She closed her eyes and listened. Ironic, that this was where all the songs came from, this stillness and quiet, only to be fused to harsh licks and unleashed within a building full of screaming people. But the balance was necessary. Danae had tried writing music in the camper and found it impossible. Too much outer influence, invasions of all kinds, however benign. She needed time away to recharge, and found it in the form of a national park, not too far away, according to the map.

That, and she wanted Alex all to herself for a little while. She knew he'd be right behind her when she jumped out the door.

"Nobody out on the trails today," she said.

"Good. It's the best we'll get for some time." He squeezed her hand, pulled her to him. "When we get home…a locked door. A real bed. Nowhere to be for awhile. Whole days to do whatever…we…want."

Out here, the kiss felt timeless. She hadn't said it—neither of them had said it—but she hoped he could feel it, in the grip of her fingers, the greed of her mouth.

I love you. I love you. I love you.

Was that what he was saying to her? She could sense it in his touch, the way he held her tightly and didn't let go. That little smile he sometimes threw her onstage: *we're living the dream.* Late nights driving through strange towns; waking up in his arms. What would their future be? All of it came tumbling out now that there was room to uncramp, space to think. Affection and melancholy and terror and ecstasy all knotted up in her mind, as hopelessly snarled as the thorns, looming as huge as a tidal wave. He'd claimed so much of her heart when she wasn't looking. She hadn't realized just how much.

She pulled her face away, and led him further down the path. Ground and center. Ground and center.

"Are you OK?" She could hear the edge of a laugh in his voice. No. Say nothing.

"It just feels so weird, a chance to relax. It's all catching up with me." The tangles gave way to a small hill. Halfway up, a monster tree loomed with a small cave opened through the roots, the kind of fantasy hideaway that beckoned little kids on nicer days to come inside, search for fairies. Two smaller trees flanked the sides, standing guard. So perfectly placed, but there was no sign of human presence anywhere. Not one Tommy + Susie scratched anywhere. It drew her up, forward.

She sat down on her knees. Alex settled down next to her. Silence as they both cast off the outside world, reached down into the earth. She stared into the rich brown bark and threw it her fear. Almost immediately, the sun came out. Sudden heat shone down on the top of her head. Her eyes drifted shut as new emotions flooded her mind with light and warmth. A deep sense of calm came over her, absolutely necessary to live a life as extreme as this. It was in the letting go that she was able to keep it together. She felt her tendrils unfold, flex, spread out across the woods.

Deeper, and deeper, falling into the voice of the trees.

(What have you learned?)

The night in Pam's apartment, lighting that white candle. Everything she'd wanted, she'd gotten.

Hadn't she?

(What have you seen? What have you tasted?)

The cadence climbed, asked her to follow as it plunged into her innermost thoughts. She'd been away from the woods too long.

(Have you gotten the knowledge you came for?)

Just being asked the question, she knew the answer was no.

(Do you dare more, Danae?)

The question was asked not with threepenny mockery, or melodrama. Just honesty, thrown plain and unadorned to her feet. She returned it in kind.

More.

She opened her eyes and inhaled, exhaled, came back to reality. She leaned forward on her hands, clawed her fingers into the wet dirt. Up she crawled into the base of the tree, turning around and holding her hands out to Alex. Together they slipped into the little patch of darkness, hot kiss through the cold air as hands unbuttoned jeans, sought flesh, release. Her blood stormed as she bared herself to him, so starving for his embrace, too fast to answer yes. It never occurred to her, as she ground her body against his, that she hadn't asked the price.

* * *

Tight miniskirts, and spiderwebbed stockings, and pointy boots. Teased mops of electric blue, deep plum like the plumage of exotic birds. Leather jackets, but thrown over bustiers, pants that laced up the sides. No jeans or t-shirts at all. And all the boys were in eyeliner.

Let's go somewhere eight billion people won't be asking you to listen to their demo, Catrinel had said, scanning the nightlife section of the local alt paper. *C'mon, I need a break from all this bashing away,* getting out her sewing box and shredding one of Danae's stage gowns into a passable piece of clubwear. Catrinel herself had swapped out her long dresses for a tour uniform of black BDU's and an ever-present French braid, dying to get back into something lacy and sweeping. The guys had dropped them off and gone out to get hammered at a pool hall.

A girl in a silver bob wig and long matching claws collected their cash through a tiny window, pointed them towards a heavy black curtain. They emerged by the side of a dancefloor lit up with twisting bodies, spinning and stomping wildly to the meanest beats Danae had ever heard…by a keyboard. Her first thought, which she was forevermore glad she'd never uttered aloud: *wow, disco's really changed.*

A deceptively simple electronic melody—three, maybe four notes total—bounced up and down the inhuman drive of a drum machine. Totally synthetic, pleasingly groovy. The singer's voice held all the necessary gravel for metal—rage and strength were there all right—but much more measured. Refined. And totally right now. This was defiance targeted not at some corrupt priest or malicious spirit, but the Financial District. A whole different way to get fired up.

"Who is this?" she asked Catrinel.

"Nitzer Ebb."

A quick trip to the bathroom, clandestine slugs of whiskey from the flask in Catrinel's hobo bag, and they were back out on the floor. The next song snuck up in a catchy, mean slink, the hip-grabbing beat the honey for an anti-consumerist slap in the face. Multiple singers, one of them female, her voice right out front through the chorus.

"OK, who's this?"

"KMFDM. Don't you ever listen to anything besides metal?"

"Um…I used to listen to some classical music…no."

That was going to change immediately, although it was going to take some time to digest this new pantheon. Where to start? Flyers were scattered on the bar listing the club's upcoming events, the kind of bands they spun. EINSTURZENDE NEUBAUTEN. MEAT BEAT MANIFESTO. DIE FORM. NEMESIS RECORDS GIVEAWAY!! A cheat sheet! She snatched one of them up, folded it in half and shoved it in her bra.

She scanned the room as she sipped a coke. Piercings, tattoos, stuff she'd seen all over back home, but gathered together here like a human art gallery, framed in lovely black clothes. Short dresses of vintage lace, red stiletto boots rising to a pair of gartered thighs, necklaces of cobwebs and pyramid spikes and coffin nails. Everywhere, cleavage, heels, dramatic blends of eyeshadow, suddenly she realized there were as many women here as men. Maybe more. Whether those were dagger eyes or merely curious glances thrown her way, she couldn't tell, but there was no solid wall of testosterone to fight through to get to the bathroom, or the bar, or anywhere. A couple of girls in dominatrix gear were making out in a booth, and on the floor, two vampire punks danced together, pretty boys in black hair, black lipstick. She watched them move, the slide of a hand across a leather-belted hip, the gentle biting tug on a lip ring, a tenderness brave and breathtaking in the way they touched.

Nobody here was going to ruin it with *you fucking fags*. Something in her chest relaxed that she'd never known was wound so tight.

A second round of illegal whiskey was making its way through her system when Catrinel grabbed her hand.

"Come on. I'm dying to get out there."

"I don't know how!"

"Just follow what I do. You're a pretty girl, nobody cares." And she let Catrinel drag her out.

Yet another thing to learn: *what are my moves?* She let herself bob along the surface of the beats in a shuffle that probably looked stupid but felt good. She glanced around the floor, back at Catrinel's face, eyes closed and bathed in red light. Danae moved close, ran the back of her hand down Catrinel's temple, down her neck. Her eyes opened briefly, closed again as she rolled her head, accepted the touch. A different way to be close with someone, how wonderful. Two girls in cutoffs and fishnets and long black hair danced around them.

Power drills. Rap lyrics. B-movie dialogue. You could throw *anything* in here. The whole set was a gateway drug, it was going to take months to dig through all these bands. She'd managed a passable two-step when she spotted Alex at the edge of the dancefloor, heard last call get yelled at the same time. Gnash strode by, caught Catrinel by the hands, and tilted her down in a flawless ballroom dip.

"These are the most beautiful girls I've ever seen," said Matt, who'd grabbed a beer and was trying to look in twenty different directions at once. A blonde in a tight black dress and a pillbox hat walked by with a peacock feather, stroked it beneath his chin and smiled mysteriously on her way to the last drink of the night. He immediately turned to join her at the bar.

"Hey." Danae wound her hands around Alex's waist, rocked against him to something light yet angsty, but he stayed still on his feet. "I heard so much good music tonight. Catrinel! Who is this?"

"Front 242," from across the floor.

"Dance with me, Alex."

"You've had a *lot* to drink."

"And I'll take your hangover herbs tomorrow. Right now I don't care." She slid down against him, but he didn't move. She turned around.

"What's wrong? Are you mad?"

"No! No. You're very cute when you're trashed. This just…it's not my thing."

"Dancing?"

"Well, that, yeah, but the music…I don't know, it's not…I just like a heavier sound, you know?"

It came as a bit of a shock. She was so used to their aesthetics lining up seamlessly. Dancing, fine, she'd been pretty reluctant to try it at the start of the evening herself. But the beats? There were whole *worlds* in there. Once she got past the novelty of the sound and could tell the good from the mediocre, learned how to listen to it, she'd be able to find the right stuff to play for him. The stuff that had a lot of guitars in it, definitely.

Gnash spun Catrinel over. "We should get going. Ronnie had to be the sober one tonight and you know how he gets."

"Two more minutes won't kill him," said Catrinel.

"No, it won't. It'll kill *us*," said Danae.

The lights came up. Smudged mascara, sweat-flattened hair, no more darkness to hide all the flaws in. They joined the throng heading for the doors.

"Matt!"

"Uh, yeah." One cheek smeared with red lipstick, a high heel hooked possessively around his leg. "Mistress Sasha wants to take me home to her dungeon. Pick me up tomorrow."

The blonde scribbled an address on a bar napkin and handed it to Gnash.

"Goodnight everybody," said Mistress Sasha, waving her peacock feather at them. From the back of the crowd, Danae stuck out her tongue and flashed Matt the devil horns.

* * *

Backstage, somewhere in the midwest. It had been a difficult show. A tech failure blew out the momentum in the middle, and a couple of relentless hecklers kept disrupting Danae's concentration. On the bright side, there had been hot water in the sink, and soap, too. Right now everybody was scattered backstage while the second band was on.

Danae sat next to Alex at a table full of deli trays, deep in conversation with a couple of guys from Ripegrave, local band they'd guested backstage to hang out after years of trading tapes.

"...a real pain in the ass to get the good stuff in the record store. And that's even the stuff that everybody already knows about. The new shit, the demos? Forget it. I swear, you've been like such a lifeline, man," said Ricky, the singer.

"It goes both ways," said Alex. "I have stuff that's just totally worn the fuck out, but I can't get rid of it, you know, it's a history."

"Oh God, my collection goes back *years* with you guys," said Jeff, the bassist. "What was it, like '85? '84?"

"High school. The only thing keeping me sane through it." Alex finished his beer, grabbed another.

"Oh, fuckin' A," said Ricky, slamming bottles with Alex.

A big guy wandered past the table. Black t-shirt, white graphic, Danae found herself staring at the figure of a woman lying on her back. Big hair, bound, screaming around a gag, nude. A huge spike was thrust between her blood-streaked legs, another buried in her heart. Every detail was rendered fine, from the pain distorting the muscles in her face to her torn labia. Across the top: SLAUGHTERED SLUT.

She fell silent without realizing it.

"What's the matter?" asked Alex.

She gestured with a jerk of her head.

He laughed. "You're bothered by *that?*"

This was not the sketch of a sexually frustrated middle-schooler. This was someone whose talent for realism she couldn't help but respect—whoever they were, they were *good*—who in return, labored hard to show how much they hated her.

Quietly, "Yeah."

"It's just bad taste. Look, there's a bunch of these guys at every show. Just take their money and laugh at them."

Sounds like something Pam would say.

But I'm not here to dance around in a fucking bikini. And I'm making a lot fucking less than five hundred dollars a night.

"That's a real cute way of telling me to swallow disrespect."

"No, I'm telling you to be realistic. We're at the next level now. You're above all this, remember?"

Was she? Easy to blow off when they were loner creeps, losers, the fringe element that always meant a few unbalanced minds would be coming along for the ride. But there was at least one pro-grade artist out there harboring graphic fantasies involving her tender flesh. How many were in the audience she sang to every night? Writing reviews, mixing albums, playing drums, she'd met so many people through Enspelled, cold hard numbers meant at least a few of them were hiding it behind a friendly smile.

The Slaughtered Slut guy was walking past the table again. Danae got up without a word, ducked into the dressing room to grab her boombox, and looked for the stairs to the roof.

Traffic, wind, and Frontline Assembly. She put the music down, rolled her shoulders, and spun, spun, spun beneath the starlight. How good it felt to stretch out beneath infinite, welcoming night. Around her, a bar's blinking martini glass, a supermarket's 24-hour red arrow, a bank's digital clock. Beneath her, the roar of the crowd. The third band must have taken the stage. She threw a headroll into a two-step, imagined trouncing that fucker's head. The image made her laugh and she twirled around again.

Clock and arrow and boombox and a dark figure stood at a distance, tall and thin and clad in concertgoing black. The hood of his sweatshirt was pulled up over his head. Fellow musician looking for a quiet spot? Weird deranged guy? No way to know, until he pulled that zipper down. Which he did, slowly, as he walked towards her.

Chin-length, pitch-black hair, framing brilliant green eyes. No way. No way.

Devon Fucking Dare.

What the fuck? What was he doing *here*? She was speechless before a libido-seizing smile.

"Dan-ah-ee. Your name's supposed to have an umlaut in it. Why aren't you using the extra metal points you were born with?" His famous voice, teasing her.

Damn you, Mom.

The zipper was all the way open now, revealing three lines of Theban across the chest of his t-shirt.

"'Die Yuppie Scum.'" She started to laugh.

"You're the only person I've ever run across who knows what this says." Sly and seductive, a touch of honey at the bottom of every word.

"I have a past life in occult retail. It was either this or tarot readings."

"Stick with this. That was a hard show, and you dealt with it well."

"Are you here for Nemesis? I didn't know you guys were signing for death metal."

"We're not. But I'm friends with the headliners. Their guitarist wanted to use a drum machine for this album and everybody said no. He's thinking about leaving. By the way, tell *nobody* this."

"Most of these people hate glam, I'm surprised any of them are talking to you, honestly."

"Not everybody's gonna hold my past against me. Not when so many of them were twelve years old and my album was the first place they ever saw a pentagram." The grin when he said, it, shit. Smoking hot.

"Now they're trying to one-up you by dreaming up exciting new forms of sexual torture. Well not everybody, actually not even all that many, but…"

"Yeah, I saw that asshole downstairs, too. You'll only get so far in this scene with that shit, you know? I mean, come on, raping somebody to death with a jackhammer is going to find a very limited audience. The ones who are open to change, who want to push it further, those are the ones to watch. The smart ones."

Man oh man, to jump into the heart of the aggro-dance crossover that was just starting to wake up, she envied the hell out of that guitarist. The tour was coming to an end, they'd be heading home pretty soon, where the next album was waiting to be written…Alex would never go for it. She'd been handing him cassettes, this band, that album, *just see what you think* but he'd never get around to cracking them open.

Frontline had come to an end. She went to flip it over, but he pulled a cassette out of his sweatshirt pocket.

"Here. Somebody we're about to sign out of Toronto, I can't stop listening to it."

The tune came to life, stuttering bass and buzzing keyboards, anchored down by a slow, vicious whomp.

"It's good, isn't it?"

"Yeah. *Yeah.*"

"So let's dance."

He dropped his sweatshirt and took her hand before she could protest. He smelled like cool water, wet skies, lean and light on his feet. The beat was irresistible, a relentless pounding that caught her feet in its hypnotic trap. Silently she thanked Catrinel for teaching her how to dance, blasting the boombox in a parking lot or pre-show venue emptiness, the two of them stomping away through the Wax Trax! roster. He angled around her, a sensual brush of muscles, freestyled a pas de deux that made it easy for her to follow. Step flowed into step, balance-stealing pivots and turns coming clean and graceful in his arms. What utter bliss to dance with someone hand-in-hand, full-body.

"You move so stiff. I bet you're really amazing when you let go."

This was heaven. This was murder. Arrow and boombox and 11:58 and *time to go.*

"Oh shit, I've gotta get out of here. The camper's about to leave. Wonderful meeting you." She tried to disentangle herself from his grip, but he pulled her close and made her feel like a deer caught in bright green headlights.

"What you're doing in Enspelled is cute. It's campy, like Elvira. Think they'll ever let you do anything more than that?"

She heard command in his voice, felt it in his hands, he fully expected her to halt wherever she was going, give in to whatever he wanted, and probably rip off her top, too—but it didn't matter, she *had* to get on that camper, her loyalty was to Enspelled, her professionalism demanded it. It didn't matter the seeds of doubt had been scattered and their shoots sprouting alarmingly fast. A couple of rubber bracelets slid off as she wriggled out of his grasp and dashed down the stairs. She ran to the main backstage area, waved goodbye to Jeff and Ricky, spotted the Slaughtered Slut guy nearby chatting with one of the roadies. She couldn't resist a detour. Ten seconds, tops.

She went up and tapped him on the shoulder.

"Excuse me. It's pretty obvious from your t-shirt that you spend a lot of time jerking off. I just wanted to wish you a long, happy life with your left hand, you fucking pig."

She heard a couple of guffaws out of Ripegrave as she ran out into the darkness.

Chapter 7

"Hey, I saw a tape of your show in Austin. I thought that asshole was gonna tear your dress off. My friend caught the beating he got by security on tape, wanna watch?"

"Here's our demo. If you could listen and tell me what you think, and be brutal, we can take it, just be honest and tell me if you think our sound has a chance with Migraine."

"Oh my God, did you *really* jam with Lemmy?"

Homecoming.

D.R.I. blared through the windows as Linda settled down on the lawn chair next to Danae's, moving slow with a very pregnant belly.

"Three more months," she said, staring longingly at a half-full bottle of Jack in a nearby hand.

"So you ended up with Steve after all." Catrinel was back in her black dresses, elegantly descending to perch beside Danae, beer bottle in hand.

"Not on purpose. But it's not so bad. I mean, he has his downsides, but I know what they are, and I can deal with them. No weird surprises."

"How's the place coming?"

"I told him he could only hang up his Judas Priest posters if he got frames for them." She sipped at a can of something lemon-lime.

"You're out in the Sunset now?" asked Danae.

"Richmond."

"The suburbs."

"Beats San Mateo."

"Danae!" Alex yelled from the kitchen.

She was off the chair before the question or request or whatever it was had a chance to form—any excuse to get out of this dismal conversation. She got to her feet and waded through bodies, stepped inside to the kitchen.

"Can you grab that bottle that Lucifyx gave us, you remember, back in Atlanta?"

She nodded and swam through to the hallway, the storage room beneath the stairs, now her bedroom. She flipped on the light. Linoleum floor, wood paneling, kind of stuffy, but it was a room of her own. And at least there was a window for some light to come in. At the foot of her mattress, a trunk held all the mementos people had given them during the tour, a treasure chest of handcrafted gifts: rose petals dried and rolled into a pagan rosary. A bottle of perfume that smelled like orchids and bubblegum. A small oil painting of a dark bride wandering through a forest, her black veil tangled hopelessly within the branches of a gnarled tree. Here was the validation, the tangible proof that what she was doing mattered, and it cheered her as much as it depressed her.

The bottle was thin and clear and painted with twists of flowers, its contents a rich dark red. The lead guitarist from Lucifyx was also a homebrewer who'd been trading botanical discoveries with Alex along with tapes, and was proud to present this concoction as they were getting ready to head north. They'd been specifically instructed to share it with September Death when they got back to town, another cluster of friends in the network. She carried it back to the kitchen, where Alex was taking down the goblets.

"You must be Angel and Sam. Nice to finally meet you," said Danae, to the two tall guys in black hair and jean jackets standing by the sink.

"Bet you're glad to be back home," said Sam. "Hot showers and beds and all."

"Enjoy it while it lasts. You're gonna have to keep touring if you don't want to go back to your day job," said Angel.

You don't think I know that, you condescending shithead, as Alex poured a little of the bottle into everyone's goblet. There would be a *lot* of sitting in that camper. And she had no idea what to do next. Everyone had already seen the blood. How to push it further, without getting cheesy? What she really wanted were the beats, but that wasn't in Migraine's realm at all. They were strictly metal, and there would be no screwing around with the sound that the fans had come to expect from Enspelled.

How to even begin tackling the thematics of the new album, when the last three things she'd written all revolved around skyscrapers? Insanity and obsession still, but the real world right now, not haunted castles and corpse-filled battlegrounds that all sounded like they were in Europe, which she'd never even *been* to, and—

Alex clinked her glass. She'd totally missed the toast but swallowed the drink anyway. It went down thick, coating her throat with raspberry velvet. A skilled blend that she should be savoring, she should be enjoying all of this, the conversational digression about the east coast sound, and all the new bands getting signed, and her place in the middle of it all. But all through the night, her thoughts kept drifting back to Linda. And the next album. And a very bright future that she wasn't sure she wanted anymore.

* * *

What came back to earth was a great rock'n'roll band…

A landscape of cold chemical-green fire. Disembodied voices flying over a grounding thump, tones as tense as a chase scene from a good horror movie. Guitars and keyboards turned ragged, echoing, abstract.

Danae was lying back on her mattress, eyes closed, headphones on. She was in *love*.

She'd never suspected such electrified decay could be wrung from the shiny tools of dance music. She was supposed to be writing new material, and all she wanted was to devour these clever new textures, five more albums in the discography stacked by her pillow.

Someone banged on her door. She reluctantly pulled off her headphones.

"It's me." Matt.

"Come in."

The door opened, and Matt dropped a couple of envelopes onto the trunk, flopped on the mattress.

"If Bobby calls, I'm not here. Tell him I moved out. Tell him I quit. Tell him I *died*."

"What happened?"

"Axenhammer want us to pull some strings, get them shows, but they're not good enough. Not professional. And if I give them the honest truth, they're gonna run around making it out that we got signed and didn't do shit to help our friends."

"They threatened you with that?"

"Well, not directly, but I *know* Bobby. And I can't really blame them, in a way—what if it was them that made it and not us? All that support, I'd totally be expecting it mutual. Think about how that sounds. 'You're just not cut out for Migraine.' Wouldn't the person telling you that sound like such a dick? I mean, nobody ever knows when they suck, right?"

"You find out when you keep playing shows nobody ever comes to."

"Right. And I've got hours at the clinic again. Between that and this new album, I'll be lucky if I get time off to see Megadeth this year."

"Just tell them what they want to hear, then let it slip your mind, we're super busy. Shit, Alex does it all the time." Immediately she regretted that last sentence.

"I've been meaning to ask you…are you OK? You haven't been the same since towards the end of the tour."

"Yeah, I'm fine, just caught up trying to write the new album and all."

Matt rolled over, pawed through the stack of cassettes, picked up *Cleanse Fold and Manipulate*.

"Oh, these guys. They're good. Weird, but good. They're all animal rights, too. I'd be up for seeing them when they come back through. Anyway, here's your mail. Anybody needs me, I'll be wrestling sick cats for the rest of the afternoon." He got up.

"Don't forget your chainmail." She waved.

"Later," and closed her door.

She leaned forward and grabbed the envelopes. One contained a brochure of rock jewelry, quick scan of crosses, pentacles, snakes, she crumpled it up when she spotted a swastika. The other was small, metallic gold ink on black paper, addressed directly to the house. This better be someone she knew. Most of the fan mail was sane, but she'd gotten a few terrifyingly unhinged letters, glad that the P.O. box had kept their authors from knowing where she lived.

She opened the flap and pulled out a piece of black cardstock within a soft burst of cool perfume. An elegant script shone up at her. In Theban.

Danae ~
Come by when I'm in town, and I'll tell your fortune.
Devon

The address was on Broadway. Date and time in a few days. Green eyes, the touch of his hands. Would there be dancing? It was hard to say no. It was hard to say *yes*.

It was just a matter of discipline to start writing lyrics in the Enspelled vein again. It was the struggle of every creative professional, to make art on demand when you weren't on fire. But she needed to pull herself together and get the work done. Prove she was more than some kind of death metal b-movie queen, but a serious artist.

Acid green dripped from the headphones, calling her back to a world of eternal toxic dusk.

She'd try harder later.

* * *

"Welcome to hour two of Metal Meltdown! Coming up: Kreator! Coroner! White Lion! We've got lots of metal mayhem coming up for ya, so don't go away!"

The blonde dipshit in the creaky too-new leather jacket dissolved into an animation of bikers on a highway. They raced past a series of billboards: a cobra flicking its tongue, and then a laughing skull, and then finally, METAL MELTDOWN rising up from the horizon to fill the screen with Olde English and a couple of pitchfork-waving demons.

"Hey, two out of three ain't bad," said Alex, sprawled out on Matt's bedroom floor. "Usually you have to wait until the third hour before they start playing the good stuff."

"Why do they need to play Warrant *again* when they've already played them fifty times today already?" Ronnie downed a shot of Jack, leaned back against the bed. Matt was out on a date that Danae hoped was going well, Gnash over Catrinel's apartment. On the TV, ads for 976 party-line numbers, crimping irons, RIP Magazine. The invite burned in her back pocket. The party had just gotten started.

"And we're back! Next up, a brand-new video from Silversin! This one's called 'Wicked in the Dark.' and it's coming at you right now, on Metal Meltdown!"

A bluesy voice came barreling out of the darkness. Five men stood on a huge soundstage in concho-studded leather, their manes moussed, exuding pure cock-rock attitude. The scene cut to a cracked sidewalk, a chain-link fence, and a guitar wah-wahed as a woman walked alone. The camera panned up her tight dress, teased black hair. Hm. Silversin were the very template of verse-chorus-verse-chorus-solo-chorus songwriting, but this video was a grittier story than usual. Spike heels descended concrete steps, a crimson glove pulled down mirrored sunglasses, and Danae's mouth dropped open.

Pam!

The normally unbearable genre of pop metal took on a whole new dimension as the camera followed Pam through a world of broken glass, spraypainted bricks, swiveling her hips and flinging her hair around. This must mean Pam was dating Michael Sin, ew. Well, better than Zolo.

You did it, Princess. I loathe this band, but you look fantastic.

"I know her! She used to come into the shop, she's—"

"She's pretty hot for a video bimbo," said Ronnie.

Pam climbed a fire escape and the camera was sure to capture the seams in her stockings, racing up the back of her legs to disappear beneath a very short skirt.

"I'd let her be my girlfriend for a night. Maybe two."

The words were out of Danae's mouth before she realized she'd spoken them, never taking her eyes off the screen.

"She was mine for a few months."

Two beats of silence.

"What?" from Ronnie, disbelief to the point of indifference, *of course you're joking*.

"I dated her when she was a dancer in the Tenderloin."

Alex looked stunned. *"You?"*

You? Little, nothing *you*? Spoken with the same undertone of laughter that had kept her mouth shut in the woods. Here she was, thinking that putting on a long black dress would turn her into a woman of mystery…no. All along, she'd been standing in a different place than the girls they'd taken upstairs, not invited to that secret part of his psyche, instead cordoned off somewhere marked Sweet and Innocent. The place where they kept the chaste, stainless maidens after the prince has had all his fun and he's ready to settle down with someone pure.

All that time on the road hadn't mattered. Getting better as a lyricist, as a singer, meant nothing. There was still a game of notched belts going on here.

I know things about Alex you never will.

Fine. She wasn't completely without pieces to play.

"Her name is Pam. She was my first friend in this city and she helped me when I was in deep trouble. She's a dominant, and she loves tying people up. I spent a lot of nights locked in her handcuffs."

No high-fives for her kinky escapades, just thick, agonizing, incredulous silence. On the TV, Pam danced before a neon skyline in a little red nightie. Michael Sin stepped into the shot, took her in his arms and pulled her down onto a leopard-print couch.

"You were right, Ronnie, I *am* a lez. I like girls, just as much as both of you do. Tell me, what's so shocking? That I'm bi? That I slept with someone that gorgeous? That I slept with anyone at all before you, Alex? I'll tell you the truth, she's every bit as awesome as she looks in that video."

The pages of the next month's calendar loomed overhead. She would not get any farther, they would not let her get any farther, she'd been so blind with the joy of joining the band that she hadn't seen the box they'd put her in. The glass box. Someone else had put her up in the window again, these guys she'd been playing with all this time, sweating and bleeding and screaming and it hadn't stopped them from throwing her back in the coffin of Starlight Occult. But, no toys and lingerie this time, instead scaled back to the rose wallpaper, the vanity, and nothing else—the empty, pink, clueless world of the little girl.

Her mother hadn't taken her seriously; now, neither was Alex. She got to her feet, on fire with the urge to *destroy*.

"It's too bad. Your little rituals sounded kind of fun. You shouldn't have stopped all that just because I showed up," she said, glaring at Alex as she walked out the door.

She ran downstairs to her room. Slammed the door, locked it, frantically rooted through her clothes. There was still time to make it to the ball.

* * *

Danae walked up Columbus Avenue in combat boots, thick platform soles that added three confidence-restoring inches to her height. Her dress was short and tight and silver, a six-dollar thrift-shop whim. She shone and seethed through the streets of North Beach, dodging drunks and catcalls.

Her destination had her double-checking the address on invitation, finding herself at the twitching line of trendy clubgoers. The number over the silver double doors, the velvet rope, matched the one in gold script. She blinked. She never thought there'd be *anything* for her inside such a pretentious place. But the hand of an aristocrat was bidding her inside, and it was his party.

She walked up to the podium and handed over the invite. A flicker of tired eyes, a disapproving glance at her outfit, *he's upstairs* and the velvet rope was unhooked. She felt a collective wave of envy aimed squarely at her back as she headed inside, climbed the carpeted curve of a sprawling spiral staircase. Another bored staff member lurked at the top, asked for her invitation before letting her through. Neither guardian of the gates had asked for her ID.

It was well into the night, when all first impressions were softened by alcohol, and yet, Danae still felt the social meter running at full merciless steam. All heads turned to check the new arrival, snapped back to their chatter when they saw she was no one they knew. Short skirts and sharp blazers, teased hair and expensive watches, a mix of business and pleasure depending on how well one could hold their liquor. A black leather banquette spanned the far wall, where a laughing brunette pulled her top down for the kisses of two slick-haired men. Beside them, a hot debate over the complications of overseas rights was unfolding over a circle of martinis.

Devon wasn't here. She got a whiskey and coke from the bar and headed up a smaller staircase to the roof. Heatlamps glowed orange beneath the night, and one of Billy Idol's softer hits played out across the small crowd. She scanned the deck for him. A pillow-topped bench, a small bar, and there he was.

He was in pinstripes, the sober dress of businessmen subverted into a formfitting vest and baggy pants trimmed with bondage rings. His head was tipped back, and he was sitting alone. A few feet away, heavy boots and facial piercings, boys and girls lounging on cushions, looking as if they were waiting for him to call them over at any moment. Danae had expected someone to fight through, covetous demoness eyes shot from a perfectly sculpted face, a test of some kind against another woman. But there was no one. As if a silent moment on top of a busy nightclub was a kind of luxury in itself, for him. She could relate.

He lifted his head as she came around, and he broke into a grin.

"Dan-ah-ee."

"It's Dan-Nay. It's too late now, OK?"

"It's never too late to become what you truly are."

Ah, fuck. She lifted the whiskey to her lips and drained the entire glass. She'd need at least two more to feel truly ready to deal with him, but she'd take what liquid courage she could get.

He stood up as she put the glass down, wrapped his arms around her in a welcoming hug, slid three rubber bracelets from his wrist to hers, bound together now with a glittery little bat, tiny gift. The scent of water rushed in, cool and uplifting.

"Shall we dance?"

"I don't know how. Not to this slow stuff, anyway."

"Put your arms around my shoulders. Like this," he said, guiding her hands into place. "Like the prom."

"I never went to the prom," she said, as he led them around in a slow circle. She looked up into his face. A layer of foundation smoothed his skin into a perfect surface, lips blackened. Totally lacquered for whatever kind of party this had been.

"That's so sad. A beautiful girl like you?"

"I never went to high school, either." The stairs swept back into view, and everyone who had been on the roof had vanished. It was just the two of them up here now. He must have made some face behind her back to send them all running. Ha, ha.

"Lucky you."

"I don't know. I missed out on all the parties. Battle of the Bands. Making friends."

"You also missed out on all the teachers trying to control you. And the bullying. Anybody who says those are the best years of your life, it's bullshit."

The lightness disappeared from his voice. She felt the glass countertop slide beneath her hands, somebody coming into Starlight in tears, just needing somebody to listen to them. They drifted over to the side of the building and leaned on the railing, the street bustling with people below them.

"What happened to you?" she asked.

"Ziggy Stardust, that's what happened. Glam rock was pretty much over by the time I got to high school, but I still loved it. To this day I still can't understand why it was so wrong to like KISS and the Sex Pistols at the same time. But the town I grew up in was all Ted Nugent, George Thorogood, shitkicker rock, none of that *queer* shit. I can't tell you how many times I got my ass kicked. I'd wake up and find *cocksucker* spraypainted on my car, written on my locker."

"And the teachers didn't do anything? Aren't they supposed to be watching out for that shit?"

"Technically. But most of them don't want to get involved. The only time they do is when they're off on a petty power trip. When you're too different. So they made it out to be my fault, not theirs."

Somewhere down in the night, a group was singing "Happy Birthday."

"I hitchhiked to Rocky Horror every weekend to get away from it all. Like, you think I'm a freak, then I'm gonna be real good at being a freak. And I'll steal all your girlfriends, too."

She laughed.

"You're not so grim after all," he said. "You in your demonic black gown, howling for the end of the world."

"I'm not sure that's what I want anymore."

"What do you want?"

"I don't know."

The woods: *do you dare more?*

"How's the new album coming?"

She snorted and wished for another glass of whiskey. A group of five girls came yelling up the sidewalk, arm in arm. The strip show barker said something to them that was met with loud, derisive laughter.

"It's not what you want to be doing, is it?"

How thrilling it would be, to shed the dress, climb into the next persona, whatever it would be. The new sound churned at the corners of her mind constantly, influencing her work in ways she still had yet to find out.

(You asked for more.)

"I want to do what's *next*."

"I'd love to see what you'd do, if you were let loose to create what you wanted. There's so much I could teach you. If you'd let me."

She searched his eyes, found an odd recognition, someone else who for all their glory was still essentially outside the system. For as righteously pagan as Enspelled was, they'd never had any problem being themselves—or finding a lot of other people like them. Devon had not only invented another life to escape to, he'd driven it straight to the stars, turning all that agony into legend.

Still, she knew the sound of a deal.

"What are you offering me?"

He pulled a flask from an interior pocket in his vest, grabbed a wineglass from the abandoned bar.

"I know everything you go through to get that mic in your hand. There's always someone there, to make sure you *know* you'll never be totally accepted. And you still do it, and your bandmates never even notice."

A blood-red nectar splashed down into the glass. He capped the flask, handed her the drink, and brought his face close to hers.

"You told someone to fuck off before you got here. I can see the rage at the back of your eyes. You came here to seduce me in that angry little dress, and go back home to whatever misery awaits you. But there's a lot more to you than that, and I'm not about to let you go so easy."

The words flayed her alive. Caught out, totally, too stunned to blush. But a backhanded compliment was still a compliment. She brought the glass to her face, inhaled.

Pomegranates.

The weight of the proposal made her dizzy. Luxury, resources beyond comprehension, a mentor with so much more experience at business, music, *life*. But the ticket went one way only, and she couldn't begin to imagine what nest of snakes lay curled at the end of the ride.

But what was waiting for her back at the house? More of Ronnie's snide insults, more disembowelled women. A storage room grafting her life on to the rest of the band. An album she'd lost the heart to write. A lover who made her feel like an idiot ingenue.

If Devon thought she was strong and talented, then she was strong and talented. No question.

(Walk away from this, walk back into your old life, and you go no further.)

She gazed into his eyes, raised the glass, and turned her back on her band of brothers.

The potion went blazing down her throat, burning sugar with a bitter depth. The edges of her vision turned black, red, black, and her skin lit up with heat. She licked a drop from her lower lip as the glass slipped from her fingers.

He brought his hand up, framed her face in a curve of black fingernails. Stomped the glass to shards and claimed her with a serpentine kiss. A flaming match dropped onto a kerosene-soaked effigy, the anathema of cheating came on with a strange, self-destructive euphoria, the sharp tear away from the person she loved and had been so stupid to love. The hurt would be coming, oh yes, but right now, her shape was changing within his embrace, already somebody else. Devon's hands raced with heartbreaker voodoo along the thin fabric of her dress, every second decimating the girl she used to be, the fit of her new flesh just as intoxicating as this forbidden kiss. No one would mistake her for a virgin princess ever again.

The tailored gabardine of his vest pressed against her cheek, not the friendly worn cotton of a beloved old t-shirt—the guise of a mortal boy, that night on the roof, the clothes of all the boys she'd ever known—but another kind of man entirely. Her stomach did a slow roll as he took her hand, led her down the stairs.

The room below was mostly cleared of people, a few couples swaying back and forth to something slow on the dancefloor, some animated clumps chewing on bits of business. As she took the first step down the spiral staircase, her mind flew back to the house. Walking out Matt's bedroom door. Weedy. Sitting by the top of the stairs, a small gold wraith watching her with those big blue eyes right before she descended: *leave, and don't even think about coming back.*

The silver doors opened out onto the street. The long line was gone by now, but a couple of fans rushed up, squealing and asking for autographs. Security guards held them back. Devon's limo was waiting by the curb, its open door a portal to another world. She looked around at the street, one last glance at life as she knew it, before she climbed inside the glowing red interior. Devon slammed the door behind them, and she vanished from the streets of San Francisco.

* * *

Alex sat at the kitchen table, left eye swelled nice and ugly, turning a cassette over and over in his hands: *The Mind is a Terrible Thing to Taste.* One white candle, and a bottle of Jack, and solitude. The flame threw its light across the black of the room, lonely beacon at the back of the house, where he waited for her to open the front door and step back inside.

He'd almost run after Danae, but Ronnie stopped him: *Hasn't she pussywhipped you enough?*

What did you say? hearing her door slam downstairs.

There'd been a fistfight. Then they'd smoked a joint. The way it always went—you couldn't take it personal. But it was probably a lot different to someone who hadn't known Ronnie nearly as long as Alex had. Definitely different when that someone was female.

The whole time, he'd been dating a fellow deviant, and hadn't known it. The remains of the high blended with the alcohol, made his mind wander into the unthinkable: Danae in Ronnie's room, lit up within a circle of black candles. Not another anonymous pit angel who'd be gone by sunrise, but a girl who knew them both, very well by now, whose sweat had dripped down alongside theirs onto the jam room's floorboards. The triad they could form, Enspelled's creative nexus…a fearsome amount of power that could be.

Just try it. Listen to it once. So much like Kaylee, and Tara, *just read these books.* Come to Wicca. He loathed being pushed. But this was Danae. His creative partner, trustworthy. She hadn't been trying to change his spirit, just share something exciting. *Just once, and I'll never ask you again.* He'd listen to it as soon as she came back. When his headspace was clear again.

And fuck it. The band had come far enough, had gotten respected enough, no more hiding their relationship. No wonder all this had been simmering beneath the surface—they'd had to spend too much time holding up the facade of friendship. No. The secrecy was over.

They'd talk it out. It would all be OK.

The moon travelled through the sky as he stared at the front door, and his body gradually slumped with fatigue. By the time the candle guttered, he'd fallen asleep on the kitchen table.

And she never came home.

Act 2

Chapter 8

1991

The bottom of the rabbit hole was covered in black satin sheets.

Danae stretched her hands over her head, arched her back, took a deep breath of ocean air. She smoothed down the antique black lace of her nightgown, the kind of clingy, delicate thing a starlet would wear. Something a starlet *did* wear, according to Devon, a tragic, beautiful woman who'd died a tragic, beautiful death. An overdose, a car crash, a jump, he hadn't said, but there were plenty of shiny exits in this town to choose from.

She sat up, smoothed back her pillarbox-red hair and looked around her bedroom for the thousandth time, still adjusting to the plum and brass splendor on the second floor. The walls were paneled with cascades of cherry blossoms, left behind by the silent screen actor who had built this hillside villa in the twenties. A marble bathroom gleamed with gold fixtures and perfume bottles. A curvy little desk sat near the door, home to an old-fashioned typewriter. Angled nearby, a nouveau vanity was cluttered with department store makeup. The balcony doors were thrown open on an amazing day, and the Pacific Coast Highway was glittering with traffic down below.

Best of all, a brand-new Fairlight. The synthesizer got the room's prime space, right by the balcony, overlooking the ocean.

A walk-in closet held treasures from the boutiques on Melrose, rock'n'roll clothes made custom, where the owners shook Devon's hand and showed off designs still being sewn together on the dummies. The rack was crammed with an array of new identities: tiny skirts covered in tabloid print, delicate lace camisoles, things made completely of PVC. No tacky silver dresses here, nor amateur dye jobs in the bathroom sink: if she was going to be weird, she would be beautified by only the best.

Near the bathroom door, a large oval mirror hovered with judgment within a spiky gold frame. What radiant faces had beheld themselves in its glass? *Are you a worthy descendant of this glorious lineage?* it seemed to ask her, whenever she walked by.

Shut up. I'm working on it, was her answer.

She had sent no word of her whereabouts back home. But the kiss would get back to Alex, news like that always did, it would filter down the rock grapevine from chic nightclub to seedy dive and…Ronnie was no doubt pouring gasoline all over that fire.

Ronnie. She couldn't help a small smile of pure relief. *Goodbye, fucker,* and quickly pushed all thoughts of Northern California aside. Immersed instead in highway lights, the sway of palm trees, 405 and 101 and flying at eighty through the world's dream laboratory, sitcom-bright and larger than life. Intense and fast and hyperreal, It was a place that pulled on a completely different set of her neurons, ones she didn't know she possessed, and she wondered what hidden facets of her personality they would summon from her.

Her bedroom door opened. Devon in tight black jeans, bondage bracelets, nothing else. Sunlight played over his pale skin. He threw himself down on her bed with a gift-wrapped box, as bright and red as her hair.

She tensed slightly. He'd given her so much already—a luxuriant space of her own, new clothes, all the necessities to start over. It was probably small change to him, just the standard way the rich spoiled their lovers down here, but she hoped he'd rein it in soon.

She pulled off the ribbon, lifted silver tissue away to reveal a heavy black leatherbound journal that held the pages closed with a protective gnarled hand, sculpted from pewter. Each fingernail held a red gemstone.

"This is beautiful." It truly was.

"The lyrics you write, they deserve a grimoire."

"But I cross things out. I erase things. I'm too messy for something this nice."

"It's coming straight out of your imagination, it should be treasured. Even the things you scratch out. It's all a record of the decisions you make when you're writing a song. Besides, nobody's first thoughts ever come out perfect."

"Thank you." *For thinking I warrant something this cool.*

One short kiss that quickly grew into a long one, and he pulled her down on top of him. She breathed in the scent of rain, thought about the woman who'd worn this nightgown long before her. Whose hands ran down the sweeping garden of intricate florals, teased by the treasure inside? A studio head, promising a part? A clandestine sweetheart whose car had to be parked two streets over? A man with a ring on his left hand, a woman clad in similar wispy lingerie, some incendiary paramour—perhaps planting the seeds of suicide within this very dress.

She swirled her fingertips inside the waistband of his jeans, but he stopped her.

"Not yet."

"Not even—"

"It's killing me, too. But let's just enjoy going slow."

He nipped at her throat, traced the lace neckline, went no further. Sweet as a boyfriend in a teen movie, showering her with all the first-base attention she'd never realized she'd rushed through with Pam and Alex. The total opposite of his perverse public persona, and yet, defying those perceptions was a kind of perversity in itself. Whatever. The way he was biting on her lower lip, he could do whatever he wanted.

The golden mirror saw all, and kept its silence.

* * *

The master suite sat above a twisted flight of stairs, on the third level, at the top of the house. A behemoth four-poster bed had rich, bright tapestries draped across its textured wood, ruling over lounges and small tables and poofy cushions scattered around the immense space. Hundreds of crystal briolettes reflected the light overhead from a monster chandelier, and the windows were sashed in cascades of silky fringe. They were pulled back to let in the sun, and the room overlooked the ocean, the trees, the rooftops and decks of the neighboring mansions. It was a lair built for seduction, torrid affairs, lustful rites, but today Devon and Danae were sitting on the floor in jeans and t-shirts, a handful of records spread out around them.

Devon had a huge collection of CD's, but these albums were relics of his old life, packed at the bottom of his suitcase like protective talismans when he'd split town and hitched out to the west coast. They'd been with him through the job at the liquor store on Sunset, through all the triumphs and treacheries on the pop metal circuit, and they'd become a treasured Fuck You when his first album went gold.

The song stuttered with pops and hisses from the needle, but the unclean sound just added depth, in Devon's opinion. They'd been in his hands since the age of fourteen, when the moondust came drifting down onto his lonely teenage face.

"1972, and Bowie was bringing us aliens. This song still gives me chills, the way he sings it."

"It's kind of creepy. But beautiful."

Devon was still Darren when he'd first heard this song, the dazzling lights of another planet beaming through his living room. The transcendence was quickly cut short by disgust, shattered between his father's angry slaughterhouse hands. It had taught him to keep secrets, start hiding everything under the bed, and these testaments to survival were more precious than the platinum records that hung in his living room.

The glitter had never been far from his heart, but his handsome pinup face hid a long, long line of daggers up his back.

"So much melancholy in it. Longing. And all this time, I thought he was just doing these political pop tunes."

"Uh, yeah, he was a much different guy in the seventies."

He'd had his fill of rocker shenanigans, now it was time to move on. Pretty he could have, and he'd had. And had, and *had*. Someone to keep up with the music, and the magick, was much more elusive.

The label had him crowning new talent, fashioning the landscape of his contemporaries around him. It hadn't occurred to him until going through Migraine's signings, when Danae's face peered out at him from a band photo, one of the very few girls on the roster, that these might be rich grounds to hunt a companion. He'd gotten a hold of Enspelled's demo before she came along. Without her, they were just another run-of-the-mill thrash band. With her, the lyrics got slightly less ridiculous, and suddenly they started dressing in black and throwing a little Grand Guignol into their act. She wasn't obvious in skimpy outfits, no vamping for the camera, no punches pulled in the words, raw power that went right up and faced her demons—she was a princess in the country of a neighboring genre, possessing all the right traits for a good union. Meant for more than the pointless noise of death metal, which all sounded alike to him, anyway.

Even though he'd switched over to a meaner, harder sound on his third album, even though he'd cleaned up into an astute businessman, the world still wouldn't let go of his early 80's past. It was time for the fourth album to etch his latest incarnation into mass consciousness. Jumping styles was tricky—not everybody had it in them to transition gracefully. But he was sure he could bring the fans over from dark fiendish rock to dark fiendish beats, and stay on top of the charts while doing so.

"'I Didn't Know I Loved You Til I Saw You Rock and Roll.' That is the best song title ever."

"Yeah, so innocent. Like kissing on a playground."

No makeup today, nothing but freshly scrubbed skin for her kisses. He didn't need to keep his mask on around her, such a relief, once it sank in she wasn't here to shop incessantly or pilfer his Rolodex. She was after something he was all too happy to give: the knowledge accumulated over a lifetime of learning how to hear music, paying him back by just listening, sometimes even understanding it. And from the kind of stuff she was writing, he knew he'd be able to bring her into the most secret room in his house. All the pieces of his armor were left on their velvets, when it was just them, alone. Except for one. Two, actually.

"What's that *like*?"

"I have no fucking idea."

They laughed, and he took her in his arms, one long deep kiss on his bedroom floor, surrounded by the shine of vintage vinyl.

Later, after she'd gone back downstairs to her room, he'd snapped on the light in his bathroom and stared at himself in the mirror. He was going to leave his twenties soon, and had to take care of his looks. No more all-night binges, he planned on staying in the game for a long, long time. Time for the nightly ritual of preserving his youth, with nothing more sinister than the best skincare products money could buy.

By the time he crossed back over the threshold, ready to crash, his eyes were brown. A small dish of lens solution had been left behind on the sink, holding a pair of green contacts.

* * *

A smear of irate keyboards for an intro, a hard-faced vocalist in a leather trenchcoat. Spiked brown hair, revving up for the first song of his band's set, eyes closed and counting off the measures above a small sea of jaded stares. Danae had never heard them—they were still unsigned—but she couldn't help a tendril of empathy towards them, wanting so badly to rock the house, earn a place within the Nemesis Records clan.

Walk in with your head up, chest out, you don't give a shit. It's one big high school, and they all would have thrown dog food at us. By the way, you look gorgeous tonight.

She watched them from within a plush semicircle of red leather, raised up on a platform above the back of the dancefloor. She was in a black stretch-satin minidress that zipped up the front, stockings patterned with skull daggers, chunky platform boots on her feet, the only kind of heels she could walk in without tottering. Devon was in pinstripes and bondage straps, and a silver wallet chain glinted around his hip. They made the drinks strong here—or, at least they did for Devon's table—and she was viewing everything through a prism of top-shelf vodka. She twisted her hand into one of his straps, tugged lightly. He put an arm around her and her head fell onto his shoulder. Half the girls in the place immediately wanted to slice out her heart.

"So what do you think?" he asked her. He was in full face tonight, black lips posing the question.

Me? She blinked. "They're pretty good."

"Why?"

"The beats are nice and jumpy, and there's a lot of oomph in the guitar."

Some in the crowd thought so, too. A few miniskirted hips were grinding away, O-rings jingling from swooping arms. Only a few, though. The rest were standing still, drinking or turning away to talk to their friends. She hadn't looked at the mass reaction first and knew she'd answered the question wrong.

"They're competent, but that's all."

"OK. What'd I miss?"

"Take it apart, piece by piece. The beats are following a template, nothing special there, no unusual rhythms or nice sticky hooks. It's what you're used to hearing, but not carving a unique place in your mind for you to come back to. Same for the guitar, it's loud but the licks aren't going anywhere new. And the vocals—he just sounds angry. And it's fine being angry, hell, Pantera built a whole new career on it, but it doesn't work if there's no real passion to it. Listen to him—do you think he believes what he's singing? Are you convinced?"

Danae thought back to Bowie's high vibrato, naked and pleading between the bursts of Ziggy's guitar. Right now, the singer was snarling out a tale of wronged love, obsession, some painful revenge but wrought generic. She tried the words within a metal context, still found them lacking.

"He's singing what he thinks he's supposed to be singing. Like they wrote the music first and then used the lyrics as filler. It's why..." Her voice trailed off. *It's why Enspelled always wrote the words first.*

Devon was a businessman as well as an artist, he'd understand that those were the dark waters in which her creative point of view had been formed. And yet it felt wrong to talk about her band. Former band. Like talking about an ex-lover, putting something close to her heart out there, only to be smashed to pieces by his professional opinion. She was still angry with Alex, but she felt strangely protective of him around Devon.

"...it's why you can't just write a bunch of shit. Could I get another drink?" So glad her twenty-first birthday was finally behind her and there was no more weirdness around getting served.

"That's one thing I enjoyed about your music. No matter what you were singing about, you meant every word, whatever it was."

His eyes were dead calm, just stating an observation, but there was a touch of something else beneath his voice. Mocking her?

"Yeah, I did. I'm sure you did too, on your first album."

"Touché." He kissed her on the cheek, and the other half of the girls wanted her flesh to fall off.

Another vodka-and-cranberry appeared at the same time as a tall, thin guy with stringy blonde hair down to his ass and a shredded t-shirt. Not part of this trendy crowd at all, more like he'd wandered in from a monster truck rally or an event that involved beating somebody senseless. His eyes were the flinty kind that weren't impressed by much.

"Who are these dumbfucks?" he said, sliding into the booth next to Danae.

"Nobody we'll ever see again. Jamie, this is Danae."

Devon's guitarist pressed close, trying to invade her personal space while shooting her a look of *and you are?* For some reason, it didn't bother her. Maybe it was all the booze, or maybe it was the pervasive testosterone she'd gotten so used to during Enspelled's tour. He came off like a mangy puppy dog.

"All right, you can be an elitist, or you can be a sleaze, but you can only pick one."

"Devon, I like her." He picked sleaze and threw himself in her lap.

"Hey! Out of my space." He grinned back at her before hauling himself up. He was a firm departure from the same relentlessly self-promotional polish as everyone else around here. She found herself liking him a little, just for that.

"So what modeling agency are you with?" He lit up a cigarette.

A compliment? A dig? An honest question? Fuck, it was hard to tell in this town.

"My last contract was with Migraine Records."

"Death metal? No way. Devon, you're finally developing good taste in women. Oh my God, so you know Stolen Hope. So when the singer lost his voice, did he really drink a bucket of his own piss to get it back?"

"No, that was a total rumor."

Metal pedigrees, favorite albums, Danae deftly turned away any talk of Enspelled onto shinier tangents. The band onstage, the whole purpose of their visit, had been relegated to the background, going no further but they didn't know that yet. Fervent and preening and trying so hard, but just not good enough. She thought of Axenhammer giving Matt hell, how they'd probably keep playing small Bay Area clubs until somebody died, and even then they'd just get a robot replacement for their Wednesday night 1am slot in the Mission. They wanted a career, everybody did, but they weren't going to let the lack of a contract stop them from getting onstage.

The singer's trenchcoat, detailed with bits of metal, must have cost at least three hundred dollars. Things were done differently down here.

Devon getting up and nodding goodnight at the end of their set was all the answer they needed. She glanced at the stage, about to show them some kind of appreciation, *hey, you tried*, and received a look of pure death from the singer.

She walked out to the limo with Devon and Jamie, felt the tension of a hundred glares wishing a painful, humiliating twist on her ankle. As the car pulled away towards a party in the hills, she crushed out the little tentacles that had been cheering the band on. She too was under the same pressure as they were, to be good enough. They didn't have it, and maybe she did. The only way to find out was to work. Hard. She already knew how unwise it was to piss off potential fans with stage attitude. That singer had a lot to learn.

Good luck at your next audition, dickhead.

* * *

Twenty-four hours since Danae had seen him last. Eighteen hours since she'd found a box from a high-end lingerie boutique on her bed. She opened her bedroom door and found a line of white pillar candles, one on each step of the curving staircase, calling her to the third floor.

The doors of the atrium were open. The full moon shone down through a canopy of glass overhead, brightening the room with a gentle white glow. It was the only other room on the third floor, across from the master suite. Her nightgown, a confection of form-fitting cherry silk, swept the floor as she walked in.

Everywhere, abstract figures stretched and crawled and roared in molten silver, frozen bronze. Insectile bones rippled up a slim torso, stretched waist-high and flanked with disturbingly human hands. A semicircle of claws rode the curve of a backbone, slicing the air. A double row of jagged, copper-tipped teeth sat upon a velvet-topped pedestal. Stripped of skin, of anything soft at all, they were terrifying. They were beautiful. She wandered through an aisle of intricate menace, stopping to drink in the motion captured in the elliptical hook of a jointed tail, the superfine detail in a line of needle-thin eyelashes.

Devon was at the back of the room. Before him, a rugged wooden table was cluttered with bowls and burners and knives. A row of white candles partitioned off the working part of the room from the figures, rising off the floor in tall swirls of iron. Behind the table, a few steps rose up to a veiled alcove.

He looked up at her as she drew close. Suspenders, a plain cotton shirt with the sleeves rolled up, a stylized version of the mad scientist's attire, more of that sharp thirties taste. He came out from around the table to admire her nightdress, welcome her with a kiss.

"What is all this?" she asked.

"They're all things I've dreamed—I sketch them down, and I send them to this sculptor in Zurich. They're designed to trigger recognition from the deep mind. You ever go someplace in your dreams, and it feels like a real place, and you want to mark it down so you can find your way back?"

Feral and organic, pulled not from anything that had gone before but directly from the subconscious. Totally off the map of recognized, established symbology. There was no book for this—he was working totally by instinct.

"I've never tried making my way back to the nightmares." She ran a hand over a silver snout. "Not while conscious, anyway."

"It teaches you strength, getting comfortable with the ugliest things you can dream up."

A gilded bombe chest squatted near the stairs, from which he brought out a coil of incense, taper candles of gray and black and white, clustered them around the table's edge and lit their wicks.

"Don't you dream anything pretty?" It felt like a line in an old-fashioned horror movie, the naive question asked by the beautiful girl, so the all-knowing doctor or magician or whoever the guy was could give her a condescending lecture on the merciless nature of reality, before ravaging her, of course. But she had to admit, the sculptures rattled her. This was an onslaught of unbridled surrealist brutality, harsh and mesmerizing, she was all for facing the dark side but there was nothing joyful here to balance them out. They were like the opposite of Pam's shrine; Devon was surrounding himself with everything morbid and hideous.

He looked at her across the table as he lit the incense, shot her an enigmatic smile as he blew out the match. Went to the stereo and hit PLAY.

A soft drone entered the room, grew louder, changed pitch through a release of distorted female voices. A bass dribbled down like water hitting the dirt floor of a cave while the women stayed blurred. It soared through the sculptures, mixed with rich, earthy smoke. His hands sought hers, led her down the aisle, brought her into the eerie low-end beat and answered her question.

That first dance on the rooftop had been light, playful, just a boy and a girl having fun up above the world. Now, here, hidden away in the darkness, the demand on her body was greater. Her silk-clad muscles pushed against his in the raising of power; soon, a light sheen appeared on her skin, musk breaking through the scent of tea tree shampoo. Purpose through pleasure, but the door swung both ways, gave the steps a substance. It was labor and ecstasy, simultaneous.

They followed each other through the cold metal menagerie, engaged in a promenade of contortion, all improvised, passing the lead back and forth. Gentle followed savage, the caress tightening into a hard grip, dissolving into the soft brush of fingertips on bare skin. The dance brought her fully into her mortal self: the blessing to be born as flesh and blood, the curse to die but what a ride, to stomp and twirl and fly while the creatures delivered from dream were bound to stillness and silence forever.

The beat melted away and left an echo behind, reverberating gradually into an ambient purr. He slowed down behind her, wrapped his hands around her waist, kissed her neck.

"It's time," he whispered.

Consummation, finally. She shut her eyes, felt her heart speed up as he took her hand.

He led her up the steps behind the altar, within the sheer drape. Here, more figures surrounded the bed, more overtly erotic. Spiny angles gave way to slender silhouettes, sudden disruptions of roundness. Mad thought: *who's been here before me?*

And then: *doesn't matter when it's me right now.*

He sat down on the bed, and she descended beside him onto rich black brocade. The way she'd twined around his body, in perfect anticipation of each other's next move, she almost felt like she'd had sex with him already. But the moment now was so weighted, heavy with all the times he'd made them wait. Now that the night had finally arrived, she was nervous.

He trailed his fingers through her bright red hair, stared at her with an intensity that was unsettling, the kind of passion that left honeymoon sheets soaked in gallons of blood the morning after. These were the last few seconds before it was all about to change, and something deep inside her almost wanted to push him away, the pomegranate wine was just a formality and here was the real binding, here was the last exit off the highway south, no turning back after this point. She trembled as he pulled her mouth to his.

One gentle kiss, and when he broke away, his face had changed yet again. A wicked grin straight out of a photoshoot, as if he knew how anxious this was making her, went back to being the Devon she knew. The Devon that all the girls knew. She ran her hands through his longish black hair, a small part of her still in utter disbelief that any of this was happening.

He pulled down his suspenders between kisses, unbuttoned his shirt in a delicious male striptease, and all apprehensions were cast aside as she watched him undress, captivated by the private show, just for her. Down, down, down, revealing more to her slowly, all while watching her eyes, crossing from glam-metal pinup to the skin the camera hadn't captured. One last bad-boy smile, and he reached for her.

Afternoons of repressed desire came bursting forth. Pale and smooth, slender, muscled differently than Alex. Hands taught by the screams of countless groupies knew just where to touch her, took control of her senses, stripped her bare. She tried to give it back, but he was having none of it, gently wrestling her hands away from him. She gave up and let him take over as he pulled the final piece of red silk from her body and unleashed the full force of his oral expertise. His eyes took in every gasp, reflected delight back to her. Slowly circling inward, taking his time learning every wet secret, all tease and torment that stole her breath when he finally hit the target, the first blissful rush nearly sending her out of her body.

He rose up and kissed her, passed her honey to her mouth. Reached towards a shelf, silver square torn open, miraculously making even the condom look sexy: *see how I'm getting ready for you.* Climbing on top, soft bites on her lips. Her eyes closed as he angled towards her, inching in, slow, maddeningly good. She wrapped her arms around his shoulders, lost herself in a deep sweet grind and a kiss that burned through the moonlight.

It was dawn when they emerged. Strange, she thought, as she descended the staircase to collapse in her bedroom. She'd had plenty of all-night erotic marathons with Pam and Alex, but none of them had ever left her feeling so completely drained afterward.

Chapter 9

Danae sat at the Fairlight, watched the waves smash into the beach down below. In her hand was a letter from Migraine.

This is official notice that your contract has been terminated…

She'd been enjoying the newfound discovery that she could play by ear, banging out favorite tunes all afternoon, when she received her first piece of mail, addressed to Nemesis. Now they all knew where she was.

First things first. Migraine wouldn't have control of her solo projects—they probably didn't care. She was just the girl, after all. If there were any legalities, Nemesis would handle them.

As for Enspelled…the form-letter split was cold as ice, but it was what she'd asked for. She was free to write her next album without them. They were free to write their next album without her. Sobering thought: all those songs that the audiences screamed for, ingrained permanently into their mixtapes and minds, could not be rewritten around her missing voice. Or, they'd completely fall back on Alex's shoulders. Either way, she'd screwed over not just Alex, but all of them.

Too late to say you're sorry now, said the mirror. *Wonder who they'll find to fill your boots.*

Devon pushed her bedroom door open, taking a break from writing his own new material. Caught the stricken look on her face.

"Yeah, I figured that's what it was. Nemesis sends out enough of them."

"I shouldn't care, you know? This was the logical outcome."

He hit the power button on her stereo. The function switch was set to Radio, tuned to some anonymous FM station. New Order came bounding out of the speakers, and he turned the volume dial way up.

She made a face. "This is dance music."

"This is good dance music. Just listen. *Really* listen." He pulled her up and out the glass doors, where the admittedly infectious beats splashed out onto the balcony, into the sunshine. No, she shouldn't care, and dancing, moving around was better than sitting here depressed. She let go and let it take her over, the pop bounce carrying a deep unease, not the usual emptiness she'd come to expect from mainstream success stories. He was right. This *was* good.

"Artists move around all the time. It's just natural, to find places where you're a much better fit. Not everybody's meant to fossilize into one band, forever." He spun her into the chorus. "Come on, I refuse to let you get dragged back into your old problems."

The breeze came up from the ocean, blew through the heat of a bright afternoon. Up above the beachgoers, the light glinting off the cars, the discovery of what might be a new favorite song, this was definitely better than anything that could be happening in Potrero Hill. Cooped up in the storage room slacking off with her industrial cassettes, or frantically trying to resurrect her inspirations within the grove, or Ronnie mouthing off, nothing good. The past was a distraction and she couldn't waste time on the road not taken. Especially when three minutes of radio glory was all too fast to pratfall into Vanilla Ice.

* * *

Candles flickered over china plates of fried banana, cups of strong coffee. The moon shone down on the courtyard in West Hollywood, on the private table veiled away from the rest of the patrons. Dreamy Britpop played in the background.

Karl's large bass-player hands lit up a cigarette, the flame reflected in his glasses. Short black hair, mouth down in an expression of perpetual wariness, one earlobe pierced completely upward in silver rings, all business. Shadow, the guitarist, was a little more relaxed. A blazer thrown over an Entombed t-shirt, long auburn hair that looked to be on good terms with a quality conditioner. Unlike Karl, he was familiar with Enspelled. Cute, too.

"Into the studio, and then a show or two in town," said Devon, elbows on the table, the tiny silver starbursts of his cufflinks sparkling in the darkness.

"No tour," said Karl, who'd been directing his questions, and interest, to Devon all night. Annoying.

"No, it's not at that level right now. We'll see."

"How far have you gotten with the new material?" Shadow asked Danae.

"The sound is still coming out, but a few things have taken shape. Enough to start on, and I'm dying to hear them fleshed out with full bass and guitar."

Nice enough guys—Shadow, at least—but it was all so arranged, not blooming from a bunch of friends playing together, but two musicians Devon thought would work well with her. The expense-account dinner on Sunset Boulevard was not helping her apprehension. It was just a small project to be released through Nemesis, an EP, she would have much preferred hashing it out over beers.

"More dirty or crunchy?" Bless him. Questions like this were an anchor, something to start building on.

"Could be either. Or both. Won't know until we start to play around with it."

"What's the tempo?"

"Mixed. A couple go faster, but I want something you can dance to, as well as bang your head."

He grinned. Yes. He looked like he was going to be fun to work with.

"So how's your new material coming?" Karl asked Devon. *Now that we're done with this silly vanity project of your latest girlfriend.* He could think whatever he wanted as long as he shut up and played decent bass.

"It's gonna be fucking epic. That's all I can tell you."

Some very subtle signal passed, and the two of them stood up, offered their handshakes and goodnights, and departed the restaurant. She flung her head back, stretched, fooled with the huge lace bellsleeves on her minidress. A little sleepy—the food had been a fusion of French and Asian, out of this world, and worth the breakfast and possibly lunch she'd have to skip tomorrow.

"What do you think of them?"

"I won't know 'til we plug in. So let's get it going, soon."

She was excited, but under no illusions. They were totally here for Devon, her solo album just a potential stepping stone into his band, or some other up-and-coming outfit that was missing a member. But it was all she had to go on for now. She was glad Shadow had some ideas of what she was trying to do. It made the process feel a little more genuine. A tiny creative fire to warm her hands by.

"So if they work out, we'll go ahead and hire them."

Hire. Not jam. Not wail, nor shred, and definitely no half-skyclad boozed-up audition full of candles and incense. She nodded—she needed to get back to work, and this was the way to make that happen—but the word was cold and sterile and sank her mood all the way back to the house.

Ever the consummate professional, said the mirror.

She wandered out onto the balcony to stare helplessly at the ocean. The music she needed to write—there was so much expectation to get it right, deliver on the trust Devon was putting in her. This whole setup was just a temporary measure while she got her shit together. Someday she'd form her own group, it would happen organically, and she'd be one of the founders. No accusations of riding the coattails of an existing group, no paying people to come play with her.

Devon had her thinking in four-minute units. Radio-friendly with big loud beats, catchy hooks. *Marketable*. She understood perfectly. It also paralyzed her.

No more fantasy trappings, on to the modern she'd wished for. But what facet of it to pull down and chew on? The fans—and the critics—would be watching to see what shape her radical departure would take, if she'd succumb to the temptation of current trends. She wasn't sure what her place on the landscape was. Definitely not the resistance of governmental propaganda. Nor the disappearance into a soulless machine. This was her chance to get out from behind the boys, writing not just the lyrics but the music as well. Where to focus?

No grove to go running to now. But that could be part of the journey, forced from the comfort of the earth, into the unfamiliar realm of water. Back home, it had always been the woods. Never the beach.

She lifted her arms, let her consciousness drift into the salt air. Dark and vast, a black horizon, but close enough to hear the pounding of the surf. Wasn't a human body composed of seventy percent water? She closed her eyes, envisioned the coursing of her blood. Like to like. Thick pulsing red swimming around and around her body, let loose from the shield of skin to burst from her fingertips and toes, pour down the balcony and speed towards the sand, hit the spray.

A breeze ruffled her hair, gentle as a loving mother's hand, as she dropped into the voice of the sea.

(Choose wisely.)

Cups represented emotion, and water ruled over music. As badly as she wanted the trees, the ocean might be a better element for navigating a heartless business.

(If you succeed, they'll credit him. If you fail, they'll blame you.)

She wondered if that's how Devon saw it, too. A touch that golden, he'd *have* to.

(Use what you have here. For the moment, it's yours.)

Truth. She placed her palms together and bowed slightly in gratitude, and went back inside. Soon, the balcony was ringed with white candles and glasses filled from the bathroom tap. She settled down inside the circle of fire and water and opened the witch book, and stared at the first blank page, let the emotions come.

I hate Alex.

Pissed, yes, but this was not going to be a breakup album.

I dig Devon.

It was not going to be a load of love/romance/fucking tunes either.

I don't know if I'm happy or sad.

The first idea flared to life. Red and angry. Then shining and victorious. All of it, scary.

So why decide, and the rest of them came tumbling forth, onto the page.

* * *

White curtains. Lots and lots of white curtains. Danae found herself walking through walls of gossamer, following the soft angles of a fragile labyrinth. Something glowed up ahead, wherever this diaphanous maze ended. It got brighter and brighter as she pushed the draperies away, and she ended up standing in a boudoir tailor-made for a thirties starlet. A vanity was set to one side, a huge starburst mirror at its center. Beside it, frozen rain fell from a glass floor lamp. A satin lounge sat in the center of the room, where a woman reclined in a white lace dressing gown. Finger waves of bottle-blonde hair framed a lovely face drawn with thin eyebrows, a cupid's bow mouth, the very portrait of Golden Age elegance. Orchestral strings soared, the kind of music that got played during love scenes in black-and-white movies.

She was reading a script. Its cover bore something in Theban. Her face lit up with a rich, warm smile as she looked up and spotted Danae.

"So you're the next one."

Her voice was soft and formalized with the era's upper-class enunciations. She was a lover, a sister, a mother, but always perfectly porcelain, whoever she was. She stood up, script in hand.

Lights flickered around her head. Her lacquered hair began to grow, spilling down her shoulders, the careful curls losing their shape and quickly fanning out into ragged maiden's locks. A triangle, point up, beamed out behind her head, surrounded by a circle of shimmering stars.

"I was wondering when you'd come."

Shapes of power danced all around her, everything she had learned from her thespian-occultist paramour. They made the air vibrate, and a couple of the bottles on top of her vanity knocked together.

"I'm afraid you'll end up like we did."

The whole table started to shake. Small things feminine and delicate struck up a nervous clatter, began to change form. The back of a silver comb stretched jagged and taut with the sudden growth of a new spine. The bulb of a glass atomizer rippled with tiny veins, started beating like a miniature heart.

"Like we all did."

A frosted bottle flew at Danae's face. She threw her hands up just in time, before it smacked against her arms, hit the floor and shattered. Another bottle came sailing over. Before she even realized that a weapon had appeared in her hand, Danae fired a small handgun and blew it to pieces. The actress's fingertips went to her face as Danae shot out the rest of the vanity, taking aim at jars of face cream, boxes of powder, saving the final bullet for the starburst mirror.

Tears of rage came streaming down the adept's face, caught in one last glimpse before Danae woke up with a gasp. She clutched the sheets as her eyes raced around the bedroom, sought reassurance in the cherry blossoms, nobody else here.

She took a few deep breaths to slow down her racing heart. Felt stickiness between her thighs. She pushed the sheets aside. Just her period.

She got up and walked to the bathroom, changed out of her stained bedclothes. Let visions come and go across her half-awake state. Lyric material, always. All was grist.

A room full of malevolent sculptures above her. A city of dead starlets, around her—all the girls who had come before her. And how much of their blood had darkened the bed, the house, the streets beneath her.

* * *

Strobelights, and heavy chugging riffs, and screams. A standing coffin held a writhing brunette, naked but for a garnet necklace and a pair of fangs. On the dining room table, a threesome was splattered with stage blood. Predators and victims sprawled on curvy little sofas in various states of undress. And throughout it all, the industry chatter never ceased. Danae stepped over a long black wig that had been lost in the heat of someone's passion, surveyed Devon's living room, the deco antiques and platinum records that had been strung with bats and cobwebs. She was dressed in a glittering black gown that looked as if it had been clawed up one side, a fitting look for a party hostess of the damned. Devon was all in leather, black eyes, black lips, and the guests couldn't get enough of him.

You've gotta check out my friend's band, they're amazing. Do you have a costume designer lined up for your tour? I'm doing a horror movie and I'd love to cast you as the villain. Sharp fingernails tugging on his arm, coke-fired eyes angling for a minute of his time. Lots of introductions to people whose names she immediately forgot. A smooth-talking puzzle into which she didn't fit, there were a few grungy musicians around but the guests were mostly the people inside the shiny buildings, the pros with their degrees and world travel and business cards. And enormous carnal appetites—she hadn't expected the inhibitions to fly out the window so quickly. Technically it was her party too, but she found herself out on the terrace, knocking back vodka and staring out over the twinkling electric landscape. Danzig blared behind her.

"So you're Devon's protegé."

The voice startled her, and she turned. Adrian Payne. Adrian Payne!

He was leaning on the railing beside her, beer in hand, in person, *wow.* Spiky blonde hair, also in black leather but much more futuristic, sleek and studded with hardware, the protective shell of a computer hacker. One of the hard-pop upstarts, not one of Devon's people at all. Unlike Devon, he had no infamous eighties past to transcend, just a lot of hard work playing every instrument himself when he couldn't find a band of like-minded misfits to manifest the sounds in his imagination. His success made it easier to sit down at the keyboard and figure it all out, that it was possible to create something good that didn't hinge on the right people coming together—not everybody got that lucky. His presence on the scene meant you could work totally alone, and still be in the game. And make incredible angry noise that went straight for the reptilian brain and lodged there forever.

Protegé. She liked that much better than *girlfriend.*

She got down to talking shop. "I've just started messing around with a sampler. How did you get that weird smashy beat on 'Broken So Beautiful?'"

Whatever he'd been expecting from her, this was not it. His eyebrows shot up and she went on, amused, also glad for the three cocktails stewing her nerves. She was a *fan.* "I've been remixing some of your songs as practice. I've never composed music before, just written words, and it's a whole new world opening to me. Your stuff feels like a good place to start figuring it out, I guess I've taken you on as kind of imaginary mentor." Whoa, shut up. Quit rambling, idiot.

"Devon's not helping you?"

"Devon's busy with rehearsals, and besides, it's better if I figure this out myself."

"Smart. Especially when you're dealing with him."

"How so?" Weird, everybody was so deferential to Devon. Then again, Adrian wasn't part of the Nemesis court.

He was silent a beat before he spoke. "Just give as good as you get."

"A strange thing for a friend to say."

"Oh, we're not friends. It just looks bad for both of us if I don't show up."

She started laughing.

"What's so funny?"

"I'm sorry. I just can't imagine my old band having those kinds of problems. Putting in an appearance, and all that. The worst thing we had to deal with at our parties was somebody pestering us with a horrible demo. Or throwing up."

"The night is still young."

"Yeah, but these people have their heads screwed on straight. Too straight, I think."

He took a small rectangular case out of his jacket, silver etched with a tribal pattern, and handed her a business card. White on black, all lowercase.

"Stay in touch. I'd love to hear those mixes sometime, from someone with a background in death metal."

He knew who she was! Well of course he would, now that she was dating Devon, but still.

"It was great meeting you." And she meant it. She couldn't stop the smile from spreading across her face.

He winked and disappeared back into the party.

The ice cubes in her glass tinkled from the shaking in her hand. Adrian Payne. She tucked his business card into her evening bag.

"Hey."

Shadow came up from behind her, hands cupped around a lighter. The ocean breeze picked up his reddish-brown hair. A tight black t-shirt trimmed with D-rings on the shoulders, boots laced up to his knees, very nice.

"Oh, hey."

"I have a couple ideas to run past you. I mean I know you're writing everything, but if you're open to it…"

"Yeah, I'll hear it. Beats or riffs?"

"Both, actually. More of that raw sound, throwing a distorted edge around everything."

"Oh, yeah. I've always liked it better when it's not too clean."

"Me, too." He dragged on his cigarette, exhaled. "Thanks for being open to it, usually nobody wants to hear jack shit from a session musician."

"Actually, it's great, you know what I've done before, so you know what I'm trying to do—"

"When Devon said who you were, I knew this was going to be a good project. I *want* it to be heavy."

"Cool." She grinned, spotted Devon coming towards them. Jamie was with him, and a girl with short black hair teased up off her forehead. Her eyes were shadowed red and lined in heavy black, her thin gray blouse tied at the front to reveal a rosary twinkling with red glass beads, draped over the black satin cups of push-up bra.

"Danae, this is Colette."

Devon glided behind Danae, slid a hand over her hipbone. Danae saw a look pass from Colette to the devil at her back.

"So lovely to meet you," said Colette, raising a lace-gloved hand to caress Danae's face. A parade of covetous emotions flickered through the girl's eyes: lust, challenge, laughter, a definite history with Devon.

"She thinks you look good enough to eat," said Devon, low, stroking Danae's hip through the fabric of her dress. Jamie sipped his beer and smirked while Shadow blew a smoke ring. Neither of them moved.

Danae had known this moment would be coming, that their bedroom doors would open, and other lovers would walk in. Now that it had arrived, she was half thrilled, half petrified. It had not arrived quietly, to unfold playful and discreet in a sensual hideaway, but a challenge thrown right here, out in front of the guests: *are you a prude, or are you a whore?*

Tension thickened the air as she stood between them, felt a growing number of eyes take peeks in their direction. It was like skinny dipping—Devon was making sure she got her freshman year hazing after all. But at least that was in front of your friends, people you knew. These were all strangers, who all wanted Devon's undivided attention. They'd been indifferent to her all night, since they couldn't be outright hostile, but they were plenty interested in her right now. Shadow standing here was especially troublesome—their relationship was professional. Sure, he was attractive, but he was tied to her career. Anything sexual was a line not to be crossed.

And yet, the line was blurry here. This was a culture where the shedding of clothes was so casual, doing who you had to in the steady climb upward, or just blowing off steam from the workday that never had a true ending, pulling your clothes on in the morning and going back to the grind like it never happened. No sentiment, no hangups to stop the train.

Still. His presence made her hesitate.

Devon said nothing, just caressed the small of her back, the spot he knew was one of her erogenous zones. *I know you want her.*

Danae did. She adored him for the generous hand that didn't grasp hard on her affections and imprison her on a pedestal of forced fidelity, instead dressing her in starlight and taking her along to the bacchanal, bringing her a stunning jewel of taboo. She hated him for giving it to her in this way, at the cost of her pride.

Or was it? Perhaps this was a chance to prove she could run with the rest of them. Another trial.

Jamie lit up a cigarette. She could feel the clock ticking.

I'm down, if you are, said the look in Colette's painted scarlet eyes.

She'd lose either way. A stupid slut if she did it, written off if she didn't. If she had a dick, none of this would matter. She went deep inside herself, centered, asked herself the question that always settles everything: *what do you really, really want?*

To have climbed the stairs of Enspelled's house with Ronnie and Alex, towards a circle of candles. Devon was giving her something very close, something that her former bandmates never would—up here in the lights of the hills, something that they never *could.*

She hadn't come this far, given up this much, just to say no because she was afraid of what people would say about her. Although she hoped that Adrian was far away from this little spectacle.

And, ultimately, most importantly, saying no would not take her further.

She returned Colette's gaze.

Let's play.

She brought her hand to Colette's chin and caught her in a kiss. She breathed in the dark fruit of Colette's perfume, discovered the tiny kink of a tongue piercing. Soft murmurs of approval from the guys, but she ignored them, tilted her head back onto Devon's shoulder as Colette bit along her throat.

Devon was slowly inching down the straps of her dress but she beat him to it and pulled down the top completely, *you wanted a show, right?* He gently pulled Danae down into a lounge chair, backwards on his lap while Colette undid the knot in her blouse, the clasp on her bra, and slid onto her knees. The red rosary sparkled between their bodies as they made out and everyone watched. Girl lips, girl skin, a softness she'd missed. Colette was a fantastic kisser.

Colette's fingers slid beneath the black glitter, up the straps of Danae's garters, traced the edges of her panties. *Ready to go further?*

An R-rated scene at a private party was one thing. An all-out X was too far. She didn't want Colette to stop. Saying no, pushing her away, getting up, any of that would shatter the mood. She just wanted everybody to go away.

Just give as good as you get. Yeah.

She turned around and ran her hands over the waist of Devon's pants. Rock hard. She undid the button and pulled the zipper down, enough to expose a little fur.

"You're going to join us, aren't you?" Kisses so innocent on his stomach, *I'm just including you,* stroking him through the leather. Out of the corner of her eye, she looked back across the terrace. Jamie and Shadow were gone. So was everyone else.

She disguised a laugh inside a gasp and turned back around. Sat up and leaned back against his chest, felt his breath at her ear. His hands reached to cup her breasts as Colette pulled down the lace wisp of her underwear, parted her damp thighs. Devon sank his teeth into the back of Danae's neck as they tiny silver bead traced her exquisitely, summoned forth her cries almost embarrassingly fast. Caught between two gloriously profane mouths, she soared above the hills, turned on almost to the point of tears.

She found her hands caught in Devon's as she came back to earth. Colette sat up. Another look passed between her and Devon, and she got up, wiped her chin with a smirk, and walked back into the party.

More. She ground her hips onto his lap.

"Are you ready?" she asked.

"I'm always ready," he said, pulling down leather, smoothing down rubber. She straddled him backwards and sank down, gazed out over the black ocean. Thrill Kill grooved loud and lascivious from inside the house. Fast, deep, his delicate fingers reached down to strum a second surge from her. He wasn't far behind, nearly simultaneous.

"It's so hot, how game you are," when their breathing slowed, when he gathered her into his arms to lie sated, a few stolen moments before putting the facades back on and heading into the party.

"Something I've been picking up from you."

Two Brides of Frankenstein drifted onto the terrace, nude but for black stiletto boots and white tatters fluttering from their wrists. They leaned on the rail, lit cigarettes, stared out over the night.

"Good, because the one thing you can't have on tour is shame."

Chapter 10

He's coming, He's coming after me. He's somewhere in here. Oh my God! Oh my GOD!

A light beat pulsed beneath a shimmering disco-style high-hat, slowly gathered heavier momentum within a bright planetary hum. A small sea of eyes gazed up at the stage, expectant, waiting to see where this spacey intro would take them.

A keyboard chirped and flickered at the edges, the caress before the punch, before shooting forward into the darkness. The beat filled in with low-end, gut-grabbing riffs, intoxicating blend of both worlds Danae found herself in. Bodies began to move, heads banged, feet two-stepped. *Yes.*

Bless my hands with a weapon
Curse a mind without remorse
Blood on both our faces now
Never doubt I'll kill you first

Bodice, hotpants, knee boots, all PVC. Freeing her to walk around so easy, no more minding the folds of a voluminous dress. Her red hair streamed down her back like a waterfall from hell.

The boys flanked her, also in shiny black. Karl was in his element, lit up with a job going well. Shadow was playing to the crowd, having a good time out of the studio. No other visuals, time to try it without any gimmicks. Especially when she was behind a keyboard this time, not roaming around the stage but back behind the equipment.

She opened her mouth, dropped into a lower register, reached down the back of her throat for a voice that did other things besides growl. Deep clean sound came out, another surprise waiting for her inside her voice. Next stop, Linda Ronstadt.

Let me in, let me in! Please, I'm desperate, I'll do anything, anything, you've got to help me...

Samples from horror movies, the girls learning how to fight their own battles now. An updated version of what she'd been doing with Enspelled—the same witches and outcasts, but walking the streets of today.

It was a beautiful night beneath the stars, Bar Sinister's tiled fountain reworked with pillar candles and mists of dry ice. The crowd turned out to be more goth than metal, more women than men, although a lot of that was due to the club's usual menu of darkwave acts. But the switch was falling on enthusiastic ears, aggressively so. Girls in velvet bustiers and black tights were whipping their hair around, stomping their platform boots. Their eyelinered boyfriends were digging it too. She spotted some metal folk down among them, even a couple of people in Enspelled shirts, who were also getting into the new direction. A couple of them tried to start a pit but quickly got stopped by security. Good, they didn't all hate her.

Too late, when the rampage goes both ways
Nothing left but the law of sweat
And when I'm standing on your lifeless corpse
I won't forget
I won't forget...

The EP had been released through Nemesis, more of a solo project than an official band, which made the rent-a-bandmate aspect easier to bear. The reviews were surprisingly good, some rock mags and a couple of alt weeklies she'd had no idea were following her career—or, Nemesis had fabulous PR clout, she'd never know—critics who understood she was going her own way, taking metal towards the dancefloor. Although she could have done without the condescending praise of *maturing sound* and *growing up*. It was going over great, much better than she'd expected.

And Devon was nowhere to be seen.

I have some work to do at the studio but I'll definitely be there in time for your show.

She frowned but channeled it into her stage demeanor. Kept her focus on the faces turned up to her, rocking out, wanting more. She sent them wave after wave of thumping beats, tricky bits of percussion, a lot of Shadow's suggestions had been good ones and she made sure he got songwriting credit on the liner notes, something to add to his resume.

It was exhilarating to remember she had fans, too. A base that was relatively small, but passionate, and cheering on the sound she'd created.

Nobody left, I'm the last one. Just me and the gun, ha! Me and the gun. Me and the gun. ME AND THE GUN!

They finished up to a loud round of applause, yells, hoisted cocktails. She put her arms around Shadow and Karl and they all bowed, before descending the steps down into the crowd.

Jamie handed her a shot of vodka. Both t-shirt and jeans were shot full of holes, honest distress standing out against the crowd's artful rips of black.

"It's solid. Good. Like totally evil dance music," he said from around a cigarette.

"That was the goal." She tossed the drink back as a couple people shook her hand, *good show* on their lips. She nodded her thanks to them and immediately ordered another. "All this talk of sales was throwing me off, I just did the record *I* wanted."

"Better to fail your way than someone else's."

"They'll still give Devon the credit for it."

"And he'll gladly take it. He's really into you, but you're still talent. Another score for Nemesis."

And if she'd been that much of a coup, his ass would have been here for sure. Fuck. She knew she was at the lower end of the totem pole, shortened album and no tour, but she'd put so much of herself into it, it still hurt to feel the undeniable chessboard beneath her feet.

"If it's any consolation, Devon does *not* bring junk to the label. *Ever.* He wouldn't risk his reputation, so whatever he's doing with you, in terms of music, it's all real. And you're the first person he's ever had living with him."

"Really? Nobody else in that big old house of his?"

"Never. Did he ever give you the history? Make him tell you sometime. There's been this whole succession of people living there, like outcasts in one way or another, you know, like total geniuses at their art, but totally retarded at real life. Devon lived in the same shitty apartments as everyone else on the Strip, back in the day, but as soon as he could afford it, he went off by himself. Until he shocked everybody and brought you home. It's probably because you have other things to talk about besides clothes. Speaking of which, nice pants, dude."

Shadow had drifted over, in his stagewear of a fishnet t-shirt and glossy black jeans. He looked Jamie up and down, rolled his eyes at Danae as Jamie's attention turned to the pink-haired amazon next to him at the bar.

"I couldn't tell if that was a compliment or an insult, either," she said.

He signaled for a beer. "Whatever. *We* match."

"Harmonious visual interest."

"Sounds like something Nemesis would put in the employee manual."

"You mean you haven't read it?" She feigned shock, and they laughed.

"The show turned out really well. More than I'd hoped," she said.

"Yeah, well, back to reality." He plucked the lime out of the neck and swigged half the bottle.

"Don't you have your own band or something?"

"Trying to, but it's hard when I've got other people's ideas in my head all day, no room left when I go home and try to write out my own."

She wondered where he lived. All too easy to envision a small, off-white apartment box full of dirty clothes and empty beer cans.

"You're not gonna be doing anything for a while now, probably." He tossed his hair out of his face, glanced around the room.

"Just because I'm not recording anything doesn't mean I stop writing."

"That's good. It means when it's time to do the next one, you're ready to go. No panicking over the theme, oh my God, what image am I gonna project this year?" He smirked.

"Am I gonna worship the devil, or am I gonna drape myself in rosaries? Hmmmm, lemme flip a coin."

"Seriously, though, we should jam sometime."

Jam! That happy word! Nobody outside of Enspelled had ever asked her to in San Francisco, no restless minds in other bands curious to play with new blood, no lone noodlers looking to goof an afternoon away in front of a tape deck. And she could play keyboards now! What shitty timing.

"That would be so much fun, but I'm leaving for Devon's tour soon."

"That's too bad." Something shifted in his eyes, narrowed to a gaze that seared through the thin black plastic of her dress. She saw herself on a messy bed, pinned nude beneath him, his hands clamped through hers while sheets of handwritten lyrics spilled to the floor.

"It is." She stared right back, meaning it.

"Hey!" Devon called from across the room. She looked over and Shadow took a step back, quickly blended in with the bar crowd. Devon descended on her in a cloud of pinstripes and apologies and lipstick kisses.

"I'm so sorry. I got tied up with the way this track was coming out and I totally lost the time. How'd it go?"

"Good," she said. No more.

"I knew it would. You don't need star power to help you out, your stuff stands on its own. Besides, you can't expect everything to always be under control. That's the nature of the business."

The words made her uneasy. Was he telling her not to trust him? Or tweaking a hope way, way in the back of her mind that she'd been relying on his celebrity to boost her along? Half angry at him for not helping her, half ashamed she'd even had the thought at all, she finished her drink and took pride in the fact that she'd done fine without him. Which was the way it should be. She forced a smile, hurt anyway that he hadn't seen her perform. She was a much different artist now, come so far from the growling ghost in the opera gown.

"I knew you wanted me here. What can I do to make it up to you?"

"Let's write together. Some afternoon, let's *play*."

"Aw, babe, I can't right now. It's all gotta go 100% into the new album."

"Not even on a day off?"

"I don't want to tamper with your sound when you're still discovering what it is."

Vision, like something precious in a bottle, something fragile—how weird. She'd always thought of it as akin to a set of muscles, something to be worked and explored. She wasn't due to record again for a while, what was the big deal? She was about to ask when Jamie broke in.

"There's a party at the beach. Let's split."

Devon took her hand as they walked out of the club, wove around knots of new fans smiling at her, telling her she was great. As she passed beneath the arch to the sidewalk, she spotted a longhair in an Enspelled shirt. Not one of the pair who were banging their heads to her set, somebody else. He leaned towards her, hissed in her ear as she smiled appreciation at him, so low she didn't realize what he'd said until she was climbing into the limo.

Sellout.

* * *

Flowers from the garden were still wet in Danae's hand when she walked into the atrium. She cut a path through the forest of hell-forged creatures to the table, where Devon was poring over a huge leatherbound book, its pages inked red with hasty Theban.

"It's gorgeous outside. Why don't we do this in the yard?" She came up behind him, scattered the blooms across the table, rubbed his shoulders. "We could build a fire, hang up a cauldron…"

"No," he snapped.

She dropped her hands, stepped back.

"It was just a suggestion."

He turned, and his look softened. "I'm in the middle of trying to remember a dream I had, ingredients in a brew. You know how fast you forget things when you wake up."

"I was just thinking, you're so lucky to have outdoor space. Even just a yard at all. A place to practice, directly beneath the moon…"

"I prefer it in here. Where it's consecrated, it's been building up through all the seasons. I'd hate to disrupt the momentum."

"Ah." Weird. Every witch she knew would have killed for a private patch of green, direct hookup into the earth through roots and ponds and the sweet squish of mud beneath bare feet. Especially when there was landscaping left over from the Twenties. Devon had enough room for a decent-sized Spiral Dance out there, if he desired. The possibilities: vegetable beds, the paws of barking, meowing familiars, branches dripping with chimes, Alex would totally go crazy…

Alex wasn't here.

"…a gift from my friend Julian," Devon was saying. "But I just feel silly putting it on, you know? Velvet cloaks really aren't my style…"

She nodded along as she watched him pound seeds to a red paste in a marble mortar, add a few drops of something clear and pungent. She knew all the stuff you could order wholesale from the occult suppliers, and none of this was familiar to her.

"…when we head up north. He's a trip."

"What is all this?"

"Wouldn't you like to know." He grinned, knocked a swirl of paste off the pestle back into the mortar. "It's better if you don't."

He caught the frown on her face, backpedaled. "I'll tell you tomorrow. Right now I just need your belief that it's fairy dust."

"Must be some pretty fiery fairies. Don't piss them off, please."

He laughed, went over to the stereo, hit PLAY. Bells came shimmering out of the speakers. Light and sweet as laughter, making her see blue. Water. Emotion.

He drew her close, lifted her up onto the table and kissed her, ran his hands along her thighs. She wound her arms around his neck and pressed against him, instantly hungry. His hands twisted in the straps of her gown, azure silk tonight, slowly pulled them down. She followed with the buttons of his shirt. Soon, nude, light perspiration, bells washing over their bare skin. Time for protection. Time for the rite. Devon dragged the mortar over and dipped his fingers in the red paste, took her hands and covered them in vermilion.

"Don't let go."

He slipped into her, and she shut her eyes. Shit. Shit. He knew she couldn't come from intercourse alone, didn't he? And: the fire painted in her palms was a total mismatch to the flood of cool tones pouring through the room. Deep throbbing bass was a much better accompaniment to the scarlet arts, that was the realm of stringed instruments.

This doesn't feel right. He's so successful, what he's doing must be right, there must be something wrong with me that this doesn't feel right.

Fingers locked together, power concentrated, she understood the directives of sex magick but it felt like such a prison of discipline, all affection and delight reduced to the functional, sparkless pursuit of a goal. Not at all like that dance, that divine symbiosis of work and play. She concentrated on her breath and desire and let the energy build, *tried*. She boosted herself against him for more stimulation, shut her eyes and silently invited fantasy lovers to join them. She wanted so badly to reach down, set herself free, but her hands were trapped in his.

She'd never faked it. She really didn't want to fake anything beneath a full moon, lie to the cosmos. But the wood was hard against her back, and she was beginning to feel tired. She lifted her jaw, closed her eyes, let out a soft gasp and arched her back slightly. Just enough to suggest the moment had struck, with the barest minimum of guilt.

She felt him speed up. His hands clenched hers as he pounded into her, a satisfied moan as he left her stranded on a lonely, frustrated plateau. But there were clouds here, thick and soft as pillows, wrapping her in a warm, calm fog.

Her eyes stayed closed when he left her body, and she barely felt the swipe of the cloth against her wet hands. Forget mere exhaustion. Within a ring of cups and candles and blossoms, Danae had fallen asleep.

* * *

The bar was tucked along one of Hollywood Boulevard's side streets, dirty and loud. A line of motorcycles was parked outside, and Bon Scott welcomed

Danae and Devon inside a hideaway of cigarette smoke and spilled beer. A night off from working, from opulence, they'd both been thirsting for a change in atmosphere. Devon spread his old leather jacket from his Strip days across the back of a barstool for Danae to settle into, and a bartender materialized before them instantly. Bald, muscular, crudely tattooed forearms that promised a hundred good stories.

"Chazz."

"Devon."

A bikery handshake, and top-shelf whiskey was brought without another word. Danae felt jealous eyes carve bloody runes in her back. Her hand strayed to the holes in Devon's jeans, toyed with the stringy edges of velvet-soft denim. Memoirs decorated his leather: a tapestry of faded embroidery, a length of sparkling chain strung through one of the epaulets, a lipstick kiss painted purple over the heart. The glam version of the studded, thrashed-out patchfests that dotted the shows back home. They never would have painted their skull pins in glittery red nail polish.

Over on the jukebox, dirty deeds gave way to early-eighties pop evil. Devon smiled.

"They can't get past my second album," he shook his head, half-disgusted, half-amused as he threw back a shot. "All I did was butch up glitter rock, made them less threatened to rock out to a bunch of guys in lipstick. I look down on them as much as I thank them for making me what I am."

"No evolution here."

"Nope."

But Danae found it the most comfortable place down here in L.A. she'd been so far. Bathroom doors stickered from traveling bands, stained wood, it reminded her of all the places she'd played back home, familiar divey grime. Which ended when she caught the patrons staring at Devon, then trying to act nonchalant. As usual, the girls wanted to scratch her eyes out. But this was the kind of atmosphere she could relax in, nothing upscale to throw her off balance. Copies of *Rock Town* and *Hit Parader* littered the bar among burning tealights and an overflowing bat-shaped ashtray.

"Hey, I knew you'd show up here eventually." Jamie came walking up, pool stick in hand, beer in another. Chalk dust blued his chin. "What was that shit at the studio today? You know Bob's right."

"The fuck he is."

"Talk and play, asshole."

Danae reached for the latest issue of *Big Bang* and nodded to Devon as he got up, grabbed a stick, and bitched all the way to the table. Time to catch up on the outside world. She turned to the news section in front, a long piece on three guys from Seattle. Tangled hair and baggy clothes departing from the leather pants of eternal partytime, their faces sardonic and self-possessed in every shot. Interesting. She'd come back to them when her concentration was better.

She flipped onward. Metallica vs. Megadeth, the feud that had no end. A piece on the Lollapalooza festival. New albums from Prong, Cannibal Corpse, Primus. She turned the page, and Alex, Ronnie, Gnash and Matt stared back at her.

It was so sudden, so unexpected that she nearly dropped the magazine. Of course they were looking at the photographer but the glares from those four somber faces shot right through her.

Four. Four of them. No replacement.

It was all back on Alex now. Back out there facing the audience alone. But they loved him, there was never any question that he belonged. She drained her glass and ordered another as she scanned the words, found her name. Held her breath as she read the sentence that contained it.

"…left the band due to creative differences." Matt. Another twist of the blade, the official explanation given by someone who must have been utterly blindsided by her sudden departure. And such an awesome friend, too.

The payphone outside flashed in her mind. Quarters in her purse, filthy receiver beneath her brightly painted mouth. To say what? Worse, to *hear* what? *We all hate you. Fuck off, poseur. Traitor. Whore.*

She started over and drank in every word. There was a new album. There was a tour with a couple of other Migraine acts. The picture was professional, all-white background, real money spent. The feature was short, she could dig up more underground mags to find out what they'd been saying in more detail, but the new album would tell her all she needed to know. That would happen when curiosity won out over dread, which would not be for a while.

She closed the magazine and threw it back on the bar. Her hands were shaking.

Other magazines, safe rock mags that didn't dare stick their toes into the raging waters of death metal, she tried those. Let her eyes run over paragraphs about Riot Grrrls boldly decorating themselves in sexist slurs and the fashion rage for Doc Martens, while absorbing absolutely nothing. Eventually she gave up and grabbed a few band flyers, turned attitudinal band poses over to the blank backs, tried to write the shock out of her system. That wasn't happening, either.

The end of the second whiskey scorched her throat as she hopped off the barstool and made for the pair of doors marked BITCHES and BASTARDS. The ladies' room door suddenly flew outward, bumped hard against her knuckles. A tall redhead in a black tube skirt and cinch belt stepped out, glanced down at Danae shaking off the pain.

"Sorry," she said, in a tone that meant anything but. Danae glared back as the girl walked away. She stepped inside the tiny bathroom, locked the door, found herself surrounded by graffiti-covered tile. Here, the mirror was cracked and badly lit. But it kept its mouth shut, let her brood in peace. She dug into her purse for mascara, lipstick, the calming focus of refreshing her war paint. She'd give herself two minutes to get it out of her system.

It was so much easier when she didn't know. Now she did. And it came on in a torrent, the scent of sweet earth, deep rich laughter. String-toughened fingertips, and kisses like fire...

You?

It still stung.

She tossed her makeup back in her purse, leaned back against a scribbled list of Strip-star penis sizes, and sighed. She could hear Dio outside on the jukebox, something from *Dream Evil*, and her fingers absentmindedly tapped out the melody against her thigh. Her eyes wandered the turf wars unfolding in different shades of lipstick, threats scrawled in sloppy pink cursive, always someone pretty lurking at the edges, Devon had been nothing but awesome with her but the threat of replacements always hovered nearby.

But this was the life she'd chosen, the sacrifices she knew she'd have to make for transformation. To be harder, colder, less gullible. Alex's full-color face still burned in her mind, not going away easily. It made her feel like being an asshole. Best to take it out on someone who'd just been an asshole to her.

She pulled herself up off the wall, ran her fingers through her hair. Shame wasn't the only thing she was leaving behind for Devon's tour. She straightened her spine and opened the door, and headed off to drop the right words in the right ear and get the redhead thrown out of the bar.

* * *

Pale blue tiles were cool beneath Danae's feet. They led towards a huge puff of steam, a shifting cloud of wet heat that summoned the sweat from her face. She swiped an arm across her forehead as she walked into its moist heart and blinked her eyes. Something was shining up ahead. The sultry wail of a saxophone echoed across the ceramic surface, noir and brazen and full of sensual danger.

Gold. Curved. The mists drifted away as she walked closer, revealed an old-fashioned clawfoot bathtub. A woman lay within it, eyes closed. Her long black hair floated on red water. Beside her, a white rhinestone g-string was strung across the back of a swirly chair. A pair of matching tasseled pasties sat on the pink cushion.

Behind her, the wall was covered in erotic paintings. Every brushstroke immortalized a moment of longing: unabashed nudes with forthright stares, passionate twists of limbs and trembling flesh, seductions and escapes and cherub-graced idylls captured in gilded frames. Danae's eyes caught on the quiver of a muscular bicep, and didn't see the dancer's eyes open.

"Well, hello, baaaby."

Danae jumped. The dancer's voice was low and husky, deepened with nights of cigarettes and strong cocktails and empty promises. Golden eyes pinned Danae in place as she rose from the tub, her hourglass figure covered in blood.

The sudden weight of steel in Danae's hand snapped her out of her daze, and she fired wildly. The bullet hit one of the paintings, and a French courtesan screamed as oily red dripped down her thigh, over the frame.

"Haven't lost your mind yet, have you? Don't worry. You will." The dancer's feet hit the blue floor with a splatter. She brought her fists up, held them out before her body. One hand overturned, opened. A dove fluttered her stained wings and cooed. The other hand brought forth a dancing flame, startling the dove, who flew towards the ceiling in a blur of red and white.

Danae fired again, and hit Saint Sebastian, threw the first wound into his milk-white chest.

The dancer made the flame jump from hand to hand. She'd learned well from the stage magician who'd taken her as a lover, molding her bump and grind into the essential distraction skills of the attractive assistant, a whole new repertoire of manipulations against the audience.

A circus strongman. A bathing sprite. A warrior unbuckling his armor. Their faces twitched as Danae shot them, took on the snapping teeth of the atrium's creatures, Devon's angry dreams. The flame grew bigger in the dancer's hand, leapt from her palm towards Danae, singeing her hair—

and she came awake, the sheets flung off into a satin pool on the floor.

She jumped up and paced the room, tried to walk the terror off. It was like those *things* had been coming for her, not tools of the deep mind but rather its masters. She couldn't imagine going back up into the atrium. Good thing they were leaving for the tour tomorrow.

She noticed an envelope had been shoved beneath her door. She picked it up, walked out to the balcony, into the cool pink light of dawn. Opened it with shaking hands.

She sucked in her breath as she recognized the graceful handwriting.

Dear Danae,
 Be careful.
 Love, your mother

Chapter 11

Skin as sweet as candy
A confection I adore
But can you take me deeper, baby
Can you give me more

So deceptively gentle, his voice.

Dulcet poison dripped into the microphone as violet lights swept the stage, picked out Devon's slender form in the darkness. Before him, thousands and thousands of black-clad fans swayed their heads, revved up for the drop into the hard beat.

Beneath the bite of sugar
Bitter strychnine's never far
Offer up your flesh to me
A taste of every scar

So clever, so carnal, the dark slink calling forth the lust hidden beneath the rage, kids raised on rock so very very ready in their sex-shop cuffs and collars. Their faces were beatific as the drums crashed over them, pulled their deepest desires to the surface, delivered an escape from boredom, abuse, the abject terror of a mundane future. Teeth gritted, eyes shining, hair sweat-pasted to their cheeks as they sang along.

Decay beneath your angry kiss
Always the same fate
Gift me with your rotted heart
Infect me with your hate

The hooks were out in full force for this one, channeling the double-album grandiosity of the seventies, paying the debt to glitter rock through a fetish spectrum, angelic androgyny dressed up in black leather and thrusting away on an angry riff. And all swagger. No ardent debasement here, none of the self-loathing, painfully introspective, crawling-across-the-stage confessionals chosen by other electronic artists. Instead, the circling of bondage-ringed hips, flaunting kink, all pride. Before him, the front row crushed against the stage, hands reaching for him wherever he went.

They'd all seen the first video. An abandoned cottage in the woods, filled with fire, shot in black and white. Long hair, guitar strings, well-cut torsos on everybody, attitudinal glares into the camera while two spike-heeled fetish brides made their way into the house and stole kisses from everyone in the band. Then each other. The part that had gotten the world's attention was towards the end, the five-second shot of Devon making out with Jamie. The veejays played it fifty times a day. The religious fundamentalists clutched their pearls and vowed boycotts. Ticket sales went through the roof.

Devon flipped his hair back, clawed down his longsleever to stand stripped to the waist before the masses. A volley of screams answered him.

Behind him, the band. All in loose black, cargo pants and glints of fetish silver, sexy in that all-night-in-the-studio way. Jamie on guitar, a blonde windmill of hair, shirtless. Antonio's curly mane was back in a skull bandanna, his bass slathered in stickers like the rock version of a globetrotting suitcase. Ceth was at his keyboard, black hair buzzed to the texture of velvet but for a wisp of bangs, absentmindedly gnawing at his lip ring in between synth stabs. On drums, Max was a one-man brawl, teeth clenched behind streaks of green that kept getting in his face. All of them radiated power. Enspelled had too, but it was different with them. They'd been on the climb upwards, needing to display chops, show they were good enough to share the stage with bigger bands. Right here was the view at the top. The proving had been done.

Danae watched them from the side of the stage, caught up in the same hypnosis as the fans. Breaking out of the west coast industry bubble, rolling through the repression of the heartland he'd been raised in, had opened a whole new dimension on the debauchery. Back in SoCal, Devon had been product. Here, he was a messiah. His cult members came swarming in from the suburbs to pack the stadiums, bringing him their belief, their utter aching need for another world, one that would last for only a few hours.

The lucky ones were the pretty ones, as always.

Backstage, Devon's crew circulated the party room, broke the ice with vodka and Faith No More while everyone waited for the band, lit up nervous cigarettes, chatted with each other. The couches were full of studded bracelets, tightly-packed bustiers, beestung lips of black and red and blue, combinations of local rocker shops with the Frederick's of Hollywood catalog. Torn pantyhose and someone's BITCH t-shirt and eyes starving for some kind of transcendent experience to take back home into whatever kind of tomorrow awaited them, miserable family or soul-destroying job while the carnival moved on to the next city. Each one tagged with a backstage pass, culled from the herd, Danae leaned in the doorway and idly wondered who they'd left behind on the arena floor—friends, siblings, boyfriends, *ouch*—when she caught a brunette glaring at her. Long moussed hair, fringed suede jacket, snakeskin boots, regal in an overstuffed armchair, the arrogant bearing of a frequent favored guest within these hallowed cinderblock halls. Her eyes traveled down Danae's fishnet minidress, back up to roll her eyes, dismiss the competition.

Devon stepped in, fresh from the shower, makeup back on, black jeans and engineer boots and the spectacularly aphrodisiac glow of someone who just rocked a 25,000-seat stadium. All heads turned in his direction, fingers reflexively smoothing back locks of hair and rescuing fallen bra straps. The brunette wasted no time, smiled at him and lifted her shirt.

All I have to do is take off my top, and you can't do anything about it.

Devon put an arm around Danae's waist.

"You don't have to take shit from them," he whispered in her ear. "Give it."

He threw a smoldering look at her and kissed her hand, turned her loose on the room.

"Who do you want to take back with us, babe?" she asked, stage-loud over the music, meant to provoke a reaction. And it did. Shock and disgust on some faces, open delight on others. The brunette's face crumpled into an ugly pout.

Danae grinned with wolfen teeth. Surveyed the circle of lovely faces, watched the way their eyes watched her. A tattooed redhead raised her fingers to her tongue in a V, *fuck yeah, let's party!* Another girl in cotton-candy bangs and metallic black eyeshadow threw everything into one saucy, irresistible wink. Danae stopped in front of the brunette, sat down on the edge of the armchair.

"I don't know about this one, Devon."

"She seems pretty eager."

"Maybe. Let's find out." Danae put her hand on the back of the girl's neck, tilted her face up for a kiss. Relished the taste of revulsion and humiliation trembling against her mouth.

This isn't a Bon Jovi show, asshole.

Danae let her go with a smirk, wiped her mouth. "She's too bitter. Jamie can have her. She's just his type."

Danae got up and went to the redhead, pulled her up along with the vamp in pink hair. Wicked grins among the three of them, *we're gonna have fun tonight.* They walked out behind Devon, hand-in-hand, off to the bus. The girls left behind barely had a chance to exhale their disappointment before the rest of the band burst in, took aim, and covered carefully-applied cosmetics, strategically-revealed cleavage, and painfully high heels with a neon riot of Silly String.

* * *

A desert landscape rolled by, sand dotted with clumps of sage. Danae would have loved to stop and gather a few feral sprigs fresh from the earth, but they had to stay on schedule.

Devon's bus was a marvel of modern travel. Plush seats, a shower, a small kitchen stocked with gourmet food, everything that wiped out the need for pitstops, just one long roll through the map from hotel to hotel. They too had a copy of *This Is Spinal Tap*. It lay on top of the VCR, atop a stack of pornos and concert videos. Of course everybody here knew all the lines. But it wasn't nearly as much fun.

"…huge guy just full of muscle, you know, like he doesn't even have to do anything but just stand there, and he starts it anyway, with a shove, and the other guy just, *bam*, *bam*, and it's on. Seriously, if you'd seen this, you would have been late for the sound check, too." Max, acting it out.

"Fuck, I would have paid to see that." Antonio, mouth around a cigarette. "That asshole runs his mouth just 'cause he's mega-pumped and looks scary, about time somebody called him on it."

"All that power, and that's all he does with it," Danae chimed into the conversation unfolding behind her seat.

Silence. Then a whisper, then a laugh. The same dismissive response she'd been getting, over and over. By this time she was trying out of sheer boredom than any actual shared interest. It was crystal clear that they were not going to let her in, and her pride was beginning to pester her that she really should give up.

The fact that Devon hadn't said anything, or smoothed it over, was kind of annoying, too.

The strange relaxed vibe she'd always felt around him was getting strained. At first she blamed it on the lack of a home base. As luxe as everything was, despite the lengthy provisions of the tour rider, there was no place to ground. He was away from the atrium, his place of power. He could not be the magician. He could not be the businessman, either. He was an artist now, and suddenly back under that critical microscope himself. And while the initial reviews of his new album were good—some of them fantastic, actually—it bothered him that after a decade in the business, he was still being written off as a lightweight.

If they were home, he'd be turning to her. But they weren't. The band technically had their own bus, but they had yet to hang out on it. And she wasn't in the band. The camaraderie did not extend to her. Even Jamie was shrugging her off when they were all gathered together.

The only other girl on the bus was a groupie. Her laugh shredded Danae's nerves.

This is not what I ran away for.

She shrugged off the doubt, rummaged around for fresh tunes within all the industrial CD's she'd played to death by now. She put on her headphones, started up Sepultura. She reached for a drugstore notebook—the witch book was gorgeous but totally not portable—and opened it to a blank page.

Nothing came.

Not surprised. It wasn't just the collective cold shoulder she was struggling against—there was something else in her bag that was eating away at the edge of her mind. She didn't dare reach for Enspelled's new album. Devon's band members were not the kind of people to risk a full-blown depression around.

She closed her eyes and leaned her head back on the seat, settled into Brazilian thrash. Dirty streets she'd mentally walked a thousand times, the grit and the grind and she was back in the camper. All the comforts modest and makeshift, held together by the glue of each other's company. Their feet had touched the ground of every state they rolled through. One strong, peculiar memory came floating up from the past. Not Alex. Not Matt.

Ronnie.

Somewhere in the south, out in the middle of nowhere. Catrinel pulling off the road to fill up at a gas station tucked away in the woods. Danae had practically jumped out the camper door in the rush to the bathroom, the hostility in the eyes of the store's cashier barely noticed as she grabbed the keyring and ran around the back of the building. Gray and squalid, rotting, so filthy that not washing her hands had been the cleaner thing to do. She opened the door back out and nearly collided with a scruffy, muscular guy in camo shorts. She tried to get around him but he blocked her path.

"Hey. Hey. You worship the devil?"

She went to step wide but he grabbed her forearm. Strong. Blocked from view.

"Let me go or I'll scream." Drilling the threat directly between his eyes, but he just laughed, tugged her off the pavement into the dirt.

"I bet you scream real pretty."

"She does." Ronnie was walking up, hands tensed. Ready. "You couldn't handle it."

All hate forgotten as he stood by her side, made it two against one. She would have done the same for him, and he knew it. Every misfit kid since the dawn of the hippies knew it, the ones who'd ducked bottles flying from passing cars, the ones who got singled out by the cops. Three kids in Tennessee were in prison, one of them on death row, for horror novels and heavy metal and dressing in black in the wrong place at the wrong time. *We've got each other's backs.*

The guy let go, backed away, hands up, *only joking*. Ronnie spit at his feet. And then, the shock of his arm coming up over her shoulder as they walked back around. And it had felt so good, totally unexpected backup. She impulsively returned the half-embrace, *why do you have to be such a dick?* Just a few precious seconds of solidarity, before she broke away to toss the keys back on the store's counter. Ronnie was already headed back towards the camper, wind rippling the freak flag of his long black hair.

Something wet hit the side of her face. She wiped away a blotch of chocolate. She pulled her headphones off, twisted around in her seat. The groupie was down to her underwear, squirming in Ceth's lap while the others pelted them both with handfuls of pudding.

"Hey, watch where you're throwing that shit."

They just laughed.

* * *

Down on the floor, jeans and combat boots and a baggy Psalm 69 t-shirt borrowed from one of the crew, no makeup, hair scraped back in a ponytail. The lanyard of Danae's backstage pass was dropped down the front of her shirt, safely out of sight.

Backstage had gotten boring. Every night, the same dressup for local rock reporters who asked her nothing about her solo album but who suddenly paid attention when Devon dropped hints about her bisexuality, wanting to know all about the antics in the groupie corral. The band's continual brushoffs, the look-I'm-cool attitude of laminate-flaunting guests, everything exotic and forbidden was turning stale with repetition. An arena show as seen from the floor had become the novelty.

Some Nemesis band she didn't recognize was being pumped through the speakers as people milled around. She drank in the ambient buzz of a hundred different conversations. Someone's history class tomorrow, a test on the French Revolution, a ballbreaker of a teacher who was also really hot. Someone else's meeting, sales reports and an upcoming convention in Hawaii. Abusive customers returning stained dresses. Autoclave certification. Tomorrow they'd all be slapping at their snooze buttons, getting up exhausted to scrub leftover kohl out of their eyes, swallow caffeine as they made their way back into the 9 to 5, but right now, palpable excitement, wide grins above the fetish spikes. Happiness. She'd gotten so caught up in a nearby drama involving pirated horror movies and a garden hose that she was caught off-guard by the lights going down.

The cheers went up, and Devon appeared onstage. The crowd compressed themselves forward—*closer! closer!*—and she lifted her hands in greeting, just another delirious fan, and felt a hand slide over her right breast and squeeze. It was gone before she could even turn her head. She tried to move but she was packed in solid.

I'm the angel grotesque
I'm the filthy burlesque
One touch of corruption
And I'll claim you forever
Tell me how you get your kicks
Tell me when I make you sick
How far down will you follow me

The intro unwound and primed the crowd. Despite her anger, the song still electrified her; she turned her face skyward and let the fury roll off her back. Opened up to the euphoria, she knew every word to the new album and she was deep down in it from the first heavy stomp. Elbows out, clearing a space to move, room to breathe now that the initial excited push had passed, and people were settling into the groove.

You're the sour meat
You're the altar heat
One night of seduction
And you'll be just as disfigured
Shroud yourself in soiled black
Once you're mine there's no way back
How far down will you follow me

A hand was rough on her shoulder, a couple of musclehead guys were pushing their way through to the front. Again, too fast to react. She could see a pit up ahead and made no move towards it. The asshole element was definitely present, and bodies that fell would get trampled.

But that was the price of admission when your reach was this huge, the fratboys who'd come to adopt Metallica as their macho badge, the older fans who didn't understand all this weird stuff about gender-bending. Here to enforce conformity at a fucking rock'n'roll show, what irony, muttering behind the high school girls with their arms around each other, *look at those fucking dykes.* Danae made sure to throw her two-step wide, full weight coming down right onto the speaker's sneakered and vulnerable foot.

Eyes closed, rolling her head, body thrown completely into the beat. A circle had spontaneously formed with a few other people she'd heard talking around her, the exhausted grad student and the bodypierced masseuse and the kid who didn't get the part in the school play. The familiar, comforting sheen rose on her skin the way it did so many nights at metal shows, so good to be back in the crowd, burden of creation off her back, no need to get anything perfect right now, just the sheer enjoyment of someone else's performance.

Onstage, Devon fell to his knees and crooned, the preacher performing the mass exorcism. Out here, it was surreal that she'd be making her way back to his side, that she wouldn't be walking out to the parking lot and starting up the pumpkin of a secondhand hatchback, inching through the stereo-blaring crush to the highway, back to a ranch house, a day job, a cute boyfriend or girlfriend or maybe even a dog.

The reverie followed her back over the threshold of security guards, through the door of Devon's dressing room, dissolved in the surprise of his anger.

"Where the hell were you? And why are you dressed like that? The press are here and you are totally not ready." Shower-damp, sitting at his makeup table, hastily painting on a fresh face for the cameras. Beside him, a rack full of stage leather.

"I was out in the crowd. Watching your show." She flopped down on the couch, nibbled on a piece of cheese from a catering tray.

He did a double-take. "*Why?*"

"Because I've already seen it from the side of the stage. I wanted to see it for real tonight. You know, like the people who paid twenty bucks to get in?"

When had they last talked music? She couldn't remember.

"How fast can you pull yourself together?"

She sighed. An interview while he was in a bad mood, this was going to be fun. She looked around for a bottle of whiskey. "I'll start now."

She reached for her traveling bag and rooted around for her platform heels, a red lace tube dress. Slowly. She wasn't in a rush to wash the show off, the handprints of excited strangers who for a couple of hours had become temporary friends, sweating and laughing together. The people she'd remember along with the show itself.

She flipped her glittery red compact open.

Maybe down in general admission is where you belong, you fraud.

And quickly shut it.

Jamie walked in as she pulled the rubber band out of her hair. Took one look at her grubby tomboy camouflage and high-fived her.

* * *

A pipe organ blended with the sound of the wind, rose up into a cold night. The moon shone brightly among the stars, and the ocean added its chill to the air, only a few blocks away. Danae's old-fashioned laceup boots clacked up the warped wooden steps as she held the hem of her velvet gown out of the way, hand in hand with Devon, bare shoulders shivering. Miniature silver birdskulls adorned the wrists of Devon's silk shirt, and he carried a leather overnight case.

A two-day break had been scheduled for the west coast leg of the tour. So many memories as they'd cabbed up from the hotel, through the chiming glide of cable cars, the thick mist creeping through the streets. She was home, and it felt bizarre to be seeing it in Devon's company, cordoned off in her hometown. Although an exclusive invite was the only way into their current destination. Occultists from all over the world were dying to set foot in here, and the master of the house was very particular about his guests.

She took a deep breath, and caught the scent of gingerbread.

A curly-haired brunette in a frilly black minidress opened the door before they reached it. An inverted pentacle hung from her neck, and her red lips smiled in welcome, not just at Devon, but sure to include Danae as well.

Inside, everything was red and slightly dusty. Brocade panels set into the walls, fringed cushions of armchairs, heavy curtains to keep out the eyes of the tourists. And art, everywhere. A couple of cute Halloween devil masks were hung on the wall, flanking a framed oil canvas of a contemplative, beautiful Lucifer. Day of the Dead skulls brandished pitchforks, while a sci-fi demoness glowered within airbrushed hellfire. Bronze sculptures, velvet paintings, the highbrow and the kitschy were equally welcome in this house, it seemed, as long as it was diabolical.

There he was, sitting at an electric piano in a pinstriped suit. Julian. Yet another famous face materializing before her in real life, the bald head and arched eyebrows and mustache so iconic, another one of Devon's friends. But, to her, a local. Another figure on the magick scene. Countless kids had come into Starlight asking her about him. Respect for the strong and scorn for the weak, his philosophies had never interested her: *I don't know.* Celeste had refused to stock his books. Later on, snippets of media interviews, metal friends talking about his writing, she'd caught footage of his ritual chamber, which was somewhere beneath this roof. Psychodramatic theater, mostly, a form of ceremonial atheism that would laugh her off as a naive tree-hugger. But Julian's self-elevating laws meant inevitable ego clashes. She'd seen enough back at Starlight to know what ugly battles could transpire when everyone was a practitioner, and everyone thought they were right, no matter what form of magick they practiced.

He finished off with a flourish before rising from the bench, greeting Devon and taking Danae's hand in his, staring into her eyes and pressing his rings into her flesh. Taking her measure.

"Julian, this is Danae." Devon's arm curled around her waist, possessive, proud.

"A pleasure. Devon's told me about you."

Really? Why? There was a familiarity in his face that she'd never noticed, but she'd never spared more than a glance at his photographs anyway. She smiled politely at the arrogant gravel of his voice, wondered what the hell Devon had told him as they settled down on a loveseat across from him. Suddenly she was back in the atrium, restored to that hallowed hall in his affections. Devon the Magician was with her tonight. Her suspicions melted—she'd missed this aspect of his personality too much.

Stained-glass lamps burned dim from the corners, threw a soft glow onto each face. The brunette brought flutes of red wine on a silver tray, and they each took one.

"So how goes the tour, Devon?" Julian's voice was slightly slowed and strained, as if he was having trouble breathing. But he was in his sixties by now.

"Breaking attendance records. No problem getting them towards the new sound."

"A different form of the same fire. I never had any doubt."

Devon just smiled and drank the wine.

"And Danae…I understand you're writing your own music as well?"

She was caught off guard. What did Julian care what she was doing? Weren't they just here for the rockstar? She'd gotten so used to the band's exclusions that she'd expected nothing more than another night of men talking, sips of booze to stave off the boredom. It was weird to suddenly feel their interest. And on her work, too.

"I just did a solo album, it came out right before Devon went on tour. He's been teaching me stuff about music, about composition and emotion, maximum impact. I've been learning so much."

She said nothing more, just waited for Devon to correct her, contradict her as he'd been doing so often lately.

"She's really evolved since I first saw her perform. She *listens*, and you can hear it come out in what she does. So many people do only what they think they should do, but she does it her way totally."

No laughing undertone, all sincere. She hid her grin behind a mouthful of wine, at the same time pushing down a deep dislike for the way he talked about her in the third person, like a trained seal. Julian was gazing at her with approval. She wondered what he wanted from her, as they launched into a discussion of Julian's new book, and all the celebrities he wasn't allowed to quote in it.

The brunette sauntered back into the room.

"Dinner is ready."

The trio of taxidermied crows on the dining room table took Danae's appetite away, and she cut up the reddened meat on her china plate, forced down a couple of bites, pushed it around to make it look like she was eating.

"So you've been experimenting with the dark side of the dreaming?" Julian asked Devon.

"Started another grimoire with it."

"I told you it was fertile soil. A whole realm at your command, which comes to you alone. All within yourself."

Danae wondered how much of what Devon did in the ritual chamber was on Julian's advice.

"It's on hold during the tour, of course."

"Why? You don't want to let your discipline rot away on people you'll never see again, who will figure nothing in your life but one night of pleasure."

That was sound. *You tell him, Julian.*

Devon shrugged. "There's only so much I can handle on the road, the performance comes first. I don't have energy for both that and serious workings. As you've said, it's a balance of negative space."

Breaking in would probably make her sound gauche, but she was too curious. "Negative space?"

Julian turned to her. Surprisingly, no disdain. Like Devon, pleased for a hungry audience. "He's referring to the principle of negative space in magick. As in a well-composed picture, all the distractions are gone so you concentrate on what's most important. What is *not* there speaks of your decisions, just as much as what is present. What you push away is just as important as what you embrace."

"What you criticize is as important as what you praise," added Devon.

"What you hate is as important as what you love," said Julian.

"The great motivator, hate." said Devon. "Nothing gets you off your ass like anger. It's what kept me going through the Strip. Flakes and thieves, pay for play, it's a lot of fun watching them all start to fall down now."

Her mind wandered as she thought about the glam-metal circuit in the early eighties, so unlike Enspelled's world of death and violence and fury and yet, all the bands were totally supporting each other. What it must have been like to fight through that hairsprayed jungle—a time and a place much too competitive for true friendships to flower. What a miracle he'd been able to ascend, and now, score rave reviews on his latest album, when all his contemporaries were in the midst of a full-blown panic.

She flashed on the atrium, the utter magnificence of those sculptures, brought into existence by sheer animosity, the painful arc of his life. His family, and then the bullies. Then Los Angeles. Now, the industry people, and the fans. Cold contempt, the sharp machete he'd needed to hack through each new treacherous tangle and keep going. No friends to put things into perspective, instead letting the mandates of the business guide him towards the sweet revenge of success, nothing less would suffice. He'd done it, but ended up imprisoned behind a larger-than-life persona. A handful of personas. What Jamie had said about a mansion of eccentrics, loners…there had never been a point at which he wasn't fighting to be himself, one way or another.

She imagined Devon at fourteen, sitting before the stereo, face shadowed by the approach of an angry adult, the lovely creature that nobody knew he was, yet. She thought of kids coming into Starlight, not the empowered hippie offspring but the ones who'd had to keep secrets, rare in the Bay Area but definitely there. Burning their candles behind locked doors, hiding their knives and cups in pillowcases beneath their beds, leaving their how-to books with friends in more tolerant households. Coming in to replace an altar tool that had been destroyed in a fit of righteous parental anger, or find a candle to ease household tensions, a safe place where their curiosities were respected, encouraged. Sure, Devon was loaded, but it would not buy him a scrapbook full of loving memories. Daughter of Celeste, she understood completely. Her own personal collage hadn't really started until Pam. And then Enspelled. A history she wouldn't trade for all the money in the world.

She came back to the present moment. Julian was laughing, pushing back from the table. "I need to be up early for a flight down to Los Angeles, another talkshow. I'll most likely be gone before you wake up. I've had a room made up for you upstairs." He got up, clapped Devon on the back. Took one of Danae's hands between both of his own.

"Danae. It was truly a joy to meet you." His eyes sparkled with secrets. Charming and perturbing.

He disappeared up the stairs, and the brunette started clearing plates away.

Devon refilled their wine glasses and led her up the blood-colored staircase, across the landing to the guest room. She was slightly drunk, and something made her want to grab Devon and sneak out. Not that there was anything stopping them, but she felt a weird itch of transgression. Against Julian and being under his roof, against Enspelled, who were away on tour, city temporarily hers to reclaim. *C'mon, let's go out, we'll put our hoods up, nobody will know it's us.* Out into the dark, away from the hotel rooms and concert halls and the endless drive, out to the streets, a long winding walk through this steep, foggy genesis of a thousand California cults. Every block another row of mysteries hidden behind Victorian doors, vibrant with hallucinogenic wisdom, when enlightenment had once descended to earth in garlands of flowers and clouds of hashish. He'd played her all those old glitter rock records, how well she could return the favor now, back in her old stomping grounds, rich with the footprints of kindred seekers.

Back to the square of Haight-Ashbury sidewalk where she used to lay out her cards. A side trip to Starlight. *Hey Mom, look who I brought home.* (Yeah, right.) A trip to the grove. A much-needed connection with the raw earth, a release of everything that had been building inside, her fingertips curved in craving. Sitting down on one of the stumps, facing Devon…suddenly the flood stopped. No. The grove belonged to her past. It belonged to Alex. Bringing Devon there would be a desecration.

The fireplace had been lit for them, throwing flickers of light across the faces of the pictures across the mantel. They put their glasses down on the nighttable, and all thoughts of going outside vanished as soon as he touched her. Hands electric on her flesh, shoulders caught in his palms, his face painted in moonlight from the open front window. Calm intensity that brought out shades of the man on the North Beach rooftop, the one who offered her the chalice of a rare future, tempting her to fall and succeeding. Now, coming to seduce her, only her.

His kisses were hot on her throat, the wide neckline of her dress coming down easily in his hands. Teeth bared as she went for his shirt. Intertwined and sweating in the cold night air, by the warmth of the fire, wish answered wish. The lonely girl she'd been was the one locking her legs around his waist, just as the beaten boy had been grinding against her hips, all this time. The boy who didn't know yet what was waiting for him on the Strip, or after success. Still believing there might be an enchanted world waiting for him, one that held a little compassion somewhere, beneath the dazzle.

She reached up to smooth a lock of hair out of his face, realized she was changing shape again. But this time, so was he. He slowed down a little as she saw him catch it, recognize it in her face. Overwhelming, his eyes, brightened not with lust or smug satisfaction, but clear and direct with understanding. Being understood. This, she realized, was the end of his striptease. The final reveal.

It was too much. She pulled him down for a kiss before he could slide any further into her heart.

Chapter 12

The slight burn of chlorine, small price to pay for a swim. No salty primal voices here in this painted pond, a cool concrete rectangle chunked out of the earth. But it would do. The watery lights caressed Danae's skin as she treaded the deep end, temporary hiding place from what was going on by the lounge chairs.

The hotel had closed the pool off just for Devon's entourage, thrilled by their rental of the entire thirteenth floor and the marketing opportunities for name-dropping. A few fans had come back with them after the show. A boy with eight rings through his lower lip, a girl with a spiral of razor slashes from wrist to shoulder, their drunken friends, all of them debasing themselves for the rock god, dreaming up all kinds of shit to get his attention. Max and Jamie were sitting within a circle of half-empty vodka bottles, egging them on while White Zombie played from a boombox.

Devon, these people are a waste of time.

The children in black, running from their schools, their churches, whatever menacing form authority took in this part of the country. During the last wave of youth hysteria, they were filling up news reports with animal sacrifices and teenage corpses and some pentagram graffiti to blame it on. And still probably were, in some places. But now they'd slid into the new decade, found shinier ways to prey on each other, new libertine philosophies to misinterpret. All the rebellion, but no critical thought, grasping the surfaces and going no further in the race to be the most shocking. A kid in blonde spikes had swallowed a ball chain and was making it come out his nose. Every city had this kid in it. Twenty of these kids. Fifty.

You're from San Francisco. How the fuck could you even begin to understand?

Devon was sprawled out in nothing but jeans, watching the show from behind his bandmates. The magician had gone back into hiding once the routine of bus-show-hotel had started back up again. Now the bitterness was back, creeping further across his personality.

She climbed out of the pool, just in time to catch a splatter of blood hitting the ground. She grabbed a towel, dried off her hair, knotted a red mesh sarong around her black bikini as she walked inside to the bathroom. Copper tiles glittered beneath her bare feet like the lipstick of a corporate whore. A mirror spanned the length of the lounge, a few faded pink chairs parked before it. She slumped down into one of them.

Oh, you think you'll be the one to change him, do you?

She winced, but continued to stare at her reflection. More and more nights were passing like this, Devon mostly withdrawn with the occasional splash of acid hurled in her direction. It was almost as if the trip to Julian's had made him worse. But what was out here that could possibly sustain that part of his personality? Self-confidence was in serious short supply around the cult, and forget about dignity.

Devon had so much, and watching his fans torture themselves for his amusement was not making the most of it. Shit, she thought, if I had that kind of money, I'd travel the world.

You are, idiot.

Shut up, mirror.

But they weren't really seeing it, were they? Everywhere they went was like an extension of the mansion, luxed-out and hemmed in by security guards. She'd kill for a trip to a dive bar. A park full of knotty old trees. A dingy little show put on by fifteen-year-olds who barely knew how to play their guitars. But there was the problem of getting mobbed by fans, who went way beyond the typical enthusiasm of autograph hounds into the risk of indecency charges.

Perhaps somewhere outside the usual channels.

The tour was heading into the northeast. Cold weather. Piling on jackets, scarves, a thick layer of warmth that could also hide his identity. She envisioned cups of coffee in their hands when suddenly she had the solution.

She got up and flipped the mirror off, headed back towards the pool. Slid onto Devon's chair, glimpsed a thick piece of metal glinting up someone's nose, turned her head away quickly.

"I'm sorry. I didn't mean to insult your roots."

"I know they disgust you." Arms flung out overhead, bondage rings shining from his wrists. Fatigue in his voice. "They disgust me, too."

A few chairs away, a girl was lying on her back, clad only in green panties. Jamie was burning a line across her stomach with the cherry of his cigarette. She heard Max daring the blonde kid to swallow something.

"They're what I could have been."

"But you're not."

The shade of a smile crossed his face.

"They just want to be accepted. They'll remember this night forever."

Maybe this was why Devon had turned to empire-building for a spell, the work of evaluating new talent a safe place to put his mind. Now he was back out in the wild, and it was messing with his head. This was not the same person she'd lived with in the mansion, who could hold it all at a steady distance. The icon, the most immortal of all his personas, was also the most fragile. She brought her feet up and sat opposite him, slid a bare calf over his thigh.

"There's time off coming up."

"Soon, yeah."

"I have a radical idea." She started twisting her hair into a long red braid. "Let's go be *normal*."

"What?" A bit of laughter, surprised out of his voice. Her heart leapt at that one sweet note.

"I got an idea from being at Julian's." Ugh, she hated having to bring his name into it, anyone else's name at all, she should be able to do the convincing all on her own but anything, anything to pull Devon out of his misery. "There's someplace we should go, I think you'll be into it."

"Normal. What does that even feel like, anymore," he said, as the kid who swallowed everything threw up in the pool.

* * *

Red paint wept from furious brushstrokes, disrupting a gray, rainy canvas with a jolt of violent color. It could be a body thrown against a windshield, or a back-alley stabbing in a thunderstorm. Danae stood before the giant painting and let it wash over her, let it sink down into her subconscious, caught every possible meaning on the pages of her notebook.

A newly-divorced archaeology professor visiting from the east coast had told her about this place, rambling on excitedly about the utter smorgasboard of cultural treasures while Danae rang up her bag of attraction oils. And it was all that the customer had promised. Up above the city, hall after hall of visions, brought to life in gouache and clay by expert shamans. Not the feral churches of nature Danae was used to, but the open grimoires of fellow travelers. Plentiful stimuli that energized Devon's esoteric curiosities as well as his creative acumen.

They'd meditated in the temple wing. Four hundred years of reverence, fifty pillars of carved granite, each telling a story of Vishnu. A small circle of martial artists were absorbed in graceful katas when they'd walked in. They'd found a stone bench out of the way and faced each other, hands to hands, eyes closed.

Heal, heal, heal, thought Danae. *Him. Me.*

Us.

It was the first time she'd thought of them that way. Together. But he was being very good at being somebody else today. The Philadelphia Museum of Art was a place where nobody really knew who Devon Dare was, and if they did, they weren't likely to freak out over it. But it was best to take no chances, and the disguise had become part of the fun. Hair pulled back into a short ponytail, lean frame obscured beneath the bagginess of a hooded sweatshirt and BDU's swiped from Jamie, a pair of glasses Danae had picked up from the drugstore, thick black Clark Kent frames. He'd initially refused.

It's not your job to be handsome today.

He'd paused. *I never thought about it like that.* Slipped them on, looked in the mirror.

You look really cute in them anyway. His face had lit up with a smile, and it was like Devon was another person completely, his past erased, some other life path taken besides rockstar. Who would he have been, if he hadn't made it? If he hadn't been so driven to make it in the first place, and chosen something else to be? Now, today, he was a student, another artist coming to drink from the well, one more member of the public walking through the museum's doors. It made it thoughtlessly easy to slip her hand into his, blend into the crowd like any other couple coming to see the exhibits.

They'd spent the day softly calling each other towards intriguing works. Prometheus tortured by the eagle for all eternity, captured somewhere in the seventeenth century. New Orleans double-exposed in a haunting celestial noir. Before her, a giant pop-art toe lurked next to a suspiciously breastlike orange, not her aesthetic at all but somehow incredibly charming.

Devon was folding the museum map, nodding towards a doorway.

"Let's go that way. Sculpture."

The room they entered was dazzling. The afternoon sun streamed down from a skylight and bathed marble bodies in warmth. Human forms emerged from stone, glowing, the minute details rendered in exquisite, painstaking detail: the strain of a tendon in a pointed foot, the flawlessly smooth curve of a hip, the miracle of wavy hair chiseled from bright rock. Radiant, so temptingly tactile. Antidotes to Devon's atrium of nightmares.

"These are amazing," he said. Before them, a woman stretched upwards, back arched, hands behind her head, glorious. Nearby, two lovers wrapped around each other, limbs tensed with passion, their muscles telling the story.

Danae sat down on a cushioned bench. Being in this room, where all was flesh and exuberance, felt like medicine for her spirit. She hadn't realized how much her own negative space had filled up while living with him, and it was a wonderful sensation, and all too rare: to be deeply shaken by something *beautiful.*

"Who would I be, if I started surrounding myself with...this." He sat down next to her, spoke as though he'd heard her thoughts.

She almost made a crack, *I don't know, but your fans would be screaming for your blood.* But, no. Their greed, their demands were not invited along today.

"Not everything has to be dark and dramatic all the time."

"Feels like it, for me. Like all of this is some kind of really good life somebody else gets to have. Every time I try it, every time I start to believe in it, something goes wrong. This is all for someone else." His eyes flickered back to the lovers, their all-consuming need for each other so clear in the sculptor's steady hand.

"Someone who gets to be human," she said.

He was silent. Took her hand, held it between his. Today he could trip and fall, and nobody would know. The deep sadness she'd glimpsed in the gingerbread bedroom was up on his face now, in the slight slump of his body, successful beyond his wildest dreams, and still so damaged.

"Maybe you could try dreaming this kind of stuff. See if there's anything that wakes up with you into a sketch. If it's got such a strong hold on you now, it must be part of who you are, just as much as the nightmares. Stand up and fucking *claim* it."

He lifted her hand to his mouth, brushed his lips against her knuckle.

"The way you handle things, you're not handing me bullshit platitudes, you're giving me...occult homework assignments."

Some habits die hard, she was about to joke, but it disappeared behind honesty. The moments of bliss were too fleeting. "This is the most relaxed I've seen you, I think ever. It's wonderful."

Her hand remained in his through the rest of the exhibits, and picking up postcards of their favorite works in the gift shop, and walking down a street of brick, filled with flowerboxes and stained glass and antiquity. A world outside of Nemesis, and Los Angeles, and rock'n'roll, another reality entirely. Devon was in no hurry to shed his costume, instead content to wander around the creeping dusk in search of a cafe, *oh wow, like a date*. Another gorgeous smile that made her blood surge. She realized that when she finally fell into bed with him tonight, what they'd inevitably end up doing could very well be called making love.

The thought was astounding. A cobblestoned alley opened up beside them, bright with yellow blooms, and she pulled him inside. She really wanted to go straight back to the hotel, but that would end the charade too quickly. For now, just one kiss to feel the change that had stolen over her, that was throwing a slight shake into her fingers as she traced his jawline, stared up at him. Whatever had gotten into her was in his eyes, too, seductive defaults blown away by something a lot more raw. She took off his glasses and their mouths met in a new kind of passion, more tempestuous for being more gentle. The potions of her body burned with the need to cure him, and she saw the night before her, up in the plush glass box, the hours changing color outside as she gave, and gave, and gave.

She broke the kiss to hug him hard, and he held her tightly for a long time, and there was nothing but the soft evening wind, and a bus rumbling past, and the clanking pot from someone's kitchen window.

You're allowed to be happy, too.

One more kiss before their hands came back together, disguise back in place and they were out on the sidewalk again.

The curling ironwork soon gave way to graffiti, weedy lots. Mosaic walls covered in shards of glass and mirror shimmered beneath the setting sun. Storefronts began to appear, video rentals and used furniture and Rasta gear, definitely the environs for a coffeehouse, although Danae would have to do all the ordering. This part of town, South Street, was a lot more likely to recognize Devon.

Trees lined the sidewalk, Christmas lights strung along their branches. Loud cheers erupted from the doorway of a sports bar. Skate rats whizzed by, deftly maneuvering around the other couples and the drunks and the cars. Up ahead, a loose cluster of people was gathered on the sidewalk. Heads all turned in the same direction, staring at something in the universal expression of Something's Going On.

A filthy white van was parked at the curb, headlights facing them, a pit bull mix running around the back. A guy in college sweats was yelling at the dog.

"No! Go away! Go away! He's killing it!"

As they came closer, the shape of another dog came into view from behind a back door. Stiff. Brown and beige with a white underbelly, fluffy. Front paws lifted off the ground. Not moving, just rocking back and forth slightly. Closer. Blood on the white fur of its chest. It was only standing up on its hind legs because a tangled leash was holding it there. The other dog wasn't what killed it. What happened was already over.

Danae couldn't look as she walked by. No reason to turn her head and scar her mind by the sight of a dog that had been tied up inside a van, sensed a beautiful day outside and jumped out the window only to hang itself.

Someone inside a bookstore was on the phone to the police. The guy yelling at the other dog was still loud behind them. The dog still alive would most likely be euthanized, no matter what happened.

They walked in silence, all thoughts of cafes forgotten, through shoppers and clubkids and everyone else oblivious to the horror down the street, straight down to the waterfront. The day had already passed into memory, its edges stained red; there would be no way to remember the museum's splendor without the gruesome spectre awaiting them in the alt district. Devon was far away again now, back in his father's abattoir, where else could he be, the air thick with animal blood and the stench of fear, the corpse a warning, *you will never get away from your past* and she'd already cursed the van's driver for their sickening negligence, cursed them again for shattering the one good afternoon on this tour, precarious hope that hadn't a chance now to grow strong.

She said nothing. Closed her mouth on comforting words that would all come out cloying. If only they'd gone down another street, or ten minutes earlier, or ten minutes later, or *maybe we should have gone back to the hotel anyway, fuck, fuck, FUCK.*

The grueling schedule was starting up again tomorrow. This chance would not be coming again anytime soon.

Back in their suite, she went through the postcards while he took a shower. Found the one of the lovers' embrace but that was way too much, she selected the one of the stone woman arching her back. Futile, but she leaned it against the lamp on his nighttable anyway, to watch over him as he slept.

* * *

It was time.

It was dusk in whatever part of the country the bus was rolling through, Danae had lost track. She'd only ever seen skies like this in Arizona, lilac clouds glowing in a soft brilliant ceiling above an empty landscape. The rushing view outside the window would be the closest she'd get to the desert, good company to keep her steady through what she finally had to do. Silently she vowed one day to come back, find a quiet place within that golden dusty heat, and find out what the element of air could teach her.

The routine was back with a vengeance. She was sleepwalking through her role as Devon's consort, throwing her emotions on hold as she searched for a crack in the wall of his black mood. Somewhere to scatter seeds and call forth the selves that had a much stronger grip on the world. She encountered nothing but acrimony, worsened by a couple of stinging reviews from critics he respected.

There was officially nothing she could do. Best just to stay out of his way, and get back to work on her own career, which had fallen completely by the wayside.

Everybody was off in the back playing Super Mario Bros., jumping on Goombas and smacking coins out of brick walls, no interruptions while they were stuck to the game console. More importantly, no curiosity. If she got caught, it could be masked behind purely professional interest, what her old band was up to, just checking out the creative differences they'd headed off in, sure. It would be weird if she *didn't* listen to it. But she was not up to any kind of discussion about it. Especially not from Devon.

Pink light blurred into the oncoming dark, and she paused to watch it vanish slowly. The cost had been gnawing at her heart ever since she'd left, like a stack of bills sitting unopened on the kitchen table and a new one coming every month, piling up, time to find out how exactly how much she had to pay.

Oh, this was going to *hurt*.

Nobody was sitting in this section of the bus, but she still opened the compact disc inside her messenger bag, the red glitter vinyl flap shielding it from any inquiring eyes, and slipped Enspelled's new album inside her Discman.

A moody landscape on the cover, a bonfire up on a cliff's edge, glimpsed through a violet fog. Lovely.

Alright, boy. Let's have it.

She took a deep breath and hit PLAY.

Deep bass set a mournful intro for the lead guitar to skate onto. Rhythm joined in, slow and threatening, and it all rose up into a mountain of harsh strings, quickening drums, slamming off into a mean pit-anthem tornado. Clean and hard, it broke with the brimstone of the past and moved into something arctic and heavy. Still full of speed, but not the hot blast of aggression—this was a great wall of requiem ice. They'd fully embraced the introspection that a lot of extreme bands were going for these days, abandoning demons and gore for polluted ruins and mushroom clouds. Growing up, in their own way.

So this is what it sounded like when it was just Alex and Ronnie, again.

Once so strong, but now it's over
The sacrifice made much too late
Once alive, but now it's cold
A world of rust and graves

Hurling knives shaped like words. They tore straight through her as she pondered what happened on the other side of her disappearance. She flashed back to Matt's room, walking out the door. Weedy. Down the stairs fast, so fast to shut her door against them, ignoring what had sounded like a body slamming against the bedroom wall.

She'd never given Alex the chance to explain. But, Devon hadn't given her the chance to go home and think through his offer. His timing had been uncanny, the one night she could be spirited away from Alex. Because they would have talked it out the morning after. Definitely. It was all too easy to see what would have come next, if she'd said no, if she'd walked away: coffee cups and plates of homefries, her eyeliner smeared in the 6am sunlight, his rings laced through her fingers across the table. *Yeah, that's right, man, Devon Dare, can you fucking believe it?* They would have gotten it all out, depleted Ronnie's arsenal, made their bond stronger.

The outcome spilled itself across her imagination like ink. The next day, and the next, and the slow dawning horror that she would not be coming back. And the moment he found out she was with Devon—*how* he found out, unknown—she lost all feeling in her knees.

> *Nights of ash descending*
> *Come to choke my life away*
> *All in ruins, such a bitter taste*
> *As everything turns gray*

His songwriting had gotten a lot better. It had to. It would have been too obvious, too humiliating, to draw his targets sharp. The anguish she'd caused was concealed in metaphor, transformed enough to be sung safely. But shit, she hadn't meant to hurt him this badly. He'd stung her. She'd annihilated him.

Alex, who'd thought she was beautiful before any makeup had ever touched her face.

> *Eternal winter comes*
> *With its killing quiet*
> *Nothing left but*
> *A future of blood and silence*
> *Nothing left but*
> *A future of blood*
> *and silence...*

Pitch black outside by the time she reached the end. Fifty-three minutes of full-body torture, scalded by his voice. She felt like that video game with all the glamorous fighters, standing dizzy and glass-eyed, the way he'd just reached into her mouth and yanked out her skeleton. FATALITY. Yeah. Contrite and dazed and nauseatingly horny.

She got up from her seat and staggered down the aisle, into the bathroom. Grounded herself on the metallic turn of the lock, solid click, assured privacy. Hit PLAY and gently tossed the Discman into the sink, put one foot up on its edge, leaned back. Alex's voice came roaring out of the headphones as she pulled up her loose black minidress and slid her fingers down. Breath jagged, knuckle up between her teeth, the bump of the road jarring her against the wall as she conjured up his body, his rhythms and scents, his rings sliding down her breasts, her hips, and she bit into her skin, Alex who didn't have Devon's problems, didn't have that kind of real-life trauma at all, *he does now, bitch!* and she came hard against her lover's ghost, drawing blood on the sweet pain of his memory, tears streaming down her face.

* * *

Whiskey. There had been plenty of it in the party suite, but there were too many people blocking the way. Antonio knocked into Danae and spilled soda down the front of her dress, a mumbled apology as his girl of the night laughed like a harpy. Three strippers from a local club had jumped on one of the beds and Jamie was pitting them against each other, *come on, show me how you make your money.* The road crew, a couple of Nemesis bands in the area, fans and groupies and booze and noise and idiocy. Danae was pretty lit, but not as much as she wanted to be. She went back to Devon's suite to change into jeans and a t-shirt, tie her hair back, no idea where the rockstar was, no need for hot concubine drag.

Down to the hotel bar with her notebook, thinking about catching a cab to a dive bar, someplace with thrash on the jukebox and people who could debate the merits of My Dying Bride. She charged a double to Devon's room, wondered if the pool was open, wondered how long before the thirteenth floor came down to spoil it. Over the speakers, Stevie Nicks was singing about witches.

"Danae."

She turned. Adrian Payne. He was sitting alone at a cocktail table in the midst of a few other night owls, dressed in plain black, typing away at a small folding computer. She grabbed her drink and headed over.

"Hey! What a place to cross paths, right? What are you doing here?"

"I've been corresponding with this guy who's doing the most incredible shit. He lives in his mother's basement, he writes video games, and now he's putting together amazing stuff out of found sounds. He's *good*."

"Someone to make an album with?"

"No—collaborate on a game soundtrack. He refuses to come out to LA, so I'm stopping by while I'm in town."

"That's…really fucking awesome." And something Devon would never do in a million years. The line was too firmly drawn between fan and star. Adrian Payne, shattering yet another paradigm of the old ways.

"So what have you been writing lately?" he asked.

Oof. "Just noodling, experimenting, nothing concrete." A notebook full of half-baked ideas, actually. A bad answer when one of your icons asked what you were up to. Once again, she kicked herself for letting her discipline go to shit.

"That's touring for you. It'll come back when you're on steady ground again."

"It can't come fast enough, to tell you the truth." Ooooh yeah, she had a nice buzz going now. "I just wanna get back to my keyboard."

"You could, now." He nodded towards the bar's piano.

"Wanna?" Before he could answer, she was up and making her way to the empty bench, pushing aside the skirts of an invisible ballgown as she settled boots and denim down upon its gleaming black lacquer. He followed, computer back in its case.

Ohhhhhh, the feel of keys beneath her hands, she'd never played on a real piano. The strike of fingertip on smooth cool ivory, no electronics, all manual, the bar staff left her alone once they realized she could do more than just annoy everybody and actually play for real. She plunked out some Fleetwood Mac, reveled in the expanse of rich, full sound.

"I should be asking where Devon is," said Adrian.

"You don't wanna know. *I* don't wanna know. Now. I know you came all this way just to rock out on Billy Joel tunes."

They took turns, banging around on Todd Rundgren, the Police, some Velvet Underground. Laughter smoothed out the hesitations in her voice, which rose higher and louder through every cover. All around them, late-night travelers were smoking and drinking and grooving along, drawing close to the spark of humanity lighting up the bar. One of the patrons came up and requested Carole King, a tired-looking woman in a rumpled dress who'd been sitting alone. Sure, sure, she knew *Tapestry*. It was one of Celeste's favorites. Danae could sing the whole thing in her sleep. *Lemme work my way to it, alright?*

"It's that time of night, when everything gets schmaltzy. Time for confessions and the golden sounds of the seventies." Whoa, she was nice and loaded. So *what*. She pulled the rubber band out of her hair, let it fall bright red down her back. You kind of needed to be a bit of a diva at the piano.

"What's the stupidest thing you've ever done?" she asked him, fingers in a holding pattern of idling melody.

He paused a moment. "I passed on the chance to go to Caltech."

"Why?"

"Didn't wanna leave the girl I was in love with."

She brooded on that a bit. They'd broken up, obviously.

"What's yours?" he asked.

She laughed without mirth. "I think I might be doing it right now."

"What, being on the tour?"

"Being here at all." It was a shitty thing to say, but she was too wasted, and too weary of Devon's sniping, to hold up her mask. Which had already started to fall down anyway. "Maybe I should have just stayed in San Francisco."

"Maybe. But would you have learned to play keyboards there?"

"Probably not. No. I wouldn't have. Not that kind of band, and definitely not that kind of label."

"Then it was worth it. If you go back, you have skills that weren't there before."

She was quiet a bit before she started up again.

"Did you ever fall in love again?"

"Are you asking me if I'm single?"

"You're talking with the wisdom of giving it all up for love. Of *course* you're gonna say the road not taken was the better one."

"Your art can't ever decide to pack up and leave you. And yeah, I did."

"Awesome."

*So far away…*the keys were pathways back to bright afternoons, back to her mother's arms, of all places. The roots of giant trees, and the scent of soil, and Celeste's larger hand closed over her tiny one, mother witch, Rhiannon to the core.

She opened up, and her voice came clean over the keys, gentle. A hush descended over the bar, now that the sound had gone from two goth drunks fooling around to someone really meaning it. She went deep into the melancholy, the inheritance her mother had passed down to her, now that Danae had a great lost love of her own to cry over. Maybe two of them, if she counted Devon. Fuck, this was all so confusing.

The song faded out beneath her hands, to a small round of applause. A woman in a business suit walked up to the piano and dropped a ten in the oversized cocktail glass. Nice to know that if she couldn't make it in industrial metal, a lucrative career awaited her in Vegas.

One pair of hands kept smacking together, slow, obnoxious. She looked over. Devon was slouched down in one of the nearby armchairs in his hooded sweatshirt. He stood up, staggered over, and looked to be about as smashed as she was.

"Adrian."

"Devon."

No bikery handshake between those two. A dreadful tension hung in the air, like she'd been caught doing something wrong. She felt terrible getting Adrian in the middle of it, whatever it was.

"It was great seeing you again." Adrian kissed her on the cheek. "Take care." He got up, computer case in hand, nodded to Devon, and jogged up the steps to the business center on the second floor. She envied him the boring, earthtoned, drama-free space he was headed off to. *Can I come? Please?* Devon slid onto the bench, wrapped his arms around her, too tight, too hard.

"Are you screwing him?"

"What do you care?" She shrugged him off, hands back on the keys, freestyling something jazzy. *I can do something you can't.*

"Because he's an asshole."

"Because you can't control him."

"We're not doing this here." He grabbed her hand and tugged her up off the bench. She glanced at the ten trapped inside the cocktail glass: *you have fans. Stop forgetting about them.* He hauled her towards the elevators, stabbed the Up button and glowered.

"Why? Jealous when someone else gets the spotlight? Wasn't Madison Square Garden enough? No, now you want to blow away the Marriott lounge?" She should be fuming, the way he'd taken something fun away from her, but his anger was having the opposite effect. The doors opened, and he pushed her inside, her laughter coming loud and helpless all the way to the thirteenth floor, where full-blown chaos greeted them. They stepped over bodies towards their suite, opened the door into pastel luxury. A few clothes rumpled on the bed, a few cosmetics scattered across on the bathroom counter, every new hotel room pristine and posh and slicing her roots off a little more. She collapsed onto the bed while he paced in front of the window, the lights of a highway whizzing red and white behind him.

"That asshole's just playing you to get to me."

"Fuck, Devon, you're so used to getting stabbed in the back that you're looking for a knife on me. There isn't, but that's not gonna stop you from finding one, is it?"

"I could tell you a thing or two about your new friend and you wouldn't be so fast to cuddle up to him."

"Is that really what you think was going on? Let me ask you something. Just shut up and let me *ask*." She sat up. "Have you ever played music just because it's fun?"

"You're not listening. I've been through this. A *lot*." His face was contorted with genuine warning.

"Not everybody is out to get you."

"Enough have."

"You're not answering my question. Yes, I know. Everybody on the Strip fucked you over. I *know*. But have you ever played music just for the sheer pleasure of playing music? Because I've never seen you doing it off the stage, or outside the studio."

He went down on his knees before her, thrust his face into hers.

"This is a business."

She glowered right back, her thrash past right up on her face and blazing. "So if you're only doing it for the money, then yeah, you *are* a poseur."

Two seconds of stunned silence, as if she'd struck him in the face, as if she'd made up the insult just for him, a blade of contempt she'd never hurl against anyone in her former band, and then he shut down. His eyes narrowed, glinted with a new emotion she mistook for mere anger as he threw open the door and went back to the party. She fell to the pillows, unconsciousness coming fast, too trashed to realize what she'd just accidentally invoked.

* * *

Somewhere in Northern California, a pair of callused hands held a red glass candle. It was covered in love oils, and enchantments were scratched down its sides seven times.

No charge. You were good to my daughter, after all.

The second album. Another tour, much longer this time around. The candle had sat untouched beneath his altar all that time, still wrapped up in its paper bag. It would spin everything around again, when there had been so many overwhelming changes already. But he could only bleed so long. The moment had finally arrived to light the match.

Out of its newspaper wrapping, and then tipped out of the glass jar, turned over for a last little bit of witchery. A scrap of notebook paper was pressed into the wax, both a last gasp of hope and an upraised middle finger.

A tall flame leapt up from the wick, and released the scent of night-blooming flowers into the air.

Done with the pain. Fucking *done*.

Chapter 13

Sickness.

It permeated the sheer curtains of the club, circulated through the cool, chatter-filled air. Blue lights gave off the illusion that all was sterile and clean, so did the dark techno soundtrack, but Danae couldn't stop seeing disease. It crawled over the sparkles of someone's elaborately beaded gown, across a silver tray of rock shrimp. It squatted at the bottom of her lungs, made it hard to breathe ever since they'd gotten back to Los Angeles. She felt trapped within the stretch satin of her little black dress, cut tight to fall in sheer handkerchief pieces.

She shifted on the silver leather banquette, people-watched. It was too polite to be a real party, more an industry thing with Nemesis, the kind of bash for celebrities to polish their edgy cred. Faces she'd only seen on TV greeted Devon by name, shook his hand, chatted with him about their own various dabblings: *see, I'm dark, too.* A sixties bestselling author sharing stories of his trips with a SoCal acid cult, a producer working on a pitch for a Witchcraft Today primetime special, she needed to break away when a wisecracking sitcom child star, now well into awkward adolescence, started asking about Baphomet.

The atrium doors had remained closed through the full moon, the stairway empty of candles.

Jamie came over and sat down next to her, lit up a smoke. Back to his busted clothes now that the tour was over, companionship now that the rest of the band had scattered. She wanted to tell him to fuck off, but she was too lonely.

"Here they are, the so-called beautiful people. Trying so hard to be down with it, look at them. As if. Thinking they can flash authenticity around like money. What a joke."

Devon was talking to a pair of starlets, not stereotypical blondes with silicone chests, but indie actresses with good movies behind them. Some kind of real. Other girls were clustering around, waiting, watching for the moment they could break in and snag his attention.

"How fucked up the star system is, if it lets in someone like me," said Jamie.

One of the girls drew Devon close to whisper a secret. He'd said he needed to work the room tonight, which meant not having her on his arm. And taking every opportunity to stoke her jealousy.

The DJ shifted into a nice hard beat, something with a little slink, easy to prop your hips on. If there was going to be any little bit of enjoyment in this evening, this would be it. She dropped her evening bag to the banquette and headed to the dancefloor, not intending to match Devon's game but well-dressed partners came gliding up to her anyway. She circled her shoulders into the rhythm, closed her eyes, spun the hem of her gown around in a fluttering circle. The remedy against the affliction, getting up and moving, she was feeling better already. Someone's hands slid into hers. Her eyes flew open. Devon.

He stepped into her path, right into the beat with her, twirled her into a spin. The familiar push and the pull, she'd missed this so *much*. Yes. Yes. His body around hers, all the moves where they intertwined for just one tight second before twisting apart, individual selves again before coming back together. She started to loosen up, maybe this would be a good night after all, they were back home now, and things could stabilize. She looked into his face. A smile on his black lips, but his eyes were ice cold. Suddenly his leg was not where it was supposed to be, and down she fell.

She hit the floor hard, right on her knee. A gasp went up through the crowd, and a couple of them stifled laughs. All the girls who'd fantasized about her death just got their wish.

He got down with her and lifted her to her feet.

"So sorry. Usually you're so good at keeping up with me."

How juvenile, how *shitty*. She wished she had a drink she could throw at him, but even if she did, he was the one with Nemesis. He *was* Nemesis. The one with all the power, and plenty of people to back him up, all of them watching her reaction. She forced a smile and walked off the floor, grabbed her bag and headed upstairs. Whoever wanted him could have him.

The upstairs lounge glimmered red with velvet and brass, full of sparkling people. Devon's people. Nowhere to hide. She stepped back out into the hallway. A black leather bench sat inside a dimly-lit alcove. Here. She settled down, pulled a tiny notebook out of her bag, hid herself inside the half-light, just a dark form you'd never notice on your way to the balcony bar.

"So what the fuck is up with Devon tonight?"

She looked up. Shadow had followed her up the stairs. Black silk button-down, baggy black pants, hair back in a ponytail. The closest person she had to a friend, at the moment. She scooted over on the bench, and he sat down beside her.

"He's in a bad mood." Her knee throbbed.

"Uh, *yeah*. Over what?"

"Over being Devon. I have a bad habit of forgetting he's not a real person."

"Of course not. He's a rockstar. His emotions are miles above ours. We're just mere mortals."

"I don't envy your job."

"The smart ones don't. I've actually been looking to switch out of Nemesis. I got a couple of guys together, we're working on writing stuff. I need my mind back, you know?"

"Yeah? I wanna hear it."

"Find time to come over. I'm sure it won't be hard, the way he's treating you."

She looked away. That was a little too honest right now.

"Hey."

His fingers curled beneath her chin, brought her face back to his. All apologies but she didn't care about that, not when she hadn't felt the touch of another man besides Devon in forever. The scent of good cologne reached out and drew her in, yeah, she wanted to hear what he'd been doing. She wanted to run away from the hills, off to his apartment, tear his clothes off and fuck him for three days straight and get up and jam and then fuck him some more and then her mouth was on his, arms snaking around his shoulders, famished. Not Devon, not some groupie, but an equal. His hand slid down her neck, down her breast to clutch her hipbone, bring her closer. It practically hurt, she wanted him so badly.

His hand slipped beneath her dress, crept up her stocking, traced her garter. Skin to skin, it brought her back to reality. Any number of wagging tongues in this club would be thrilled to catch them in the act and dutifully report back to the master. Shadow didn't have to go back to Devon's mansion tonight. She did.

And, what a coup for him, Devon's current girl, too easy to hear the gossip around the Nemesis office. This was a world that turned on self-interest, and everyone was suspect. The chessboard burned beneath her feet.

It killed her to turn her head away, push his hand back from beneath the elegant tatters.

"I can't."

"Why?"

"I really want to, but I can't, I'm sorry."

"Yeah you can. I won't tell." He reached for her but she moved back.

"Look, I really like you, but I fucking *can't.*"

"Oh." His hand descended on her arm. "So you only whore around when Devon tells you to."

She tried to get up, but he was strong and he didn't let her go.

"And lemme guess, only girls, right?"

She tried to wrestle away but he pulled her back. She could scream, but who would come? Someone who would tell the truth, or who would benefit from twisting the story? How much would Devon believe her? No, she was on her own, and if she didn't win this battle, she was in deep trouble.

"Stop it, stop it, stop it," she breathed, chanted, a steady stream of *no* and his hands went back up her dress, desire from seconds ago telltale through the lace of her panties. She shot into a full-blown panic, too close, he was much too close to her body and her elbows winged out in a pit reflex—*get out of my space*—his grip faltered and she tried to jump up but he snatched her back, tried to pin her down and she smashed her forehead into his nose. Blood hit her face and she kicked him in the balls for good measure—*I said, get the fuck out of my space*—grabbed her bag and ran down the stairs, out to the line of limos outside.

She knocked on Devon's driver's window.

"I need to get back to the house. Some bitch just fought me in the bathroom. Please don't tell Devon, I don't want him to worry, just tell him I wasn't feeling well."

The driver got out, opened the back door for her with a wink and a smile. The lie was a good ego-stroke, something for Devon to laugh over later with another man. She settled back into the butter-soft leather, reached for a bottle of vodka with shaking hands. Deep swigs to make her forget, make her sleepy. The sooner the night was over, the better. Or so she thought.

* * *

Chains swung in metallic partitions before Danae. Cool and heavy through her hands, shining beneath a harsh white light beaming from the darkness overhead, she pushed her way through as her boots clacked against the scuffed boards of a stage. Someone was playing a piano. Classical. Strauss. Soft tinkling that sounded like wedding veils, christening dresses, a sound wrapped in white chiffon and fresh lavender. Deceptive. The tranquility was that of final rest. This was a song about death.

A woman in a green velvet gown was sitting at the bench. Her long black hair was parted in the middle, huge hoop earrings shining gold beneath the merciless light, huge chunky rings on her hands. She looked ready to call down the lightning against all foes, imposing and noble and battle-ready. Instead, she poured a sweet, soft voice out over the notes, played with a restrained passion.

Grand and haunting, the song gently swept through the space. Danae stood at the edge of the chains, watched silently as the woman painted the picture of a couple's long life lived together, together still as they headed for eternal peace. Tears started up in her eyes. It killed to hear this, with no one beside her, hands empty.

The keys dropped into silence, and the woman looked up.

"You thought you could get away from us, could you?"

Her speaking voice was deep, strict like a tough teacher. She stood up, started walking towards Danae.

"He was beautiful. Played as powerful as Paganini. I thought I'd been kissed by the muses when he swept me up and brought me here. He told me he'd be my mentor and teach me what he knew."

Closer, Danae saw red marks on her neck.

"He took away my voice. His need destroyed it."

The rings shone on her hands as they came up, wrapped around Danae's throat. No gun in her hand to save her, this time.

"This is the only way I can warn you." Gold dug into her windpipe, hard. Danae tried to speak but those elegant hands were strong, forcing her to face the audience. They made the point: cutting off words, all song, the sheer terror of all expression gone forever.

"This is the only way you'll fucking listen."

Red velvet seats filled the darkened music hall before her. All empty, but for one. A boy was sitting in the front row. Devon. Somewhere around fourteen or fifteen years old, in blue jeans and a plain white t-shirt.

The singer beside her had vanished. And suddenly Danae was dressed in her old operahouse gown. Her hands brushed against packets of corn syrup.

Devon got up and walked towards the stage, into the light. It caught the glitter shining on his handsome teenage face, and the starvation in his eyes.

He stood directly beneath her, at her feet. Bruised hands curled against the top of the stage, slurs bloomed on his arms in black marker. He didn't know yet what was waiting for him on the Strip, or after success. And he was looking to her to sing him something. Asking to be seduced, empowered, vindicated. Demanding it, the way true fans did. This was the moment she could reach him, and within the confines of a costume she'd outgrown, she was tongue-tied.

You want sparkle, and all I've got is blood.

It was not a good answer, but the only one she had to give. Hers was a genre that happened long after he'd gotten his shit figured out, a genre that he didn't even really like. It didn't make sense, the way he was reaching out for her. His expression didn't change, but she sensed his disappointment, the hurt at another letdown. And there were so many more to come. Her heart broke, and she reached out to touch his face.

He turned against her hand and kissed the base of her thumb, the gesture of a cultured gentleman. Her younger self would have *loved* him. That's who he should have been asking. The girl who didn't even know how to get into a metal club. Someone just as alone as he was.

He spread his hand out behind hers. Warm. Soft. He angled their fingers towards his eyes. Hooked them over his lower eyelids and pulled down. The skin slid away, pulling red strands of gore from his second face, the one hidden beneath the pinup smile, cast from a lifetime of relentless pain. Silver and sharp, spiked teeth, no soul whatsoever in the two green voids before her.

Nothing. Nothing. Nothing.

He dropped the scrap of flesh. It hit the floor with a wet slap, as he reached for her throat.

She awoke screaming, peal after peal tearing loose from her body, well after her eyes opened, just to prove she still had a voice. Her hands flew up to her neck just to feel freedom, no constriction, she was not dead today, she could continue.

She got out of bed and threw open the doors of the balcony, walked out to face the ocean. Still dark. She raised her trembling hands to the descending moon, mouthed two desperate syllables as a predawn breeze chilled the sweat on her skin.

Help me.

* * *

"More coffee, hon?"

The gray-haired waitress in cateye glasses was poised at the end of the orange booth, holding up a black-rimmed pot, the magic wand of the caffeine fairy. Danae pushed her cup over for a refill, loaded it up with milk and sugar. Canter's was fragrant with the scent of pastrami, animated with overlapping conversations and the chime of the register. Outside, a bus roared by.

She nibbled at a plate of the diner's free pickles, stared at the steady march of handwriting across the lines of her notebook. She hadn't gotten much writing done on the tour, and what had made it to the page wasn't very good. Frustrations and anxieties, most of them circling around Devon. If this notebook had gotten left behind on a park bench somewhere and picked up by a total stranger, it could have been anyone's story, any woman wondering why her man had grown so cold. Strip away the dark rockstar glamour, and there was nothing special about it at all.

What had happened to all her notebooks she'd left behind in San Francisco? Another angle she hadn't considered, accepting Devon's offer. Right now, another huge loss. Her hands started shaking again. Perhaps putting the pieces of her career back together wasn't the best way to get focused right now, too much cold hard reality to handle in her numb state. Maybe she should have just said Fuck It and gone to the beach.

Van Halen picked that precise moment to come streaming out of the speakers, the happy partytime thump of the David Lee Roth era lifting up her chin into a completely different California, the one full of bikinis and convertibles and eternal summer, straight into the eyes of a beautiful woman walking up the aisle.

Pam!

That strut, those sexy thick eyebrows, those glossy lips, an oversized white t-shirt over a pair of black bike shorts. She blazed through Danae's gloom on orange spike heels, about to pass her by until Danae caught her arm. She whipped around—Danae caught the scent of strawberries in her hair—and then, those painted eyes were looking down on her.

Three seconds of open astonishment before Pam sank down into the opposite booth. How much did she know about Danae's life here in the rock scene? How pissed was she still? Danae was too shocked to even form a greeting. All that mattered was that the first friend she'd ever made was right here, someone she'd hurt and who could have walked right by with her nose in the air and she didn't, she was sitting here, maybe ready to talk, and that was enough.

Danae got up and climbed into the booth beside Pam, wrapped her arms around the strawberry scent, and buried her face in her neck.

Please don't make me let go.

Pam managed to light a cigarette around Danae's fierce embrace. "So how bad is it?"

"It's pretty fucking bad," Danae whispered. *Thank you.*

Danae heard Pam draw breath for a response, then heard the words disappear in her throat. Maybe just as uncertain what to say.

"I'm so sorry, Pam," she choked.

A bangled hand came up slowly behind her back, returned the tight hug. Danae fought back tears.

Thank you. Thank you.

"You know, when I said you were running with a bad crowd, I didn't mean go find a worse one."

Pam knew. Of course she did, she'd starred in a video with Michael Sin. Danae had gotten so caught up in Devon's life she'd completely forgotten about Pam's move to SoCal. Oh, *idiot.*

"How would I have known? Pop metal wasn't my scene at all."

"That's probably what he was banking on. Danae. What *happened?*"

"I'll tell you only if you tell me how you ended up on Metal Meltdown."

Pam snorted. "Oh, what a sordid drama *that* turned out to be."

"I saw you. You looked amazing. So amazing that it started a huge fight when Ronnie wouldn't shut up about you, and it all came out, about us, and…that's when everything changed."

"Let's get out of here," said Pam. Danae got up and walked the check to the register, Pam pulling a ring of car keys from her fringe bag. "I'm not due on set until late tomorrow, and we have catching up to do."

"You're acting now?"

"Let me save the happy ending for the end, OK?"

* * *

The shrine was on fire. Loads of new photographs cluttered its surface, new people in Pam's life. A cameraman flashing the peace sign. A group of women in leotards smiling along the barre of a dance studio. Three devious-looking girls posing among a small garden of whips and floggers. A few scripts were stacked beneath a brochure: *Yoga With Pamela Black! Thursdays at Seven!* Shells from the beach, sugar skull necklaces. Life had changed all around her, but Pam remained a stalwart magpie.

She was being fought over by two telenovelas dying to have Pamela Black ham it up in runny eyeliner, and she was tempted—Hollywood would never take her seriously as an actress, why not—and between her exercise classes, and the hopscotch of fetish paramours, her hands were pretty fucking full. She counted herself extremely fortunate to have fallen into such abundance after the split from Michael, but every beauty queen needed a backup plan, sooner or later.

Danae needed a plan, now. Her morbid, sarcastic little witch from San Francisco had been reduced to a nervous wreck. Pam leaned back into the vanilla pillows of her couch, wineglass in hand as she heard the whole story, pieced together the angles to put her friend back together, not-so-secretly delighted in the airing of rockstar dirt.

"Devon Dare. I would have thought his ritual room would be wallpapered in black leather." A mouthful of white wine and a glance out the bay window, the lights of Echo Park came on one by one in the creeping dusk. A couple of white candles burned away next to the bottle on the coffee table, KNAC turned down low on the stereo.

"It's full of bad dreams. Really beautiful bad dreams." Which had to be awful, if Danae got freaked out by them.

"Dreams that filtered over into your sleep. And then the sex that was knocking you out when it was over. I don't know, the whole thing sounds like he was using you as some kind of food."

"And I'm gonna sound *so* naive if I say it felt like he wanted me there for more than that, right?" Danae refilled her glass.

"He made you a bargain. Did you ever think to ask what he was getting out of it?"

"I think it changed, from whatever it was at the beginning. He was just supposed to be like a mentor. A really *hot* mentor."

"Oh, tell me about it." Pam lit a cigarette. "I went through the same thing with Michael. It gives you a taste for screwing really stupid people when it's all over—whatever problems they have, they won't be trying to outwit you ."

"But it ended up going deeper."

"And it vanished once he saw something ugly outside his little velvet rope, the perfect excuse to run back to his misery. How all-powerful can he be if he can't handle one dead dog? Not everything is a sign from the universe."

"But it was amazing to discover he even had that side within him, I don't think he even knew—"

"You could wait around forever for him to show that face again, and he knows it. It's the chain he's keeping you on. Don't you get it? He's suspicious of everybody, it was just a matter of time before you made him paranoid, too."

Danae put her glass down, shifted her body, and put her head in Pam's lap. Normally Pam would have gotten pissed at the presumption of space, but this was someone who knew her from San Francisco. Who hadn't been stuck-up with her knowledge, the way a lot of witchy people could be. And hadn't had the best grip on social maneuverings, first with that speed metal band, then running off with Devon and really learning the hard way. But the promise of transformation hadn't been without worth. She caressed Danae's hair, thought about how much *more* there was to her now.

"I let things slide so much while I was down here," said Danae.

"We're all vulnerable in the hands of the wrong teacher. Trust me, I know. And if you're going to get fucked around by somebody, better someone like Devon than Zolo." Danae sucked in her breath as Pam's nails softly raked across her scalp. "You know that Devon and Tommi hate each other's guts, right?"

"Devon pretty much hates everybody from that scene."

"Devon has a reputation for being spiteful. *Really* spiteful. Don't know if you knew that, but how would you? You're in the girlfriend role, it's all hidden from you, what goes on at Nemesis."

"You came out of all this to be a pretty shrewd businesswoman yourself, with all this stuff you've got going on." She grinned up at Pam. "I want to see all your movies."

"They're just little indie things, bit parts, they're no big deal."

"But I wanna see them. And I want to know when your celebrity workout tape is coming out. By the way, you're teaching classes in yoga, aren't you not supposed to smoke?"

"I'm down to one a day."

"This is your second one."

"Today is special."

"Is it?" She ran her hands along Pam's thighs, arched her back.

Oh, yeah. Lots more to Danae now. *Let's see what else has changed,* as Pam stubbed out her cigarette, took a swallow of wine, and brought her mouth down to Danae's. Lips and breasts and hair rippled beneath her, and she slid her hands over Danae's wrists, found the familiar spots of control.

Big smile on Danae's face.

"What's so funny?"

"You'll kill me if I say it out loud."

"Oh, just say it."

Danae exhaled, stared into Pam's eyes. "I'm about to get fucked by Pamela Black. Everybody can go to hell."

Pam laughed. "Only you, darling. Only you." She took Danae's hand and led her into the bedroom.

A soft *whoa* out of Danae as she took in the web of chains suspended from the iron canopy, falling down into four posters of fetish rain. Restraints of red silk were tied into a few of the links, matching the shimmering bedspread.

Pam gently pushed Danae down onto the bed, felt the need in her ravenous kiss, knowing what was coming—oh, she *thought* she knew what was coming—but for now, pure affection to counter the wounds, someone to trust. Their hands clasped together overhead, and Danae's hips lifted up to grind against hers, and it was afternoons in the lower Haight, for just a little while longer.

A slow crawl down Danae's body, stripping her clothes off as she went, leaving her in nothing but the black mesh of her lingerie. Lifting her hands into the red silk and knotting her in. Flashed her a mischievous smile before getting up and walking to a mirrored deco cabinet on the other side of the room, flung the doors wide on a staggering collection of toys.

Danae strained against her bonds. Always so impatient, *that* hadn't changed. "Why'd you tie me down first? I want that one! And that one! And that purple thing!"

"Why don't we work our way through, slowly?" Pam lifted a flogger of ball-chain fringe from its hook and brought it over, ran its cool tendrils across Danae's stomach.

"One thing, though," said Pam.

"What?"

"I want your permission to do healing work on you. Counteract what Devon might have been doing. Make you strong. I've been doing some... experimenting."

"Yeah. You've got it." She broke into a grin. "That's a hell of an athame collection."

"Such a smart mouth."

Danae smiled back up at her, but her face grew serious.

"Thank you," she said softly.

Pam leaned down and kissed her. *You're here, you're in my very capable hands, and you're safe.* And began.

The talent to call ecstasy up through someone's body, to make their flesh shiver, helpless with passion: a kind of magick in itself. The cabinet gradually emptied through the course of the night, the contents spilled all over the bed as new tastes were discovered, new pathways awakened. Never had Pam tormented someone's flesh so thoroughly, expertly wringing out all doubt and fear. Through it all, her mouth and hands and words remained as soft as they had always been, but the techniques had been refined: strikes delivered between deep breaths, sensations placed upon the chakras. Pam could feel the lightness entering Danae's spirit, and she sent wave after wave of pleasure through her body, uncramping the places where the anguish had been.

When it was over, and they lay side by side, covered in each other's sweat, there was nothing left but gratitude.

Danae rolled over and laced her hands through Pam's. They stared at each other for a little while, wordless, while dawn light broke through the curtains.

"You can stay here, if you need to," said Pam.

"I need to go back. It's not over yet."

"But I'm here. You're not alone in this city."

Danae brought Pam's hand to her mouth and kissed it, held it to her heart.

"Always a flame."

Pam squeezed her fingers.

"Always a flame."

Chapter 14

Firelight flickered against the stone face of a mermaid, the living flesh of the nude girl curled around her.

Devon's garden had once been a temple to early-century ostentation, the lavish tastes of the burgeoning motion picture industry stamped firmly into the soil. In his care, it had been left to run wild. Square stones sunk a path around the side of the house, bordered by elegant urns up on pillars, stubby little trees, the weathered faces of maidens and cherubs who had seen the wild parties of every decade. The foliage was thick at the edges, completely obscuring any sight of the neighboring villas. Circular flowerbeds were set among the stones, and one of them had been dug up and replaced with a fire pit by a previous owner.

Devon was out by the blaze, one leg thrown over the arm of a scrolled iron lounge chair. Acolytes in black ringed themselves at his feet, employees scattered themselves across the stones in their eternal clusters of business talk. A stereo had been moved outdoors, and Iggy Pop belted attitude from the huge speakers.

Danae lay on her back beside him, stared up at the stars. Pam's magick was circulating through her veins, but she was back on Devon's turf, where his influence was stronger. Her mind knew an escape was needed. Her heart was lethargic, too easily seduced by his smile popping into her room, inviting her downstairs, a few people were coming over. And how wound up he'd been from the tour, and how patient she was to put up with him, and how there was a bottle of good whiskey awaiting her out in the yard.

From the long-dry fountain, the girl who had shed her clothes lifted her chin and barked at the moon. Jamie was out in the trees, getting high with a cluster of Nemesis people. The whiskey made Danae mellow, but didn't shut her anxieties off completely. They were just pushed off to the side by that persistent hope that Devon's good side was coming back.

"This isn't kissing on a playground," she said.

"What?"

"The sound. This is totally not that seventies bubblegum innocence at all. This is like the filthy underside."

"Some people consider Iggy the first punk rocker."

"Yeah, I can see that."

The track ended. Three seconds of black silence, and then a guitar opened up, the notes played light but mournful. *This* one.

Devon started singing along, soft at first, but then picking it up, getting into it. He got up and stood in front of one of the speakers, started to sway his body the way he did onstage. Opened his voice up over Iggy's, and sang it with a strength that knew this song inside and out. His eyes locked on hers, aimed it straight at her.

I'm giving you what you wanted.

Danger.

The conversations all around the yard came to a grinding halt.

She was astounded that somebody back in 1973 could put it all so well, their story. And Devon was a master storyteller. He sketched a portrait of grace with his body, the prop of the mic stand not needed, no background of a slick video or an arena of screaming fans. Up close, all his moves beheld from a distance of just a few feet, it was an offstage performance that had one of the Nemesis people loudly cursing the lack of a camcorder. The pain and passion blended so smooth, offered up to her in a smoldering gaze. She was mesmerized, held captive by the star power that came coursing off his body, dropping to his knees to channel Iggy's exquisite torture.

Cheering applause greeted him at the fadeout. He ignored it, crept forward to her chair, and kissed her. Her arms went around his neck, how could they not, only somebody with no soul could sit unmoved through that level of intensity.

He broke away, lipstick smeared. "Happy now?"

"That was amazing. Like a gift."

"It wouldn't be a gift if I did it all the time."

There was a strange undertone in his voice.

"Time for the next band. Let's listen to something really heavy."

Devon stood up and went back over to the stereo, rooted through his case of CD's, swapped out the Stooges for the next party soundtrack and dropped back down on the chair. He stretched out next to her, took her in his arms, and the opening chords boomed across the stones.

Enspelled's new album.

She froze as her old band's new sound spilled across the ruined garden. A couple of the acolytes got up and started moshing around the fountain, tearing up the dirt around the stones. Their enthusiasm was cold comfort, the way Devon caressed her face, pinned her with his best photoshoot stare.

"You were screwing him, weren't you?"

"No. Adrian is a friend. You're still not over this?"

"Not Adrian." His eyes went icy above the smile. "Alex."

Her stomach did a slow flip. He pulled her to him, held her close, spat venom in her face between kisses.

"Oh, yeah. The look on your face tells me *everything*. Nights of ash, rust and graves?" He laughed. "I did this to him." He glared at her, grinning. "And so did you."

She tried to pull back, but his arms tightened around her. "Can't you hear it? His loss? His utter desolation? I believe him *totally*."

Someone knocked against one of the pillars. An antique urn hit the ground and shattered.

"And it's so over. You want to run back to him, don't you? You think he still loves you. But you're not the same girl anymore. You came with me to change. And change you I did. The way you speak, the way you think, the way you fuck. I transformed you into somebody else. And you *loved* it."

"Shut up." She could barely breathe.

"It's all true."

"Shut up."

"Hurts to find out you're not so strong, doesn't it?"

She pushed away from him, and he let her go, falling back on the chair in a loud burst of laughter. She ran over the stones to the house, slid the glass door aside. Through the kitchen, up the staircase, into her room.

She ran to the closet and pulled out a leather satchel, one of the bags she'd had on tour, a big sturdy thing of beaten black. She threw it onto her bed and started taking inventory. OK. All the notebooks. Fresh underwear. Toothbrush. She went into the bathroom and suddenly doubled over. Cramps like butcher knives came slashing across her abdomen. She fell to the marble floor and convulsed, vomit hot up the back of her throat. It tasted like sugar.

Pomegranates.

On her hands and knees to the toilet, lifting up the seat, hands against the bowl, ready to expel it from her system. But it didn't come. She stuck her finger down her throat, but nothing moved. Her head was pounding, and her eyes were wet with tears. With shaky hands she pushed herself away, stripped down to a t-shirt and panties, crawled back out to the bedroom.

She climbed up onto the bed, shoved the bag to the floor. Curled up into the fetal position.

The mirror, snide as ever, had the last word before she dropped into unconsciousness.

Ever get the feeling you've been cheated?

* * *

The door to Devon's office on the first floor was wide open. Nothing to hide.

Sunlight came in through the floor-to-ceiling windows. A huge desk dominated one side of the room, dark carved wood from the early century. A collection of gargoyles was spread out across the front to glower at his guests. By the sofa, an antique liquor cabinet, topped with decanters and glassware from the thirties.

Danae picked up a gold-rimmed tumbler and poured herself a shot of bourbon, wandered his sanctum, let the drink burn a path through the fog. Coffee-table books on performance, stagecraft, acting in the cases behind his desk. The fax machine and printer, squares of unfortunate beige sterility. The wooden box of petty cash, only someone who was assured of having plenty of it forever would ever call any kind of money *petty*. CD's all over the place.

She sat down in the throne of his leather swivel chair, the place where a sizable chunk of the dark-rock market was decided. And so richly rewarded. It was unimaginable that her creative endeavors would ever put her on such a velvet level. But they'd brought her so many other good things. Things she needed to ground herself on right now as she tried to find a way out of the binding, now that Devon's malice had seeped in, irreversible.

Her eyes swept his desktop. Paperwork. A letter. Handwritten to the address of Nemesis. She gasped as she caught the name signed at the bottom.

Catrinel.

Oh, no.

She picked it up, felt herself shrink smaller and smaller as she read the words.

Danae ~
  I don't even know if you'll get this, but I have to try. Alex has gone missing. He's out of his mind. I know what happened. We talked about it. I can't say it because you need to hear it from him. But if you get this letter, please, please come back.

No date, but there didn't need to be. Devon's words came back to her, the day the letter from Migraine had shown up, dancing on the balcony: *I refuse to let you get dragged back into your old problems.*

He'd known all this time. Last night was just telling her in the most devastating way possible.

Beneath Catrinel's letter was a cassette. A serpent wound around a skull— Enspelled's first demo. Beneath that, an old Migraine catalog, turned to the page with their graveyard picture on it. The family portrait. That hilarious day in Colma trying to pick out the most menacing tomb, turned to mere research in Devon's hands, like she'd been some kind of death metal mail-order bride. Was this what he'd been getting out of the bargain? She flashed on the rough wood of the atrium's worktable, the candles and herbs laid out. Her professional curiosity wandered out from behind her horror to wonder what exactly he'd used to draw her forth, bring her here.

But it didn't matter, when she'd come willingly. High-pressure, sure, but it had been her choice to leave. You couldn't blame a red candle for *that*. The guilt was squarely on her shoulders, and she accepted it, gladly. Because he'd left all this out here for her to find, all the cards of her remorse on the table, and there was nothing left for him to torment her with. Now it was time to make a move.

She took the letter—that was *hers*—and the demo, precious collector's relic he didn't deserve to keep. Let it go to someone else who'd be thrilled to listen to it, the way she'd been. She ran back up the steps to her bedroom, slammed the door, and locked it.

If I can't get out, you can't get in.

She popped the cassette into the stereo and spun the volume to ten. Rewound back through Devon, through Migraine's tour, San Fran dives, back to that first club in the Mission, standing outside so anxious and unsure, but knowing there was something amazing waiting for her on the other side. The four opening cymbals were carved into her heart and her muscles twitched along with them, priming her for the fight.

Alex. I call on you not as a lover, not as a former bandmate, not even as a friend, but as a fan. I need your strength to get through this.

The guitars slid down, and the room flooded with brutal riffs. She was back in the dark, dingy bars, back within the manic energy of other thrashing bodies. She threw herself around the room, raised the power needed to answer the question: how the *fuck* do I get out of here? She was back in Starlight's window, which had changed again: the vanity was draped with expensive dresses, the walls patterned with cherry blossoms, the faces of nosy reporters and jealous groupies fixing her with envy, greed, hatred.

The gilded deco lamp on her nighttable came crashing to the floor. Blood rose up on her fingers, painful, familiar as she tore apart the panels, kicked over the desk, turned the bathroom into a snowfall of glass.

To be trapped again behind a wall, where you couldn't move and everybody could stare at you: no, *no*, she willed the image over to the eyes of fans, fellow believers, nuzzling stage blood from her hands and singing along with the words she'd written. Not a storefront but a stage, where you were free, where you were doing what you wanted.

The most barbaric of them all, said the mirror.

FUCK YEAH!

She picked up the typewriter and threw it into the gold frame, shattered its vicious tongue.

The tape ended, and the wreckage was complete. Ten different perfumes rose up shrill and stinking off the bathroom floor. She staggered out to the balcony. Filthy, bruised, her adrenaline soaring just like it had so many times after a good show. She gripped the railing and threw her head back, and sent her loudest guttural howl out across the hillside.

* * *

The salt water was cool on Danae's toes, lapping at the black lace of the starlet's gown. The lifeguard was looking at her strangely. She ignored him.

There were cars in the driveway as she'd walked down to the beach. Devon was making his move, whatever it was.

She took a deep breath and started the walk into the water. Purification was cold. Purification was fucking *freezing*. And it hurt, too. Every open wound stung.

Black lace swirled around her body as she passed through the crash of the waves. When she got waist deep, she kneeled down and ducked her head beneath the water. Opened her mouth and swallowed the antidote. Sea salt washed down her throat, down to her stomach. Nausea took hold of her system, and searing pain shot through her belly as the salt water began to boil. Down on her knees, the nightgown billowing out around her, she crossed her arms over her stomach and rode it out.

And then, gone. The pain trailed away and she gulped down fresh air.

(It is done.)

It was dusk by the time she ascended the staircase back to her room, the nightgown half-dried to her skin. She heard the sounds of a party coming from the third floor. A few candles flickered on the staircase, calling her. She softened her tread and continued walking up, and found the door to his bedroom cracked. From within, Nemesis beats, laughter, female moaning. Lots of female moaning.

Across the landing, the atrium's doors were slightly open. She peeked inside. All the sculptures were gone. The pedestals had been pushed to the edges, exposing a huge gold pentacle laid into the marble floor. It shone in the starlight.

The humiliations so far hadn't been enough, apparently. Devon had some kind of little spectacle planned for her. Let him wait. She had work to do.

First, all her DNA. She ascended to the alcove and stripped the bed of its silky linens, carried them down to the laundry room and threw them on the hottest cycle. Then, a quick rush around the house to gather some ingredients, before heading back up and locking the door behind her.

Sugar, sage, rosemary, she'd cleared Devon's worktable and scrubbed it down counterclockwise. Doused the entire surface with rubbing alcohol and tossed the empty bottle down as a warning. She only meant to cleanse, not get the house torched the next time he lit a candle.

She picked up a brass censer and filled it with 151-proof rum, struck a match and dropped it in. Put the fire in the center of the pentacle. Went to Devon's stereo and sorted through the tracks, hit PLAY on her favorite.

The starlight, the pentacle, all hers for the moment. There was no way she could leave this house without one last dance in this beautiful place. No sculptures, no man. Alone.

Devon could not take away the woods, nor the ocean. They were hers. They were everybody's.

She lifted her arms and let the rippling chimes descend through her flesh, spill down into her muscles. The beat kicked up and snagged her feet, spun her around the pentacle's points. The lace flared out all around her like an elegant dress in an occult ballroom.

She pivoted across the floor, luxuriated in the freedom of all that space to move in, tilted her face up to the moon as she sailed widdershins across the giant star, ready to leave the chessboard.

* * *

Black jeans, a plain black t-shirt, the combat boots she'd left San Francisco in. And an armor of sea salt. The party had gotten louder.

A pair of travel bags were packed by Danae's bedroom door. All her notebooks, including the witch book. A few favorite CD's. Some clothes pulled from the closet, which had stayed shut and safe during her rampage. The contents of the petty cash box. She'd departed NoCal with nothing but a cheap dress on her back, and he'd stolen autonomy away from her when he'd hidden Catrinel's letter. He violated the agreement. He owed her the seeds of a new life.

The Fairlight would have to be left behind. She'd weep later.

She imagined the scene awaiting her on the other side of Devon's door. He could have called her down to his office and handed her a termination letter, as the businessman. Or summoned her to the atrium for some kind of breakup spell. He could have absolutely killed her by being the mortal boy in the hooded sweatshirt. But by putting it here, in his bedroom, he'd chosen to bring the axe down in the guise of the sex symbol.

If I can't have you, neither can he.

She was not about to walk into another humiliation.

The world was hers. She could go anywhere, leave the west coast behind completely, if she wished. But her heels twitched. Fog, cool summers, secret forests hidden within the concrete. The city by the bay, her history wound within its twisting streets. She needed to go back and face the destruction she'd left behind, as this older, hopefully wiser version of herself, and then she could decide if it was best to keep going.

Devon was probably in his bed, covered in women, surrounded by his nightmares. Some shocking tableaux that was doubtless annoying him to uphold, she should have been in there by now, shocked and crushed and *done* with already. She quite enjoyed throwing a wrench into his plans by grabbing her bags and running downstairs, ringing a cab and waiting outside for the yellow chariot. One last glance up at the villa as she was driven away to the bus depot, opulent doom growing smaller and smaller behind her, locked back behind Hollywood mystique. As if she'd never been there at all.

Nothing left behind to say goodbye, but a line of dead candles down the stairway.

Act 3

Chapter 15

1994

"Sin will send you straight to hell. For all eternity! Because God sees all. He sees all the fornicating. Hey, Jesus loves you!"

"Hare Krishna," replied Danae.

She squinted her eyes against the late afternoon sun. The Powell Street cable car was getting swung around for a trip back up the hill, a line of tourists ready with their cameras. A drummer was banging away on a cluster of overturned plastic buckets, a few panhandlers held up cardboard signs, and the garrulous fundamentalist who was always here with his giant handpainted-hellfire sign extolled the horrors of premarital sex.

It felt good to be back on the streets of her hometown. Bleach-splashed jeans with the knees torn out, hair chopped to her shoulders, the party dresses were stashed away while she got down to business. She'd done her best to cover the remaining red—which looked like shit as it was starting to fade—with a box of Autumn Ash from the drugstore. An approximation of her natural shade, nice and anonymous.

Dirty pavement beneath her combat boots, a chill in the air. Beneath her trepidation, a deep, deep sense of satisfaction.

I am not who I was.

Let Devon make it sound revolting. It *was* what she'd chosen his fata morgana for. Devon, who through all his incarnations, remained a scared little boy. Mistakes she'd made, sure, but not that one.

But this swaggering optimism would not last. That Enspelled fan who'd cursed at her on the way out of her solo show—*sellout*, it was just another word for *asshole* if you played metal—there would be a lot more of them up here than in L.A. She'd been keeping her head down while she got settled, staying invisible for the past few months while she got used to life back on the other side of the velvet rope. Quarters for the bus and the washing machine and the payphone, pots of ramen, yeah, but long walks through the glittering night, liberated from the tyranny of the freeways. Sliding back into her lo-fi circuits had been pleasingly easy.

Limbo had its comforts—no confrontations, nobody else's bullshit to disrupt her—but the wreckage had to be faced sometime, and besides, she was curious as hell. With the blaze of one white candle, and the nightlife ads in the *SF Weekly*, she'd stepped back onto the web.

OK, I'm here.

The cosmos had answered throughout the day. A Sutter Street jazz bar had poured Motorhead at her through its stained-glass doors. A couple bike messengers hanging out at Battery Plaza blasted GWAR from a boombox in someone's basket. It was just a matter of time before she encountered the first spirit from her past life. No, two lives ago.

In the meantime, she had a sacred site to visit.

Up past the concert hall, towards Civic Center, left onto 7th, down into Potrero. A block away, and her hands started to shake. Confidence was bulletproof when it was never tested.

All the memories came flooding back, from when it was her battered old hi-top sneakers treading this sidewalk. Heading to an exhausting afternoon in the jam room, or a kitchen full of headbanging drunks. Running up the stairs to Alex's bedroom, throwing on the latest death metal score and locking the door to spend the rest of the day making each other moan. A holy house of blood and sweat and sex and most of the best days of her life. She rounded the corner, and there it was.

The van wasn't in the driveway. A silver sedan was. She walked closer, and the red tricycle on the porch made her stomach flip over.

Alex! You became a...

The front door opened, and a shorthaired guy in a polo shirt walked out, talking on a cordless phone and holding a toddler's hand. He smiled at her and she returned it, weakly, mentally fanning herself back to a state of calm. They'd just moved. OK. It hurt to see that it wasn't Enspelled's house anymore, but nobody's future had changed *that* drastically. Whew.

Westward towards the Mission, over to Valencia. A little girl wandered down the street, her long black hair spilling down a white blanket pulled around her shoulders. Behind her, the rest of her family wrapped themselves in quilts on their front steps, piled pillows in their doorway. Mariachi blasted cheery from somewhere. Danae nodded at them as she pulled her keys from her pocket and unlocked her door.

Up the decrepit steps, one more lock and she was inside. A mattress lay on the hardwood floor, mussed with thrift-store sheets and a shabby comforter. Her CD's sat in a box next to a cheap pawnshop keyboard, and her notebooks were stacked in a corner. The witch book lay propped against her pillow. Austere, and rotted at the edges, but she was making her royalty checks—and Devon's cash—last as long as she could while she figured out what to do next.

She shrugged off her secondhand moto jacket and dropped it on her bed, switched on the cauldron of her boombox. Jotted down a few lines about the new family living in Enspelled's house, scowled at how inadequately they conveyed those two seconds of pure gutwrenching shock. What came off as soulburning pathos in the late evening kept waking up as stinking melodrama in the morning. She'd learned things, but she was having the hardest time putting them into words.

She tried again, and again, and again, and finally threw down the pen. Fuck it. It just wasn't coming. She stood up, pulled her jacket back on, and headed out to slake a sudden mad craving for whiskey.

* * *

Painted black cats arched their backs and hissed above flickering tealights and loaded ashtrays. Danae perched on a barstool near the door, notebook open and pen uncapped, soothed by the ambient burbling of other drinkers, the distant clack of the pool table. Something was going to happen here, definitely. On her way over to Lucky 13, a car had turned in front of her, blaring Public Enemy. Right at their shout-out to Anthrax.

A nice throat-scorching slug of Jack, and she ran a hand through her hair. Black Flag started having a nervous breakdown on the jukebox. From the corner of her eye she saw a guy walk in, all in black, short. Saw him do a double-take and she wondered how many years it would take for her reputation to fade from loathsome betrayal, settle into bemused infamy, one more Barbary tale of tawdriness. But then again, metal wasn't the scene where a guy got crushed to death by a piano while screwing a go-go dancer.

He came up, sat down on the barstool next to her. She steeled herself—*here we go*—and turned to look at him.

Matt.

He'd cut his hair. The wild curls had been shaved down to a half-inch of dark golden brown, and a silver ring glinted from his eyebrow.

"Hi," was all she could manage.

"Hi."

A loaded silence, and then he spoke. "So, are you out slumming while Devon's in town?"

She shook her head, finished her drink. "No, that's all over."

"And now you're back home."

"What's left of it. This all still looks like San Francisco to you, to me it's scorched earth."

A small laugh as he signaled the bartender, a girl with black bobbed hair and Celtic knots tattooed on her wrists, and ordered a beer. Danae chimed in with another whiskey. This was going to be the start of a very long, painful, extra-sticky band-aid, and she wanted to be well anesthetized before the flesh started coming off with the adhesive.

"What happened to you? I walked by the house and thought somebody had a kid."

"Jesus, somebody's raising children in there?"

"I can't believe it, either."

"Well, you're in for more shock, if you haven't heard. Enspelled is over."

Their drinks arrived, and she reached for hers with an unsteady hand.

"I didn't know." Shit.

"My hands are done, you know there's only so long you can play drums like that. We came off tour and everything was starting to ache, the doctor said I'd better start looking at another career. So I'm back in school, I'm studying to be a full-time vet, big surprise, right? And I have a girlfriend now, I met her in class. She's not into metal at all. Well, OK, she likes some Soundgarden. Her name is Lisa." He pulled out his wallet, brought out a picture of a girl with long red hair in a green crop top, holding a tabby and smiling. Pretty. And anybody who loved animals was automatically kind of cool.

"She's lovely."

"She is." He glanced at the image before putting it back into his wallet. "What I've been looking for, I found it with her, like what you had with—"

She looked down. "Yeah, I know."

"Do you? You didn't even know the band broke up."

She took a deep breath and looked Matt in the eyes. "Tell me everything."

"You seriously don't know? Shit, this is all like old news now."

"Not to me. You're the first person here I've talked to."

"Really? You haven't been out? You don't have people here—"

"Being with Devon was really not as great as it may have appeared. And no, I haven't made up with my mother. I'm totally on my own right now, and I need to know what I left behind. I want to hear all of it."

Sympathy softened his initial anger. Oh yeah, this was gonna *hurt*. "All right."

"Thank you." On with the show.

"So while you were gone…" He flagged down the bartender for another round. "This is gonna take some time."

She nodded, and he began.

"All right. So, at first, Alex said you'd walked out after an argument. I came back from a really bad date—really, do I look like the kind of guy who's gonna be into Debbie Gibson?—and I found him sitting in the kitchen with a black eye."

"He *did* get into a fight with Ronnie."

"Yeah. They talked it out but he was still pretty shaken up by you walking out. He'd been up all night drinking, he was waiting for you to come back. I had to wake him up in the morning, he'd fallen asleep on the table."

And I was off with Devon.

"Neither of them would tell the rest of us what happened—but Catrinel got into it with Alex. She asked him what he'd done to you, and they stayed up all the next night talking about it, and she straightened him out on some shit, I don't know what, but she came out all like, *finally, he's listening.* But by the third day, you still hadn't come back. We weren't sure if we should file a missing persons report, if something really bad happened to you. Alex went into your room, went through all your stuff, trying to figure out where you went. Just…look, we were starting to assume the worst, OK? Like maybe the Zodiac Killer came back or something. But then this little card showed up in the mail, no return address, the message part in Theban."

Danae went cold as fresh drinks appeared on the bar.

"It read, *I'm safe. Danae.*"

Devon, calling off the dogs, using an arcane alphabet to disguise handwriting that wasn't hers. Angry as she was, it was smart of him to make sure the cops hadn't gotten involved. Smarter than she was, bewitched as she'd been, her first weeks in the City of Angels.

"It wasn't until Catrinel got all her rock magazines the next month that we found out where you went. There you were, right between the updates on Def Leppard and Skid Row. Getting real cozy with Devon Dare. Let me tell you, the word *shock* doesn't even begin to describe the reaction *that* got. How the hell did you even *know* him? It was just too bizarre. I mean, we could all understand if you were mad at Alex for something, but not the rest of us. Catrinel particularly, she thought the whole thing was too weird. We both drove down to talk to you."

"You did?" Danae nearly choked on her drink.

"'A good high priestess breaks her friends out of the evil castle.' I had to talk her out of bringing her sword. 'Just as a talisman, I'm not actually gonna use it, I'm just gonna leave it across the backseat.' Yeah, the California Highway Patrol would have *loved* that. Anyway. The plan was to stake out

Devon's house, but that neighborhood is full of celebrities, ready for all kinds of crazy fans, it wasn't happening. We went to the Nemesis building, we couldn't get anyone to talk to us. Went around to all the Sunset clubs, nothing. Went back home, and found out now Alex was missing, too."

"I didn't get Catrinel's letter. Devon hid it from me."

"I just wanna say, Catrinel always had your back. She always had suspicions about your disappearance. She said that you might be cut off from all outside communication, that Devon's the kind of person who likes a lot of control."

"Did everybody know this but me? Who knew I could avoid such a tragic fate, by reading pop metal magazines."

Matt raised an eyebrow at her. "Don't even. I hate that fucking poseur and I think it's fucked up you left Alex for *him*."

Yeah, that was about the typical reaction of your average death/thrash male. The death/thrash women would all say the same thing, but half of them would be lying. It sucked to hear it, but she blessed him for his honesty. Matt would not lie to her.

She sighed and finished her glass, silently thanked whoever had cued up the Plasmatics. "Go on."

She could tell there was more he wanted to say about it, but he went back to the story. "So, we're like, oh great, now *both* our singers are gone, and Migraine's getting antsy about when we're coming back to work. We're waiting for a phone call from jail, or the hospital, or the morgue, but no, he came back to the house a couple days later. Got all of us up to Strawberry Hill, like the time we'd all first jammed together, Catrinel, too. He said he was ready to get to work on the new album. He'd take on all the vocals, we'd go back to having one singer again. I called Migraine and told them you wouldn't be coming back. As far as whatever happened between you two…all he said was, 'Don't hate her. She had her reasons.'"

Danae ordered more whiskey.

"So we did the second album, and we went on tour. Everything was really off. The vibe between Alex and Ronnie turned strange. It wasn't fun anymore. My hands started acting up, and that was the end of Enspelled."

She knew there was more to it than an injury, but that was as far as the story went, with Matt. Fresh booze arrived, and she was glad her apartment wasn't that far away.

"We all moved out, went our separate ways. Ronnie got snapped up by Stolen Hope when their guitarist quit, he doesn't even live here anymore, he's in Phoenix. Catrinel got a job doing costume design in L.A., she moved down to Echo Park and Gnash went with her."

Danae wondered how close they lived to Pam's apartment. The funky boho underside of the city that she'd totally missed out on, circles she hadn't moved in at all.

"As for Alex, he's bartending now. Moved to the lower Haight. It turns out he really liked your industrial tapes after all."

"I *knew* he'd like them if he'd give them a chance."

Matt went quiet and finished his beer.

"Alright, look. I know you well enough that you wouldn't have taken off like that without a good reason. And I don't know everything that happened. But you hurt him badly when you left, and it was a long time before he came back to reality again. He stopped burning his candles, he stopped everything. What was the point, how strong could his power be, if he couldn't bring you back?"

She killed the pain of that thought straight down to the bottom of her glass. "There's always things that are bigger than what you can handle, stronger than you are. You can't affect everything. Alex knows that."

"Sure, his mind knows that, but not his heart. He was a real dark person before he met you, believe me. There was a whole side of his personality you brought out of him that nobody else ever did. I don't know if you ever knew that—let's face it, he's Alex, we all know how oblivious he gets—but you made the darkness go away for him. And I'll never understand why you turned your back on what you had with him."

Her head was spinning, from both the liquor and the story. She stood up.

"I need to go home and...process all of this. Thank you for not hating me."

She leaned forward and hugged him, and he hugged her back. She hoisted her bag up from the bar and smiled at him, turned towards the door.

"Oh, Danae? One more thing you should know."

She paused on woozy feet.

"He's moved on." Expression impassive. Nothing else.

She plastered a smile on her face as it sunk in, too drunk for a response, and headed out into the palm trees of Market Street. The night breeze was cool on her face as she crossed over Church, hands in her pockets, thinking about how maybe she should have taken off for a brand-new city after all.

* * *

Soaring keyboards and the rhythmic smash of a hi-hat came pulsing out of the speakers, a heavy three-count throb that prompted cries of *gotta dance* and a small stampede of combat boots to the floor. Boys in blackened eyes and electrical tape wrapped around their forearms, girls in long velvet gowns with billowing sleeves, every other patron in fangs. The dark romance that the clubs had evolved into was a much more welcoming place right now, theatrical and baroque. The goths didn't really know Danae's backstory but dug her solo album—and tended not to be nearly as obsessive over the lives of musicians as the metalheads were. She pulled herself out of the wallflower garden of candelabras and clove smoke, and joined the dancers.

It felt good to move. A column of black ruched ripples hugged her tight from her strapless bustline to her lower thighs, set off with a coffin locket. She spun on her platform heels, the boots that had carried her through all those nights with Devon, all she'd survived. Out for more.

She'd officially given up. It was time for her to move on as well. Start over with someone totally new, with a totally different life to get lost in, her past nothing more than a crazy story told over drinks. The stings of consequences, the ache of guilt, over. How intoxicating it felt to break free, the burden of one huge, hastily-made decision lifted off her shoulders by nothing more than a change of atmosphere, as if spirited away by a pair of ragged black wings.

Black hair, painted lips, lots of pretty, pretty faces tarted up in their funeral best. She wound her way through the floor, through ankhs and chainmail, glancing around at the other dancers. Someone to take home with her. Better yet, someone who'd take her back to their home, through a strange doorway, into a strange bed, tangible panting proof that the people in her past didn't have a monopoly on the world's pleasures. She clenched her fist, felt the peorth rune light up in her palm. The dice cup. Yeah. Ready to roll.

A tall guy in a strappy longsleever and long blue hair was checking her out. So was a girl in a white medieval blouse and thigh-high boots. The song beatmatched over into the next number, another thumpy thing. The DJ ran down the steps from the booth to dance to her own set. Danae caught her face just as the robotic vocals began.

Cat-shaped blue eyes peered from beneath platinum dreads streaked with lilac. A pierced nose, a light dusting of freckles across her shoulders and face. Her physique was thick and solid, muscular, clad in a tight tank top over huge pants full of pockets and zippers. Three thin white lines were painted straight down from the corner of her left eye. Most captivating was her look of utter bliss, standing out in her own private trance among the serious, serious seductions going on around the rest of the floor. Danae moved into her orbit and soon caught her eye.

An absolutely beautiful smile shone back at her as the girl shifted her body, moved closer. It was like dancing in a warm spring, an exuberance to her movements, graceful shoulder rolls and circling hips. No lascivious turn to her mouth, or challenge in her eyes, just childlike glee. She smelled like fire.

They spun and twisted around each other like two dynamic puzzle pieces, finding new ways to fit their bodies together. The crowd drew back a little and made space for them. It brought Danae back to Catrinel, the first night she'd ever danced at all, but now, moves refined by Devon's embrace. Something else she'd come back with.

The song shifted into its final verse, and the girl ran back up to the booth, cued up her next track. Danae drifted over to the bar, pawed through the flyers until she found one printed with the club's calendar, scanned it for tonight's date. DJ Dahlia. She folded it up and shoved it in her bra.

Hard beats flowed continuous from the speakers, no break to catch a breath or a drink or a phone number, just relentless with sweet, mean sound. Dahlia darted out to dance every other song or so before running back and pulling her headphones on, deciding on the next track to pull the next sheen of sweat from the crowd. Strong drinks and lust and plain old exhaustion gradually carried the other dancers off into the night. A small but intense crowd was still carrying on when the lights came up, only giving up when Dahlia spun the last track of the set, something from *Jesus Christ Superstar*.

Danae laughed and glanced up at the DJ booth, genuflected in the shape of a pentacle. Dahlia's grin broke up into raised eyebrows. She snapped her CD case shut, threw on an oversized black jacket, and bounded down the steps for the final time.

"My mom used to play that record all the time when I was a kid," said Danae, as they walked towards the door.

"Mine, too. I was going through all her old stuff trying to find something to chase everybody off the floor, you know, *go home*." Her voice was deep and Old Hollywood-sexy. "Last week I did 'American Pie.' You'd think that would be a really good song to kill the floor, right? *Huge* backfire."

"That's…kind of cool, actually."

Up close, those white lines were not paint. They were scars.

"It is. I just get so tired of the posing, I forget a fair number of them have good taste in stuff other than daaaaahkness.."

"Oh, you mean like the guy who has to out-goth everybody."

"Or the guy who has to out-industrial everybody, but he's cooler. Usually."

"Because he's not all like, 'my bats are bleaker than yours.'"

"No, *blacker*. They're blacker than yours, and they're not songs, they're incantations. And they're only available in expensive limited editions."

They reached the sidewalk, and the streets of SoMa were full of drunken clubgoers hobbling around in high heels, hailing cabs, starting fights, laughing hysterically.

"Count me out of that shit. I practice witchcraft with a Casio."

Dahlia's eyebrows lifted again, and she reached into one of her cargo pockets. Handed Danae a flyer, winked at her, and walked off towards the loft buildings.

Did she have to go so soon? Danae wanted to talk to her for about five more hours, at least. She wandered beneath a streetlight to get a closer look at the invite. A woman's cool sci-fi face peered contemptuously from behind a rubbled skyline. Just a few years ago, she would have been traced in neon, the buildings lit up, the city exciting. Not now. She presided over the desolate urban wasteland like an enraged deity.

Rite of the Full Moon
presented by The Temple of Lunacy
BY INVITE ONLY
No spectators, all participants.
Choose your companions with care.
Everything is permitted.
Everything.

Danae would be there. She would *so* be there.

She was ready to drop by the time she got her key in the downstairs door. A black envelope was sticking out of her mailbox, and she unlocked the silver metal door to free it. Up the stairs to shed her sweaty dress, take a quick shower before hitting the sheets, but first…

A delicate red script, no return address. Oh no, not Devon. She tore the back open and froze when she caught the scent.

Gingerbread.

Chapter 16

Combat boots on rickety steps, black jeans, a faded Ministry t-shirt, Devon wasn't here this time to tell her how to get dressed. A brunette in ruffled black opened the door before Danae reached the top step. Straight-haired, not the same girl as last time but so similar in dark visage, exchanging polite smiles and leaving Danae to be leered at by the devil masks.

Julian rose from the couch to greet her. Same exaggerated arched brows, same haughty charm.

"Danae." He took her hand in his, trapped it briefly between his rings.

"Hi, Julian." She felt strange, here alone, no one else to share the spotlight of his undivided attention. She settled into the couch across from him.

"I'm glad you decided to come. I wasn't sure if you would, after you and Devon…"

"Yeah, it's done." *Maybe I should rent a fucking billboard.*

"Yes, I know." Danae inwardly cringed at how *that* conversation must have gone. She flashed on an image of Devon in his office, on the phone with Julian, describing in graphic detail all the stuff they'd done together in the atrium. She tried not to blush.

"I heard his side of it, but I know you have yours. And that it couldn't have been pleasant staying by his side, the way he gets so ugly when he's depressed."

To hash Devon out with someone who knew him, understood him, to slide that weight off her back, *closure*, so tempting. But…

"No offense, but I was just his…girlfriend? Protegé? Companion? I don't know how he described me to you. But whatever it was, why do you care what *I* have to say?"

He rose. "Come with me."

He took the stairs slow, leaning hard on the bannister. She followed him up to the bedroom she'd shared with Devon, the bed where it had been so good. As hateful as he'd turned himself at the end, there had been an undeniable connection between them.

Yeah, and Pam probably tells herself the same thing about Michael.

Julian beckoned her towards the cold fireplace, the row of gilt-framed pictures across the mantel. They captured him in various defining moments throughout his life: young, sprawled out within the brightly painted sleigh of a carousel. In a red velvet nightclub, winking at the camera, fingers dancing along the keys of a grand piano. Up in a forest, sitting on a rock, a woman in black lace leaning against him, holding hands, beautiful in a dark-bohemian way. Long blonde hair, and thick black eyeliner, and...

Holy shit.

Danae turned back to Julian, dumbstruck as she searched for resemblance.

"You got more of her in your features than me, lucky you. She was gorgeous, wasn't she?"

"She never told me..."

"She wouldn't. She never let me see you, she didn't want me to be a part of your life at all."

"I don't...uh..."

"Wine?"

"Please."

Back downstairs on the couch, a glass of chardonnay trembling in her hand, she heard the story. The girl who'd come up from San Mateo, light as sunshine, black of heart. The prettiest girl in the go-go club, dancing to his tunes, eager to hear all about his philosophies over cocktails.

"But weren't you married?"

"My wife and I had an arrangement."

The sixties were so much more...*distinguished* about it.

"Your mother knew, going in, that I wasn't going to end my marriage. She seemed to have forgotten this when she became pregnant with you. I wanted to make provisions for you, teach you, have a hand in your life, but she was angry I wouldn't get a divorce and marry her. So she hid you away from me, told you nothing. But I kept a watch on you. Sent my people into the store, and you were always so polite to them, even though you didn't carry my books. Then you disappeared, and one of the girls found you in a rock magazine. Devon Dare. Well done, daughter."

"How come you didn't tell me when I was up here with him?"

"It was much too big a bombshell to drop during a casual visit. Best to have you all to myself for that kind of news, no other social obligations to distract us."

"You know I was in a band, right? I write, and I sing, and I can play keyboards now…"

"Oh yes. I'm very, very proud of you."

The magic words Celeste had never said to her.

"Danae, I'm nearing the end of my life. I've had a couple of heart attacks, and I need family around me."

He sounded so much like Devon. An older version.

"What do you want of me?"

"Stay with me. Here."

She looked down into her wine flute, exhaled. She'd just gotten the ground steady beneath her feet again, made a potential new friend. And now the past was threatening to swallow her back up again, not even her own past, but that of her parents. Family, yes, but not present since birth like Celeste, not built through art like Enspelled. Family, claimed by just blood, nothing else. Julian was a stranger.

But how good it would be to have someone at her back, up here. A pretty powerful one, too, in terms of local celebrity. Whoever hated her wouldn't fuck with her too hard.

"I need to think about it."

"Of course you do. But whatever you decide, I'm glad we talked."

The proud parent inside the devil's house. It was all too much. She finished her glass of wine, and her face lit up with what she never knew was her father's smile.

* * *

Danae was dizzy as she climbed up out of Noe Valley. The weed-covered stairway beneath her boots rose up into the next street and took her past secret gardens, enchanted cottages nestled into the hillside. Bright blooms dotted the steep landscape here and there with yellow and purple. Above, lounge chairs perched on rooftop decks, where barbecue grills and lanterns the color of sunsets awaited the next intimate party. The ambient motor noise from the road was hushed by distance, nothing but bedroom quiet in these hidden paths. A tortoiseshell cat perched in a branch and meowed down at her as she passed by.

Julian. Celeste. Her mother poised atop a glossy black piano, her father gazing up from the keys, their affair budding before an audience anxious for the flesh show. Backstage trysts had run in the family, it seemed. And then the gatherings at Julian's house, the ceremonies. She'd always assumed her mother was so strong, capable and knowledgeable in her array of earth magicks. But those hadn't been enough, if something had drawn her into the black Victorian.

The air began to hum, like the low end of a woman's vocal range. A breeze caressed Danae's face and lifted a cluster of nearby windchimes into song.

He's the other half of you, it's true.

Blonde hair, blue eyes shimmered in the glare off a tall window. Thick black lashes framed a cool stare. Danae glowered at the apparition and kept walking up the steps. Of course her mother knew she was back in town. Stepping onto the web alerted everybody, including the ones she had no wish to see.

Another reflection appeared from within the round window of another pastel house, like a spirit speaking from inside a crystal ball.

And now you know who you are. What will you do with it?

Head down, moving faster, she would not be baited. What business was it of hers? Danae grimaced. So many lies, and what a passive little mannequin she'd been. A mannequin dressed in lingerie, her feet circled in dead roses, on display to all who passed by.

A showroom dummy no longer, though. A quick tally of her survivals revealed a trove of weapons beneath her skin: poisons, blades, bombs, each one earned dearly. Clearer sight. Map-drawers of strategies. She'd come back armed.

But right now, it all stayed dormant beneath Celeste's gentle assault. Already rocked from the sudden discovery of family roots in the Richmond, fragile, Danae was outmatched beneath the blue skies. Getting her when she was vulnerable—her mother's style, always.

A third visage peered out from the sliding glass doors of an ivy-covered balcony.

How much do you think you know, daughter?

Danae jogged up the steps. Where the fuck was the street? She looked up and saw the stairs breaking off into multiple directions, twisting all over the hillside, an endless maze sprawling through hundreds, thousands of little houses. Flowers, stairs, and sky, nowhere to hide.

How much do you really know?

She broke into a run, *just leave me alone*, up through picket gates and twisted little trees, she missed a step and fell hard on chipped stone, scraped her palms, scrambled to get back on her feet and she couldn't look up into that insane labyrinth, just keep moving, up and up and—

An angry honk woke her out of her trance, narrowly missed hitting her. She jumped back onto the curb, kept the cars to her left, people, humanity. Interference to jam Celeste's signal. Breathe, breathe, ground and center, calming herself down as she walked along Market. Up in the land of the hulking apartment buildings, where every tenant received a spectacular view. She slowed down, came to the break where the skyline opened up, stopped to rest her torn hands on the railing and gaze out over the city.

Some subconscious part of her mind really had thought it had all stood still while she'd run away to Los Angeles. Down in those streets, no Catrinel, or Gnash. But, no Ronnie. The enemies had changed, as well as the allies. Another chess game was mapping itself out over the landscape, perhaps even worse than the one down south, now that two of the pieces shared her blood.

* * *

Up in the folding seats of a homemade theater somewhere in SoMa, one of those lofts that also served as someone's home, judging by the toothbrushes

Danae spotted by the bathroom sink. The walls were painted black, and the room was curved amphitheater-style around an empty space in front that served as the stage. Layers of tattered green velvet formed the backdrop, softening the room's edges. A keyboard, a bass guitar, nothing else.

She'd donned a piano shawl of deep red burnout fringe, skillfully wrapped around her body into a dress. A similarly well-dressed couple nearby were passing a flask back and forth, and the people behind her were definitely on ecstasy. So it was a show where nobody was going to tattle. Okay, but she was very curious to see how good the band was, especially after that stellar set of Dahlia's.

The house lights went down, and one bright spot went up on the stage.

Metallic breath seethed from the speakers, and Dahlia walked out from behind the curtains, straight into the light. Layers of soft white net were knotted all over her body, heavy bronze cuffs on her wrists. Two figures dressed in black came out behind her, and took their places behind the instruments, in the shadows.

The keyboardist started up a chattering midtone beat. A soft screech rippled out over the rhythm, and gold glitter fell from the rafters in a small shower on the left side of the stage. A deep thump brought in the low end, and Danae envisioned the gears of a grand machine beginning a slow turn. Dahlia stood in the center, arms out, palms up, fingers splayed. Eyes wide and fixed to the crowd. A celestial cacophony skittered around the high levels, balanced by a cold echo from the bass. Much like the warming up of an orchestra, the prelude, grounding the crowd. Tiny lights flickered to life among the velvet rags.

And then a melody came striding up out of the dissonance: strong and steady, the anchor, the heart flooding the room with the rhythm to dance on, and Dahlia's shoulders began to circle. Louder, rising up above the chaos, and her hips came into it. More lights woke up, bigger and brighter, matching the crash and boom along the edges. Rockets of dirty gold noise flared up into the night as hot and fervent as prayers, exploded into a sizzling veil of sound. Dahlia closed her eyes through a headroll, moving like a snakehandler, she *was* the snake. Energy came coursing off her body as she lifted her arms in benediction, opened herself to the crowd. The flock. The congregation.

Los Angeles had been a major, major wrong turn. *This* was what Danae had been seeking out in her industrial cassettes. The music a ritual, not commercialized and chopped up for three-minute dancefloor bursts, but long, long wanders through the atmosphere, layered and complex for lots to get lost in. It was incredible to hear hard beats outside of aggression, anger, any violent emotion at all—instead, the smash and bang exuberant, taking everyone into a sky filled with fireworks, through the giant footsteps of manmade gods.

"Lift up your hearts!"

The voice of the divine feminine, from the throat of a mortal woman.

Some in the seats started to rise, channeling the rhythm within their own skins. A cluster of three were slowly shedding their clothes, ambient light turning their flesh amber as they twisted around each other. Strange bottles emerged from bags, communion wine shared freely, and the air grew rich with exotic smoke.

Dahlia climbed up into the seats, gently pulled people out with her onto the floor.

We are all priests and priestesses. Dance with me.

It was…stunning.

And Dahlia was climbing up, up, right in front of her. Eyes painted copper, ablaze with the rite. Calling her with open hands, *come down to us, bring us what you've got.* Yes. Yes. Danae descended, and her feet were quickly covered in gold glitter. She twirled beneath the bright lights, gliding through the curling hands and dreamy eyes of the other dancers. All around her, opulent gowns, everyone's best clothes worn to be sweated, lived in. Like dancing in the atrium, but the music live, the sculptures softened into sparkling skin, elated smiles.

Dahlia drew Danae close, and she felt the warmth of her body moving sure and strong behind her, her arms coming around to hold her, *someone accepts me, this insanely gorgeous creature wants me here,* and Dahlia was winding around the other dancers, caressing faces and whipping her dreads around, and she moved to the back, hugging the keyboardist, and then to the bass player, sliding her hand into his long hair, grinning as she tilted his mouth to hers for a deep, passionate kiss, the room lit up bright as day for just a second, and…

Oh no. Oh no.

Danae stopped moving, the music played on rapturous but it wasn't for her anymore, none of this was, she was sick as Matt's final words tore through her mind, and the bassist turned and met her eyes and it was too late to beat a graceful exit.

Alex skipped a couple of notes as his jaw hit the floor, and Dahlia's arms were still wound around his neck when she realized he wasn't moving, turned to see what he was looking at and caught Danae's look of horror, back to see open shock reflected on his face, then back to Danae. Surprise, then realization narrowed her eyes slightly.

Yeah, I'm the bitch who tore his heart out. That's right, I'm the vampire. And you invited me over your threshold.

And Danae stepped back, and let the crowd block her out, and threw total mad power into her movement, because the music was intoxicating, like nothing she'd ever heard, and she had only one charmed night before it would all disappear.

Chapter 17

Sunlight fell across the sleeves of a black velvet gown. The sky outside Danae's bedroom window smoldered orange-pink, caressed her upturned face with burning hands. Her fingertips were curled over the sill, sitting in the path of its burning glow, but all she could feel was cold, cold, cold.

The fireplace crackled and hissed, and a sunflower rested in a vase of water on her nighttable. Beside her, the witch book lay nestled upon red brocade pillows. Notebooks, keyboard, CD's, clothes, all here. A much more decadent hideout after her cheap Mission shoebox, definitely, but it was the patter of footsteps outside her door that eased her spirit the most. The tones of a distant conversation, or dinnertime scents from the kitchen, it was the closeness of other lives going on around her that made her feel sane again.

Julian? I'm sorry, it's really hard to call you Dad. But yeah. Yes.

Deranged. Callous. Inane. Different interpretations of the same social verdict: totally fucked up. Why not just go all in on the dark side, be whatever they were going to accuse her of anyway, and find out what her birthright meant on the other side of her family tree.

Halfway home from the lunar rite—she'd lasted only ten more minutes—she'd ducked into an alley and hurled herself against the brick, bruising the red fringe on the slow slide down, crouched and breathing hard and thinking about that canine corpse hanging from the back of the van, that Devon may have had a point. You couldn't outrun your past, no matter how much you changed yourself.

Devon. *Fuck.*

She'd dreamt of him her first night here. Down in the depths of unconsciousness he'd reached for her, his wicked smile melting into an incendiary kiss. No harsh words or dignity-stripping spectacles, which would have been much easier to handle than the caress of her face, the soft whisper of the word *cherish*. A mirage, potent and intoxicating. And dangerous in this wounded state of mind, one that would have to be destroyed. The sooner, the better.

But the black Victorian was a very good place to accomplish just that. It took you into biting winds, crystalline ice, and made you like it there. It was a sanctuary to learn self-reliance now that everybody hated her, learn how to turn isolation to her advantage. She flashed back to her younger self, scrawling away on the rolltop desk while the noise of the Tenderloin flowed through her bedroom window, the world outside like a mystifying blank page. Now she was back in that seclusion, but there were a few things she'd taken along with her.

Fresh flowers in her bedroom. A plate full of avocado rolls. A silver necklace shimmering with tiny stars. After a little while, dining on the same table as the taxidermied crows didn't seem so disgusting after all. Julian was feeding her small earthly pleasures, trying to make her happy, but it was the one sympathetic shoulder in San Francisco she could cry on, that she needed the most.

"Wait, are you sure you wanna hear all this?"

"You're my daughter. I want to hear everything."

"Devon was just…so strange. Like it was all okay to encounter horrible things in his dreams, totally insane alien things with their skins turned inside out, but in real life? One dead dog? He couldn't handle it at all."

"Unfortunately, the pattern set in him, long ago. He doesn't recognize the same sad occurrences as part of life, just because he's had so *many* of them." He spoke with an arrogant wheeze.

"I feel like I really fucked up. I don't know if I should have gone off with him at all. But then since I did, I should have been the one to break that pattern and help him through it. And I failed, because…I wasn't strong enough."

"No. Whether you know it or not, you're a warrior. You drank down whatever was in that chalice without *any* idea of what was coming next. That's bravery."

"You're the only one who thinks that. Everyone else thinks I'm a bitch for betraying Alex."

"Were you supposed to pass on that opportunity, give up your future, just to make someone else happy? You have the right to determine what's best for you, and you must always put your own interests first. Especially because you're a woman, and the world wants you soft and passive."

You could wait around forever for him to show that face again, and he knows it, Pam had said. She'd ended up soft and passive with Devon anyway.

"And what would Alex have offered you, anyway? Not the chance to play music yourself, not companionship over your interests. You would have been sacrificing your life for his, and you would have resented him in the long run. All this guilt you're torturing yourself with, it's ridiculous. You really did make the best choice."

At least one person was on her side. She'd sighed, and smiled at him. "Thank you."

If she could shut out the sun, she could close her heart. Surround herself with only the strong, those who would not need her to nurture them. No one to eclipse the full blast of her capabilities.

There was a knock at her door.

"Come in."

Charlotte poked her head in. "Hey. Are you going out to the club tonight?"

"I don't know yet." Danae went to her stack of notebooks, dug out the flyer with the calendar. Some New Romantic thing, synth stuff from the early 80's. No Dahlia. "Yeah, sure."

"Cool." She stepped into the bedroom, followed by Lacey. Julian's caretakers sat down on her bed, doll-like in their black velvet babydoll dresses, shiny combat boots, long necklaces of inverted pentagrams. Lacey was the one with straight hair, where Charlotte's was curled. But they shared delicate faces china-white with opaque foundation, eyes brimming with overheard knowledge, a giggle they passed back and forth in one long, continuous secret.

"First the club, then the park," said Lacey. "Out to the circle of headless trees."

"The spot with all the stumps?" asked Danae.

"The hidden place, yeah."

So they knew about the grove, too, a whole other crowd of witch-people doing their thing out there in the dark. Spider silk spun through her imagination, wound itself around tree trunks, tightened towards a certain encounter that was going to happen sooner or later. Would she run into Alex in a club, or on the street? Would he be alone, or with Dahlia? She realized she had to clear the air, so much inevitable pain and awkwardness, best to seek it out before it found her first. The black Victorian to come back to when it was over, somebody here acting like a loving parent, she could handle it. She'd go, but not with the girls.

"I'm up for dancing, but I'll probably call it an early night."

"Some other time, right?" asked Charlotte. "We were hoping you could…"

Lacey broke in. "We know all about your history. With Starlight, with your bands. It would be an honor to have you with us."

"Julian's not doing well," said Charlotte. "We volunteered to care for him when his health started to decline. Every day he grows weaker, and he's so glad you're here, someone of his blood to pass his knowledge down to. We're not his true children, but we intend to carry on his legacy."

"Here," said Lacey, handing Danae a chapbook. "This is something we all worked on, it's kind of our manifesto."

Exquisite calligraphy flowed across the cover in silver, across an image of three red candles. Inside, the same careful, exacting hand laid down their thoughts on the nature of energies, of the earth, acts of will and personal responsibility.

There is nothing wrong with worshipping the self, when the world wants us to hate ourselves for being different. Hold your head up and be proud of your strength!

It was a painstaking piece of work, from the poetic diction to the perfectly sharp points on the serifs. Danae turned it over. On the back, a black-and-white photo of the authors: Lacey and Charlotte with two handsome boys, all of them in formal black, posed across Julian's front porch. This was their version of a band, Danae thought. Keeping Julian's work alive through beautiful art, taking it into a darkly elegant future.

"We're very interested in what you have to say, what you've learned," said Charlotte.

"What you could teach us. We think that women should definitely be taking more of an active role, not just serving as the altar," said Lacey.

It was flattering. It was unnerving. She'd accepted Julian's invitation for the promise of mutual companionship, a safe, supportive place to resurrect herself while picking the useful pieces out of his ideology. Ascending the throne of diabolical heiress had not entered into the equation at all.

She had no intention of taking up Julian's mantle. What she needed was a band, the right people found as quickly as possible, to make up for all that time she'd wasted with Devon. To find out what else she had inside, besides horror movies.

This polite but intense desire for her expertise was a form of pressure she didn't need right now, the spectre of Wise Woman something she was in no way equipped to live up to. Lacey and Charlotte saw album covers, rockstar kisses. That ending up in this house was some rare and glorious door opening by the luck of her birth, and not a dubious featherbed to stop a terrifying fall straight into isolation and creative death.

But the way their eyes gleamed, Danae was not about to shatter the illusion. Or push away any kind of camaraderie. There was much she had yet to learn, herself.

"Some other time," she said. "The afterparty in the park, anyway. So, what are you guys gonna wear?"

* * *

Into the woods of Golden Gate, through the curving streets. Past the giant Celtic cross and the strange little stream that flowed upwards, past birthday parties and barbeques and a patch of asphalt that was being used as a roller disco. Up the path to the last place left from her old life.

Danae heard an acoustic guitar, and slowed her steps.

How tongue-tied and nervous she was the first time she'd seen him, and it turned out she didn't have to say a word.

And totally plain, no makeup, no style, NOTHING, of COURSE he would have been totally shocked to hear you'd slept with Pamela Black. Give the guy a fucking break.

She flashed on Ronnie's smirk. Whatever her missteps, there was no way she could fit back in the box of innocence ever again. She was too gnarled, too knowledgeable by now, and the total obliteration of purity would make for an awesome metal album—if done by a woman, of course. A guy would make it all about the entrails. Again. She took a deep breath and walked into the trees.

His hair shone in the afternoon light, gathered back in a ponytail, skull rings still dancing along the strings. He'd gotten inked: a graytoned tree spread its branches along the muscles of his left bicep, the roots curling around his elbow. Still so boyish, but fully grown into his adult self. It *had* been a while. She wondered what changes time had wrought in her own body when she hadn't been looking.

He didn't look up when she sat down on a stump across from him, didn't acknowledge her presence at all. But she knew he knew she was here, as he wove a melancholy tapestry of chords through the forest air.

She closed her eyes and heard the story of loss. Theirs. She wanted to reach for her notebook, flip to a blank page and catch it all, but she left her bag propped against the stump. The least she could offer him, in this moment, was the respect of total attention. Let him speak uninterrupted in the language of raw sound as he trapped her heart in intricate spider strands, gently ripped her to shreds.

The song trailed off, and it was time to open her eyes and face him. But the breeze blew across her face, and the sun was warm on her skin, and she was near him again, and she held the moment in her head for just a few more seconds before coming back.

Cool gray measured her evenly. Not hostile, not disgusted. But definitely changed. They stared at each other across the grove, and she felt the tension building in her chest, no idea how to begin.

"Hi," she finally said.

"Hi," hands folded across the front of the guitar. That low baritone, still weakening her knees.

"So I guess you know I'm back in town now." Duh.

He nodded once, slow, silent.

She thought back to Devon's arms around her, a phantom prom dance, the red of the underworld poured into a wineglass. All Alex knew of that night was her feet walking out the door.

"Catrinel sent me a letter that said you went missing. I never got it. I don't know what happened, after…" Her mouth went dry. "Where…did you go?"

His mouth turned up in a small, bitter grin.

"Starlight Occult."

Danae felt all the blood run out of her face. Oh no. She'd never told him about that either, the sleeping draught, the glass trap. Just that she didn't get along with her mother. So much he hadn't known, and she'd blamed him for it anyway.

"Yeah, I met her." Another grim little smile. "'So you're the one who stole my daughter's heart. For a time, anyway.'"

"Like she'd know!"

"Oh, she does. A lot of it, anyway. She knew all about Enspelled, you know, people coming to see us and then going over to buy their incense and stuff. Not spying, just chatting with her. She's making it out like everything's all cool between you two."

Of course she would. Of course she would. Danae rocked back and forth on the stump.

"I knew you hated her, but what could I do? You'd been gone a week. You've said she's real good at her stuff, and she knew who I was from the minute I walked through the door. She turned the sign around, closed the shop down. 'I've been expecting you,' she said."

No matter what, there would be an undying flair for drama going on in the Tenderloin. Danae pictured a tarot spread across the glass counter, or worse, Celeste trying to flirt with him. The horror.

"She ended up giving me a red candle."

"To bring me back?"

"No. To find someone else."

It hit her like a boot in the stomach, stole her breath.

"'She's with someone who can give her more than you ever could, so just let her go.'"

Just like Julian. Subtle but unmistakable hurt in Alex's eyes as he recounted her mother's words, and maybe believed them. A torrent of all the things Enspelled *had* given her built up behind her lips, but easy to say that now, after getting to live in Devon's house, now that her fingers carried tunes in them.

"I didn't know what she meant until Catrinel got her rock magazines. I just couldn't deal. With anybody. I came back here. Figured some kind of answer would come to me if I just spent enough time out in the woods."

Just like I did, once upon a time.

"Everything I was feeling, I put it into the album. I didn't light the candle until the tour was over."

"And then you found...Dahlia."

"She was the first person I could touch, without it feeling empty."

She wondered how many women Alex had tried to forget her with.

"She's beautiful," said Danae. No guile, all honesty. "I love what she's doing with the full moon rite. It figures it's the first place back in town that I'm happy, it's the first really good energy I've felt in a really long time, and...I guess it had to be someone else to get you into the music I loved, right?"

He said nothing.

"You realize I was absolutely dreading writing that album, right? There was no room to do what I wanted, I know Migraine wasn't gonna go for that kind of thing anyway, but...Nemesis did."

Silence. She was dying to touch him and she couldn't, and it was making her want to hit him. She started to do it with words.

"You know I can play keyboards now? It probably means nothing to you, but I'm not just the girl singer anymore. Think *that* ever would have happened if I'd stayed here?"

He sighed, long and low, holding back some immense frustration. He lifted the strap over his head and opened his guitar case.

"So where are you staying now?" he asked.

"With my father." She scrawled down her number, crumpled it in a ball and threw it across the strings. "In the Richmond." Relished the look of shock as she gave the exact address.

"No way."

"My mother got around, back in the day. Seriously, I can't be surprised anymore."

"From Devon to Julian." His voice dripped with disgust.

"What are you gonna do, put me up? You and your girlfriend? I have nowhere else to go. Dahlia gets to have you without Ronnie around to needle her. And she also gets to have you playing in her band, the genre of which you *totally* hated when you were with me. And it must be great to date somebody and not have to hide it from the rest of the world. Everything I wanted, you're giving to somebody else. So don't fucking judge me."

He stood up, eyes going cool again, and she thought about the red candle Celeste had given him. The person she'd been when she'd worked at the shop. So hard to believe it was inside that gawky, clumsy girl, the power to wound someone as beautiful as Alex. She shut her eyes again, willed herself to keep it together until he left.

She heard him draw close and drop something beside her, and then the swing of the hinges on his guitar case, and the fading sound of his footsteps. Out onto the trail, wherever his home was now, the lower Haight, Matt had said. A much closer walk than Enspelled's house, that's nice, and she shuddered, tears welling up, wanting to run after him, but Devon's chalice had taken away any right to scream *come back*. On the insides of her eyes, the trees turned to smoky black, blasted and covered in ash beneath a blindingly white sky. The bleach of an inner shriek scalded her throat, rose up above the wasteland in a death-wail of hopeless loss. The place Alex had already been, and written about, and left behind when he'd found someone else. Now she shuffled onto its dead grass, to sit alone within the forest tomb.

The wind, and the light, these things never hurt her the way people did. She focused on the sound of the trees, the distant yells of a ballgame. The things that never changed.

She opened her eyes. Lying on the stump beside her, neatly folded, was her old jean jacket. Sitting on top was her Rider-Waite deck.

A fresh wave of desolation came crashing down as she realized what else she'd lost: one of the best friends she'd ever had.

* * *

Black fingernails curved over the bannister, and black-lined eyes took in the party. Chic cocktail dresses and turtlenecks were accessorized with silver pentagrams, all inverted. Wealth and taste, in abundance: Danae had already recognized a few local celebrities milling about the crowd. A pair of fondue pots bubbled beside the three crows, and she wondered if that was due to Julian's retro tastes, or because stabbing things with elegant little forks made everyone feel extra evil.

Her mind's eye saw the altar setup clear as day. A man and a woman made of black wax, back to back, moved farther and farther apart during seven days of the waning moon. Throw yourself in there as the red woman he's walking towards, if you're doing it to get him back. Yeah. Plenty of other places besides Starlight to grab the goods, if she wished. If she wished.

Consequences, the bitter aftermath she'd always known was hiding inside the pomegranate wine, it all came flying up in shards of jealousy. What beauty, what cool; no doubts about the hold Dahlia had on Alex, with Danae caught in the same magnetic grip. It was bad enough when another woman was mesmerizing in ways you could never be, utterly confounding when you wanted to sleep with her yourself.

It hurt like hell, but it also felt good to hit the bottom, the end. She'd faced him, faced her. She could move on now. On to things that wouldn't make her feel pathetic, like breakup spells.

Julian was holding court from the couch, deep in conversation with two stylish women in silk blouses and upswept hair. He looked stronger, more energetic, as if restored to good health by all the ass-kissing. He frowned on talking about problems, or processing emotions, anything that wasn't ego-boosting. But, as she watched him settled back on his soft throne, contentedly expounding his theories to a sophisticated, attractive audience, she couldn't help but think back to Dahlia's loft, how inclusive and powerful her rite had been. Refreshing.

"Hey, Danae." Charlotte was ascending the steps, holding two wineglasses of something dark. "Try the Gremlin Punch."

Rum, citrus, grenadine. Tasty.

"I think it's so sad that Julian's not doing the black masses anymore. Figures, the lowest common denominator had to show up and ruin it before I got a chance at it, fucking perverts. Everything was so much cooler back then. Although I totally would have had the guys getting naked for a change."

Danae had seen the videotapes: candles and incense and wine, altars of smooth curves and big breasts, she'd tried not to think of her mother. Julian loud and self-important, but wasn't that the point? Self-importance? Overall it felt very staged, lots of protocol, much like the Christians. Much like a lot of the Wiccans, too. It made her think about how she'd much rather raise her energy by playing a show. Which she was very hungry for.

"But I think it's all in flux, right now," Charlotte continued. "It's so important to preserve the history of that space, all the power built up over the years. I wonder what the house will look like, when you're running things."

Danae sipped her drink. "I haven't really thought about it."

"You should, you're the new blood. You've brought so much passion to the things you've done, I really want to see what you'll do when you're in charge."

"I don't know if that's where I'm headed."

"I get it. You're still thinking about Devon."

Not really, but it seemed best to leave Charlotte uncorrected.

"Lacey and I have a couple of people we'd like you to meet. Come with me."

She dragged Danae down the stairs, through the crowd to the dining room. Miniature slices of fondue bread, tiny cupcakes, the girls had been busy in the kitchen all day. Sitting at the end of the table were two more delicacies: a pair of boys dressed towards the aristocratic end of the goth spectrum. Brocade vests and silk button-downs, long black hair, jewelry covering their hands in an armor of rugged silver. The vampire bluebloods from the back of the chapbook.

"Danae. This is Erik, and this is Galen." Both of them rose to greet her, each taking her hand to kiss it. Danae arched an eyebrow at Charlotte, who leaned over to whisper something in Lacey's ear. They giggled, and Lacey got up from her seat beside them.

"We need to have a chat with one of our guests, he invited us on his TV show to discuss our book. Public access, but still. That guy over there, in the sport jacket? Time to put on the charm. We'll leave you all to get acquainted. Here, take my spot."

Danae settled down between the boys—brothers? They sure looked like it, but midnight-colored locks made all the children of the night siblings of the bottle job. Erik refilled her wineglass.

"Lacey was telling us you've started working on another album," said Galen.

Frustration, some crumpled papers, thanks for the faith, Lacey. But that's where all the notebooks were eventually heading, right? Towards the next project. No. *Band.* The next band. The next family.

"I'm not so much into straight-up metal, but I loved your second album. The solo thing. Is it gonna be anything like that?" asked Erik.

Danae wasn't going to fault Lacey for talking her up, especially to people who turned out to be fans. Amazing where the people who had been following her career turned up. Or that she had such good-looking enthusiasts. Fuck, the punch was strong.

Julian caught her eye from across the room, and winked.

"I don't know," she said. "Staying here, the energy's so different. I don't know how it's going to come out yet."

"I can't wait to hear it, whatever you do," said Galen.

They were attentive, they were mannered, glass after glass of punch and their company soothed her ravaged heart. Time slid quickly towards the small hours, and a subtle but distinct vibe rose through their talk of favorite acts, and travelling the country, and the inevitable turn towards esoteric theorizing: deference. Danae realized that all four of them were looking to her as a leader.

The way Galen was tracing his fingertips into her palm, Erik's claw rings curling into her shoulders, Danae glanced towards the kitchen. Lacey was standing in the doorway watching them, regarded her curious look with one slow nod.

Please. Fuck them and get Devon out of your system, so we can get to work.

Something was uncurling itself from Danae's chest, something that was getting very, very tired of suffering. It was shaped like a scarlet letter, and it glared at Alex's thoughtlessness, Devon's icy temper. Her eyes flickered from face to face, strong jaws and heavy brows, smooth skin and full lips. The Temple of Lunacy was the nourishment she craved, but couldn't have. That didn't mean she had to starve.

She got up from the table. "I'm ready for bed," she said, grabbing a bottle of wine. She started to walk away, and turned around, let the words drop soft from her siren mouth. "Are you both coming?"

They rose up behind her, graceful as ravens, and trailed behind her up the steps. She knew Julian was watching, and approved, but she couldn't bring herself to accept a high-five from her own father.

The bedroom door locked behind them. She made Galen light the candles, and Erik pour more wine, while she hit PLAY on Type O Negative. She sat on the bed and watched them, and when the flames were dancing, and the glasses refilled, they kneeled at her feet. Galen sat before her right foot, and she had the overwhelming urge to kick him in the face. Would he still want her? Yes. Like Devon's groupies, they'd swallow any humiliation just to get closer. Groupies of her own.

She was the first person I could touch, without it feeling empty.

But that didn't stop you from whoring around on tour, did it, Alex?

She lifted up the tie on her halter.

"So who's gonna help me with this?"

She bit down on a smirk as they crawled up onto the bed with her, four gentle hands sliding beneath the black webs of her dress, stripping her down to garters and boots and nothing else. Hands that remained gentle through slaps, and bites, and blood-calling damage aimed at other skins. She glutted herself on their submission, the infliction of pain, her bed never so boundless, no consideration to slow her down in any way. No one to assuage, second to none. *None.*

When dawn lit up the window, when she'd finally fallen asleep, the boys dressed quickly and silently stole away to the room across the hall, the embraces of Lacey and Charlotte. Sharp fingernails trailed over their bruises with glowing approval, a job well done on the exorcism of their priestess. *Soon*, they murmured to each other, *soon*, blowing out the candles and pulling up the bedsheets, four heads of black hair spilling across the pillows, four dreams of a gingerbread cabal walking at the very front of the left-hand path.

* * *

Damn him, thought Dahlia.

Damn that beautiful silm-fingered man who'd spiked her nipples with stainless steel, the first barbell hadn't been so bad but the second had torn the breath from her chest, sent her consciousness into a couple moments of blinding darkness.

Everyone I pierce, I say a little prayer for them when they leave my studio.

It was a sentiment she'd carried with her into the pulpit of the DJ booth, when she built the night's setlists, the stars by which she'd navigate the journey, lead everyone deep into the dancefloor. But playing in someone else's church hadn't been enough for her. Nor for her roommate and comrade in experimental media, Wiest. Not when the only intoxications were overpriced, watered-down, and served by a snotty bartender. Not when the law forced you to keep all your clothes on. Not when cash was the only currency that allowed you to attend.

The Temple of Lunacy gathered up the trustworthy and adventurous for a series of underground parties—parties? no, they were way more than mere *parties*—offering their home to spend the full moon with as little inhibition as possible. Ceremonies of tradition carried out as performance, the invocations and chants given over almost completely to music, crafting intricate textures of sound to say it. Letting that sound possess her like a spirit at a seance. Blessing everyone who walked through her door as another member of their consensual community.

And now, that guiding sentiment had driven her up onto the neutral ground of Corona Heights, to sit beside Danae and stare out over Market Street. Alex's ex or not, you couldn't exactly take benedictions back. Not when whatever happened onstage made the I Ching coins fall, turned over the tarot cards. Danae's arrival had been no accident.

And after dancing with her that night at the club—it was too late to hate her. Although she couldn't imagine picking a cheeseball like Devon Dare over Alex. But then, not long ago, she couldn't imagine picking anybody in death metal at all.

Theirs was a passion born when their eyes had met across the vet's office, through the stink of a thousand feline fears.

"OK, so probably what the doctor's gonna say is to scale back Curio's food so she can't bolt it. Small scoops all throughout the day, so she knows there'll be more coming and not scarfing it down. That should take care of the bulimia," said Matt, scritching a tense, nervous Curio below the ears.

"Good. Because at this rate, I'm ready to bottle it up and sell it. The barf of a black cat's gotta be good for a really nasty hex, right?"

Their eyes caught across the steel table in recognition—*hello, fellow pagan!*

She'd been waiting at the front desk to pay the bill when Alex walked in. Wow. Hella cute, a cool drink of tattoos and leather after the fight she'd just had with Damian 23. Matt had come out, caught them staring at each other, didn't even wait for Alex: *do you need a ride home?* They'd chatted about music as they'd dropped Matt off, and then Curio, and went out for drinks, a conversation full of bands and magick that ran until dawn. Up on her roof at 5am, when all the bottles were empty and the soundtrack had drifted into chill ambient, when the words gave way to long, hot kisses.

It had only been going on a few months—still so new—and he was guarded, most likely terrified of being betrayed again. He'd given her the overview, the bare outline, but mostly pretty quiet about the enigmatic Danae, the kind of quiet that admitted some blame as well. Which wasn't exactly a bad thing, after Damian 23's rants over all the sluts and psychobitches he'd broken up with.

Afternoons spent up in the sky, getting drunk and watching the clouds while the cats jumped up into the lounge chairs with them. Taking him through the city on her found-sound rummages, going up to Tamalpais to his hiding spots in the woods. Long jams of keyboards and strings that meant his interest in her music was genuine. What a relief to play with someone who didn't demand she pepper her tracks with sex moans, or throw his screeching noise experiments into her carefully crafted DJ sets. And to play with someone who had a fucking sense of humor, too.

All going pretty smooth, until Danae walked back into his life.

"What, am I some kind of placeholder while you were waiting for her to come back?" Dahlia cringed inwardly right after she'd said it. Fuck, she may as well have asked where their relationship was going.

"No." Beneath the moon, candles and whiskey and cats, college station rolling through a weekend marathon of dark trance, he turned her face towards his. "You're a totally different planet." And drew her close, kissed her. Did she love him? It would hurt horribly to lose him, she knew that. She pulled back to lie down on his chest.

"I know she was a huge part of your life. I don't want her to hurt you again."

Or me, either. Daughter of Starlight Occult's proprietess. The other singer in Enspelled. Devon Dare's squeeze. And now, Julian's child. It was a lot of things to be, plenty to swell her head, but how down to earth she'd been at the club, a who-cares smile that was both ridiculous and hot through all the goth vamping.

"I don't think so. More like the other way around. It's like she was bleeding, and it wasn't easy to see her like that."

If Alex fell in love with her, she had to be kind of cool.

"Gimme her number."

"Fuck, Dahlia, just close the lion's mouth. You don't have to stick your head in it."

"I'm the priestess, I gave her an invitation. I have a responsibility to everyone who walks through the door, to just talk to them once."

Besides, I'm curious.

A honk from the traffic below brought her back to the present moment.

"Here." Dahlia passed Danae a flask. "Blackberry homebrew, someone brought it as a gift during one of the rites."

Danae tipped the flask into her mouth. "Mmmm. This is good. Like something you'd drink from the skull of a vanquished enemy." There must have been an interesting look on Dahlia's face, because then Danae said, "Sorry. Being home is bringing all the metal back out of me. So, the full moon rite—are you the one who's writing all the music for that?"

"Yeah. It's my own thing, I know it's not the militant hard-edged stuff everybody's into, but I like it."

"I thought it was gorgeous, I didn't know industrial could sound like that—like, beautiful. Not the same old shit about information control or fascism or whatever." Danae passed the flask back, and Dahlia took a deep slug.

"Or shock tactics. My ex *loved* shock tactics. Any excuse to throw porno into it."

"Oh, fuckin' A. And I bet he was all, oh, don't be a puritan, right, when nobody ever fantasized about jamming a chainsaw up his ass."

"Well, *I* did. For a little while." They laughed, the liquor throwing a warm glow over everything. A couple of guys ascended the rocks next to them, let out a *whoa* at the view and whipped out a camera.

"I really dig what you're doing, though. The stuff you spun in your set was all amazing, and then what you played that night, your own material, you're not just some dude hiding behind a vocoder. Just hearing a raw human voice within all the machines, a woman's voice, I loved where you were taking us."

There was no faster way to Dahlia's heart than talking about her music. She suspected Danae was the same. An impulse came bubbling to her lips, one that was the blessing and curse of the experimental musician.

"We have to go into the studio together. Right now, come on."

* * *

The theater stood empty and sunlit as Danae followed Dahlia past the bathroom and up into the residential part of the loft, up a staircase where the living space was tucked away.

A window dominated one entire wall of the living room. A bookshelf was crammed with VHS tapes, neatly hand-lettered with bands and dates, set back from multiple television sets. The cats were a pair of suspicious black loaves on the worn red sofa.

"So this fluffy one is Oophi, and the sleek one is Curio. And back here is my roommate, Wiest." Dahlia led the way past an open kitchen and a spiral staircase, to a back room that flickered with three more television sets stacked against the wall: 80's New Wave robot-women dancing beneath blue lights, long pans across a smoldering forest, tiny glass bottles getting whipped around a conveyor belt. All hypnotic.

"Danae. Danae!" Dahlia waved her hands and snapped her attention towards a guy sitting at a computer. Short dark hair, a five o'clock shadow, a t-shirt that read SOYLENT CORP, and a smile that looked like pure trouble. Danae liked him instantly.

"This is Wiest. He does the lighting at the rites."

"Enchanté," he said, taking her hand and charming her with a wry look.

"Is this…all your work?" asked Danae, nodding towards the TV sets.

"The one of the woods, yeah. I never go anywhere without my camcorder. But the others are some found footage I'm playing around with, right now I'm doing a video installation for this sculptor's gallery opening, this guy who works in mixed metals. He wants to have something projected on the wall behind his stuff. I don't know, I'd think it's distracting, but he says it'll make it more dynamic. Whatever, he's paying me for it."

"Yeah, although he'll probably kill you if you use the one with the bottles. I can't stop staring at it," said Danae.

"Oh, those kinds of tapes are *very* useful for inducing trance states."

She returned him a knowing look of her own, definitely someone she'd have to talk to at greater length, as Dahlia made noises about bad horror movies and her friends getting sucked into television sets and led the way back into the theater.

A strange and fantastical doll, poised at the center of her insanely cool dollhouse, thumping down the stairs with that lilac-streaked hair. Art and energy thrummed through every room, the vast spaces ready to change at the drop of a hat to whatever scene they wished. Danae's envy multiplied a thousandfold when Dahlia pushed aside the velvet rags and revealed the studio.

About ten different sets of wind chimes came to rest silent against the far wall. Sheets of metal, a box of broken bottles, bits of rock and machine were scattered everywhere. The equipment rose up out of the mess to dominate the room like the consoles of a spaceship: Yamaha, Akai, Roland. Danae was trying to keep from salivating. It was candyland.

"A lot of it is stuff I find on the street—making sounds out of things that show up randomly when I'm walking around." The zippers on Dahlia's pants jingled as she went around the room, shoving boxes back into corners, straightening up.

"And it's like the weirder and cheaper it is, the better, right?" A total contrast to the expense of Devon's music: earned from hours of experimentation to wring out just the right sound, the lucky accident of being on the right street at the right time to find it.

Dahlia grinned at her, *that's right*, hit the power that brought the machines to life. A beat started up beneath her fingers, minimal but twisted around just enough to be interesting, skeleton awaiting flesh. Danae stopped at one of the windchimes. Cheap drugstore Halloween ceramic thing made of mummies that yielded surprisingly rich tones when she lifted one up, let it go against its dangling dead cohorts.

Dahlia caught it, played it back on the keyboard. Threw it against the beat, gave it a place within the rhythm. Danae lifted a bottle of thin glass, waited for Dahlia to nod *go*, and dropped it into the box with a light crash. Together they built a skyscraper of sparkling percussion, wove it through with a deep warm bass like a thick amber ribbon. They added their voices, the ghostly whispers of two sisters lost at a metallic crossroads, looking for the way home.

It was dark by the time Dahlia led her up the spiral staircase, past her little green bedroom, up onto the roof. They sat down on the lounge chairs, and Danae looked out over the city as Dahlia popped the tops off a couple of beers. Oophi appeared, twitched her ears and jumped up beside Danae.

"This is…so totally *not* how I thought today was gonna go," she said, as she ran a hand through the cat's thick fur.

"Me neither," said Dahlia, handing her a bottle.

"I mean, I didn't know what you wanted when you called me, I'm pretty sure I know, but…I just wanna say…"

Dahlia didn't quite freeze, but she slowed down. Tensed slightly.

"If your keyboardist ever quits, let me be the first in line to replace him."

Chapter 18

Danae coated the night in eerie tones, the organ's keys vibrating beneath her fingertips. She'd been aching to play it since first stepping over the threshold with Devon, and this was an older model, vintage, like her father, ha. The notes reached into every nook and cranny of the black Victorian for every last page of its dark history, brought the excesses of isolated counts and scandalized magicians into the Richmond. She imagined herself ascending the steps of a great castle, somewhere in Europe, a grand train of black velvet fanning out behind her. Coming to play a show, a concert, brought in to hypnotize an audience of nobles. Powdered faces and glittering jewels, greedy hands caressing flounces of lace, sharpening their teeth on her enchantment, ready to descend into an orgy, or a massacre.

A presence loomed behind her. Julian? Yes. He eased himself down onto the bench and took over the left side, the lower end, deeper notes chasing her lighter ones. He flipped a switch and turned the tune dark and smoky, like some hot number from the jazz club of the damned, a stunning woman gyrating towards her doom. He cocked an eyebrow at Danae, flashed her that famous half-smile. He was a man who had, no matter by fair or by foul, seen much.

"Tell me about my mother," she said.

"Celeste."

"Yeah."

Thinking with his hands, the way she'd started doing when someone asked her a question at the keyboard. He flipped another switch, and the rest of the chord filled in around the one note. Did he always play with automatic generation? She frowned slightly.

"Your mother wanted to be my scarlet woman. A Crowley term. You're familiar with it?"

I think I may have lived it, but she just nodded.

"She had a fiercely independent spirit. Very competitive. She always had to be the best at whatever she was doing, above all others. Demanded the best from life. And she never lied. It set her apart from a lot of people who came here for the surface glamour—she was for real. She practiced true magick and intended to earn her way in."

His face softened with memory.

"She didn't believe in the illusions of the straight world, its hypocrisy, turned her back completely on her suburban upbringing. Her parents disowned her for becoming a dancer. Probably disturbed by the power she had over the men who came to see her, not their docile little daughter anymore."

Danae tried to envision her mother ever being any kind of submissive, and couldn't. No pictures around their apartment of her grandparents, nothing from that former life at all.

"But, ultimately, her talents manifested as an affinity with nature. Not what I do, not what this house is based around. I knew it was going to be a problem when she wanted me to come with her into the park, into the trees."

Danae thought about Devon in the atrium, the wonderful ritual space he could have fashioned out of his yard, if he'd wanted to.

"What we were doing here was not the best place for what she was good at. It suited her darker urges, but not how her actual practice manifested itself. Although I'll give her credit, she never hid her appetites. She was proud of them."

"I know. I lived with her all those years."

"She was honest. Not like your new friend. The one with the dreadlocks? You know she's only calling it the lunar temple to disguise her ability to manipulate people."

Danae's hands twitched on the keys.

"Drawing them into her home, so she's got the advantage of having them on her turf."

"The way you do?" Enspelled had, too.

"Yes, but I don't hide it behind a pretty spiritual name. I understand the attraction, the erotic subversion of changing your body in the name of art. But these tattoos and piercings, withstanding suffering for some ill-defined enlightenment—it's merely an extreme form of New Age fancies."

Danae reined in her anger. Dahlia was the first good friend she'd had since Catrinel. Another rogue female, making her artistic way in a world of men. The only person she felt relaxed around—not judging her for her past, although she was sure Dahlia was dying to ask about Devon. (And Alex.) Strangely accepting Danae, just as she was. Dahlia was everything Danae had loved about the hard sound, the path she would have taken instead of Devon, if only she'd known it even existed.

The burning-leaf scent of her skin, the rich depth of her voice. Danae couldn't stop thinking about her.

"These aren't the same lost kids that Devon brought back on tour. They're not aimless."

"Tell me, if she loves them all, how much does she have left over for the ones who matter the most?" And he flipped another switch, and the jazz club transformed into a calliope, light and sweet as cotton candy, leaving the chord generator on.

You're not as fine a musician as I thought you were, you cheater.

She got up, slightly disgusted, and headed up the stairs. Galen bumped into her on the landing. Velvet bondage jeans, a Cradle of Filth t-shirt.

"Hey. Where've you been?" His arms went around her, and he leaned her against the wall for a kiss. Her body craved warmth and she gladly took it from him.

"Busy," she said.

"With that DJ."

"Oh, now you too? Aren't I allowed to have my own friends?"

"We just want you with us, too. I just got interviewed for an occult journal."

"Mmm," not really caring. She hooked her fingers through his back beltloops and drew him close. Hers at the crook of a finger, a secret alcove of gratification to sneak into, whenever she wished. He wouldn't be near her, if he didn't want to be. And guys did this all the fucking time.

She broke the kiss, peeled herself off the wall and swayed up the rest of the stairs, gazing back over her shoulder at him.

Over the threshold, inside her bedroom where the fireplace blazed, she turned to face him. She ran her hands through her hair, down her hips, reached for the zipper on the back of her tight black dress. Down it came, slowly pushed from her shoulders, landing in a soft crumple at her high heels. The flames stroked dancing light onto her skin.

Her fingers curled against the edge of the door, she stared at him and started to push it closed, and he was up the stairs in three bounds. His mouth descended on her neck, armor rings scratching down her spine. She laughed silently as she kicked the door shut.

Behind her back, his eyes were open, sweeping her room, and narrowed slightly when they reached the witch book.

* * *

"So if they've heard the demo, and thought it was good, they probably would have told you, right?"

Somewhere in the Mission, Matt rolled his eyes at Alex and evaded a response behind a slug of beer, feigned a show of great interest in the second band's equipment setup.

"I don't know. They're really busy, it's not like Migraine's a huge label, you know?" Alex had already gone through some version of this conversation with Angel at least three times already.

"Hey, isn't that your new drummer? Weren't you saying he owes you ten bucks?" Matt gestured at a hulking tattooed guy walking through the door.

"Oh yeah. 'Scuse me." Angel shoved off through the crowd.

"Do *not* tell him about the Ripegrave signing. At least not tonight," said Alex.

"It's too bad you turned them down for the vocal spot. They're a fun band to play in."

"Not my style."

"So…what *are* you gonna do next?" asked Matt.

"Aw, fuck, you too?" Alex scowled.

"You can only coast off the last album for so long. And you can still play."
I can't.

Alex leaned against the bar, let the first band's guitarist grab Matt's attention away over a dog that had eaten a toothbrush. It didn't matter he was off the musician's market for good, the guy was a born networker. Somebody would always be coming up to him for *something*.

The same tentacles reached out for Alex. When Enspelled had disbanded, he'd been tapped for bands left and right. But none of them had the sound or chemistry for a seamless fit. Stepping onto a stage, being able to command the crowd with his voice, what a rush—and what a loss. He'd never realized how lucky, how *spoiled* he'd gotten with Enspelled, until it was over.

Drinking heartsease to stitch himself back together, while the red candle burned away. The phone rang constantly, lots of persuasions and temptations over beers and nights of road-story camaraderie. Two good albums in his bio and tour-tested, solid, *pro*. Someone who knew what the demands were at this level, and delivered. But whatever the offer, it was someone else's project. Not his own. And not the right people. In metal, anyway.

Dahlia. The girl the candle had drawn forth, the first person to make him feel truly alive again. Solace with hard edges, filtered through a weird, blissed-out smile. A knowledge of music as catalogued and cherished as his, fun drunken nights finding the bridges between their album collections. They were different from each other the way Gnash and Catrinel had been, and like them, somehow, their roots had gotten tangled together. The feminine principle, miraculously manifesting again.

Bring your guitar over. Let's play. And they did. Strange, experimental worlds away from the conventions and constrictions of death metal, which was all starting to sound the same.

The second band plugged in, got going, offered him nothing new. Yeah.

The full moon rite, initially a panicked last-minute request to stand in for a missing bassist, became a totally unexpected sanctuary. Music for music's sake, not to get on a label but still enthralling a crowd. It kept his discipline from falling into atrophy, this form of service in her pagan church, a way to be supportive of her in the most direct way he could manage: gratitude for bringing him back to life. Between the dive bar he called a job, and nights at her loft, and drives up to Tamalpais, not bad. Time was ticking on his Enspelled laurels, but not bad. It beat running off to Half Moon Bay to start a pumpkin farm. And—yeah—probably end up dealing.

Matt banged his elbow with his beer bottle and jerked his head. Danae was standing in the crowd, wearing her jean jacket and ignoring a fair number of cold stares. A messenger bag was slung over her shoulder.

What was in that bag was the reason he'd told everyone to back away from her.

He caught the eyes starting to glance his way, everybody watching to see how he'd react. If he didn't go over and say hi, it would look like he was holding a grudge. Sure, they'd kept their relationship secret, but that never stopped everyone from speculating. Keep it casual, *hey, how are you*, just saying hi to an old bandmate, no big deal. Why not, Dahlia had already hung out with her.

The second band finished and the lights went up along with Darkthrone. He nodded at Matt, who shrugged. *Keep me out of this.*

Walking up to her, everything he'd buried was clawing its way back to the surface, helped up by the booze. He settled his stage mask over his face, the one for facing massive crowds, shutting down egomaniacs in other bands. Getting his pulse to shut up.

He tapped her on the shoulder with his bottle and she turned, scowling, ready with some verbal shrapnel that metal chicks armed themselves with against the inevitable creeps at shows.

"Hey," she said, kind of surprised.

"Hey."

Not distraught like she'd been in the grove. Stronger now, pulled together.

"I saw what happened to the old place, on the way over," she said.

"Yeah. Cups of coffee where we used to scream our lungs out."

"Pathetic."

She was about to say something else, but quickly closed her mouth. He glanced back at Matt, who was deep in conversation with Angel's new drummer, turning his back on them completely. Smart man. Others weren't so disengaged, and more than a few necks suddenly snapped back in other directions.

"I need a drink," said Danae.

"You haven't started yet?"

"Oh, I did. Before heading out. I could use more."

Back to the bar, whiskey for both. Doubles.

"I heard your new album," she said.

"The last album."

"The final album. Yeah." She sipped her drink while he silently waited. Like her first visit to Enspelled's house, investigating the living room, same tenterhooks. "I listened to it while I was going through the desert. It was—"

"Hey, an Enspelled reunion!"

If Alex hadn't wanted to kill Angel before, he did now.

"Angel. Nice to know some things never change," said Danae, the edges of her words tipped in acid.

"Now that you're here, maybe you'll get him off his ass to do something hella brutal, instead of fucking around with that raver church bullshit."

Danae's expression turned to ice.

"Alex has more talent in his fingernails than you do in your entire being. So does the priestess of that church, my friend Dahlia. They're making music the rest of the world doesn't even know *exists* yet. But you're still praying for Scott Burns to produce your album someday, aren't you? The whining of a dying breed, oh, how *hella* brutal, man."

Angel's mouth opened and closed, about to spit out *bitch* but not in front of Alex, stomped off in the direction of his band.

"I never liked that fucker," she said.

"I never knew." Holy shit.

"What do I have to lose? It's not like I have four other people to think about anymore."

"You never told me."

"How could I? You'd just want to kick everybody's ass. It would make it look like I couldn't handle it myself, like some kind of damsel in distress, and it would give it away that we were…you know."

"No. I would have gotten your back. We all would have."

"And how long would it have been before you'd started to resent it?"

"Enough until everybody knew never to fuck with you."

She paused, sipped her whiskey before she responded. "I was the girl in the band. I was always on probation. It doesn't matter what *you* do, they'll always respect you. No one will ever say you slept your way onto anybody's coattails."

"You never gave us the chance. You never gave *me* the chance!"

The sudden silence around him made him very aware he'd gotten much louder than he'd intended. He knocked back the rest of his drink, tried to ignore all the ears dying for the next part of this exchange.

She smirked. "Yeah. Some things never change, do they, Alex."

Low, getting a grip on his anger. "Outside."

"Fuckin' A. Let's go." She slammed down her glass and headed for the exit, and he followed, smoothing a glare over totally blown nonchalance.

Taquerias and laundromats and check-cashing joints, their brightly-painted eyes closed for the night. Ahead, a city bus rolled to a stop, doors squeaking, coins chiming. The night wind was full of burnt sugar, and exhaust, and a radio softly playing salsa up in someone's window. Never truly asleep, this part of town.

"I did give you the chance," she said. "Several chances, and you ignored them all. Others didn't."

"You mean Devon."

"Yeah. *Devon.*"

She swung into a narrow alley splashed with murals all the way to the end of the block. She turned around with a hard smile, raised her arms up in a slightly swaying cross. The rays of a psychedelic sunset formed a fiery pink corona behind her head. Her eyes glowed, and for a second, she was the spitting image of her mother.

A week, missing. Desperation. Starlight, the last resort. A blonde woman behind the counter in a long black dress: a dark, wily, older Danae. The woman she would become, a possible future self. She'd listened to him, told him all about her daughter while she carved a red candle. Only at the end did she tell him its true purpose.

Trust me, you're going to need it.

He'd picked up the glass jar, about to smash it against the floor, sanity snapped by this point, but she'd caught his arm, quick as a flash, blue eyes on fire.

You want me to make sure you never see her again? Go ahead. Destroy my shop. I have locks of her baby hair, her first shoes, her first drawings. If you really care for her, you'll back off. She's with someone who can give her more than you ever could, so just let her go. And if you're smart, you'll set that candle on fire as fast as you can.

Knowing Danae, the way he had, was like watching a painting color itself in. He pictured her behind the counter, she would have still been a teenager, explaining spells and suggesting books and being helpful in her sarcastic way. *Why* had he never gone in? The girl she'd been, what could have been, hanging on to his BMX while he rode them to the park, lighting bonfires on the beach, sharing traded tapes and pilfered beer and their virginity probably, no, *definitely*…gone forever.

All the spite came back into Danae's face, but she wasn't bleeding anymore.

"Go on, take your shot. I know you want to. Everyone else does. I ran away with the big bad rockstar, and they all wanna punish me for selling out. Never mind how pissed off I was at you, that's not important. Come on. I'm ready for it."

Now, she had her own secrets locked up behind the bones of her face. Straightening her back, arrogance in the way she carried herself now. A sordid past of her own that he'd have to accept, just as she'd had to accept his. Her time away had changed her, made her more curved and cruel. How much of this was Devon, how much of this was her father? Her mother? It was like watching her evil twin. This new Danae was practically licking her lips to do battle against him.

This new Danae had also gotten his back pretty fiercely against Angel, but he pushed that thought aside.

"You want a word for it. The way you've always written everything down, always pushing for just the right word. Alright. *Chickenshit.* For not speaking up, not saying anything, and then leaving and not telling anybody where you were. And then you show up with...*him.*"

Danae burst out laughing, wrapped her arms around herself and slid down the wall, off-center from the corona, crooked halo.

"What's so fucking funny?"

"Just listening to you two talk about each other."

"What the...what the fuck does that asshole even *know* about me?"

"He hates you with the fire of a thousand white-hot suns. Yeah. The mighty Devon Dare. Rock god extraordinaire, and not half the man you are."

She rose up from the ground, and her laughter faded.

"The final Enspelled album. Amazing, even as I knew what I'd done to you, that it was me who tore all that pain out of you. Do you really want to know what I thought of it? I cried over it. I jerked off to it. I played it to death behind Devon's back. But he heard it anyway. He kept excellent tabs on me down there, he knew all about us. He made sure I was good and tortured over it."

"Why would he give a fuck?"

Two beats of silence as she looked him straight in the eyes.

"Because I never loved him."

Up to the wall, *I'm sorry Dahlia* as he took Danae's face in his hands and kissed her.

That hungry little mouth like she'd been starving for him, his hair clenched in her fists. She still smelled like cookies, but ripe summer fruit, too, sharp and tart beneath the sweetness. Shaking as she pulled him close, those hands, those lips that knew so many secrets about him. He ran his hands down her back, stopped just above the curves of her hips, familiar, one of his favorite places on earth. Being right here felt too fucking good to stop.

She broke the kiss, pulled away.

"I can't." She looked up at him. "I want to, you don't know how bad I want to, but this hurts her the way I hurt you, and I'm never doing that to anyone ever again. I'm sorry. I'm *so* sorry, Alex." Her arms went around him, held him tight for just two more stolen seconds, and she stepped back, spun on her heel and walked back down the alley, fast, around the corner and gone in the blink of an eye.

He ran a hand through his hair. Confusion and guilt and desire: the seeds of so many good songs were such a mindfuck when they collided in reality. He started the walk back to the Lower Haight—pointless to go back to the show—back to take refuge in the strings. Write it out of his system. Everything Dahlia feared had just come true, he hadn't lit that candle just to hurt the girl it called. But right now, a bassline was trying to crawl out. Life had just turned into a mess, and it had given him the first real inspiration he'd had in forever.

* * *

Squint your eyes, and you can see the women in the trees.

Hand in hand with her mother, long ago in the time of the folk singers, the framed photographs in Celeste's bedroom coming to life inside Buena Vista Park. Sepia-toned sylphs from the early century stretched their pale flesh against the knotty branches, their tangled hair wild in the wind. Raising their arms skyward, skin bared completely to the elements, they wound themselves around the trunks of a different grove, one with more darkness, more fog. The place they'd gone for picnics, and walks, and songs, which had abruptly stopped after Danae's first period.

Let Alex and Charlotte and Lacey and everybody take Golden Gate. It was full of tourists, and none of its swingsets gave you a view of the bay.

Holy Moses played on Danae's Discman, resurrected back into rotation. The witch book sat inside her bag. Before her, choice characters from the major arcana were laid out on the grass at the very top of the park.

The return to San Francisco made her feel as though she'd developed a split personality. Merciless inside Julian's house, twelve years old inside Dahlia's. It made her almost want to call Devon. *Hey, it's me. Well, one of my personas. One that got along well with one of yours. Tell me, how the hell do you handle it? Being all these different people?* Death, the new life she'd started with him, and abruptly ended. She wished she could have seen the look on his face when he discovered what she'd done to his workroom.

Strength, beside The Hanged Man. She'd really thrown Alex into it. *Good going, lush.* She'd hate him for a dishonest shitty guy if he didn't tell Dahlia, but if he did, goodbye Temple of Lunacy, goodbye sonic playground. She'd found out Alex still had feelings for her—incredible, she'd thought he hated her—but at what an awful cost.

Both of them, she wanted both of them. The boy who held so much of her past, the girl who was building a dazzling future. She closed her eyes, and two wax figures stared back at her. A man and a woman, both red. Maybe. Maybe.

Beneath them, three cards that represented possible phone calls.

The Empress, Pam. Wisdom, sensuality, crash space. Solid help in getting her shit together if everything fell to pieces up here. But she'd just run away from Los Angeles. Her name would be blackballed all around town, doors closing in her face, loyal to Devon. She wasn't sure the kind of life she was after even existed down there—she liked walking around in the night too much. And it was a pretty big fucking favor to call in, much too soon after the last one. She'd leave it as a last resort.

The Magician, Adrian. No. Not when she didn't have real material. She'd position him as a goal, a guide, the focus to streamline her energies into finished work. A downside to Julian's house—the organ in the living room was loads of fun, but the overall atmosphere, and her crappy little Casio, did not make for a good place to write music.

The High Priestess, Catrinel. Someone else who'd lost the thread of Danae's journey, but fought for her anyway. Danae realized how much she missed Gnash, too. The Tall Blonde Control Tower, how much she'd love to talk to him, feel his grounding gaze keeping an eye on her, keeping her safe. But off the map, no longer here, off in another, sunnier story. She'd be a voice from the past, catching up, too much work to be done to get that spider thread current and live. Worth it, definitely, but best not done in the midst of all this turbulence. That call would be placed when this all shook out, however it did.

No card for Matt. She'd lost him.

Two more cards. The Moon, and The Devil. Mom and Dad. Hard to chart the twitches of her psyche without feeling their distinct influences, the dark gifts they'd bestowed upon their lovechild. Within the features of her face, the whorls of her personality, she dove for the subtle signs of lineage. Uncovered charms, and muscles, and knacks. And flaws. Her birth had formed the discord between them, a tension she didn't care to repeat within her own love life.

She knew who to call next.

At the bottom, one more card. Representing the way she'd followed her own path, and hoping to avoid a fall off that cliff just a step or two ahead.

Even though this wasn't a reading, it was still a habit of hers to look beneath the deck at whatever card ended up at the bottom. The very last word. She turned the deck over.

Ten of Swords.

Also known as Deep Shit.

* * *

Two dark forms in thrift-store prom gowns sat parked on barstools, box purses sitting beside cocktail glasses. Black lips sipped at whiskey, black eyes surveyed the Xymox-swirled dancefloor of DJ Thirteena. Cobwebbed sleeves and glittering eyeshadow, jingling belts and platform-soled boots all swayed in time to the singer's divine baritone. Behind the bar, the drink specials board offered a bloodsucker cocktail made with cranberries, rock videos played on a television set, and a skeleton was decked out in a red sequinned bikini. Trippy concert posters bathed the Red Hot Chili Peppers and Jane's Addiction in neo-sixties neon nouveau.

I need to get out. Come with me.

Alright. Let's do the makeup and everything!

Was it guilt over that kiss in the alley that made Dahlia look even more lovely tonight? Tiny silver bats wrapped themselves around the dreads that formed her bangs, and the runs in her black stockings had started well before they'd walked through the club's front door.

"So Les is making noises about other projects. Things that might pull him away from playing the rites."

"Really." A pigtailed girl wandered by in a Hello Kitty backpack and baggy jeans, a sparkling pink pacifier in her mouth.

"Just putting you on notice. Nothing's definite yet, but it might happen."

"Are you sure you don't need two keyboardists?" Danae laughed and spun around, caught the lace-bustiered bartender's eye and nodded for another drink. Was about to turn back around, until she glanced at the television.

Devon Dare was kissing a girl in a long black gown. Her hair was long and bright as flames.

Dahlia noticed Danae's sudden silence and looked back in time to see a sneering domme dressed like a fifties pinup tear the gown from the girl's body and rip it to rags. Down to shredded black lingerie, cheeks filthed with mascara tears, black claws flexing with helpless anger, her face faded into the smug visage of Devon.

Danae whipped back around. The drink came, and she didn't mean to slide the bills into a small puddle, but she couldn't bear seeing any more.

Dahlia said nothing. Curious to hear it all, of course, but too polite to ask outright—much like how Danae wanted to ask about the three scars streaking down from her eye. A sympathetic presence beside her, having dealt with her share of assholes in bands. The fact she was Alex's current squeeze just threw one more surreal layer on top of it all. Danae was ready to spill.

"He knew just what to tempt me with, so I couldn't walk away," said Danae.

She looked up at Dahlia.

"Sex wouldn't have been enough. Nor a Nemesis contract. It was both. And he offered it to me right in the middle of my first big fight with Alex, ever. He invited me to a party in North Beach that I wasn't even sure I was gonna go to, and I was furious, and I don't even know what I meant to do there. Say hi, get drunk, flirt a little bit to restore my ego, which Alex had just smashed into the ground, come back home and talk it over. I didn't know..."

Do you dare more? She had, and bringing up the woods would sound utterly batshit. Some things weren't meant to be spoken aloud, to anyone. She smoothed back her hair and continued.

"I didn't know enough to make Devon wait for me, accept my terms. I just blindly jumped for his. Back at Starlight, I always tried to direct all these confused women towards the more empowering writers. Live your life for yourself, don't contort yourself for some self-centered asshole. And that's totally what I did, when I was down in Los Angeles. I knew more when I knew *nothing*."

Dahlia signaled for more whiskey, face bright with her own stories to share, just as Danae suspected. Every girl in showbiz had them.

"You know, Damian 23 demanded that I come to all his shows. So that he'd teach me, right, brainwash me was more like it. Everything had to be hard, pounding, fast…and yeah, he was like that in bed, too," catching the amused look on Danae's face. "So he'd get to brag about how everything I knew, I learned from him, while he got a girlfriend oohing and aahing over his every performance."

"But he didn't teach you the stuff you're doing with the lunar rite."

"Oh, no. That was all my own experimenting. Which he took credit for, until his friends would make fun of it, and then suddenly it was all weak bullshit."

"Why'd you stay with him?"

"Well…the sex *was* pretty amazing."

They laughed, and Danae felt a hand run down the side of her face. Fingertips encased in metal. She looked up.

Galen, in a tight black t-shirt, set off with a silver dagger necklace. Lacey and Charlotte were right beside him in coats trimmed with what Danae hoped were fake fur collars, over PVC ballgowns.

"Dahlia, these are the girls staying in the house with my father, Lacey and Charlotte. And this is Erik."

Faces plastered with obvious fake smiles, met with one cold nod. Charlotte angled Danae away, while Lacey got the bartender's attention.

"I've been designing a line of jewelry," said Charlotte, bringing her hand beneath one of her pendants, lifting up an intricate silver goat's head. "I want to do stuff that's beautiful, not cheap, not pewter, but real silver. Really capturing the detail." Which she had, in the texture on the horns, the inverted star on the forehead, right down to the haughty look in the half-closed eyes.

"That was you doing the handwriting in the chapbook, wasn't it?" asked Danae.

Charlotte smiled, pleased. "I'd like you to have this," she said, lifting the chain over her head.

Danae smiled, but curled the pendant back into Charlotte's palm, no. "It's amazing work, but I can't take that from you."

"But it's a gift."

"But it's not my symbol."

A brief flash in Charlotte's painted eyes: the sting of rejection, recognized from countless people in other bands who didn't really like hearing honest feedback after all. It didn't matter that Baphomet was absent from Danae's spiritual universe. *You just told me I suck.*

But if the Gingerbread Four were serious about being leaders, of any kind, respecting differences was a lesson they'd have to learn, and learn early. It wasn't up to Danae to hold their hands. Which they probably didn't want anyway, drawing from pride and intelligence and strength and not a lot of room for a stumble.

Bauhaus came on. A groovy bass and Peter Murphy's vocals immediately doubled the dancefloor population. Lacey downed her drink, ran out and joined them, Charlotte right behind her. Erik reached for Danae's hand.

"Come on. Dance with us."

But Danae shook her head, leaned back, half-hoped Dahlia wouldn't guess how intimately she and Erik knew each other.

"No, I'm not really..."

"We're on our way out," said Dahlia, grabbing her purse from off the bar and getting up. "Charming to meet you."

"Likewise," said Erik, mirroring her flat tone.

"I'll see you guys back at the house," said Danae, turning away and heading towards the door, while Erik's eyes bored holes of annihilation through the back of her companion.

The night sky simmered with an impending storm, casting down the first drops of rain down onto their bare arms like cold wet jewels.

"Should we get a cab?" asked Danae.

"Fuck that! I don't live that far, come on!" And she grabbed Danae's arm, the two of them off down the street, running as fast as they could in heels. They made it two blocks before the world flashed with lightning and the downpour came on with a boom. The streets disappeared behind curtains of water, slowing the traffic with icy chaos. Hand in hand, they darted between inching bumpers up onto the next block, not far now, there was the building, they ran inside and slammed the front door and up the spiral staircase to Dahlia's bedroom where they took one look at each other's ruined outfits and burst out laughing.

Green draped along the walls, spread across the bed, thrown down over the hardwood floor. A couple of antique-looking wooden chairs were dusted with cat hair, and a curvy dresser served as Dahlia's altar, bottles and powders among twists of metal, chunks of wood, candle stubs. Decorating the place she slept like a wild garden, fae and enchanted and not what Danae had expected at all from someone into hard grinding beats. But, just like writing metal songs in the woods, probably a much-needed counterbalance. The moon shone down through a skylight.

Kicking off heels, peeling down wet lace, down to lingerie and damp hair and smeared lipstick. Dahlia rummaged in a drawer, pulled out a pair of striped pajama bottoms.

"Here, these are huge on me, they'll definitely fit you."

Danae took in Dahlia's strapless bra, black boyshorts as her gracious hostess rooted through the laundry on the floor, grabbed something huge and gray and hopped up on the bed.

"All my t-shirts are dirty, this one's really comfortable if you don't mind I slept in it."

"I don't mind."

So soft, that edge making its way through Danae's voice, very okay with the sleep-funk of Dahlia's unconscious flesh. The cold was turning Dahlia's skin to goosepimples, and Danae reached out to trace a path of warmth along her bare thigh. Dahlia shuddered, and their eyes met. Just one kiss. Just one, to even things out against Alex. Danae leaned forward, and lightly bit Dahlia's lower lip, and her arms were suddenly filled with girl. Face ghouled with black eyeshadow, skin textured with chill, Danae pulled her on top and immersed herself in fire.

Hands in the soft scratch of her dreads, down her back. Thumbs on Dahlia's hipbones where Danae knew his hands had been, nuzzling against her neck, she wanted to *be* Alex, search out how many erogenous zones they had in common. If Dahlia too loved soft nips along the undercurves of her breasts, if a deep growl got her soaking wet. It didn't count when it was two girls doing it. Right?

But this was still going on behind his back. Now Danae was Devon, tempting someone to fall, and too fucking bad for whoever got left behind. Just like in the alley, it was going too fast, already farther.

She wanted so bad to pull down Dahlia's boyshorts and hear what her screams sounded like. It killed her to stop, but she did. Confusion in Dahlia's eyes, but a kind of relief, too, and Danae softened the break by not letting go of her hands.

"Can we..."

There's another way we can be intimate.

"Can we go jam?"

An incredulous look, before the part of Dahlia that created the lunar rite seemed to understand what Danae was asking. The priestess part. Up on the same wavelength, not blowing her off as crazy, or a tease, the way most anyone else would have.

"Please?"

Down to the studio, still in their underwear. Dahlia dragged a space heater into the center of the room, switched on its small sun and blasted it towards the keyboards. One, and two, she powered them on. Danae banged around in the dark while Dahlia threw down a beat like clay on a wheel. They filled the room with a wall of shimmering dissonance and swam in the sound. Blew it up like a bubble and let it go, ready for the next layer.

Danae took the microphone and whispered into it, started a chant. Words not for storytelling, but hypnosis. Lyrics like percussion, repetition to focus. Shifting the studio from playground to pentacle. She shuffled to the center of the floor and lay down on the warmed concrete, right in the spot where all the sound converged. She looked around for Dahlia but didn't see her. She closed her eyes, let the heater gently burn her stomach, savored that strange, sweetly unexpected reality when you've drifted much, much further into the night with someone than you intended.

She felt a presence looming over her. She opened her eyes.

Dahlia was squatting beside her, smiling. Her hand uncurled to reveal two white blotter squares, one printed with Ren, the other with Stimpy.

Her face glowed orange.

Let's

keep

GOING.

Chapter 19

No. *No.* This could not be happening. Danae glared across the three crows at Julian.

"Devon's coming up for a visit? You've got to be fucking kidding."

"I'm not." Steak tonight, rare. Julian was halfway through his plate.

"You're putting a celebrity before your own kin, is what you're doing. Did you even *see* that video he made? How can you expect me to stay in the same room with him and not kick him in the face, let alone make up with him?" She got up from the dining room table, strode into the living room, collapsed on the couch. Thought about classified ads. Apartment shares. Maybe Dahlia knew someone from one of the lunar rites who might be in need of a roommate. At least they'd be pagan, a major hurdle cleared.

"You're going to give him all kinds of advice on nightmare magick, and negative space, while all you ever tell me is to act sexy," she said.

"Do you know how many girls would kill to have what you did, with him?"

"Yes. Because they all wanted to kill *me.*"

A small clock sat on the coffee table, a gift from a local artist who rescued broken antiques and reworked them into bits of macabre decor. Black wood, brass details. She idly wondered where the gory surprise was in this one.

"You'd rather I be the groupie than the rockstar." She put her feet up on the table.

"You had a good future with him. An excellent future. You want to live the rock'n'roll life. And that's fine. But how many people, realistically, end up making their living from it? There's only so many years before their dreams hit the ground, and they wind up in day jobs. They become slaves. That is not the life I envision for you." His knife clattered against his plate.

Because you care about me, or adding one more jewel in your crown? She thought about Alex shaking a perfect martini. Matt mastering the art of getting a pill down a cat's throat. What was so great about climbing to the top, if it meant living in a splendid mansion, all alone?

There was more than one way to be a slave. Many more.

"You're acting like the relationship I had with him was more important than the albums I recorded."

"Heavy metal, belligerent disco. You've carved out a niche for yourself as a cult figure, but what did you do with it? You sing your heart out, and then everyone goes home at the end of the show. Haven't you ever tried to harness all that power? Channel it towards some productive end?"

"Yeah. Charity gigs."

He snorted.

"Everything we did, everything we got, we put back into the music. We weren't after domination, or being the best, we didn't need to crush all the other bands because we were dying to hear what they were doing. Making it in music means nothing if you don't have a ton of friends to share it with. Living the life was the goal. And we did it."

"And nothing more."

"If you call that failure, I feel sorry for you."

His eyes lit up with anger for just a moment. Just a moment. And then his face relaxed, right back down into that infamous smirk. He remained seated, didn't move a muscle, but his voice melted into sweet carnival-tent hypnosis.

"Spare me your misguided pity, daughter. Save it for yourself."

Loud, and sly, and knowing, it was as if he'd risen to his feet, sprouted massive wings, grown taller and taller to tower over her, all by the power of sound.

"Save it for when you're thirty, forty, fifty, and the world can't remember your name. When your records are dusty at the back of the shop, lost among everyone else who couldn't rise any higher. When your health gives out, when you weary of the travelling life, one way or another, it will end."

The little clock chimed the hour with a spill of blood down its white face.

"Devon will be up here in a month. It's your choice, of course, whether you smartly grow a spine and resume your place by his side, or continue to squander your gifts on people who can never take you as far. Whatever you decide, my friendship with him will continue."

Of course Devon would want her back, now that he knew whose daughter she was. One more pair of claws coming for her. She flashed back to Celeste, Zolo leaning on the counter, there was always someone else who meant more than she did.

A cold rage lifted Danae's chin, and she squared her shoulders against her father's smooth brutality.

"If you let Devon walk through the door of this house, I'm moving out. It's me or him. Admit it, he's the son you've always wanted, right?"

She got to her feet, saw the nerve she'd hit in the way his face darkened with fresh hostility. Good. He shouldn't be the only one allowed to make threats. Danae charged up the stairs and almost mowed down Lacey.

"Danae. I've been looking for you."

"Not now, Lacey."

"But Erik and I have been invited to give a lecture on alternative spirituality."

"That's great," said Danae, trying to get by, but Lacey wasn't moving.

"It is. Academic credence, more acceptance of other worldviews. I thought you'd be...more *excited* about this."

"I'm...I'm just..." Worn out from all this drama.

Lacey stepped close, put a hand on Danae's shoulder. Soft, seductive. "What do we have to do, to bring you closer to us?"

"I appreciate that, but I really need to go my own way." She tried a smile, but Lacey didn't let her go just yet. She brought her face close, her perfume all dark florals.

"I worry about you. You spend all your time with a girl who sticks X-Acto knives in her face. We just don't want you to hurt yourself," she said, almost a whisper.

One cold nod from Danae, and Lacey stepped aside.

"I hope you know we consider you our sister," she said, as Danae ascended the stairs into her bedroom, and shut the door.

* * *

Exhaustion. Calm. The cotton tatters of Dahlia's dress were soaked through as she knelt down on the last strums of Alex's bass, lingering before the rite's fadeout. All around her, congregants slowed their dancing, stilled their bodies into the cooldown, the return home, guided by Danae's hands back to earth.

Back to earth. For Dahlia, it was an inner twist of emotional labyrinths where the end was still hidden, somewhere up ahead.

Danae's pro face had gone up when Alex walked through the door, stayed plastered on all through setup and a soundcheck, ready for the improv. It hid the girl who'd walked with Dahlia even deeper into the music, two maidens running through a forest of windchimes, building houses of smoke and crystals for each other to walk into, forging their bond through an eight-hour ambient marathon captured for the ages.

"I've never played like that with *anybody*," Danae had said, Dahlia murmuring agreement, before dozing off in the light of the next afternoon, their arms around each other like children.

Later, when Dahlia dropped in on Alex at work, three whiskeys to get her confession over with, she found out he had one of his own.

You're right. It is hard to watch her bleed.

It hadn't occurred to Dahlia, until Les backed out, that Danae had to know keyboards to even be standing here at all. Staying in San Francisco, and never getting to break beyond lyrics and vocals, would not have led her onto the temple stage.

Danae and Alex, their first performance together since Enspelled. Totally different roles this time, different instruments in their hands, and no words at all. The lunar rite sounded pretty fucking amazing running off death metal power. Not to discount the people who had come before, who played for the love of playing, without any dream of national fame, but damn. After recording an album, and touring, they were strong and solid behind her, sending out serious voltage. Whatever was happening, it needed to be kept together.

Dahlia's eyes traveled the theater seats, picked out various members of the community. There was the pastry chef whose husband had divorced her for a younger woman, who always brought a basket of crescent moon cookies. There was the mechanic who'd been cut off from his entire family as a teenager, after his father had thrown him out for kissing another boy. He danced like a wraith, movement like a dream. The two animal rescue volunteers, Matt's friends, girls in fairy wings who blew bubbles out over the crowd. No problems she'd had to listen to there, just happy, although they surely had heartwrenching stories to tell.

Nights in dive bars, days on park benches, just listening to them. All of them. Performing the holy service of just being there. Cheating bastards and judgmental assholes and love finding so many ways to go awry, she was doing the little bit she could to put the world back together, her little corner of it. Not ordained, not sanctioned by any official order, but fuck that. The practice of compassion needed no one's approval.

Now it was her turn to need tending. Sacrifice was part of being a good priestess—sure, it could be glamorous, but it also meant distraught phone calls in the dead of night. Stiff-backed chairs in waiting rooms. It mandated a generosity of spirit that didn't inoculate against further demands, further tests.

Like right now, between her bassist and keyboardist.

Theirs was an old story that had suddenly started back up, and she wasn't sure of her place in its pages. Back at the bar, she'd asked Alex to dig up Enspelled's scrapbooks, the history. *Show me what Danae meant to you.* Purged of secrets, they'd gone back to his place, and soon his floor was covered in fanzines, interviews, stage shots. Danae screaming into a microphone, covered in corn syrup, a snarling girl who wasn't afraid to get dirty.

"All these pictures, and not one of you together."

"Actually, there's one. Only one. Catrinel took it." He lifted up a manila folder near the bottom of the box, lifted out a color snapshot and handed it to her.

Collapsed against a wall covered in graffiti in the back of some club somewhere. Danae still in her stage gown, Alex shirtless, their faces shining with sweat. Their eyes were closed with exhaustion as they leaned on each other, hands laced together. Beautiful.

Applause and kisses brought her back to the moment, she caught Wiest ascending the stairs to the DJ booth, club classics to smooth the crowd's transition back into reality. Another gift to the attendees: favorite tunes enjoyed off the leash of the cabaret laws. Already a couple of requests came hurrying over as he took control of the speakers.

Dahlia knew one thing, for sure: she would not make Ronnie's mistake of trying to tear them apart, only to end up losing them both.

She slipped behind the instruments, to her band. Both clad in total black, Danae in a sheath dress, Alex in a plain t-shirt and dress pants. Their damp angel faces flashed in her mind for the thousandth time since she'd first seen that picture. She took a deep breath, drew on the strength of the congregation at her back.

"You both have unfinished business with each other."

Danae glanced at Alex, back to Dahlia.

"You have a bond that's been broken. It's not supposed to be. Go put it back together." *And don't forget me*, as she brought her mouth to Danae's, long and deep, *don't leave me back on my own*, the same sweet kiss for Alex.

"Come over," Danae breathed, "when all this…is done."

"I'll be there at dawn."

Dahlia turned her back, walked through the dancers up the stairs into the house, up the spiral into her room. A story she was not a part of, and the very real chance it would go on without her. She threw herself down on her bed, grabbed a tasseled pillow and wound herself around it while the party raged downstairs. Curio nuzzled her hand, offered the matte satin of her fur. Like petting an evening gown, Dahlia thought, fighting back tears.

A couple of minutes later, she heard feet clonking up her stairs. Wiest.

"Hey, aren't you supposed to be in the booth?" she asked.

"Don't worry, it's 'Temple of Love.' The extended version."

She smiled at him as he sat down beside her. Wiest, the other lunatic. She cast aside the pillow and rolled over on her back to look up at him, up at the moon.

"I did it. I set them free."

He pulled her head into his lap, smoothed back her dreads. "The smartest thing you could have done."

"Or the stupidest. The most clueless and naive. Hella fucking crazy."

"Oh, and holding on hard would have been better? Don't stress over it, you did the right thing and there's nothing else you can do right now. Don't make me put on the crayon factory video to get your mind off it. Come on. David's here, I want you to meet him."

"The sculptor?"

"The showing went really well," he said. "*Really* well."

She hugged him. "I'm glad you're happy."

"I think everything's gonna be fine," he said, getting up, pulling her up with him..

"How do you know?"

"Because when you walked out of the room, they watched you go."

* * *

Sweetshop houses sat atop painted staircases, flanked the street. Danae drank in the lower Haight as Alex found a spot, commenced the teethgrinding joy of parallel parking on an incline. Fog came drifting down as she stepped out onto the sidewalk. Not far from Pam's old place.

Janis came wailing from someone's open window. Ecstasy, or despair: her voice could be either kind of erotic omen.

The ride over had been quiet, in the black Firebird with the MEAN PEOPLE RULE bumper sticker and the red feathers clipped behind the rearview mirror, Alice in Chains filling up the spaces between small talk. Permission granted, but it wasn't that easy. The tension came back, a live wire that neither was in a rush to trip, not when there was more to be said. Not when things were just as fast to tip over into an argument.

But, underneath it all, contentment from a good show together. That hadn't changed.

Not a house, but an apartment over a liquor store, up a ratty staircase to a studio that was even smaller and grimier than her crash landing in the

Mission. He threw his keys on the kitchen table—the kitchen table from Enspelled's house—and put the bass case down by his bed. Plants along the windowsills, two guitars in their stands, empty beer bottles scattered along the kitchen counter. Altar still minimalist with pieces of the woods, taper candles.

A pair of green-ribboned hair clips sat among the show flyers and cologne bottles on his dresser. Dahlia, here before her. Jealousy flared up like a vestigial tail. Another woman who was now across town, a sparkling creature up in her bedroom, hopefully back in her party by now and having a good time. Danae wasn't sure she'd be able to, if their roles were reversed.

She sat down by the strip of sink and fridge and stove that passed for a kitchen. Picked up his keyring and fiddled with it, the bottle opener, the penknife, the tiny wooden coffin a fan had carved from a rotting farmhouse that he'd kept all these years. How awful it must have been to stay here, live inside the memories, while Los Angeles lifted her out of her past.

He lit candles, hit the stereo to resume a Dead Can Dance cassette.

"This reminds me of Catrinel."

"Yeah, she got me into them."

He poured two glasses of wine, something white, and sat down. Scratched wood familiar beneath her elbows, CD cases and bottle caps clustered across its surface, she'd come back after all, even though the table was in another part of the city now. The man beside her was still dark, but a touch more elegant in his classed-up black: silver across his hands, hair tied out of the way, looking as if he'd spent the night in a jazz bar. A suit would look really good on him, mad little thought as she looked into his eyes, unsure where to begin.

"When I saw Enspelled for the first time—that day in the grove, when you handed me the flyer, and I came to see you—I never ever dreamed I'd be part of something so *good*. And then I was, and…I never saw this kind of an ending coming. It's supposed to go on forever, right? And I caused it. And I can't believe I caused it."

"No." He shook his head, fidgeted with a bright red guitar pick. "Ronnie did."

Her brows furrowed. What?

"Honestly, Matt's hands were an excuse to leave the band. I'd been looking for an exit, I couldn't stand playing with him anymore. Forget living with him. I can understand why he was pissed at you—at both of us, really—but he handled it totally wrong."

"You fought him."

"Yeah, I did. It wasn't the first time."

"I never…I always tried to just get along with him."

"It didn't really matter who you were. You were the girl who…disrupted things."

She hid her reaction behind a sip of wine, that was an interesting way of putting it, but she was nowhere near ready to tackle that particular head on the hydra. She let him continue.

"And I wish you would have told me things had gotten that bad, but then again, I wasn't listening. To you, or your music, or anything that wasn't about the band. But…" He looked down, exhaled. "Danae, what the *fuck*."

She wanted to reach out and touch his face, but not yet. Not until she'd told him the whole story. She poured another glass of wine, and it all came out. Pomegranate wine and glitter rock. Moonlight shining on grotesque silver creatures, nightmares full of stunning, tormented women. A huge bus shooting across the country, her feet never touching the earth.

"I was really happy with the way my solo album came out, under the circumstances. The way it was all put together, it was so…sterile."

"It was good."

"You've heard it?"

"Only recently. Really recently, like a couple days ago. I mean…this was the album you ran away to make. I couldn't bring myself to listen to it. But Dahlia asked to see pictures of us in the band…I figured it was time. And yeah. It's really fucking good. Horror movies, that's totally you."

The ocean, and the art museum, and the arena floor, new places of magick revealing themselves to her. Afternoons up above the beach, fingers growing confident on the keyboard. Jamie. Colette. Pam.

"If I ever run across this Shadow guy, I'm going to fucking kill him."

"No need, there's better ways to fuck with him. I know where he works."

The mentorship slowly souring over the miles as her role changed from eager student to camera-ready courtesan. A sumptuous world that only magnified her isolation. Learning what she wanted, by getting more and more of what she didn't.

"…and I came back up here, and figured I'd destroyed everything, that there was no way you'd ever speak to me again, and I'd just start over. Again." Her wineglass stood empty. "And then I met Dahlia at the club, and she gave me a flyer for the full moon, and…now I'm here, and I'm still…I can't believe I'm here. With you."

She fell silent, somewhat exhausted in the telling. But he said nothing. She searched his eyes for a reaction. A little pain, maybe, but it was more like he was truly taking in everything she'd become, both battle scars and victory toasts, all shattering the blank slate forever.

One more thing.

"So was there anything else you wanted to talk about, that night?" she asked.

He got up and walked to the closet, sliding mirrors, odd touch of luxe in an otherwise dismal apartment. He grabbed a box off the top shelf, brought it back to the table. Sat back down and watched her eyes go wide with Christmas-morning elation.

Her notebooks!

She tore through the box, running her loving hands over their broken spines. Flyers, backstage passes, souvenirs from other states came tumbling out from their pages. Black and white composition books, a Muppets journal Matt had gotten her somewhere in Florida, tiny notepads in desperate moments when there was nothing bigger to write on, poems and lyrics and sketches of life all around the country, all here, all safe. Safe. Her innermost thoughts, private moments, deepest fantasies…

She looked up at Alex, her hands slowing across the top of the box.

"Did you…" Her eyes wandered down to all the diaries, so much let out on paper that was so hard to say in real life. How exposed she'd be, if his answer was yes.

"Yeah, I did."

She ran a shaky hand through her hair, unable to meet his eyes. She felt scooped raw, this coming, right after telling him everything that happened in Los Angeles.

"Danae."

Fingers trembling, it was a frightening amount for one human being to know about another.

"Danae. Look at me."

Breathless, she raised her head. Vulnerable beneath those gray eyes, caught out in that smoky storm and nowhere to run.

"I love you, too."

Three seconds of stunned silence before she reached out for him, and he pulled her into a kiss that sent her reeling. She climbed over into his lap, legs catching in the fabric of her stage gown. He lifted her up and carried her to the bed.

Back in that familiar woodland scent, so slow in this second first time. Lips that couldn't get enough of his kisses, the taste of his skin through the unravelling of their clothes. She flashed back to Devon, the night in the hotel room that never happened, she'd never been this tender with Alex because he'd never needed it. Now, the elixirs unleashed to send his blood racing, the taking was in the giving, the way Pam had healed her. All pain exiled by the touch of her hands, the joy in her eyes, the magic words so plain but so terrifying to say

I love you

letting it out, the strength it took to say it, how insane, two vocalists who wrought chaos on crowds of thousands but hadn't been able to speak such a simple, obvious truth to each other, straddling his hips, as deep as she could hold him, his face in her hands and

I love you

back to her, and she dropped forward onto him, locked together, breathing hard against his ear, saying it again, and again, back and forth, forging the bond that would not be broken this time.

Dawn found them wrapped in the sheets, her body half-spooned into his, tilted up to face him. Dreamy and glowing and ready to walk right into the most dangerous part of the fight.

"I hated the way it felt like snooping, but I was trying to find out where you'd gone," he said.

"There's nobody I trust more around my stuff."

He kissed her temple.

"The whole time…I was afraid you were laughing at me. That night in Matt's room…it was like you'd called me an amateur. Which is like, why didn't you just call me a poseur. Like it was so shocking that I had a past too, a little one compared to yours, but still. And I was so angry that you considered me some kind of inferior, and when Devon made his offer, it seemed like something that would put me as equal to you."

He was quiet for a moment, throwing a cold fear into her spine that she'd said too much.

"Catrinel told me that the worst thing you can ever say about a rock chick is that she's not tough," he said.

Danae exhaled. It was all out.

He continued. "I didn't mean to shut you out, if that was what you wanted. You came along, and…I just forgot anyone else existed."

"You do that when you get caught up in anything. It's your fatal flaw."

"Yeah. If anything, I was surprised you knew Pamela Black before she was famous. Like, we don't know anybody who *ever* goes on to that level of fame, you know? The rest of it…is actually pretty fucking cool."

"Yeah?"

"Yeah. You're…adventurous."

A key turned in the lock.

"What perfect timing," Danae murmured.

Intentionally loud, slow push of the door and Dahlia stood framed in the doorway, still in her ragged stage dress. Stock-still as she took it in, the lovers staring at her from the rumpled bed.

Yeah, it happened.

Danae rose, a sheet wound around her body. Went to Dahlia and kissed her, pushed the door shut behind her and let the sheet drop.

And you're coming with us.

She pulled Dahlia towards the bed, no room for confusion, or hurt feelings, or even talking. Danae undid the tattered ties of her stage dress as Alex kissed her. Ran her hands over the velvet leopard of Dahlia's lingerie, lit up when she discovered the piercings. Small tugs on silver rings, first with fingers, then with teeth, carefully finding the boundaries between small moans.

Soon, between them, Alex sinking his teeth into the back of Dahlia's neck as he took her from behind, Danae kissing her lust-smeared mouth, gliding a crafty hand down between her thighs. Bellydance groove rippled through Dahlia's flesh as her hips undulated and her cries grew louder. Alex started to growl and Danae growled back, Dahlia caught between them, a pair of wolves surrounding her, bringing her into their pack, tearing her apart with pleasure, and when her body seized on the highest, sweetest notes, her bliss was twofold: deep shuddering gasps, streaked with laughter.

* * *

Danae bounded up the steps of the black Victorian, pulled the housekey from her messenger bag. Tangled hair, crumpled black gown, but she was beaming. Walk of shame? More like walk of fucking *pride*.

Three days. They hadn't left Alex's apartment for three glorious days. He'd called out sick from the bar, and Dahlia had thrown a gig to an extremely grateful DJ Thirteena, and the hours flew by through the dark of the moon. Danae's head was still spinning, stopping to light on moments throughout. Climbing into the bathtub with Dahlia while Alex was still asleep, taking turns washing each other's hair, pouring a mug of warm water through her dreadlocks. Alex's arms circling her waist while she seasoned a pot of spaghetti sauce, sitting down at their first dinner together, *can you believe this is happening?* Hand in hand within a circle of candles, any weirdness about being skyclad completely out the window by now. Two other hearts to live within, two other people to get her back. And catching their reflections in the closet-door mirrors....she couldn't wipe the smile off her face if she tried.

It was time to move out, Devon or no Devon. No running away this time, actually planning it out. She had to figure out a roommate situation, tell Julian, but she could do that later. Right now, her thoughts were veiled in incredible distractions. Back in a band, with two beautiful lovers…she'd get back to reality tomorrow.

Nobody in the living room, nobody on the staircase and she pushed the door to her room open. She pulled this week's *Bay Guardian* from her bag and opened it to the classifieds when there was a knock at her door.

Galen and Erik. Both dressed in elegantly rumpled suits and combat boots, coming in to settle on her chair, her bed. Charming smiles on their faces. Two total interruptions she didn't feel like dealing with now.

"We've hardly seen you at all, lately," said Galen, arms crossed on the chair's back.

"We've missed you," said Erik, reaching up to caress her cheek. Danae drew away.

"Why so shy?" asked Galen. "What's changed, are we no longer welcome in your bed? You know Erik's still got scars from what you did to him."

Oh no. Not now, not ever. But it wasn't like she could shut the tour bus door and leave their city behind. But then again, with her imminent move, her bedroom door wouldn't be nearly as accessible in the future. She feigned a headache, rummaged around the couple of notebooks on her nighttable, tried to brush them off with the vibe of more important things to do.

Galen got up and went to the mantel. Found the picture of her mother and father, ran a metal fingertip down the edge of the frame.

"I see where you get it from," he said.

"Beautiful," said Erik.

Danae's heart picked up a little speed. There was no overt threat being made, and yet she sensed she'd better move carefully. And quickly. She'd call Dahlia as soon as she could get rid of them, ask if she could crash over tonight.

"You can be what she couldn't," said Galen.

"Better," said Erik.

How do you know what I truly want to be?

Galen walked to the door. "Come with us. Every time one of us has accomplished something, you've waved us away. There's something we want to share with you. Please, just this once."

Just this once. She'd check out the writing, or the crafting, or whatever dark project they were up to now. And then they'd leave her alone, because she was leaving, period.

"Alright. But I've got a lot of work to do, I can't stay long."

"That's fine," said Erik, getting up from the bed. "We're happy to get the little bit of you we can."

Galen exchanged a look with Erik as he led them out into the hallway, ascended the staircase up to the third floor.

To the ritual chamber.

The room was small, much more modest than the TV clips had made it out to be. The ceiling slanted at the edges from the contours of the pointed roof. In the center, a marble altar, empty, a black pentagram painted on the hardwood floor beneath it.

Lacey and Charlotte kneeled at the edges of the circle, both clad in black velvet robes and gentle smiles. Behind her, Galen locked the door. Danae's heart raced a little faster.

Her eyes flew around the room. The walls were completely shrouded in black, no outside light at all, no tourists to spy but no neighbors to hear her scream. A ritual was laid out around the circle, and she cased each compass point, took inventory. A dish of incense was smoking away in the east, strong and floral and headache-inducing. Red candles were clustered in a small forest of swirling ironwork to the south. In the west, two chalices. One was crafted from hammered metal, the other of glass, banded with gold and holding a measure of red wine. A cut-glass vase of red roses sat at the north.

At the head of the altar, atop a velvet-covered pedestal, seven shiny pennies circled an armor ring, jointed to bend with the knuckles, etched to cover a finger with delicate baroque curves. Something white was scattered around the pennies. Most likely sugar. Because what they'd laid out was a love spell.

"Danae." Lacey rose to her feet. "I apologize for the somewhat false pretenses we've used to lure you here. But we've been so concerned about you."

"We feel you need to be empowered," said Charlotte. "These people you've been spending so much time with—these, *lunatics*, at least they're honest with their nomenclature—you're not your strongest self when you're with them."

"You shouldn't be so free with your favors," said Lacey. "With people who aren't worthy of them."

Four of them, one of her. Still. "Don't fucking talk like that about my friends."

"We're your family," said Lacey. "Not those parasites."

Danae took a step back but Galen caught her. "I'm sorry, but it's for your own good."

She tried to wrestle out of his grip, but Lacey lifted the dish of incense, brought the smoke directly beneath her face. Danae's temples throbbed and her knees went weak. Galen lowered her to the altar, where she fell back, all resistance draining from her muscles.

Charlotte kneeled down beside her.

"This spell is for you, darling. For you to fall in love with yourself. You're a prisoner of your own guilt, and you've been letting other people hold you back, for far too long."

"When this rite is done, you'll be with us," said Galen.

"You'll be with us, finally," said Lacey, putting the incense down beside the altar.

Danae tried to get up, but her head was killing her, nearly blinded by pain from the smoke. Nausea cramped her belly, and she tried to at least roll over, maybe sticking a finger down her throat would splatter the whole rite into failure, but she couldn't move at all.

Lacey lifted her arms, and each of her captors shifted into position, each compass point filling up with their voices, their energies. She raised her voice in a language Danae didn't recognize.

"*We all come from the goddess…*" Danae murmured, disrupting the priestess.

Lacey dropped her arms, spun around with an annoyed look. "Charlotte, maybe we should do that particular part now."

Charlotte took up the glass chalice and crouched before Danae. Didn't even try to lift it to the clamped lips. She motioned Erik over with her eyes, and his metal-shod fingers pinched her nose shut. Danae's eyes watered as she felt her body struggle and lose the battle against air, tried to take a breath as quickly as possible but red wine slipped past her grinding teeth. She felt her tongue shrivel, her throat dry out with soreness. She spat out a few drops, cursed—and found she had no voice.

No talking. No singing. Or screaming. What was left?

Her body. Her hair, her eyes. Her silence.

The glass box came slamming back against her palms, not smashed to pieces at Devon's after all, but so exhaustingly resilient, inviolate. The vanity was dropping squat into an altar of marble, the phallic toys standing up and elongating into burning candles, the dead roses disintegrating into a scattering of herbs. Not a sex doll, not a child, nor a courtesan…but a sacrifice.

She felt Erik winding silky ribbons around her wrists. Another pair secured her legs together. The incense was driving her mad. Bound, and gagged, all they needed was to whip out a blade and she was the Slaughtered Slut. Her eyes watered.

I fucked up. I fucked up so bad.

Danae listened as Lacey started the chant again, and it flew from mouth to mouth deosil around her, aiming to bring something in, towards her. Each one of them was wearing an armor ring on their left index fingers. Their athames. How were they not falling over dead from this incense? The pressure in her head nearly screwed her eyes shut.

Another round of chanting as they stepped forward and held hands above her. The invocation. Erik was bringing the metal chalice forward.

"Galen, your connection to her is strongest. You're the best one to do it," said Charlotte.

Galen's right hand, bare of jewelry, descended into the cup. His fingers emerged, tipped in red. He brought his hand to Danae's sleepy face and ran his fingertips along Danae's lips. Not apples. Not pomegranates.

Blood.

And now he was taking his athame off his left hand, replacing it with the ring from the pedestal, dipping the sharp end into the chalice. Erik rolled

Danae onto her side, exposed her hands. Galen's touch was soft on her left wrist, uncurling her index finger.

One deep, fast slash split her fingerprint in half. The metal chalice came up and swallowed her wound.

"Now you're truly our sister," he said.

Danae closed her eyes. Julian and Celeste, younger, clad in the velvets themselves. The marble grew warm with the heat of their passion, the place of her conception fast becoming the killing floor for her spirit. The faces of her parents grew sharp, disdainful, abandoning her to whatever fate was planned next. The ascendancy straight into Julian's throne, after all. Or a transformation into Devon's dark bride. She was helpless in the face of whatever metamorphosis they had planned, that was certain.

Lacey's voice rang out across her dizziness.

"Now. Let's get the rest of her coven."

Chapter 20

Alex lay back on his bed, within the prints the angels' wings had left in his sheets. Night nibbled away at the edge of the moon as he toyed with one of Dahlia's silver dread cuffs, and he could still smell them, feel their breath against his skin, their fingers in his hair. A pair of woodland creatures, wolfen and feline, staring at him with their dryad eyes. Sirens, and queens, and sorceresses. His hands itched to write, to play.

Danae had left first, and then one last tryst with Dahlia, just the two of them. She'd been throwing things into her bag for the trip home and how hard that decision must have been for her, to trust him like that, trusting Danae. Catching her arm and then her mouth in a kiss, easing her down, trying to touch him back but he'd gripped her wrists: *let me*. Her dreadlocks spilled across his pillow as he told her what she meant to him with his hands, his mouth. She accepted every adoring touch, springing up and hugging him tight when she could take no more. All doubts vanished, she was along for the ride just as much as Danae.

He felt like calling Matt. *Dude, we worked it out. It's all okay now. Fuck yeah, is it ever okay now.* He felt like calling Catrinel. *All that shit you were saying about Devon? You were right.* He felt like calling Ronnie. *Danae came back, and now I have two girlfriends. Two beautiful women, yeah. So how's Phoenix?* Maybe even stopping by to thank Celeste. Because the new love had come into his life, all right, but she'd brought along Danae.

All the notebooks, gathered from around her room in a frantic search for clues where she'd gone. Dated, thankfully, and he'd shuffled them into a quick chronological order. Along the way, his mind got blown: how much she cared about him, how her words were reaching for him, ever since she stepped into the grove and changed his life. Those notebooks, that first little mirror in which he'd seen the other side of his music, had gone on to reflect his own face as well—so many different ways he'd seen himself described as beautiful. He'd never known she'd felt that way, never known that he *was* that way. To anyone.

Right before he'd lit the red candle, he'd pulled down the first notebook. The day up at Tamalpais, the song about the burning witches, where his handwriting joined hers. Right by her side as they both discovered her voice. He'd carefully cut out the first lines they'd ever written together, folded up the scrap with a swipe of whiskey and pressed it into the bottom of the candle. One last chance. One little bit of personalization inside someone else's handiwork. He wasn't letting Celeste dictate shit about who got to date her daughter.

The phone rang, startling him. He glanced over at the digital clock on the nighttable. Midnight, exactly.

He groped around on the floor, grabbed the receiver.

"Yeah."

"Hello, sweet prince." A girl's voice, high and sultry. Neither Danae nor Dahlia.

"Who's this?"

"True love waits for you within the circle of headless trees."

"…what?"

"You think we'll let her go to the light side? Let her die inside all your New Age delusions? Not with her bloodline. No way will we give her up to a pair of moon-gazing lightweights. If you want her, you fight us for her."

"Who the fuck is this?"

"This is your chance to be a hero. I wonder, will you wear your warrior gear to the park? Bring your guitar? I can't wait to find out how you'll save the girl."

She hung up.

The park. Headless trees. The grove. Boots on, grabbing keys and leather and he was out the door, running down the steps and sprinting to the Firebird. Alice in Chains jacked back to life on the stereo, at the start of this song Danae had been sitting beside him, in some kind of deep trouble now and he pulled away from the curb, down the hill to swing over onto Page and head back up towards Golden Gate.

Speed slowed, pool after pool of streetlight white to guide the way. He turned the stereo down, stopped a good distance away from where the path hit the road—best not to announce his arrival, nor draw outside attention to what would surely be evidence of occult activities. He parked and set out into the pitch black beyond the road. Not a problem, he could find his way to the grove in his sleep.

The woods were thick with mist, the shrinking moon icing pale light across the branches, the shivering leaves. Darkness to get lost in, never to emerge. The hum of the earth felt angry, buzzing beneath his boots, something malevolent in the cold air. All these years he'd been writing songs about evil, *evil*, a stand-in word for will, for power, for living as one pleased. They'd all written about evil, all the bands, as they'd shared the sound, helped each other climb the ladder. Nobody who truly embodied the word's real meaning would have lasted a minute in the scene.

Firelight, as he drew closer. Through the trees, he glimpsed burning candles, black wax melting down the stumps. On the ground, within the circle, a woman in a black dress, her hands and feet bound.

Danae!

* * *

Head throbbing, throat burning. Danae had watched the Gingerbread Four desecrate the grove with a controlling spell. The herbs were scattered among the grasses, the brews spilled into the ground. Nothing she could do while she watched them work, from her position as bait. No warning she could call, as she heard the rushing of boots, as her captors slipped into the woods.

Alex went down on his knees beside her, looked into her face.

"Are you OK?"

Half-closed eyes could tell him she wasn't dead, but could not stop him from tearing at the silk around her wrists. Could not stop the sudden stabs of pain behind his eyes.

"Fuck!" A sharp intake of breath and she could see his temper flare to life, more people to kill on her behalf. Just what he needed. Bits of silver glimmered from within the trees, behind his back, the promise of more pain to come.

His face came down beside hers again. "What's going on?"

She shook her head. *Can't help you. Can't help myself. And I don't know what they've got coming for you.*

"What's wrong? Talk to me!"

From the darkness, one of the girls laughed.

He sat back and she watched his eyes fly around the trees. Nothing.

He sat up and looked around the grove. At the crude pentagram scratched into the ground beneath her. At the black candles dribbling down the stumps, nine of them. She summoned all her will and tapped her bound hands against the dirt. *Look. Look.*

The armor ring. He lifted her hands. Ran a thumb along the slash.

What had she seen the first time she'd come here, when he'd taken her on that spirit journey? The first question he'd ever asked her, and the answer...

Blood. Lots of blood.

Suddenly he was grabbing his keys from his leather, flipping through for the penknife. He opened the blade and sliced down through his palm, wrapped his hand around her finger and pressed his blood into hers. She felt the binding twitch, her headache lift for just a moment as he poisoned the stream, jammed the system of the spell.

The draught had silenced her, but it hadn't taken away her ability to smile.

"No!" A dark form hurled itself out of the trees and tackled Alex. Erik, in a long velvet coat, boots glinting with metal shinguards. Alex rolled out of his grip and kicked him in the stomach. Sprang up, grabbed Erik by the collar and smashed him in the face, one, two, about to land a third when Galen jumped in and grabbed Alex's arms, twisted them back. Erik got up, face bleeding, fingers shining with sharp edges, eyes on fire.

Brute force when their magick didn't hold. No honor in that. No honor, no honor, she thought, as a steel toe slammed into Alex's solar plexus, and a fistful of armor rings tore his jaw open. Her pit muscles flexed, raged—how badly she wanted to jump in and help. Nothing she could do but watch, and curse herself for leading him into a trap.

Lacey and Charlotte emerged from the trees. Long velvet dresses, glittering eyes. The punches stopped but Galen kept Alex's fists wrenched behind his back. Charlotte kneeled next to Danae, ran an affectionate, proprietary hand over her forehead. Not enough strength left to even flinch.

Lacey strode up to Alex, licked the blood from his lower lip.

"Sweet as candy."

Alex spit in her face. And got a silver-shod punch in the stomach from Erik.

Lacey just smiled. "Don't fuck with us. We're stronger."

She stepped away and stood beside Charlotte.

"When we're done with you, Danae will be free. She'll wake up tomorrow and have nothing to do with you, ever again. Your hold on her will be broken, and she can come into her true nature."

"You think I'm just gonna let that happen," Alex snarled.

"Right now, you have no real choice, do you? Don't worry, sweet prince. You won't care for her very much either, when the night is over."

Lacey gestured around the grove. "This is where it all started, isn't it? True love. We had so much fun reading her diary while you were besotted with the pleasures of the flesh. Did you ever know she wove a spiderweb here, the day before she met you? It shouldn't be too hard to tear it apart."

No. No. I finally found my family, I just found them, and now they're taking them away from me. Danae tried to lift her head, felt nauseous and immediately crashed back to earth.

"It's time to charge the circle. Pain is power—but I think you already knew that. Galen, Erik, get him on his knees."

Down to the ground, Alex refused to look up at Lacey. He tipped his head forward, hair falling over his face.

"You would destroy her, all that she is, all that she could be. Look how far she went when she got away from you. And now, at this point…you're regression, nothing more. A step backwards."

The pointed tip of her boot connected with his chin in a fresh burst of red.

"That's what you get, for trying to take her life away."

She grabbed his hair, tried to force his face up into hers, but a soft jingling of zippers was making its way into the grove. Everyone froze.

Dahlia walked out of the darkness, into the light. The woman fashioned from black wax, the rival, the competitor for Alex's affections. The road not taken, the girl not banished. Her face was a portrait of total calm as she looked down at Danae, over to Alex.

Charlotte got to her feet. "Oh good, you're finally here. Now we can *really* begin."

Lacey grabbed Dahlia's arm and hauled her over to Alex, forced her to her knees beside him. Charlotte came over to stand before her.

"I'd like a turn, sister," she said.

Lacey smirked and stepped back, and Charlotte hit Dahlia, armor ring gashing open her cheek. Dahlia stared back, through the blood, no break in her serene expression.

"The path of razors. Forcing needles into your flesh, how much pain you can take, like your piercings are some kind of spiritual trophies. I've never been impressed by all of that. Quite sickened, actually. Agony's really not so noble as you seem to think—look where it brought you, *priestess*."

Pure reflex had Alex lurching for Charlotte but the hold on his arms was too tight, and he got a boot in the stomach from Lacey.

"You'll just fuck her over, waste her time with your church, all those people who can't get their shit together. Bloodsuckers that could have killed her, all of you."

Such a long hard road out from that one white candle, so much savored and suffered, only for the journey to end here.

Lacey gently swiped a little blood from each battered lunatic face, lifted her left hand, and the reddened athame whistled through the air as she walked the grove widdershins. Danae felt the web rip apart, saw her circle's faces suddenly blur. The kisses disappeared from Dahlia's lips, the excitement of shows faded from Alex's eyes, all the memories started to trickle away within a spell of erasure. Friends, turning back into strangers with each vicious slash of Lacey's ring.

She wanted to reach out, hang on as their features lost familiarity. Their names vanished into a black fog, forgotten, never known. Their voices, their scents, the touch of their hands, gone.

But, warmth. A red glow. The promise of fulfillment that beckoned Celeste into the black Victorian. Family, Danae had cast for—her hand lit up with the swirls on the ring, like the damask walls inside a magic castle, a brocade pillow inside a haunted house, a tiny slice of a fine home to be worn as a talisman by those who lived there. Her brothers and sisters with black hair, protectors, guardians—her clan was watching out for her. Love and honor, a place in this city that would always be hers. Making sure she would never be alone again.

Two people kneeled on the grass, bleeding, and they were important, but she couldn't remember why.

Another blow and the girl with the dreadlocks was still impassive through the pain, red spattered against her scars. The guy in the leather was struggling, cursing, vowing they were dead, fucking dead, and one of her sisters was laughing—

and the girl with the dreads took a deep breath, threw back her head, and flooded the grove with deep warm vibrato. She was answered by footfalls. Lots of them.

Figures in black stepped out from behind the trees. In twos and threes, eyes glinting by firelight and very, very pissed off.

Danae was jolted back to reality just in time to see about twenty of Dahlia's congregation gathered around the stumps. Witnesses to assault. Wiest was among them, camcorder balanced on his shoulder, eye to lens, the recording light a game's-over red in the darkness.

Stunned faces from the Gingerbread Four, before they all went crashing through the woods. The lunatics gave howling chase, and the park filled with havoc.

Alex and Dahlia crawled over to Danae. Tore apart the silk, which came away painlessly now. Danae's head still hurt, but her circle was here.

"She can't speak, I don't know what they did to her. I got a phone call, I came out here and found her like this," said Alex.

"And they beat your ass hella good, too. Gimme your keys. We're going back to my place first." Dahlia curled an arm beneath Danae's shoulders, lifted her up.

"So you got a creepy phone call, too."

"Yeah, some guy. But I've seen enough horror movies to know, you should always show up with *numbers*."

* * *

Flu herbs, blech. The familiar, dreaded taste flooded Danae's throat. It was like drinking the woods. *All* of them.

Alex was sitting across from her, Curio on his lap, while Dahlia packed away her first aid kit. Painkillers had gotten rid of Danae's headache, but her vocal cords were still dead. No surprise.

The skylight poured down the moon onto their faces, their bruises. Alex's hair was wet from a fast shower, enough to check his injuries. His jaw was bad, but not enough to need stitches. Dahlia was handling her damage pretty well, shrugging it off as another occupational hazard. The way Catrinel probably would.

"That cut on your finger, all of them wearing those rings. They were trying to make you one of them." Dahlia crawled up into the bed, lay down on her side. Oophi curled up on her hip.

"I didn't think the flu tea would work, but you know, cross it off." Alex sighed.

"They wouldn't have made it that easy. They meant to get us out of her life permanently and have a good time doing it." Dahlia played with the armor ring she'd pulled from Danae's hand.

"OK. Think. Think of everything."

"All the candles were black."

"Shooting pain when I first tried to undo the restraints. They freaked the fuck out when I cut my hand and put it on hers."

"*That's* what started the fight?" Dahlia snorted. Slid the ring onto her left index finger, flexed. "They obviously didn't want *you* getting into the family." Curio got up and stretched, walked into Danae's lap to settle on her thigh.

"Some family."

Family. Once upon a time, that had been Celeste. Then, Enspelled. The bond came from the music—blood hadn't been necessary.

Except once. To get Ronnie under her skin, to control his anger. *Hurt me now, and you hurt yourself.*

Maybe the reverse could work to get her voice back.

Heal me now, and you bring us closer.

Danae put the mug on Dahlia's nighttable, dislodged Curio, reached for Alex's leather. Rummaged around the pockets for his car keys, grabbed the ring.

"What are you doing?" asked Alex.

Danae held up the pocket knife, pulled out the blade. Before either of them could react, she slashed the ring finger on her left hand, and let the drops fall into the mug of woodland tea. Tiny clouds of red spread through the warm green herbal pond, the grove captured in a cup.

She lifted the mug and offered it to them.

Alex and Dahlia exchanged a look. Danae nodded.

"Wait." Alex took the knife from Danae. "Shouldn't we all do this together?"

"What do you mean?"

"If one bleeds, we all bleed."

"All of us in the cup?"

"Three times as strong."

A smile spread slow across Dahlia's face. "We may as well bond as a proper coven, if we're gonna get beaten up as one." She sat up, Oophi clinging on to her cargo pants.

Silence, as Alex nicked his ring finger, and then Dahlia, and the binding swirled together. The mug was passed from hand to hand as each swallowed blood chosen. Sweat, and spit, and sex, and now the last connection, the deepest. The oath was silent in the air between them, spun from spider silk, the web alive and shining again as Danae felt her throat grow warm and the pain fade, the poison of forced kindred washed away.

"'If one bleeds, we all bleed.' Alex, you're so metal." And Danae savored the sound of her laughter booming through Dahlia's bedroom, rich and loud and free.

He tackled her, and Dahlia piled on top, and their noisy relief gave way to a fierce embrace.

No one can break us apart now.

They grew quiet as exhaustion overcame them. Warmth, and the soft sound of deep breath, both Alex and Dahlia were asleep when dawn edged into the skylight. Danae was still awake, tangled within their hair and hands, but just barely.

A black bird flew over the glass. Then another. Danae kept her eyes on the window, and when the third one came soaring by on outspread wings, she knew.

Goodbye, Julian.

Chapter 21

"I'm standing here in front of the home of one of the most infamous figures in the occult world. Many of you remember my special on the forces of darkness…"

Danae sat in the passenger seat of the Firebird, staring at the crowd that had gathered in front of the black Victorian. This was supposed to be the last trip ever, and she had not anticipated a fight through a throng of nosy reporters and candle-clutching mourners to get to the front door.

"Maybe we should just wait until everyone's cleared out," said Dahlia, from the backseat.

Tempting.

"…his sick, twisted philosophy onto America's youth. Preying on their innocent minds…"

Danae opened the door and jumped out.

"Or maybe not," said Alex, getting out, Dahlia behind him.

Danae shouldered her way through the crowd, gray tailored suits and lengths of wire trailing all over the sidewalk, noticed that the mourners were clustering in her wake. Ready to get her back, or ride it inside the house. All she wanted was her stuff, and a few moments to say goodbye, and definitely not a microphone shoved in her face.

"…his daughter. Tell me, do you plan to carry on his agenda of evil lies?"

"Julian was my father. He was family. And I thought your show was all about family values. So back off and show some respect." She pushed him out of the way while he frantically drew a line beneath his chin to stop the filming and caught up with her, inching his way towards the front steps.

"Please, please, let me in. I'll give you uninterrupted screen time."

"No, you'll just ask totally pointless questions and cut me off with some bible-beating nutjob when you don't like the answers. You have no fucking class, get lost."

"Please—"

"You heard the lady," said Dahlia. "Now get off her property before we call the police."

He headed back to the sidewalk, signaled his cameraman to shoot the exciting act of Danae ascending the steps and unlocking the front door, but the mourners formed a wall of black against him, nothing for his viewers to gawk at.

Danae turned to the crowd, plastered on a grim little smile. "I know you're here to pay your respects, but I'm not ready to deal with this yet. I don't know what to say, other than you can hang out in the yard until I get things sorted out. Don't let the press people get any closer than the sidewalk. And…we'll miss him, won't we?"

A sympathetic murmur from the mourners as she stepped inside.

A dark form was hunched over the dining room table. Alex shut the door, and the figure looked up at the three of them. A woman in her sixties, gray hair pulled back in a twist, delicate silver glasses, all business within a black chiffon dress that fell to the floor. An inverted pentagram shone from her high buttoned neckline.

"About bloody time. Where've you been?"

"Who the hell are you?"

"Julian's secretary. I'm Anne."

"I didn't know he had a secretary."

"Lots of things you don't know, and you should, being that you're the next of kin. Sit down and I'll catch you up."

Danae pulled up a chair while Alex and Dahlia tentatively wandered the living room, staring at all the infernal art with a mixture of wonder and disgust. Of course it would be fascinating to them. You didn't delve into the practice of witchcraft without running into Julian's notoriety, sooner or later.

Paperwork was neatly stacked across the table's surface. Financial statements, handwritten lists, a huge address book. Danae noticed that the three crows were missing.

"Now. The funeral's to be held in Colma, followed by cremation, as per his instructions. Obviously the service is invitation-only."

"No press ghouls. Good."

Anne paused, cracked the tiniest of smiles, *you've some sense after all.*

"Lacey, and Charlotte…"

"Those goth gits, they've cleared out. Just as well. I warned Julian about them, they don't even stay to respect his death. Honor his legacy, my arse. On to the next shiny thing."

Danae flashed back to the beautiful calligraphy, the detailed silver goat face. Grasping and greedy, but theirs was not the work of trendy lightweights. Angry as she was, talent recognized talent, and it burned to feel any grain of defense towards Anne's easy dismissal.

But they were gone. One less headache.

"Are you prepared to speak to the media?"

"I just talked to that guy outside—"

"That wanker who did the special? Consider your statement made. Now. The estate." Danae stayed quiet. "I'm afraid there isn't much left of one. Your father ran up massive debts…"

Not like she'd wanted to stay in this house, anyway. Danae's eyes caught on an express envelope, her name. She picked it up and tore it open, found a smaller envelope inside. Shiny gold ink. Theban.

Danae ~
  My condolences on your loss.
  Devon

She apologized to Anne and got up from the table, shuffled into the living room. Alex was sitting right where Julian used to, and that meant her father was truly not coming back.

Up the stairs and past her room, up the second flight into the ritual chamber, somewhere safe to perch up above the madness.

Empty.

The walls were still covered in black velvet, but all the implements were gone. The Gingerbread Four must have run back and whisked away all the evidence, probably five-fingered a few pretty things too, she dreaded finding her room ransacked. High-tailing it back to their elite enclaves, furiously casting spells to make the whole thing blow over, bury it deep, scot-free from all punishment. She'd caught Alex cracking his knuckles on the way over, but there was no one here to fight. A mercy in the midst of a harrowing day.

Danae parted the curtains to let the day inside and sat down at the center of the pentagram, bathed in a slice of warm light. She hugged her knees to her chest, turned her face to the sun and heard their voices. Chants, invocations, her father the loudest but not the only one. Not the only one. Beneath, women speaking, singing, sighing. Their bare flesh serving as the altar, manifestation of the divine feminine only when it was young and pretty and prone. Damn. Her father had invented groupies right around when the rock bands did.

"Danae."

She looked up. Dahlia.

"Are you alright?"

"Yeah, I just…needed a minute away from everybody." Danae held out her hand and invited her in.

Two witches entwined in the heat of the day, comfort embracing sorrow, further profaning the ritual chamber with the open show of emotion. The smell of fire cloaked her, and there were no words, just the quiet transfusion of strength from woman to woman. Danae's eyes shimmered, pain but joy, too, utter awe that fastened her arms tight, tight, tight around the lunatic priestess, here for her in her hour of need.

"Stay with me forever."

A room built on rivalry, designed for women to hate each other, only for the fairest of them all to serve, never to lead. Dahlia hugged her back, fierce grip all the answer she needed.

One tear hit the floor. The voices receded into silence, banished.

"I came up to tell you….there's someone asking to see you," said Dahlia.

"Who?"

"She says she's your mother. I checked with Alex and he says it's definitely her."

Danae paled one second before scrambling to her feet and running down the stairs—quick check of her bedroom, everything still there, good—and down to the first floor. Celeste was sitting across from Alex, glaring at him with pure contempt. Alex smirked back, all *yeah, I'm sleeping with your daughter again. Ha ha.*

"Mom."

Celeste rose from the couch. "I'm sorry it took a tragedy for us to finally speak with each other."

"It did last time, too. Excuse me if I don't offer you a drink."

"We need to talk."

"Do we?"

"Surely you have questions. I *know* you do."

Proud and cold, none of the fake sweetness to lure her into a trap. And a backhanded compliment—her mother saw her as a worthy opponent.

"How do I know you won't try to poison me again?"

"Afraid, are you?"

Danae smiled, let the ghost of Julian pass across her features. Watched Celeste restrain herself from flinching.

"Alex, my *love.*" Danae glanced towards the couch, *isn't it awesome we don't have to hide anything now?* "Look after my mother's handbag. She'll be leaving it here on the coffee table, with her I.D., and the keys to her house, and all her money."

He nodded back, gorgeous with pride and affection and total insolence.

"Dahlia." She curled her hand around the back of her girlfriend's neck, flaunting her. "If I'm not back in exactly two hours, call the police."

Dahlia grinned, *you got it*, before throwing a look of lascivious venom at Celeste and sashaying over to Anne's mountains of paperwork.

"I think that takes care of everything. Shall we go, mother?"

* * *

Natural. Neutral. Mother and daughter sat side by side watching the waves break on China Beach, the sun a sizzling disc slipping down into the horizon. Other families were gathered out on the sands, curled up on picnic blankets or building crumbly little castles. Danae inhaled the damp air, thought about how much this outing would have meant to her in what felt like a lifetime ago. Now, it was merely the discharging of obligation. Although it was not time to throw her gore-spattered sword to the ground, not just yet.

Back at the house, Alex was packing up her stuff and getting it into the car. Dahlia was handling the mourners, letting a select few into the house to pay their respects, take one last look around under close souvenir-guarding supervision. Anne had initially been huffy, but eventually recognized a kindred soul who knew how to take charge and would actually be a huge help dealing with the chaos.

Leaving her all alone with her mother.

"This was one of the places I liked to come, to ground with the earth. The shoreline is a doorway, an in-between place, both earth and water. A natural threshold," said Celeste.

"Why didn't you ever take me with you?"

"Because you hadn't earned it yet. Not by coasting on your bloodline, and not by your parlor tricks in the shop. But going out into the world, and seizing it. You're smart enough to receive it now."

"A test."

"Of sorts. You were on a wayward path, and needed to be kept safe from your own ignorance."

Or, pretty words to cover up Pam's unexpected smashing of the storefront window, a way to save face. An embroidery of bullshit same as those martial-arts guys Catrinel was talking about, strangers in bars who suddenly dumped all sorts of esoteric achievements in some polite girl's lap. It was with a jolt that Danae realized she'd always assumed Celeste had been telling the truth.

"You named me for a rape."

"You're the reason Julian threw me out of his life."

"He said you kept me away from him."

"He never cared to visit. He only showed interest in you when you dated that rockstar. I knew you were up here with Devon. Julian didn't tell you that time because his wife was dying in the hospital. By the time you came back for good, she had passed, and he could acknowledge you."

"So...he didn't have an arrangement with his wife?"

"He was screwing around on her, and she didn't know. *That* was the arrangement." Celeste's laugh was a short sharp bark. "Don't think he wasn't giving you a cold reading, too. Telling you what you wanted to hear. I hope you didn't buy too much of it."

Between the two of them, liars, she'd never know. But it was truth that her mother's love had disappeared around the time of adolescence, first blood, when the child she'd been started to transform into a woman... crowding her mother at the mirror.

A young woman led a small child along the sands. Going slow, letting tiny bare feet navigate the uneven terrain, chirping encouragement.

"And I don't know what you're doing with Alex, and that...creature, but I can tell you for certain that it's not going to wind up all roses and stardust."

"So you're saying I should start dating Zolo, is that it?"

A burst of laughter from the child, like strumming the highest string on a guitar.

"Don't get smart with me, I'm just looking out for you. One man, two women. You'll put him in the middle. You'll fight over him. You'll war over who says the sweeter words, smiles from the prettier face. And she'll push you down the stairs to get you out of the way."

She had a fiercely independent spirit. Very competitive. She always had to be the best at whatever she was doing, above all others.

Her mother had hidden her knowledge not because Danae was unworthy, but because she was *too* worthy.

"And that's why you drugged me, isn't it?"

Celeste went silent, quickly composed herself. "Like I said, it was because I had to keep you safe."

"No. It's because I threaten you." And Danae smiled with her father's face, and watched Celeste recoil. "It never occurred to you, did it, that all I wanted was to get close to you. Learn from you. How badly I wanted your respect—just like you wanted his. And if I was, as you say, too ignorant, then why didn't you teach me how *not* to be? You're my mother. If anyone was supposed to be guiding me towards strength and wisdom, it was you."

Danae stood up. Before her, the horizon. Sky and ocean, the union of air and water. Intellect and emotion. The last scrap of pain was fluttering the in the wind, the scab coming off the smooth wound, ready to drop off and disappear as she locked eyes with Celeste.

"But you didn't. And I'm so glad you never turned your head in my direction. I never would have left the shop. I never would have found out that working alongside you was not the only good future. And I definitely would never have learned half of what I know now. How ironic, in trying to bind me, you let me go to learn so much, all without you. I thank you and honor you for that, and nothing more."

A graying of the skies, the chill of sudden mist. The glamours of Celeste's anger were icy and dark, a soft storm gathering speed, and Danae put her hands up, barricade, and before she knew it, the sensation was beneath her fingertips, smooth and clear and so familiar. But different this time.

Because this was the glass around Celeste.

Freezing rain, and harsh wind. Danae let the tempest brew as her hands grew cold against the coffin, safely outside this time, and locked Celeste in with her connivances, her jealousies, the fruits and failures of her temper. Rage blazed in her mother's eyes, imprisoned within her own sour sorceries, the backfire only growing with each fresh torrent. Pathetic, the way she clawed at the air, choking on the bile of bitter envy, snarling and miserable and...*funny.*

A rich, victorious laughter rang out from Danae's heart, soared above the fury that was painfully realizing its impotence. This enemy, the subconscious battle-target of so many of her lyrics, had been vanquished. This long, painful dirge was finally over.

She dropped her hands. Watched the drizzle dissolve back into blue and gold warmth, leaving her mother panting. Shrunken and drained, helpless, Danae almost pitied her. Almost.

One last glance to savor the new wariness in Celeste's eyes, and Danae walked away. Healed. Free.

"Danae!" Her mother called after her. Already her voice was growing smaller. "You would cast your own flesh and blood aside?"

Danae pivoted to walk backwards, one last cold smile.

"My flesh and blood is music. Not Julian. And not you."

* * *

"Hello?"

"Adrian! This is Danae. Remember me? Carole King?"

"Of course I remember. Devon's ex. I mean, ex-protegé."

"Yeah. Ex everything."

"Good for you. I know you split town—where are you now?"

"Back home in San Fran. Jamming with a couple of people. And, ah, I think you might be interested in what we're doing."

"Still that dark sound?"

"Always. Well, almost. One of the members is trying to get us to lighten it up somewhat, but we're fighting it out in the music. I think it's a really interesting fight. Want a copy?"

"Sure, send it over. You still have my business card? Use that address, it'll get you past the crush."

"Awesome."

"You still regret leaving?"

"I think I regret the way I did it."

"There's more than a few Nemesis acts who have said the same thing. Not to the media, of course, but still."

"Well. I hope you enjoy the demo, because it'll really piss them off if you do. I worked *really* hard to piss them off."

"Can't wait to hear it. I'm gonna be up that way pretty soon, we should go for drinks."

"Somewhere with a piano."

"Definitely."

"I'll bring my band."

"You do that. I'll be in touch."

* * *

Onscreen, a skull nodded and crooked a long, beckoning fingertip above the words SEND A MESSAGE, written in an Olde English font.

"Wiest, you're a genius. These dripping bloodbar things? I love them!" Danae scrolled up and down the webpage, the little home he'd built for her in cyberspace.

Dahlia leaned over the keyboard behind Danae, her face lit up by the screen's glow. "We need to take some new pictures of you. Everybody still thinks you've got long red hair."

Watching Wiest work was fascinating, the way he conjured up these virtual worlds from lines of code, little incantations. Danae moved the mouse around the webpage, the icons like tools on an altar, activated with a click.

"Can you teach me how to do this?"

"Yeppers, I have books that can walk you through it. It's not as bewildering as it looks."

"Cool. Better day job than fortunetelling."

It was hard to tear herself away from the keyboard and the myriad realities it connected her to. The first search Danae had run was on other women in metal. Warriors and witches were adding new imagery to the pantheon: innocent in white dresses, posed in lakes. In long black gowns, circlets around their heads, swords beneath crossed palms. And the chicks in torn leather would be around forever.

Last night, she lit a white candle in her new room, built off the studio, a space carved out of the dollhouse just for her. The witch book was propped up by a synthesizer, the Old Ways safe in the temple of sound.

Alex leaned in Wiest's doorway. "I just got off the phone with Gnash. He says they'll have dinner ready when we get there, and there's plenty of booze, and Catrinel is freaking out. Danae, did you call Pam?"

"Yeah, can you believe she only lives a couple blocks away? This is gonna be awesome."

"Car's loaded. Let's roll."

Danae got up, and Wiest waved goodbye to them all, already loading *Doom* onto his desktop.

They walked out to the car and climbed in, Danae in back, Dahlia shotgun, the doors banged shut and Alex started the engine. Rammstein came booming out of the speakers as he pulled into traffic.

Six hours in the car. The trek from NoCal to SoCal, provisioned with drinks and tunes and the conversations that were lurking in the depths beneath daily routine, a pretty fun afternoon, actually. Danae leaned back on the seat as they passed through the warehouse district, headed east for Route 5 South.

The sky was summer blue perfection as the Bay Bridge came into view, light reflecting off the buildings in the Financial District. Dahlia rummaged in her purse and took out a pair of cateye sunglasses, slid them onto her nose and rocked along to the beat. Alex drummed his rings on the wheel, and they both started banging their heads when the chorus wallop kicked in.

(Family.)

There were no better people to be with, thought Danae, as the bridge spread a steely canopy above them. No one else, as she spotted the case of CD's in Dahlia's hands, and the front seat was already in heated discussion over which one should get cued up next. Because the sound came with them, always.

Wherever they went, was noise. And wherever there was noise, was home.

Special thanks to: Alan Beatts, Cassie Alexander, Roz Clarke, David J. Williams, Jocelyn Paige Kelly, Carrie Duvall, Kris Dikeman, Mercurio D. Rivera, Matthew Kressel, Devin J. Poore, Alaya Dawn Johnson, Paul M. Berger, Eugene Myers, Loren Rhoads, Claudius Reich, Seth Lindberg, Tarryn Kelemen, Danny from Malignancy, John Boone, Michele A. Feldman, and Duff's Brooklyn.

Manuscript formatted by Polgarus Studio.

Lilah Wild's dark fiction is an ongoing search for hidden cauldrons within the modern landscape, exploring the contemporary fantastic and horrific. She is a graduate of Clarion West and member of NYC-based writing group Altered Fluid, and her work has appeared in venues such as Pseudopod, Kaleidocast, Niteblade, and Morbid Curiosity. Her fascinations include bellydance dabbling, synthwave, horror movie interior decorating, doom metal, and running away to the beach. She lives in Queens with two cats.

Visit http://www.leopardmoon.com for the full bibliography and further adventures.